Wet Screams
A Monsterfucker Anthology
Edited by
Mindy Rose
Chris Krawczyk

WET SCREAMS: A Monsterfucker Anthology
Edited by Chris Krawczyk & Mindy Rose

This is a work of fiction. Any resemblance to actual persons or events, living or dead, is purely coincidental. The horror and arousal you may incur, however, is real.

Cover illustration and interior formatting by Chris Krawczyk.

First Edition Published by Little Ghosts Books, Oct. 2025.
ISBN 978-1-0695415-1-2 (Paperback)
ISBN 978-1-0695415-2-9   (eBook)

Published with generous funding collaboration from Ontario Arts Council.

Wet Screams

A Monsterfucker Anthology

Little Ghosts Books
Toronto, ON Canada

Wet Screams is a collection of Monster Erotica that blends romance tropes and horror elements, playing at your fantasies and stretching the boundaries of pleasure. We begin upon a cloud of Happily Ever Afters, with the soft touch of magic and playful scrape of teeth. As the dream continues, you will descend into the darker and more lurid depths of desire.

Each piece includes graphic sexual content. There are no closed door or fade to black romances. More detailed Content Warnings are available on the title page of each story.

Table of Contents

Stag & Stone
Megan Bontrager

She moves past a window where the night slithers, cool and wheedling, into the room. The raw bite of winter steals past the panes; no matter the heat within and the heady swell of magic that summons spring like a song, there is still cold to fight just beyond the glass. It's overstayed its welcome; there's no place for the white stag in the cold and so her father's spell swells, stinking of jasmine and honeysuckle. The heat swims over a sea of dark bodies, all undulating and masked, as she — a slip of white silk in a forest of black — lingers in the cold.

It's to be expected of the prey, of course; the predator has nothing to fear. The white stag eddies in the hopes that it might deter the hunters from their pursuit. A delicate hand lifts to adjust the headdress of pearl and gold, the crown of crystalline antlers that place her silhouette a head higher than any others. Father's always told her that she's meant to enjoy the hunt, that the pursuit is something to be relished. Tonight of all nights, the Solstice, when the arcane is at its strongest; tonight of all nights, when it swells and peaks like drunkenness, like heat, like arousal; tonight, of all nights, Soleil knows that she should be happy to be a prize. She is a wanted thing, the most precious object of desire.

But there are *eyes* on her — and too many. They keep their hands to themselves for now, out of respect for the family name she carries with her, but the hunters are in their cups and the potent magic calls. She will be someone's prey tonight. It's a small mercy that she gets to choose. Insulated and protected as she is — though a gilded cage is still a cage — it's a gift of sorts. The hunt is won by those who are *chosen.* There'll be no leaving this place tonight — and the night will wear on, an arcane suspension of ever-midnight — until an arrow finds the stag's heart. It's the only good thing about this whole damnable tradition.

Somewhat. It doesn't feel like much of a choice, primped and tied and dressed like a prized cut of meat. She is who she is, and they are who they are — and there her father stands, observing them all. His quarry, his subjects, his punch-drunk magicians, lush and amorous as they clamor for one another beneath the music, the heat, the spell.

Through the window and at the heart of the hedge maze, a single strike of limestone and marble, Magnus the Champion rises above. The clouds shift and a bar of moonlight spears into the trimmed umbrage, illuminating his stone wings, curled tail, gnarled and knife-tipped claws. At his feet, along the base of the dais on which he stands, is a bench — and underneath, a furtively stashed stack of books. His company is the only she'd like to keep; he is the *only* man, still and stone as he is, that will not intrude on her peace; Her guardian, her watcher. Visitors to the estate call him monstrous, but she thinks otherwise. If he were alive, he'd be something terribly powerful, something free.

At the balcony, her father lifts his hands. A fresh deluge of heady magic thickens in the smoke and half-light, and Soleil feels her stomach twist. On the dancefloor the spell deepens the trance in which the night's hunters twist and undulate. Sleeves slip off sweat-salted shoulders, lips find exposed throats, fingers wander into the laces of bound corsets. The night will end in her consumption, but they dally where they can. The night is for *them*.

But Magnus is for her. The moonlight. The quiet of the maze's heart. Far from the magic, far from the hunt. Far from what expectation lives at the other end of this delirious, dizzying night.

How desperately she wishes to be there now. Steal a glass of elderflower and berry wine, maybe; take a blanket from the adjacent parlors to ward off the chill, perhaps; the party will go on in her absence, because it isn't ever *really* about the white stag, the magic, the chase. It's about *them*. The men, their business, their money and power. Magic is business, after all. No matter its esoteric origins, its insular path to study and might. Spells are contracts, at the end of the day. Just like marriage. And she wants nothing to do with it.

The small mercy of Soleil's solitude is short-lived.

As it so often is. No one cares what she wants. Save, perhaps, her beloved gargoyle. But no monstrous stone-carved beast can save her now — not when a suitor has broken from the pack. He licks his lips as he approaches, the sweat that dapples his brow glistening in the cool moonlight.

"Darling!" the man calls. His eyes are round and unfocused, pupils blown wide. With a grin, he runs his fingers through the mess of ginger tangles that bear the telltale signs of being mussed one too many times already. "There you are. I've been looking for you all night."

All night? She's not hard to spot. Soleil traps something snide beneath her tongue, sucks on it like a sour candy. If he's looking, it hasn't been very hard. By the *smell* of him, he's been deep in the punch instead.

It takes her a moment to discern him, hazy as the room is; the heady fog of magic and spell smoke warps his features. She doesn't recognize him at first, and nothing's lost for it. He certainly doesn't seem offended by it; men like him always seem keen to talk about themselves in any context, even if it's the simple act of parroting their own name like a declaration of war. "Cato," he says, something conspiratorial in his voice like he's letting her in on a dirty secret by reminding her of just who he is. There's no denying that he's handsome — but he speaks like he knows it, which ruins anything that might be appealing about him. "You are ravishing."

He takes her hand before she can snatch it away. The other, lithe fingers bedecked with ceremonial rings and painted gold at the tips, knots in her lily-white skirt. Cato smells overwhelmingly of cologne and sweat, and his mouth is hot and sloppy on her knuckles. Over his bowed head, her father has turned to watch.

The blood must endure, he'd said. *The magic must be born anew.*

But if the magic, the bloodline, the family name were to carry on with someone like this — someone whose mouth clings to Soleil's skin like honey on a flytrap, someone whose staggering gait pushes her a step closer to the cold window — it would be nothing but torture. On a night made for pleasure, for celebration, for the decadence of magically goaded hedonism, shouldn't she be the first and last to indulge? Shouldn't *her* pleasure be the beating heart of the ceremony of it all?

In the crowd, the woman who'd begun to lose the top half of her velveteen gown has half-undone her corset. Her dancing partner's hands rove over her chest, dip down to the hard planes of her abdomen. She begins to hike up her skirts, turning round and falling further into the saturnalia where the magic loosens tongues and coaxes moans and whimpers from the fray like music. It should excite her. But Cato has stepped forward once more, blocking her almost entirely from the room at large.

She smacks her lips, blinking wildly as she remembers that she is meant to be a gracious host, a willing supplicant at the altar of the night's pleasures. Soleil's knees crack as she gives a shallow curtsy. "I am honored that you would take an interest in —"

"It is my understanding that the Stag is to descend into the fray, to allow her hunters a taste before the real hunt begins — correct?" The hand gripping hers slips along the slender stretch of her forearm, while the other reaches for her waist. "No good in lingering here, taking on the chill. The spell, the night, the sex is no good if you are not a part of it."

Soleil gulps. "I will join in my own time, if you would give me a —"

Again, he interrupts. For a moment, it's all she can do to keep from stomping on his tackily shod toes. "An industrious hunter would simply take you from the playing field entirely," he ducks his head to inhale loudly, a whiff of her perfume punctuated by a groan that sounds more painful than aroused.

"That would be cheating, I'm afraid." A nervous laugh slips from her, a bubbling mewl that he seems to willfully misinterpret. His hand flattens over her waist, fingers playing at the golden sash that ties the flimsy silk down.

And to her horror, his tongue lashes from between wine-purpled lips to trace the sweat that beads at her throat. Her breath stutters, and her empty hand flattens against the windowpane. Soleil cranes her neck, a shiver dancing the length of her spine at the cold. The magic shucks sweat-damp cloth from writhing bodies, coaxes legs round strong tree-trunk waists and hands between thighs. A cry rings from somewhere beneath the dazzling chandelier, and glasses rise to the display of unbridled ecstasy.

As her neck cranes from her pursuer, she finds the

hedge maze once more. As she is so wont to do, she finds Magnus amidst it all. And with a start she finds him... *different.* Changed. His head has turned from its usual place to fix directly upon the window. A trick of the light, she thinks; the magic getting to her head at last.

But then — he *moves.* Plain as day, with no sound and no great flourish, his great stone body shifts. The broad stretch of his stone torso twists; wings stretch, and tail lashes; clawed hands stretch to reach *toward* her as his eyes flash with no more light than a flame in a compact mirror. Magnus, stilling, extends a hand — and waits.

Soleil slips from Cato's grasp with a rake of sharp-clawed hands over exposed flesh, quick and harsh enough to draw blood. He hisses, reeling back — but his visage twists not into dismay or offense, but sheer delight. His lips move, and she can scarcely discern what he says over the pounding in her ears (*"A challenge!"*). She turns on her heel and slips along the wall, fingers trailing with anticipation along the ridges of cool stone.

Cato follows, calling her name as she bursts from the ballroom and hurtles along the darkened hall. Past immobile marble busts, leering portraiture, glass-cased spellbooks and tattered scrolls; she makes for the foyer, kicking off her shoes and leaping across the threshold like the doomed stag they so wish her to be.

And the night is brilliant, blistering cold. There's no time to relish it or to wick the sweat from her arms and the nape of her neck. She spares Cato no more than a glance as she slips between the towering hedge rows, beneath the rose-trellised arch that beckons visitors to the estate and bids them to get lost for an hour or two. Soleil could never get lost here. The curves and stops of the hedged paths are familiar; she knows their tricks, their subversions, their backsteps. And at the heart of it all, her solace.

"Come back, little Stag!" Cato calls. "After I spear you with my hunter's arrow, I claim you as my own —" a hiccup, a rustling of leaves as he falls, curses, rights himself. "I promise I'll be gentle the first time."

Her stomach turns. Soleil knows how this will end; the sun will not rise until she's chosen a partner. Not a partner, really; someone to carry on the family line. There needn't be any partnership involved. Archaic, barbaric traditions. They say the Stag has a choice, but does she really?

"Stag!"

Certainly not with *him*. Under different circumstances, there might be something thrilling about the chase. Were it someone desirable tracking her every move through the maze, following specks of gold and the hopeful flash of antlers, the thrill might be a *good* thing.

Soleil's feet ache as she races along the corridors of the maze. Gold fingertips trail along the manicured walls, leaving specks of paint in her wake. Honey hair haloes in an aureate swell of curls and lopsided horns at her temples. She *is* the stag, propelled by a singular need — to get to *him*. She's no idea what a gargoyle, long since left to the elements, is to do for her now, but Magnus is comfort. Magnus is quiet. And Magnus never asks anything of her. Even if his movement, his extended hand, his sympathetic look are all an illusion — the respite will be enough.

At the heart of the maze, he stands proud. The bench at the foot of the dais is just how she left it; the stack of poetry books she smuggled away is visible only to those who know where to look. The sound of a fountain tucked away amidst the leaves and roses trickles blithely. A breeze trembles at the petals that halo the circular clearing as if the flowers themselves anticipated her arrival.

Magnus stands proud, his limbs rearranged in exactly the way she'd left him just that morning. His hands have returned to his sides; no longer do they stretch to the window, and no longer does his neck crane to find her in the chaos inside. His wings stretch high, tail curled over the edge of the platform on which clawed feet stand shoulder-width. Magnus's visage is nothing but stone; no guiding light, no flash of warmth.

She wilts, falling heavily onto the bench as she rips the crown of antlers from her head. Golden curls tug from her scalp, and she winces.

"Not sure what I expected," she huffs, voice reedy and thin. And Soleil reaches out, the flaked paint at her fingertips trailing lithely over the stone curve of Magnus's calf, his ankle.

To her surprise the stone feels strangely... *warm.* Another illusion, maybe. A merciful fancy, something dreamed up by a desperate mind riding the high of magic made to overwhelm her. Disappear into it with Magnus and she might forget them all.

But there's no forgetting Cato. He's closer now, calling out her name. She can hear him as he comes, narrating his approach: first he abandons his belt over the shoulder of a marble dryad, tucked away with the gardener's prized hyacinth; next, he undoes his top buttons; lastly, as he launches into soliloquy about the sheer power of his *"hunter's tools"* — at which Soleil grimaces. His voice draws close enough that she knows it'll be merely moments before he finds her here.

"Come now, Soleil!" Cato calls. Her name sounds like a condemnation on his tongue. "I am beginning to tire of this game. Come out now, and I promise to make it worth your while."

With her heart in her throat, Soleil clambers atop the bench and reaches for Magnus's stone form. It's never mattered to her until now, until she's climbing up, up, along the bare stretch of a thigh and clinging to his waist — he is *gloriously naked.* She's always had a fair respect for art; it never occurred to her to *consider* the generous appendage between his legs. But as she climbs, there's a moment where she is precisely face-to-face with it — and at the sight of it, her stomach twists.

Soleil slips behind him, arms wrapped round his waist as she stumbles at the edge of the dais, climbing clumsily over a stone wing and a curled tail as her dress tangles round her knees. He's broad enough that Cato might miss her, broad enough that he could mistake her for an errant wind, a bar of moonlight. Soleil presses into the space between Magnus's sun-warmed wings, chest to spine with cheek just beneath the curve of a shoulder blade. Her heart hammers in her chest; the edge of the dais is high and precarious, and as she looks down she feels her head spin.

All at once rock rumbles as powerful wings shift over her head, and the great tail between her legs lifts to wrap sturdily around her thigh. She jerks, a quick enough start to send her tumbling into the rose bushes with nothing to abate the fall — but *he* holds fast, keeping her pressed to the slope of his back . And as her fingers clamp onto the stone of his arms, a rumble from deep within his torso startles her into silence. He shifts, a beast twice her size changing shape to accommodate her hiding place; at once she is entirely obscured behind a veritable wall of granite and limestone, rooted by the tail at her thigh and the shifting wings that shield her from view.

Cato appears to find Magnus entirely changed, though he'd never know the difference: wings cocooned; tail lifted out of view; and one warm body tucked away, shielded behind the stone. She can only hear Cato as he huffs, feet shuffling uselessly in the grass. Her heart pounds against the warm stone, but she makes no sound as her pursuer cries out again. He calls for her, her name and her unwelcome title interchangeable like he simply cannot decide if she is a prize to be won for the sake of it, or if she truly is something he desires. Magnus is still, but the warmth remains. Far off, she can still hear the music from the party, the swelling crescendo of a string quartet playing beneath the trilling laughter and sing-song of its guests. There's nighttime birdsong, and the tinkling of the fountain — but none of it can find her now.

And then Cato is gone. He huffs, curses, departs down another path that will inevitably spit him outside the maze on the opposite side.

Soleil slips her arms round Magnus's midsection, cheek pressed to the stone slope of his mid-back. She exhales hard, squeezing her eyes shut tight.

"Thank you," she mutters, voice lost to the breeze. "I don't know what strange magic this is, but if you're real, if you're *listening* —"

"I am always listening." His voice is honeyed, and thunderous. Beneath is the grinding of stone, like the words themselves are rough granite carvings. She can feel his voice at every edge of her. Soleil gasps, startling away to the edge of the dais. A slip, a rush of air, as her heel slips — but he catches her, spinning round impossibly fast and taking hold of her wheeling arms. The stone aches, rough and hard on the bruisable peach of her flesh, but strangely enough she finds that she doesn't mind.

Magnus's wings tremble, eyes alight with strange magic once more. The moon sits perfectly within the frame of his horns, strong brow furrowed as stone fangs grind over a hard-set mouth. Cold night air shifts to ghost her bare arms — but the impossible warmth of him scares it away. Impossible, improbable, but utterly irrefutable. Like the sun. Like flesh.

"Are you real?" Soleil whispers.

At this, he lowers her from the dais. She crumples in the grass at its base, his towering nakedness obscuring her from the voyeuristic moon— and to her wild disbelief the molten heat of arousal sparks at the sight of him.

"As real as you," he says, voice the rumble of a mid-summer storm. "I could smell your fear. Your disgust."

Soleil blinks, rubbing the heel of her hand over her eyes. Realization settles with a jolt in the pit of her stomach. "Have you been *alive* all along? Frankly, I could melt into the earth right at this very moment given all I've *said* in this place, all I've admitted aloud when I thought that I was alone —"

"Alive... somewhat," he says, dropping into the grass. He takes a knee, monstrously large as he looms over her. "Listening, yes. But unable to speak. To move. To... touch." At this, his tail tightens. The arrowing heat at the pit of her stomach twists keenly. He is made, carved, in the image of a devil. A cautionary tale; something to warn away diabolical temptation. He is a beast twice her size, his clawed hands broad enough to crush her skull in one fatal blow. And yet — *yet* — "You are no stranger to the magic of the night."

"A victim of it, maybe. I have no desire to be a part of any magic that sees me *pursued* by a half-naked lord to be fucked in the dirt."

He cocks his head. "I can smell the lie on you, too."

She blinks. He speaks with such certainty, but he isn't wrong. The idea of the chase, the idea of being prey to something strong, commanding, and tender all in one — it tickles something wanton at the back of her mind.

And so: "It's not the chase I detest. It's the predator in question. If I am to be the Stag, if I am to be hunted and claimed like the sacrificial animal that I am, I would choose."

"You chose to come when I beckoned." Again, the bluntness startles her. "My life is given and taken by the magic of this night. I chose to use that life for good. For you."

"Of course," she says. "You are my only companion. An *immobile* one, or so I thought. One that has listened but never responded."

"I could not, even when I wished to."

"It could very well be that I'm dreaming. Drunk, maybe, on magic. Better dreaming than awake in a sea of flesh and strangers. I don't *want* to be touched by someone like Cato, who sees me only as a means to an end."

"But you want to be touched." It isn't a question. At this, his wings stretch, unfurling wide enough to shield her from the moon entirely. She can still hear the music — but suddenly, the beating of her heart is much louder.

A gulp. Her head spins. "I want to be touched by someone I trust."

And that is why you came to me."

"That is why I ran."

"I would protect you again, if it came to it." His tail slips down the length of her leg, trailing the curve of her knee, her calf. Magnus extends a hand, impossibly large fingers outstretched. "I will. I have always been yours to command."

And she knows it. A stranger's hand carved him, placed him here, imbued him with magic beyond her understanding long before she ever found solace in his quiet company. But she has always felt protected here, insulated from the demands of what lies outside the maze.

Something occurs to her then, with a wild dart of thrill, of pleasure, at the core of her. "I choose you," she says. "In silence, in solitude; you are who I have always chosen. And tonight, if you are as alive as this wild dream supposes you are —" a gulp, and she takes his hand. She can't help herself; though he's been made to appear monstrous, devilish, his body is still man enough. Her eyes fall to the cut of his abdomen, to the trunks of his thighs, to his monstrous cock. Under different circumstances, this might amuse her; someone, long ago, made the choice to create him in this way, so intimidatingly endowed that her legs ache at the mere thought of it. But not now. Now, it simply makes her dizzy. "Hunt me," she says. "While the Solstice still grants you life."

A rumbling growl shakes his chest, so deep and immediate that she can feel it in her bones. Something primal, something rooted in the lascivious magic of the night. But it's something real, too. She trusts him. She knows him.

Soleil rises, and so does he. With a deep breath, she takes a step away. His head tilts, wings trembling with a rumble of stone on stone, and at his feet his tail flicks like a cat's. Tension sits heavy between them, honey-sweet and smelling of jasmine.

And then she's running, fists balled in her skirts. Soleil tugs the fabric around her thighs as she shoots, barefoot, down the path at her back, hair whipping over her shoulders. She tears past the fragrant florals, skirts around the dryad-painted fountain. And as he pursues, the electric crackle of his magic following her around every corner, she leads him to a grove of moss and pampas grass, of dancing fireflies and hyacinth.

She skids to a stop, panting. Arousal aches so deeply within her that she sways on the spot, as drunk as the rest of them. Every small sound, every snap of twig and rustle of stone over leaves, heightens her senses, loud and vibrant in every inch of her.

Magnus makes no sound as he finds her; the only tell is the absence of moonlight as his wings, his horns, his towering shoulders block it out entirely. A hard stone arm bars her waist, hauling her back. His arousal is hard against her spine, tail slipping between her legs to nudge her feet apart. Clawed hands grapple at her hip; so easily her white shift rips, exposing her hot flesh to the night air. His mouth grazes the nape of her neck, the flesh beneath her ear; even half-alive, even carved from stone, his breath is hot.

"Are you certain?" he asks, voice a low rumble in her ear.

Bold, drunk not on magic but desire, Soleil slips a hand between them. She leans against his chest, lithe fingers trailing the impossibly hard length of his cock. It, too, is warm as the rest of him; and it, too, moves beneath her touch. His cock twitches and a rumble shakes his chest once more — just like any other man. She palms him, fingers unable to fully wrap around, and she shivers.

He waits for her. Were he any other man, he would have driven her to the ground by now, forced her legs apart and fucked her into the moss. But he waits.

And so she nods. "Yes," she says. "I want *you*."

A kiss beneath her ear, at the hollow of her throat. His teeth graze her pulse and she shudders. A pitiful sound slips from her, and her cheeks redden. "As you wish," Magnus says. Overlarge fingers gather the gossamer of her skirts as he pushes her legs apart further still, tail slipping up to press into the flesh of her inner thigh once more.

Soleil pushes her hips back, pressing against him. He exhales, sharp and audible, and the heat of his breath flutters at the curls that spill from the opalescent pins in her hair, the remnants of her damnable crown. A rumble of satisfaction slips from him as his fingers disappear beneath her skirts, rough across the flesh of her hip, her inner thigh. He finds her painfully aroused, wet and throbbing round his deft fingers as one pushes inside, then two. She gasps at the fullness; only two fingers, and she's rising onto her toes to accommodate the stretch.

With two fingers hooked inside her — and how strange it is, the unyielding hardness of stone that feels so pliable as it molds to the unpracticed heat of her body — his other hand pressed flat against her abdomen, Magnus lowers her to the earth. His enormous body hulks over her, wings curled downward to shield her from any watchful eyes that might come upon them. With a grunt, the stone of his tail nudges her thighs apart further still as his fingers work inside her. She gasps, scrambling for purchase in the cool moss. Her hips jerk, nervous and trembling, and so with no hesitation Magnus tightens his grip across the front of her stomach. He lifts her, but only just; barely any weight is placed on her hips, her trembling thighs.

She finds her voice, and it's mortifyingly pitched, mewling, shaking at every syllable. "I'm not sure I'll be able to take all of you," she admits, head bowed in a curtain of aureate curls. "You are —" a gulp. " — *generously* made."

A laugh rumbles through the cage of his body. "And made of stone," he reminds her. "Not so soft as any mortal man."

She cranes her neck, struggling to find his lit-stone eyes. It's difficult to twist, her abdomen so tight from the feeling of his fingers as they crook and press inside her. She meets his gaze, and a third finger slips alongside the first pair; her mouth flies open, eyes wide, and she bucks against the heel of his hand.

"More patient than a mortal man," she huffs. Her arms tremble, wobbling as they struggle to hold her upright. "But I do want it — I want to feel as much of you as my body allows."

A hum, a twisting of his fingers. Soleil cries out, collapsing with her cheek pressed into the moss. His hand slips to her hip, steadying her as stars dance before her eyes. A whimper slips from her as she lifts a trembling hand to rest atop his. Senseless and dizzy, she guides the steadying hand round her front, tugging him down to press fully over her back. And with a shudder, she presses the very tip of a rough stone claw to the bundle of nerves at the apex of her thighs. Her head spins as she whimpers, working his finger beneath hers. She can feel herself dripping onto the carved planes of his palm, her thighs trembling as his tail lifts to knead the flesh there. It's comforting — and it's strangely human.

The tip of his cock is cool, and as impossibly hard as the rest of him. Soleil's heart lurches into her throat as her eyes fly wide, moss tickling her nose. Magnus withdraws his fingers, and without warning he presses into her. No more than an inch — she cries out, pressing her brow into cool earth as his hand slips once more to her abdomen. Her hips buck of their own accord as he leans down, pressing his cheek to the sweat-salted stretch of her back.

"Tell me," he growls, low and quick, "of the poem you left unfinished this morning."

She opens her mouth to speak, but he pushes his cock further inside and the words garble and twist into a wordless cry. The feeling of stretching, of impossible fullness, is nearly too much. "I don't think I can," she whimpers. It's only then that she realizes that her legs have gone entirely limp beneath her. It's only by the strength of his hand, the steadiness of his grip, that she is held up, propped atop the cragged stone of his thighs.

"*Try.*"

Another push, another cry; heat needles dizzyingly through her core, as painful as it is wondrous. Soleil gulps, fingers trembling as she reaches back to touch the caging stone of his thigh, his hip. "*I found love where it was meant to be lost—*" his hips move again, and she groans. Still, he holds her up, his breath hot on her back. " *— in-between a runaway's legs, flowering on prey's lips.*"

He withdraws for but a moment, pulling saccharine

whimpers from her throat as she works herself to the very edge of the unfamiliar pressure at the pit of her stomach. The foreign tumult of a climax, so lamely done on her own time and time again — it's different when it's someone else. Different when it's him.

"More," Magnus commands. "Try more."

She nods, hair splayed on the moss. "*More,*" she echoes. "*Give* me more."

He obliges. The hand pressed flat against her abdomen lifts her as easily as a stalk lifts a petal, hoisting her fully onto his lap. Magnus rocks back onto his heels, lifting her until she is positioned over his broad length, barely slick with her wetness. She falls flush against his chest, trembling hands lifting to feel at the curve of his fangs, the arch of his horns. And there, she holds fast.

Magnus holds her thighs apart, spreading her wide with deft claws. Breath catches in her throat; they're sharp, almost painfully so, as he works her open for him once more, lifting his hips to push up into her. The sound of her cries, her wonderful sing-song mewling, seem to spill life into him all the more as his own hips shudder. His grip tightens as his hips jerk, fucking up into her with enough force to fill her almost entirely. And even then, there exists a great gulf between where she wets him, grips him with all the force of her unpracticed muscles, and where he is carved perfectly to the hilt.

"Had I more time," he breathes, the sharp crag of a fang worn by time and the elements rough against her crown, "I would know every inch of you." A thrust, and another cry spills from Soleil with a flint-strike of heat and pressure so dizzying that she feels she might be sick. "And not in silence," he says. "Not in perpetual stone. Were I to live to see another night, you would never know another moment without wanting. The hunt would never —" a groan, a bucking of his hips, " — end."

A clawed finger presses to the nerves between her legs as he fucks up into her once more, pressing deeper still. And it's enough. She clenches around him, eyes flying wide as stars belonging to no known sky dance before her eyes.

Head thrown back, spine arched; she gives a tug at the horn she's gripping for dear life. Her body strains, the unfamiliar sensation of an orgasm at another's hand hot and ferocious. It's all she can do to keep from falling limp, even as he eases her down further still, coaxing another roll of shuddering thunder through her core. Something strangled, mewling, far beyond any reasonable semblance of his name skittering from her, everything pink and trembling. He holds her fast; there's no chance of falling, of slumping into the weeds or the encroaching hedges — there's only the pleasure, the stars, and the stone at her back.

It is the matter of a single nudge to ease Soleil, starry-eyed and dizzy, onto her stomach. And she's out of breath; as she opens her mouth to speak, it's a long moment before she can muster words. Only vaguely does she register the feeling of his hands on her, the rip of fabric from the hem of her already-ruined dress as he cleans the space between her legs.

"I think," she says, rolling with a groan onto her

back. The stars remain, but so does his face. Stone, familiar and weathered, but alive with magic that will wane come morning. And morning *will* come after all; her pleasure has broken the heady seal on her father's magic. What will he say when he learns that the Stag was caught and stuck by no one at his precious party? "I've forgotten the rest of the poem."

A laugh rumbles through him again as he settles over her, a cage of stone arms round her golden-haloed head. His legs nudge hers apart as his hand trails the damp stretch of her neck, her chest, her abdomen. She shivers, and again his tail flicks like an animal's.

"It's alright, little Stag," he says. "You can try it again tomorrow. And as always, as forever, I will listen."

Nyxion, Room 91
Kari Kephali

CW: Age gap, consensual dubious-consent, demon/sinner roleplay, telepathic connections, transactional sex work

Admit One (1) for Initial Interview

Time: November 29, 2054, at 11:59pm (23:59)

Location: 267 Foundry Row, Millingsford

Name: Calico Thorvascion

This invitation will not be extended again. You may reschedule once in the same manner you applied for the initial interview. Tardiness or absence will result in your name listed multiversally as non-contact and permanently ineligible.

Your pass phrase is 'Nyxion Beseeches the Abyssal Eye.'

Calico held their breath as their phone vibrated inside their hoodie pocket: one minute to midnight, and they knew they were at the right spot, but where...?

A door opened to their left, a 6-foot section of the

bricks simply swinging inward out of the rain, revealing a faintly yellow-glowing lobby. Calico immediately ducked in, dragging their boots across the scratchy welcome mat and taking in the space. Earthy hues of mahogany and forest green were well-matched with the amber-toned light coming from table-lamps and recessed fixtures overhead. There was an L-shaped desk to the right, and a small collection of mismatched sofas and armchairs to the left. A glass-topped coffee table rested in the seating area, a few magazines dog-eared and lying abandoned on its surface. With the smell of an extinguished match and myrrh wafting through the air, Calico thought there must be a candle burning somewhere.

The sound of the rain was shuttered as the door was pushed closed behind them, and then they were struggling not to stare as the receptionist moved past them and arranged themself again behind the desk. Calico had *known* what they'd been signing up for, but knowing and seeing were two very different things. The receptionist was human from the waist up, buxom and curvaceous like a classical vaudeville beauty in a burgundy blouse and white silk neckerchief; but their lower body was a full eight feet of sinuous, scaled tail, no legs to be seen. *Naga,* they were called, one of the types of Travelers that had begun to interact with humankind only a few decades before.

"Invitation, identification, and medical record, please." The receptionist spoke in a soothing murmur, and Calico fumbled their invitation and wallet out with shaking hands. The Naga didn't seem to notice or judge their reactions, though Calico thought they caught a glimpse of a smile before they managed to hand over the USB that contained their medical history. "Wonderful. Calico, my name is Maraia, and I use the feminine pronouns she and her. Your file indicates you prefer neutral pronouns; is that correct?"

Calico cleared their throat. "Yes, I use neutral they/them pronouns."

"Excellent. Now, I have reviewed your interest forms, and I am pleased to say you may have a great future here with us. Provided you remember your pass phrase?"

"Nyxion beseeches the abyssal eye."

"Perfect. You should know that line of text was enchanted, and can only be read by the intended recipient. That is for your protection, and you will receive new invitations with new pass phrases each time you visit one of our facilities. You will be immediately black-listed if you ever fail to produce the correct pass phrase upon request by a member of our staff. Do you understand these terms?"

"Yes, I understand."

"Wonderful. Now..."

Ten minutes and a handful of signatures later, Calico smiled broadly at Maraia. The Naga returned their grin, small dimples in her cheeks framing her fangs just so. As she sorted and stacked Calico's paperwork into a fresh manila folder, she said,

'Thank you for your patience with all of that, and I'd like to welcome you once again to the Nyxion family of escorts and companions. Now, if you're ready, there is a candidate who might be a good match for you tonight. I do have a few more questions to ask to be sure, but if you'd rather not, we can simply call it here and you can request your first appointment in the app at your convenience."

"No, I'd love to meet someone tonight! Ask away."

"Your enthusiasm is welcome, Calico. Alright, our client is a Traveler known as an Incubus. They are a type of Infernal, what some humans have termed demons or devils. Incubus are actually closer in kind to the concept of Vampires, but rather than feeding on blood, they gain sustenance from sexual desire and action."

"Must be a pretty popular client, then?" Calico quipped, but Maraia's slight grimace twisted their heart.

"Unfortunately, not quite. Incubus produce a pheromone that induces heightened sexual desire, allowing them to feed more easily and deeply. Some of our human escorts have reservations about this, feeling that the pheromone causes their decision-making to be altered, like a drug. Because Incubus are rare these days, we only have one such client on the books, and he has struggled to find a compatible match. Now, please don't think I'm telling you this to pressure you; this is just information, and your decision is still your own. If you are uncomfortable, we will not proceed, no retaliation and no harm done."

Calico took a minute to think it over: a being that fed on sexual desire, with aphrodisiac pheromones to aid the process. They could definitely see how some folks would be turned off by that. But Calico didn't think they had a problem with it; if anything, the thought of being out of their mind with lust and fulfilling their partner that way seemed kind of sweet. There had been a lot of times in their past when Calico had wished for a partner to be more active - even feral - in the dominant role. If an Incubus could naturally fill that desire...

"I think I'd like to hear more about him, but for now, I'm still interested."

"Wonderful! Well, let me go pull his file, and I'll be right back. Just hang tight."

Maraia swept away, passing around the corner near a glowing lamp and disappearing into a hidden hallway. If Calico hadn't seen her go, they'd have never known the passageway was there. Not even a full minute passed before she returned, a manila folder an inch thick tucked against her breasts. She sank back onto the sofa and flipped to the first page.

"Here we are. His name is Laikros, and he is 589 Earth-years old." She paused, watching Calico's face for any change of expression; they just smiled and nodded. "As an Incubus, his very presence induces physical lust by means of pheromones; however potent the effects are, once you are separated, there is no lingering or permanent change in your body's chemistry. The pheromones also cannot alter your emotions; only your body's physical responses will be changed. How are you feeling so far, Calico?"

"Like this was an even better idea than I thought!"

"Wonderful, I'm glad to hear that." She turned to another page, and after skimming it briefly, she said, "Laikros has interviewed 5 escorts before you, and only one has gone further than the initial introduction. That escort experienced some dysphoria after the pheromones left their system, and as such withdrew their name from Laikros' pool of candidates."

"What was the nature of the dysphoria, if I may ask?"

"You may, one moment, let me find the right page." She thumbed through the documents until she found the one she wanted, and read aloud, *"Escort J. M. reported Client Laikros' pheromonal presence was immediate and unavoidable from the moment of introduction. J. M., after leaving the session, expressed discomfort and regret that, had they wished to stop or withdraw consent, they feared they would not have been able to properly express that wish. J. M. did acknowledge that Laikros checked on them repeatedly throughout the encounter; J. M. states they were overwhelmed and hadn't realized the effect would be so immediate or potent. Laikros states the length of time since his last feeding - which he also acknowledges as his own error in not providing an accurate assessment of his potency - was the likely cause of the intensity J. M. reported."*

Calico, blinking, replied "Damn," and nothing more.

Maraia leaned toward them slightly. "How are you feeling now, Calico?"

"Hmm. Uhhhmmm, like I wanna meet him even more? I... Well, I like the idea of losing control of myself like that. And if that helps Laikros? Even better. I like being useful, and being used." They blushed, realizing they were rambling.

"Oh, please don't feel self-conscious, Calico!" She reached over, patting the arm of their chair, instead of touching them directly. "Your honesty is helpful, it keeps us both on track. If you need a minute, that's fine. Let me read through the rest of this, see if there's anything else I missed."

Maraia finished checking the folder a few minutes later, and Calico knew the time for a final decision had come. When Maraia asked, they confidently nodded and said, "I would like to meet Laikros, if he would like to meet me. I would like to have sex with him, if he would like to have sex with me."

Maraia nodded and swept back to her desk in a whirl. She rapidly typed out a message, then beckoned Calico to another corner of the room, where a second hidden hallway was tucked. She began to talk, throwing her words back over her shoulder as she swayed down the plain, wood-paneled hall ahead of them.

"I'll lead you down to Laikros' room. Each client is assigned a room upon signing up with us; it helps them feel more secure, and can even be a refuge of sorts if the human world is less than kind. You'll be waiting here, in the hall, outside his door until he arrives. That way, if you change your mind, you'll have a better chance of avoiding his pheromones and keeping some distance between you. If you leave the doorway, he will not pursue, and it will be recorded as a rejection in your file. Again, no retaliation, just being as clear as can be."

She slowed beside a simple wooden door with a brass number 91 tacked in the center. Her aquamarine nails drummed a rhythmic tattoo below the number, and the door swung inward. She slid a little further away, then turned tight around on her tail to gesture

Calico forward.

"As I said, just wait here in the hallway for him to arrive. You can see the door he'll be coming through on the far side. It will be a portal, so if you've never seen one before, try not to look too deeply into it; it can make humans nauseous. You may wish to provide him a safeword, and we do recommend that for most encounters. Once he leaves, you are free to use the bathing facilities and to sleep if you wish. There is no time limit, though we will check on you every 12 hours. There is a small kitchenette stocked with snacks, water, and sports drinks; those are free for your use as well.

"When you are ready to leave, simply open this door, turn right, and come straight back to the lobby. If you need assistance with anything, your Nyxion app has an emergency call button which will summon myself, a human medical aide, and a psychological support individual to you here. Laikros may also use his app's alert at any time on his or your own behalf, if he feels it's necessary."

Calico nodded, absorbing everything and checking in with themself. Yep, they still wanted this. "Got it. Thank you, Maraia, you've been great. I guess I'll see you on the other side!"

"You certainly shall! I'm on shift for the next 36 hours, so unless you and Laikros have a marathon, I'll be here when you check out! Have fun, Calico!" And with that, she slid behind them and back toward the lobby. They peered eagerly through the open doorway into room 91, excited to see how an Incubus kept his space.

It was... oddly normal. About the size of a one-bedroom studio apartment, there was a small seating area next to the kitchenette, and Calico could see the frosted glass door leading into the bathroom on the left. There were some abstract paintings on a couple of the walls: reds and blacks layered over each other in broad strokes, evoking swords or blades of grass dripping under a dying sun. The most prominent feature of the open floorplan was the bed: huge and covered in silky black sheets. It had to be four feet high, and looked at least twice as large as a California King.

The door across the room from where Calico stood clicked, and a rushing gale of sound whipped through the space. Swirling red and yellow light blinded them, and then all was silent with another click. Calico blinked and got their first look at their Incubus.

Laikros was at least seven feet tall; no, he had to be taller with those horns. Gently twisting curves of bone rose up from above his eyebrows, which themselves were thin and deeply arched. His hair was the tawny blonde of a mountain lion in summer, not quite yellow and not exactly brown. His eyes were amber but round, like cats' eyes, and set against his burnt umber skin, they seemed to glow. The Incubus wore a simple collared shirt and slacks, both in black with faint grey smudges like acid-washing. Calico stared in delighted wonder as a whip-thin tail wove gracefully into view around Laikros' hip, clinging vine-like to his leg before drawing slowly away.

Oh yes. They were going to love every bit of this.

"You must be my newest Escort. I am Laikros."

"Calico. Neutral pronouns."

"Male or neutral for me. Calico, I would like you to decide now if you want to enter my room, knowing you will most likely lose some or all of your mental faculties due to my pheromones. I promise I will be gentle and careful with you, and I will do my best to do nothing with you which you might regret allowing after I leave."

Calico drank in the tone of his voice; his words tripped and trickled over their ears like the rain on the bricks outside, smooth yet clipped, urgent yet careful. They watched as he raised one hand to brush his tawny, wavy hair behind his ear. His pointed, jewel-bedecked ear.

"I do want you, Laikros. You're gorgeous, and I would like nothing more than to share your bed tonight."

Calico stepped over the threshold and shut the door behind them. Their feet carried them into the room, angling between the Incubus and the bed, uncertain if Laikros would prefer to start standing or not. Laikros stood quite still, his eyes roaming over Calico's movements, amber gems flickering frequently back to their face to gauge their mood. Calico did their best to seem nonchalant, but they worried that they should try to be more seductive, more sinuous, more tempting.

They hadn't covered more than ten feet, their mind starting to race with excited nerves, before a tingling wave washed over them, unspooling in trailing tendrils of static fire up and down their arms and legs. The unearthly sensation traced over the back of their neck, and they felt their hair lift at the roots like a lightning strike. They almost stumbled at the jolt, catching themself on the corner of the kitchenette counter.

"Damn, that's…" Another wave of incandescent sensation swirled around their ears, sending shivers down their spine. A few prickles even sparkled across the soles of their feet, and they let out a startled chuckle.

"Is this to your liking so far, Calico?"

"Hell yeah! This is… wild…" They swallowed drily, feeling their thoughts beginning to muddle. "Um, hey, safeword. It's… um, mahogany, yeah, like the wood?"

"Oh, I know all about wood, sweet thing. Will you also use colors for me? Green is good, yellow is pull back, red is stop?"

Calico nodded frantically, the tingling, tickling drags of arousal deepening and swirling inward behind their navel. "Yeah, green, I'm green right now! Fuck, I feel high…"

Laikros hummed, and his voice hovered somewhere above a rumbling purr. "Good pet. I want to lay you out on my bed, unwrap you like the gift you are, and feast until we're both deliriously sated. You don't have to do a thing, but anything you want, I'll give to you. Do you understand me?"

"Yes, fuck yes! Green, I'm good, just…"

Laikros was there instantly, lifting Calico by their hips so swiftly it felt like their stomach was left behind. They gasped, and the Incubus covered their mouth with his own, stealing their breath and sending the spiraling tide of arousal even higher. They felt like they were drowning, and flying, and throttling a motorcycle, and dancing in front of the eyes of thousands, all at once. Exhilarating, intoxicating, rampaging *need* poured into them, stirred everything inside them, and left them barren, an empty vessel craving the fullness only Laikros could give them.

They felt the silk sheets under their bare back, with no awareness of how or when or where their hoodie and shirt had gone. Their shoes thumped to the floor, out of sight and mind, and then their pants were slowly, tenderly unzipped over their aching erection. Laikros had his face buried against the side of Calico's neck, nibbling gently with delicately pointed fangs, careful not to bruise the human with his arching horns. Calico felt a slithering slide, and craned their head up to see the Incubus' tail, weaving into their belt loops and tugging their pants down.

"*Holy fuck!*" Calico whispered enthusiastically and collapsed back to the bed.

With a chuckle, Laikros murmured, "I can assure you: nothing *holy* about me. Rather the opposite, in fact." Calico gave a delighted shudder, and felt the Incubus take a sharp inhale. "Ohhh, how lovely you are. You enjoy playing the sinner? Color?"

"Green!"

"Hmmmmm, I'll hold onto that one, for later then. I'm afraid I don't quite have the patience to roleplay right now; you're simply too *delicious*, sweet Calico..."

And with that, Laikros bit, sharp and playful, against Calico's earlobe. They jolted, but the Incubus, so much taller than them, kept them pinned to the bed. He slowly drifted back into Calico's line of sight, peering intently from under lowered lids, observing their reaction. They smiled, entranced: the Incubus wore the faintest dusting of gold eyeshadow, and his lashes were coated with a shimmering oil.

"May I use my mouth to please you, Calico? I will not use my teeth."

Calico nodded again, and fought to form a whisper. "Green. Teeth, next time."

A bright flash arced across Laikros' amber gaze, and with it, a pulse in the waves of arousal smothering Calico in sensation. Laikros growled, diving down, landing with a muffled thump on the floor between Calico's feet. They struggled up to watch in awestruck, delighted desire as Laikros slid Calico's boxers down and away, and then, with all the ease and seduction of his fabled species, licked up and swallowed down Calico's cock.

If Calico had thought the buffeting waves of pheromones were intense before, they needed a new scale to measure upon. From the moment Laikros sealed his lips around their tip, Calico forgot their own name. They ceased to exist as an individual, becoming a reflection only of the sensations the Incubus coaxed from and poured into their body. Under Laikros, their body writhed, twitched, spasmed, and flushed. Their hands, almost disembodied and moving of their own accord, curled desperately around Laikros' horns, clinging for dear life as everything *pulsed* inside their pelvis. They breathed in frantic bursts, and their mouth may have formed words, but they could not control nor remember anything beyond the piercing, all-consuming intensity happening to-within-around-upon them.

When they climaxed, they felt a flashing instant of something outside themself, both frighteningly alien and intimately familiar at once. It felt like the first drink of water from a cascade tumbling down green-etched boulders at the end of a long hike. It felt like getting a graded exam back in college, one they had studied earnestly for, and finally receiving the proof of their hard work in a bright red "98%". It felt like their mother's holiday dinners smelled, warm and comforting and layered with savory and sweet and spice.

Just as quickly as they felt it, the feeling jerked away, leaving behind the balmy, heart-racing afterglow of an incredible orgasm. All their muscles felt instantly weak, so they let themself flop back onto the mattress, flexing their fingers back and forth to ground themself. Slowly, Laikros stood up before them, and even more slowly, he began to remove his shirt and trousers. Calico hadn't even realized the Incubus was still dressed.

Calico licked their lips, watching as the Incubus' lean, wiry body was revealed. Thin lines of near-black marked their ribs, hatches and long lines scattered and puckering the skin: scars, perhaps from claws or blades. As the Incubus bent to shuck off his trousers, his spine stood out along his skin like the spiked tops of pine trees along a mountain ridge.

Calico decided they had to ask, before the pheromones swept them under again. "What... was that you I felt?"

Laikros paused, looking away before turning to climb onto the bed beside Calico. He reached a long-fingered hand down to help Calico scoot up to lie beside him. They turned on their side to face him, waiting as patiently as they could, trying not to vibrate as the proximity had their skin buzzing again.

"Yes. I'm sorry, I tried to keep myself to myself there, but... I think Maraia told you, it's been a very long time since I fed, at least on anyone other than another Infernal. And other Infernals just... It's like a human trying to live on nothing but tofu."

"I get that, and please don't be sorry! I honestly didn't mind it. I can understand if that's too intimate for you, with me being practically a stranger, but I'm green, I promise!"

Laikros seemed uncertain, watching Calico's face closely for any hint of deception. They kept smiling, letting their own eyes roam the Incubus' body hungrily after a few moments. The Infernal huffed a soft laugh, reaching over to tuck a loose curl behind Calico's ear.

"I can't help but feel inordinately lucky, sweet Calico. I only hope you'll be able to warn me before I scare you away."

Calico snorted, then pounced, rolling the taller figure over and straddling his hips. "Fuck that, magic man! You can't scare me off; I've been waiting my whole life for this. Now, why don't you put your tail where your dick should be, and make me forget my name again."

Laikros growled, and arousal crashed over Calico like an avalanche, pounding in their head like surf, surging in their veins like tidal waves. Their skin erupted in goosebumps, and they shivered in anticipation as they felt the Incubus' silky-skinned tail brush along their hips.

"Hellfire, if you insist!" Laikros snapped his fingers, and with an orange flash of light, a tube of lubricant appeared in his hand. Calico leaned down to lavish the Incubus with kisses and licks, distracting him to the point of hisses and more growls in a language that was definitely *not* English. Laikros brought his lubed fingers to Calico's opening, carefully and gently working his ring until he could slip two in without resistance.

And then, finally, Calico felt the blunt, narrow tip of Laikros' tail nudging its way inside them. With a whine, they arched their back, unspoken desire thrumming through them like thunder. The Incubus' tail was only the width of a finger, but it was so much more flexible, pressing up and down and swirling inside them with a sinuous dexterity. It was like nothing they had ever felt before, and they were instantly addicted.

Laikros had been silent for a while, but now, he quietly asked, "Color, Calico?"

Calico licked their lips, opening their eyes to meet Laikros' careful gaze. "Green."

"Good, sweet thing. I'm going to make you come on my tail, and then I'll give you my cock. Have you ever been milked before? Had your prostate stimulated so well that you just... *spill?*"

Calico whined, shaking their head and clutching at the sheets beneath Laikros.

"You're going to be good for me now, Calico. You just relax, and feel, and nothing else. You can trust me, I'll take care of you. Color?"

"Green." This time, it was a gasp, and that was enough.

Laikros pulled them down until they were cuddled against the Incubus' scarred chest, and deep inside them, his tail curled and began to prod their prostate over and over, unerringly accurate and unflinchingly constant. Calico whined and whimpered, moaned and gasped, listening with all their might to Laikros' coaxing rumbles.

"You're such a treat, Calico, letting me play with your body like this. You don't know how rare you are, how long I've waited for someone like you. You're so soft inside, and so tight. I can't wait to fill you up, make your body remember the shape of me long after we part ways."

Calico nodded, tucked against Laikros, scraping their cheek against his sleek pectoral. The Incubus hummed a laugh, smoothing his clean hand down Calico's hair and back.

"You would have liked to have known me a few hundred years ago, I think. I might have taken you home with me, kept you for a pet, my own to play with, every night. I'd have shown you off, kept you dressed in nothing but a little net of chain, just enough to jingle prettily when you wanted my attention. I'd have you on my lap, all day long at court, just sitting there, keeping my cock warm inside you. You'd have liked that, wouldn't you?"

They nodded again, shuddering as a trembling feeling began pulsing in their groin. It shimmered out in waves, and beneath them, they felt their cock dripping pre-cum like a fountain.

"I do so love a pretty pet who knows their place and

enjoys serving."

A moan tore from their throat as Calico felt something unlock inside them. They felt cum pouring out of their cock, felt their walls clamping around Laikros' tail in rhythm, but amazingly, their cock stayed erect, and their arousal did not lessen. They whined as they felt the tail sliding out of them, and were soothed with another stroking caress.

"Now, now, sweet Calico. I promised you I'd make you mine."

Calico melted as they finally felt Laikros' cock at their entrance. Slender like the rest of him, only a little more pointed than a human's would be, it slid easily into them, filling the emptiness they'd only just begun to feel.

They clung to Laikros as the Incubus wrapped them in his arms, planting his feet on the mattress and slowly thrusting up into their body. They kissed his throat, and he nipped the shell of their ear with a hiss. His claws dug into their ribs, and Calico shivered with pleasure. Arousal cocooned them, and they swam through it, languid and lazy like an eel, relishing in every sensation, every motion, every scent and taste and sound. At some point, Laikros rolled them both over, so that Calico's back was on the mattress and their knees were over his elbows.

And just as they had wished for earlier in the evening, thrust by thrust Laikros seemed to lose himself in Calico's willing submission. Growled Infernal words rumbled around their whimpering moans of pleasure, the spicy scent of the Incubus mingling with the tang and salt of sex in the air. Powerful pulses of arousal were like one heartbeat shared between them, waves cascading and drawing them further into the sea of passion. Beat after beat, thrust upon thrust, give and take and release...

Later, long after Calico's brain had ceased to form coherent thoughts, Laikros dragged one hand up their body, claws raising goosebumps in their wake. The Incubus' over-long fingers curled around Calico's neck and jaw, and his thumb pried open the corner of their mouth. They laved it with their tongue, knowing instinctively what he wanted from them.

Laikros groaned aloud, slowing his rhythm until Calico's hips began to squirm with the craving for friction. The Incubus chuckled darkly, Infernal words resolving once more into deeply accented English. "I think I'd like to see you play the sinner for me now, Calico. Do you think you can do that? Color?"

Since Laikros didn't seem interested in removing his thumb from Calico's mouth to let them answer, they mumbled as best they could around the claw, "Green."

"Wonderful." And something subtle changed in the air, enough to send a chilling thrill of fear down Calico's sweat-laced ribs. Laikros hadn't moved, but the shadows played differently down the sharp angles of his face, and his spicy scent shifted more to the realm of the ash left after incense has exhausted itself. A roll of distant thunder tolled through the room, cycling up and down with every beat of Calico's heart.

Laikros gave them one thrust, sharp and jolting.

They gasped, and the Incubus' fingers tightened around the curve of their jaw.

"Humans should know better than to play with things they call devils." When he spoke the words sounded layered, whispers and the faintest screams threading around his voice. Another thrust, with a deep, rolling grind at the end. "You came here to partake of forbidden fruit; how do you like the taste, human?"

Calico drew breath to answer, but Laikros' tail whipped around and spanked their hip, close to their thigh. They yelped instead, and the demon only laughed.

"I knew humans were depraved creatures. Courting one such as I, desperate only for heat, for *lust...*"

His tail wound gently around Calico's erection like a sentient vine, the tip aligning with their own, flicking back and forth there like a tongue. Calico could only moan, a long, shuddering sound like a thing possessed. Just as they thought they might get used to the tail on their cock, the demon pushed forward again, bending them nearly in two and pinning them to the center of the enormous bed.

"Pray to me, human. Pray, and maybe I'll spare your soul."

Calico gasped, "Please."

The demon kissed them, silencing anything else they might have said, and began pounding them into the mattress in the same instant. Calico's hand flew up, latching onto Laikros' horns, clinging to the Incubus for dear life, whining into the kiss as every nerve in their body sparked alight. Laikros broke the kiss, eyes locked on Calico's, breathing just as rapidly and brokenly as they were.

Calico caught just enough breath to say, "Please," once more.

And the demon broke, grinding as deeply into them as he could go, infernal heat marking them so far inside it felt like it was right behind their navel. Calico whined through it, their cock still wrapped in gentle coils of tail. They hadn't come again, but that didn't matter; they trusted their Incubus to satisfy them before the night was through. Being used this way, a vessel for Laikros' pleasure, was more than enough for now.

Some time later, Laikros unfolded them from the cramped pose he'd held them in, and turned them on their side. A whispered check-in, another near-silent confirmation, and their demon pushed back inside them, both unwilling to leave the heaven of pleasure just yet. Calico came repeatedly like that, never feeling the harsh bite of overstimulation, welcoming the lingering, eternal embrace of the Incubus who held them tightly.

They had no clue how long it lasted, but at some point, they found themself tucked beside Laikros, tenderly cleaned and warmly wrapped in silk sheets. The Infernal hummed an unfamiliar, gentle tune, and Calico drifted into dreams of tracing claws and slithering tails and nipping fangs.

The Red Drake of La Montaña en Llamas

D. O. Rackham

CW: Forced marriage, caning, cucking

The oracle had said she would wed a monster.

The path up the mountainside was narrow and winding. Alma watched the land below fall slowly away. Just as her town and her family's sprawling home had done, just as the only world she knew would surely do. Dark clouds were already gathering in the fresh morning, bringing a cool wind to relieve the stifling heat that had built with the sunrise. She bobbed on the back of the wagon as it rattled up the switchbacks of the old dirt road, thinking of her parents, her brother, her sisters, wondering if she would see them again. She had always felt aimless; maybe having a husband would give her some direction.

Alma toyed with the long braid she wore slung over her shoulder, pressing her fingers between the woven pieces of her brown hair, loosening the braid gently. A few short, loose strands drifted around her face. Her guide, driving the cart, was the son of a powerful matriarch her family was indebted to; it was she who had arranged the marriage, and her son who would hand Alma off.

She clambered to her hands and knees, moving to settle herself near the front of the wagon, close to the driving seat. "Can you tell me about Señor Rojo? Have you met him?"

He started in surprise, glancing back at her. "Miss Garza, here, that must be uncomfortable." He twisted around, slinging the reins to the pair of mules pulling the cart over a post on the front end of the cart and held out his hand. Alma took it, a little thrill running through her at the touch of their palms, and he helped her maneuver onto the seat beside him. "I have met him, once or twice. What would you like to know?"

Alma looked at him as he turned his attention back to the reins. "Anything. Everything. Is he kind? Is he terrifying? Will I be happy?"

"I don't want you to be apprehensive, Miss Garza, but... He is an intimidating figure. They say that a beast lives on the mountaintop, a dragon that he sets loose on villages that don't pay their tithes to him. But he's always been fair when he's had dealings with my mother."

"Is he as handsome as you are, Saiyed?" she asked, tucking a little lock of hair behind her ear. She was pleased to see his cheeks darken.

"Are you always so direct, Miss Garza?" he laughed, dark curls bobbing around his face, "I think Señor Rojo will appreciate that."

"Call me Alma. I won't be Miss Garza after tonight."

#

At the summit, the palace of El Rojo came into view. A structure that seemed to carry the mountain's peak higher, with a central tower climbing into the sky and low buildings around it. There was a high wall that wound around the entire estate, and a single open gate through which they entered. The mules whickered nervously, stamping and restless in the courtyard, as Saiyed helped Alma climb down from the wagon and moved to get her luggage.

A man, shorter than Alma expected, emerged from the tower with his arms spread wide. He had long, black hair hanging to his shoulders, and a dusting of stubble over his hard jaw. He was dressed in fine black clothes, and spurs on his boots tinkled as he walked toward them.

Alma caught the scent of smoke, savory and warm, as he approached.

"Bonita, you've made it here at last. You have my apologies for not bringing you here myself, but I was detained." He turned to Saiyed with a grin, extending his hand. "Thank you, for escorting my bride, and for taking such good care of her."

Saiyed took the offered hand and they grasped forearms in greeting. "It was my—of course, sir."

"I thought we could break fast together, and begin all the necessary ceremonies at midday. That gives you both time to eat and rest and rid yourselves of the dust from the road. And Saiyed, you should have light enough to make it back down the mountain."

Saiyed nodded, glancing at Alma. "Thank you, sir."

Rojo gestured to the small pile of belongings by the wagon, "You can carry those inside. All the way to the top of the stairs. I want to show Alma around her new home."

Alma stood uncertainly, watching as Saiyed busied himself with her trunks. "I hope I am pleasing to you, Señor Rojo?" She dipped in a small curtsy, feeling suddenly self-conscious about the dust on her dress and her hair that had come loose from her braid, blowing free in the gathering wind.

"Beyond words, Alma."

"What should I call you?"

"For now, Rojo will do. Or Señor, if you feel more comfortable."

She nodded and followed as he led her toward the low buildings that surrounded the tower.

Rojo adjusted pace so they would fall into step alongside one another. "Tell me," he spoke softly in low, rumbling tones. "Are you nervous?"

Alma decided lying would do her no good as they entered the first building. "I am, Señor. It's always difficult to find your place in a new environment. And you are a stranger to me."

"I hope I can put you at ease. You will be comfortable here. Anything you wish, you may have. In return, I expect obedience. At any point, if you wish me to stop, you only need to speak my full name. Adan Damaso Rojo. And I will stop." Her face twisted in distaste of the word 'obedience' and he laughed, waving his hand. "You will understand. Come."

The rooms were all beautifully adorned. Rojo kept

a full library, soft and plush furnishings, rare fabrics and soft silks, and everywhere the glow of gold glimmered. The tour concluded at the base of the tower, where he gestured to the winding stairs like those in a lighthouse. "Our rooms will be up there. I will let you explore those on your own while you see to your needs. We will eat soon, so do not tarry."

Alma found the rooms to be a delight, though only one large bed occupied the highest one. She found her things already waiting, and she made quick work of her bath and changed into a fine, clean dress. The room opened up to a balcony that spanned the entire outside of the tower, offering magnificent views of the entire landscape around. She wondered if she might be able to see her home on a clear day.

They ate with the polite, stiff conversation of the ill-acquainted, Saiyed stealing glances at Alma from across the polished table.

The wedding ceremony was brief and efficient, with no officiant, only Saiyed's signature as a witness. Alma waved at Saiyed as he rode back down the mountain path.

"I have some business to attend to, but I will come to you tonight." Rojo brushed a lock of her hair back behind her ear as he spoke. She felt a little shiver run through her. "I must ask that you extinguish every light and draw the curtains at dusk. Do not light a lamp after dark. Do you understand?"

Alma nodded, her eyes wide. "Why is that, Señor?"

He hesitated, looking at her carefully. "I expect you have heard about the beast on the mountaintop already."

There was a red gleam in his eyes as he smiled, and she thought, for an instant, his teeth appeared sharp and pointed. "I fear you will not stay here if you see the monster." He laughed suddenly, a deep sound. "Or, I suppose I could just say that I am shy."

She nodded again. "Very well, Señor. No lights."

#

Alma busied herself with unpacking. She was surprised by the glaring lack of staff for the estate. There had been no cooks, no serving women, no stable hands, no one besides her and Rojo on the summit. *Who does all of his cooking and washing?* she wondered. *Will he expect me to do that for him, is that what he meant by obedient?*

Near dusk, she mounted the stairs to their room again. The gain in altitude made the going slow, but she was thankful for the soft bed at the end of her trek. She considered her various sleeping gowns, settling on her finest one of soft silk. She felt curious more than afraid; she had lain with men before, though none quite like Rojo, and certainly none she couldn't set aside when she was bored. *He'll want to consummate our vows right away,* she thought.

She was reluctant to pull the curtains over the massive windows. The views from the tower were striking. The desert rolled out under the sunset in all directions. She knew the ground was hard and unyielding, parched and unforgiving, but from this height it was all soft as the fur of a lion, turning golden and pink in the diminishing light. She pulled the curtains closed and moved around the bed chamber, blowing out the candles she had lit earlier in the day, then the oil lamps. She carried one final lamp to a bedside table, crawling into the massive soft expanse, before blowing it out as well.

The darkness was sudden and immediate as her eyes struggled to adjust. She sat in the bed with pillows against her back, hugging her knees, waiting for the shapes around her to form. There was enough light to make out the grey lines of the settee, armchair, and little vanity, of her trunks piled against the wall, of the massive double-door wardrobe and the soft archway that led into the bathroom. She was resolved to wait and stay awake.

The darkness deepened as outside night fell in earnest. She felt her eyes growing tired, the lids heavy, and she stretched her legs out beneath the blankets. Maybe he wouldn't come tonight.

A sound on the stairs snapped her back out of her drowsing. She sat up again, twisting toward the door.

A rasping sounded against the steps and the soft clicking of many hard points against cold stone, conjuring the image of dead leaves in the wind and small rocks falling before a landslide. She heard low rumbling like distant thunder, and she drew shallow breaths to try and hear better over the pounding of her heart.

The door creaked open and the slithering sound came into the room. The door snapped shut again and she watched for movement.

She could hear the whispering of something large dragging across the cool tiles of the floor and the scrape of metal, or bone, as it approached the bed. *The dragon,* she thought, her pulse racing. *How did it get inside?*

She felt the bed shift with the weight of the creature.

All around her was the smell of sharp, clean gunpowder. It stung in her nose and she could taste it in the back of her throat. There was hot breath on her exposed shoulders and neck and she felt gooseflesh erupt over her skin despite the sudden warmth. The breathing of the creature mingled with soft growling.

Her eyes opened wide as she shrunk back in the bed, looking at the shapeless void before her.

"Señor? Rojo?" she whimpered, looking in the direction of the door. "Please Señor, come here!" Her voice sounded reedy and thin in her ears, and she felt her eyes begin to heat with the threat of tears.

"I am here," the voice rumbled out from the weight gliding over the bed. She could see nothing but a faint silvery glint against a hard, shining surface, and the dull glow of red like embers in the dark.

She squeezed her eyes shut. *Rojo is the dragon? Why would he come to me in this form?* she thought, *Unless, he means to...*

Tentatively she reached out her hand even as the covers slid off her body. Her fingertips pressed against the hardness of smooth, interlocked scales, surprisingly cool to the touch.

She moved her other hand to roam over the cool glassy body beside her, shifting to press her cheek into their surface, then her breasts, veiled by the silken fabric of her nightdress. Her nipples slid over the ridges that defined each scale, hardening against the fabric.

The sharp touch of talons grazed her shoulders and

thighs, creeping around to her back and round bottom, like so many little knives, delicate against her nightdress. She felt warmth rush to her cheeks as her heartbeat sunk to the place between her thighs, feeling a sudden wetness spread into the soft hairs there. She inhaled in a soft gasp, surprised at herself even as she swallowed a soft moan at the press of her nipples into the cool, hard body.

A tail lashed and swept the rest of the blankets to the floor, then moved to stroke along one leg. She brushed her lips over the scales, tasting them with her tongue. Above her, she heard the growling breaths deepen as she lowered her exploring, curious fingers.

Her fingers served as her eyes, her main sensory pathway, reaching lower along the serpentlike body until they found a bulge amongst the uniform scale pattern. With her hands pressed to this anomaly it opened beneath her, like a gateway, the scales shifting aside for something hard and writhing to emerge.

Her palms greeted it as it continued to emerge, a thick tendril of cool, firm slickness, pressing into her hands as it uncoiled from the body. "Rojo," she whispered against his scales.

His head dipped down to her own, nudging her back into the pillows and she felt his breath hot against her neck and collar bone. There was a soft scrape of many teeth, scratching against her shoulder and the fleshy softness of her breasts. He drew gentle circles with his talons, first around and over her hard nipples. Alma gasped again, a soft moan finally escaping her lips.

One talon moved to the neck of her night dress, then

drew down slowly. She heard the tear of the fabric as it gave way beneath his talon's edge, the cool curve dipping down between her breasts, across her belly, over the dip of her belly button. His talon paused in the ripping as he reached the parting of her legs, and she lifted one to hook around his lithe body. The talon dipped, pressing into her clit and urging another moan from her lips as her hips rocked into the hard shape, uncaring of its sharpness.

He swept his talon through the rest of her nightdress, pushing the fabric aside as her hands still cradled the still-emerging length of him. She felt his forked tongue flicker out at her breasts and she pulled one hand away from the snakelike girth to explore his face. The jaws were wide, his lips ridged with scales, and rough horns swept back where his hair grew on his human form. She shifted, straining toward his body with her hips, and guided his searching member with her hand.

Like a separate entity, she felt it strain under her grasp, feeling for her, the cool form probing against her wetness and arching against her clit, parting her labia with the head of his member as it rocked against her.

"Oh, Rojo," she murmured. Behind her closed eyes, she imagined his face, unshaved and sharp teeth smiling.

"Alma," he growled against her breasts, his low voice distorted by the rows of teeth. "Do you remember how to make me stop?" The forked tongue twisted around her nipple.

She pressed her lips together to stifle a moan, her hips shifting desperately to try and coax his member to enter her, the pulsing heat of her unbearable against its cold, slithering stroking. "I do—I remember."

His talons gripped into her and his tail wound around her lowered leg. The muscled body wrapped around her and she clung to him as he constricted to surround her. The stroking tendril of his penis coiled, the head slipping slowly into her.

She cried out as he filled her, stretching her a little at a time as he withdrew, then plunged in deeper with each throbbing pulse. His penis stayed arched, bent to maintain pressure against her clit as it continued to pump inside of her.

The effect was swift. She began to sob out her moans as the warm glow in the depth of her spread out to her constricted limbs, a pressure building, urged on by the flickering, twisting tongue on her nipples, the antagonizing stretch inside of her, and the thrumming pulse against her clit. She cried out, again and again, sobbing into the cool scales of his neck. Her hips rocked manically into his flexing member in deep, shuddering bucking motions as the font of pleasure erupted from her core. She came in a long, shaking wave, the throes of her body restrained by his form wrapped around her.

Just as her orgasm began to ebb, he gnashed his teeth against her breast, sinking his fangs into the vulnerable flesh. She screamed again, now tinged with pain, but she felt another wave of pleasure building behind the sharp fire on her chest as the snakelike penis burst inside of her. She buried her face into the scales of his neck to muffle her screams as she came again, her vaginal wall throbbing and gripping against the wild thing inside her until finally, trembling, she went limp, held by his powerful body.

Rojo's form loosened, but remained wrapped around her. The thick tendril of his cock eased out of her wetly, and she moaned at the emptiness within her. His teeth released her breast, the tongue softly licking around the wounds he left there.

In a growl that was more of a purr, he breathed against her neck, "What do you say, Alma?"

She sighed against the scales, her eyelids fluttering. "Thank you, Señor."

#

Alma woke alone in the tousled bed, the rags of her nightdress still hanging from one shoulder. She stretched out languidly, her toes not quite reaching the edge, and examined her body. There were soft lavender blooms of bruises on her thighs with singular points of dark crimson already scabbed over. She pressed a fingertip into one bruise and winced a little, though the thrill of it curled deep inside of her.

Rojo was waiting for her with a large breakfast already laid out over the table. He waved for her to take a seat and began to pile her plate full of fresh bread, fruits, and cheeses, setting this down before her. She picked up a large ripe strawberry and brought it to her lips.

"Ah-ah," he tutted at her, "You wait until I take a bite, first."

She put the strawberry slowly back down onto the edge of her plate. Indignation flowed first, then quiet pleasure.

"You feel this rule is unjust?" he asked, a red gleam

in his eyes.

She nodded, shaking her long hair back from her shoulders.

"Hmm." He picked up a cane that had been laying against the table's edge and twirled it slowly in his hands. "Would you like to test what happens if you break it?"

Her pulse beat suddenly in all the small wounds of her body—and between her legs. She returned his stare, debating. She wondered what he would do. How the cane would feel. His smile looked playful, despite the sudden sharpness of his teeth. She picked up the berry and wrapped her lips around the full redness, staring at him in his red eyes as she bit into the fruit.

He rose from his seat, the chair scraping behind him. She set the end of the strawberry back onto her plate and looked up into his eyes, willing herself not to.

Grasping the cane in one hand, he strode over to her, placing his other hand at her throat, stroking the soft flesh below her jaw. "You remember what I told you yesterday?"

She nodded against the flex of his hand, her heart hammering in her chest.

Good." He pushed her roughly down to the table, scattering her plate across the polished surface and pulling up the layers of her skirts to expose her bottom. She hadn't bothered with underthings and he ran the cane's hard shape against the tender flesh where her buttocks met her thighs.

She whimpered a little as he pressed his hand into her back between her shoulder blades. He drew the cane back and struck her hard and fast. Once, twice, three times. Leaving searing stripes of hot pain against her bottom. She barely had time to cry out.

Warm wetness leeched out of her, slicking her thighs, and she felt her cheeks burn as hot as the marks on her buttocks. Rojo ran his hand over the roundness of her ass and she heard a low, approving rumble. His fingers dipped curiously against her vulva and probed her aching slit. She moaned, pressing into his rough hand, and he chuckled.

"Mmm. That's interesting," he mused, pulling his hand away. "Eat. You'll need your strength for tonight."

\#

Rojo was often busy. Occupied with whatever it was he did to maintain his estate and the finery therein. She found that her days were not lonely. The library was full of more books than she could read in two lifetimes and the grounds were gently crafted, with melodic fountains and ample shade for her many strolls. Sometimes, Saiyed rode his cart up the mountainside to bring her letters from her family and take hers in return. He often stopped and shared lunch with her, but never stayed late into the afternoon.

"Why do you leave so early, Saiyed?" Alma asked on one such day.

They were walking through the courtyard gardens arm in arm while she pointed out every new bud and fresh leaf in the sheltered foliage.

Saiyed patted her hand that rested in the crook of his arm. "I would hate for your husband to think I was being untoward. Unchaperoned, alone with such a beautiful wife? I would be wary, were I in his boots."

Her mouth curved slyly, her fingers squeezing his arm. "And what of the beast? Are you not afraid?"

"Sí, I would rather not meet the dragon. I would risk it, though," he said, pausing their stroll to look fully into her eyes. "If you asked."

Alma's cheeks darkened in a blush and she tugged on his arm, pulling him back into their promenading. "Rojo would not like that, you are right, but he does enjoy keeping me in line."

"In line?" Saiyed asked, his head tilting. "Are you not free here, Alma?"

She sighed, looking out over the walls, into the boundless sky. "Is any woman free in marriage, Saiyed?"

He didn't answer her, only watched her, his dark eyes waiting for some slip in her countenance. In this watching, he noticed the bruising, just a glimpse creeping out from beneath the sleeve of her dress. His hand tightened on hers where it lay draped over his arm.

Completing another circuit of the grounds, Alma caught sight of the storm clouds bubbling out of the lowlands with the distant echo of thunder.

Worry creased her brow. "We talked too late today. It'll be a downpour." She patted Saiyed's hand. "You can't leave, you'll be swept away by flash floods or caught in the mud with your cart."

Saiyed rose, looking out of the swift moving shadow that was the storm. "But your husband—and the beast." His eyes traced her neckline, searching for more evidence of an unhappy marriage.

"I thought you would stay if I asked?" She winked. "We'll pull your cart into the garden where it will be sheltered, and you can bed down in the storeroom. Rojo busies himself with breakfast when he first rises, so I will come let you know when it's safe for you to leave."

Saiyed nodded slowly. "If you're certain. I don't want to make trouble for you."

#

Alma waited for Rojo in the dark of their room as the storm raged outside. She felt a little thrill of excitement that Saiyed was hidden away in the storeroom far below, thankful that he was not traveling beneath the riotous skies, and eager for the sound of Rojo on the stairs.

She had never felt herself to be a lustful woman, but her nightly encounters with her monstrous husband had awakened a hunger in her. Like attempting to douse a fire with gasoline, the more she came, the more she craved the slithering muscle and writhing cock of Rojo. The simple act of blowing out the gas lamps and closing the curtains brought wetness between her thighs.

Climbing beneath the blankets, her skin tingled at the light touch; she no longer bothered with another nightdress that would be ruined by their passion. She swept her long hair back over the pillows and waited

Rojo came to her as he always did. She squirmed with anticipation as he slithered onto the bed.

"My dear Rojo," she breathed, her voice low and dreamy. Her hands searched for him, wrapping around the horns on his skull as he dragged his body against her.

The growling voice heated her flesh as he spoke, "Precious Alma." His body parted her legs, flexing the bulge that hid his member against her. "How lovely, how wet you are for me. And so obedient." He slid his forked tongue along her body, a stripe of heat as keen as the strike of his cane.

His cock uncoiled from his body quickly, entering her with no pretense, and she cried out as his body wrapped tightly around her. He filled her with his whole length as his talons sank into her arms.

Alma rocked against him as his body turned, pushing her upright to straddle him, his member buried and twisting inside of her. She rolled her hips into the bulge at the base of his cock, her clit sliding wetly over the ridges of his scales.

She cried out again, as his muscled body wrapped around her own, his teeth gentle as his jaw opened around her throat.

The door flung open, clattering against the wall.

A shaft of light flew into the room from a lantern held aloft.

Alma's eyes sprang open.

Golden light spilled over crimson scales wrapped around her, black horns and talons gleaming like iron.

Rojo roared, untangling himself from her as he whipped around to face the door. Alma fell from his rising body, suddenly empty and cold as his cock slithered out of her.

Saiyed stood at the portal, his curls wet from the rain and sticking to his brow as he held the lantern high. In his other hand he wielded a pistol. This he leveled at Rojo's snarling face. "Unhand her, beast!"

Rojo roared again and Saiyed fired.

Alma screamed, drawing her legs up to her body as

Rojo thrashed, knocking the lantern from Saiyed's hand and plunging the room back into darkness. She saw the curtains part as a shadow flung itself from the balcony.

"Rojo!" she cried, leaping from the bed and running to the balcony, flinging the curtains aside. She gripped the cold metal as the rain cascaded down onto her body, steaming on her flesh. A ribbon of fire glimmered as lightning streaked across the sky.

Alma stormed back into the bedchamber, her hair wild and curling. Saiyed was lighting one of the standing oil lamps, the gun held limply in one hand.

"What have you done?"

#

Alma emerged from the tower late in the morning. Her body was sore and tired from her nightly exertions, painful now that Rojo was gone. Red and swollen, her eyes still shone with tears. She was wrapped in a heavy robe, her hair mussed, as she sat down at the dining table. Saiyed was there waiting for her.

She shook her head, sitting down gingerly. "Saiyed, how could you?"

He shifted awkwardly in the seat across from her. "I thought he was killing you."

"He's my husband. What else could he possibly be doing with me in our bedchamber?" she snapped, her eyes burning into his.

"I saw bruises on you, Alma," he protested, his voice weak. "He's a monster."

"Yes, but he's mine." A fat tear rolled down her cheek. "What will I do now?"

By the afternoon, the storm had finally abated, but the road was too muddied for Saiyed to set off with his guilt. Alma consented to him staying one more night. Saiyed insisted on accompanying her to her tower room, out of fear that she would fling herself from the balcony in her grief.

She didn't bother extinguishing the lamps, but seeing the wavering light dancing around the room she had shared with Rojo brought fresh tears to her eyes. *Perhaps Saiyed's worry is justified*, she thought.

Saiyed sat in the highbacked armchair in the corner of the room as she climbed into bed, still huddled in her robe. The curtains swayed in the wind as it howled outside; she couldn't bear to close the windows or the doors leading to the balcony.

The hours crept by in silence. Alma occasionally sobbed into her pillow. Saiyed crossed and uncrossed his legs.

Alma felt her body drifting toward sleep. Her eyes were heavy, but her limbs felt light and weightless against the softness of the bed. There was a scratching on the balcony outside, a quiet scraping.

Her eyes shot open. She sat slowly up, watching the swaying curtains.

There was a gleam of scarlet as Rojo's head parted through the curtains. Slitted eyes narrowed at Saiyed where he dozed in the armchair, and he slithered across the floor, his short limbs tipped with talons scraping across the tile.

The dragon crossed the room and glided onto the bed, coiling around Alma and growling softly. "You didn't think I had gone forever, did you?" he asked, stroking her damp cheek with the tip of his tail.

Saiyed stirred in the armchair, then awoke with a start.

Rojo hissed at him, his eyes wild, "You."

Saiyed began to scramble to his feet, but a roar from Rojo stilled him, sinking him back into the chair.

"Stay there, you fool," Rojo growled, his scales bristling along the ridges of his serpentine back.

Saiyed seemed rooted to the chair, his eyes wide.

Alma stroked Rojo gently with a trembling hand, coaxing his head back to face hers. "Rojo, you're beautiful."

The red eyes found hers, and he settled himself so the length of his body was before her. His talons crept over the fabric of her robe, pulling it from her shoulders, exposing the naked flesh beneath. Her breasts rose with her quickening breath.

"I should have let you look upon me months ago, my precious. But that one..." His tail flicked toward Saiyed. "Now that he's seen me, he cannot go. He stays here forever. Or he dies."

Alma shivered, glancing to Saiyed. "I understand. I don't want you to kill him."

Rojo's tongue darted out, tasting her breasts, splaying against her nipple. "Very well." He turned his serpentlike head to Saiyed. "You. Stay there. And watch."

Rojo turned back to Alma, dipping his head low. Alma's legs parted at the sharp touch of his talons along her inner thighs. He bared his teeth, flicking his tongue out, parting the soft curls to tickle against her vulva.

She drew in a moist breath, sinking back against the pillows, staring at him. She wanted to see. The forked tongue licked out, each half along the split embracing the shape of her clit beneath its pink hood of flesh.

A soft moan broke free of her and she bit down on her lower lip. Rojo's tongue rolled, the flickering tip teasing at her entrance as the thick base rolled against her hard bud. He slipped his tongue inside of her, talons grabbing into the flesh of her inner thighs, drawing small beads of blood.

She gasped again, pressing her hips down into the rolling of his tongue.

He growled against her, teeth scraping against the swollen mounds of her labia and pubis mons, sharp and smooth. She moaned lowly as his tongue lashed against her, swirling around her clit and licking deeply inside of her, pressing against the hot ridges of her inner walls as she pulsed.

Rojo's tongue didn't fill her the way his snakelike cock did, but it did flex and press against the best parts within her. As his tongue slipped fully into her he growled, baring his teeth tight against her clit.

Alma whimpered, grabbing at the pillow behind her head with clenched fists as her body arched into Rojo's fanged mouth. In the chair across the room Saiyed shifted uncomfortably, one hand falling to his lap.

Fascinated, delirious, Alma drew her eyes from the horned head gnashing and growling between her thighs to Saiyed, rubbing himself, his eyes rolling back in his head.

Alma sat up, her hands grasping Rojo's horns to pull

his head tighter against her as a cry bubbled up in her throat. Her hips bucked into the sharp mouth and she felt the dribble of blood join her wetness from a nick of a fang. She screamed throatily, the sound tearing itself from her depths as the waves of her orgasm began to spread from her core to the rest of her, spiraling out through her body like a mad serpent of her own. Her legs went rigid, wrapped around Rojo's powerful neck, as his tongue carried her to orgasm.

She collapsed back into the pillows as Rojo slithered up her body, bringing his uncoiling cock to her wet, bloodied slit. Panting, Alma moaned against Rojo's body as he wrapped around her, his snakelike member slithering into her, stretching her.

Alma's eyes opened, catching a glimpse of Saiyed, still in the armchair, his pants unbuttoned to free his own cock as he stroked himself, staring at their intertwined bodies as Rojo twisted her around, giving him a clear view of his writhing cock slithering wetly in and out of her cunt.

Rojo pressed her back into the bed as his thrusting quickened. "How have I not tasted you before tonight?" he growled. "The sweetest nectar." He drowned out her cries with a roar of his own, and Alma heard a strangled sound from the other side of the room. She imagined what Saiyed must be witness to, the red snake wildly pulsing and thrashing inside of her, evoking riotous screams from her as her body shook beneath Rojo's constricting body.

She came again, carried on the shuddering waves of her pleasure as Rojo erupted within her, his seed leaking out at the point of their union and seeping down her thighs. Her eyes rolled and her vision swam as she clung to Rojo's neck in the aftershocks of pleasure coursing through her.

Alma trembled weakly as Rojo unwound himself from her, pulling himself free of her to turn to Saiyed. "What a mess you've made," Rojo mused, his fangs gleaming in the lamplight. "You will live, foolish man. But you do not get to touch her."

Alma sank into bed, curling against Rojo. There was a pang of guilt knowing Saiyed would remain a prisoner of Rojo, but it would be nice to have a friend to occupy her days. She smiled against red scales and let his rumbling breathing carry her off to sleep.

Interactive Archeology
Morgan Gage

CW: Alcohol consumption

"Listen, barring any serious destruction or desecration of sacred relics, whatever you chucklefucks get up to on the dig site after hours is your own business," Marg said in a voice that reminded everyone listening that she was the only one here with a PhD. "But I will not be sticking around to watch."

"That is a perfectly valid and scientifically sound point of view," Tamryn said. She was quite proud of getting the word "scientifically" out smoothly on her first try. Words over three syllables were becoming harder to grasp the more cups of punch she had, which was weird because Jake had assured her he'd mixed it up "not too strong." Jake, with his near-legendary tolerance for alcohol, could certainly be trusted with such a determination.

Fuck it. Tonight was their last night on the dig site, and Tamryn was going to get drunk. Okay, Tamryn was drunk, and had been for probably about an hour. What she was going to get was *real fuckin' stupid.*

They were all grad students—everyone except Marg, who was their university-accredited babysitter—so even though they were all incredibly smart, driven, and proud to have been selected for this assignment, they also weren't going to take themselves too seriously. After all, when other teams across the planetary system had been sent to alien dig sites with the remains of long-dead weaponry or the shells of biological computer systems fossilizing in ancient caverns, their team hadn't been so lucky. They'd been sent to the caves with the weird horny robot statues.

The technical term for them was alien automata. With a vague sense of resentment and despair, Tamryn tilted her head back to look one of them in the eye. Well, it didn't have a face per-se, just a weird smooth surface like a helmet that curved back into a series of horns, or spikes, or weird decorative greebles whose purpose years of similar teams of archaeological newbies and misfits had not been able to determine. It loomed over their little fireside gathering, tucked into its alcove in the same position that every last one of them had been discovered in decades ago. Its limbs were long, like a gibbon, legs folded at the ankle in front of it and its arms resting over them, fingers dangling over the knees. Vaguely humanoid, except for the weird proportions and horned-helmet face. But none of that was the first thing any casual observer or fully trained scientist was likely to notice. What you noticed first was the giant dong.

It wasn't proportionally giant. About the length of

Tamryn's forearm, slender and tapered, carved with a bunch of runes whose meaning no one had been able to figure out. Interior imaging had revealed that all of the automata, despite appearing to be made of nothing but polished grey stone, were in fact filled with incredibly complex mechanisms that suggested at one point they had done more than just sit there and stare at their own boners. Decades of science had been unable to awaken them. But decades of science hadn't tried Tamryn's solution.

Probably because it was kind of batshit insane.

"Really not sure how this doesn't qualify as desecration," Calendula said.

"Why else would they have them, though?" Tamryn pressed. "I mean, come on."

Marg groaned. "There are so many potential reasons, Tam, for gods' sakes this isn't archeology 101—"

"Scientific integrity aside," Jake said. "Do you really think no one's tried it? I mean, look at the fucking things."

"Firstly," Tamryn said, "I think you vastly underestimate the prudishness inherent to most specimens of the archaeology program. Secondly, if someone did try it, they were too embarrassed to tell anyone, and that's just bad science."

"You're going to make yourself completely unemployable before you even graduate."

"No," Tamryn said, and stood up. It was a five step process, and ended with her tottering in place with one finger stabbing at the cave roof in defiance of man, god, and ambiguously horny aliens alike. "I'm going to crack the archeological mystery of the decade with nothing more than my wits and my pussy."

"That academic paper is going to be difficult to publish."

Tamryn flopped back down on the stack of bound books with a burst of compressed dust from the pages. "Not if you aren't a fucking coward."

Beside her, Calendula put her head in her hands. "You don't even know if it would be safe. What if you catch some kind of, like, ancient alien STD or something?"

"Well, Jake already tested it, the material contains no organic elements and unlikely to react to, let's say, a slightly acidic and moist environment—"

"Gross."

Marg levered herself up from the overturned packing crate she'd been perching on and went to overturn her cup into the fire. It flared to life, and she stopped a minute, maybe to contemplate the exact density of alcohol she'd been drinking in Jake's "mixed drinks."

"My official standpoint as your mentor is that this is an unacceptable breach in professional conduct," she said. "My unofficial standpoint: just clean the damn thing up afterward, and don't make me hear about it in the morning."

#

There were, in total, sixty three of the alien constructs dotting the cliff alcoves at the site. Yes, Tamryn had a favorite. Yes, they all looked basically the same. So it was probably weird to have scanned the field and decided, *yeah, if I had to pick an automaton...* But she had, basically on day one. That was just how Tamryn was.

So she made her way to that construct in particular, up the steps carved into the rock, through passages that sometimes meandered across exposed cliff faces and sometimes passed into enclosed tunnels. The steps and handholds were scaled for larger beings than her, so there were several places where the archeologists had supplemented the carved handholds with metal holds drilled into the rock. It was weird to think that the society that had built the technology to travel across dimensions and defy the laws of physics had settled for chipping straight into the rock, but they also had put massive erect phalluses on their robotic constructs, so who could say what they had in mind.

She hauled herself over the last ledge—of course, she picked one of the harder ones to get to—and flopped down, panting, in the shadow of the construct. Its head bowed towards her, faceless and almost glowing in the light of the alien moons. The automata always looked like they were waiting. Maybe it was the alcohol, maybe the moonlight, maybe the fact that it was Tamryn's last day on this planet and she hadn't accomplished one goddamn thing other than making a fool of herself and laying the seeds for an almighty thrasher of a headache tomorrow—but it seemed like the thing, creature, whatever it was, was leaning towards *her.* Expectant.

A little out of breath, Tamryn trooped up to its folded legs and stopped. Admittedly, she hadn't gotten much farther than the vague idea of what she'd come here to do, spurred on by Marg's exasperation and Jake's wry disbelief. Well. First things first, she'd better take her pants off.

She proceeded to nearly fall off the cliff. When she'd successfully kicked off her jodhpurs and her underwear, she still felt a little overdressed and so shucked off her shirt for good measure. If she was going to do this, she might as well do it right. Nights on this planet were warm, but the cool night breeze chilled her skin.

"'Scuse me," she said jovially, stepping over the construct's folded ankles into the center of its legs. Its cock was... well, it was big. There was no way she was fitting the entire thing inside of her without some serious rearranging of her internal organs. For that matter, all the carvings on it looked like they could be a bit painful going in—but momma didn't raise no quitter. She'd do what she could.

She'd need a few warm up exercises.

"Normally I'd light a few candles and put on some smooth jazz," she said. Her voice sounded oddly small in the cavernous chamber, but she threw it against the darkness and space and immensity of the being in front of her all the same. She sat down cross legged on the stone floor, mimicking the automaton's position in the center of its folded legs. On second thought, she lay back and spread her legs. It felt a bit crude—she was basically shoving her pussy in the thing's face, and normally she at least would have wanted to buy it a drink first—but she had a hard time imagining getting it up while sitting criss-cross applesauce and buckass nude in a dusty alien cave.

She closed her eyes, and slid her fingers between

her legs. Being a little bit drunk had already put her ahead, and she was vaguely relieved to find herself slick enough to get a good movement going. She tried to think about her last boyfriend—ugh, never mind—then the one before that—worse—and settled instead on thinking about nothing at all. That wasn't all that helpful. She was pretty quickly getting bored.

It occurred to Tamryn that she could just… stop. She could either lie to her colleagues about her erotic exploits with the local archeological finds, or just cop to the fact that she had chickened out after a few minutes half heartedly jerking off in front of it.

Yeah, that was pretty much unthinkable. Tamryn did not back down. So instead she opened her eyes and stared at the creature looming over her, and thought about it instead.

She'd be lying if she said the idea wasn't at least a little bit sexy in theory. Partially because these things were so weird. But they were beautiful too, and this one in particular—she liked the way some of the long spars that stretched behind its head curved forward again like a ram's horns, while others rose behind its head in a crown of spikes. Staring at its blank face now, it wasn't difficult to imagine it watching her with interest. Anticipation, even.

Tamryn grinned, a little stupidly. "Hey, handsome. Come here often?"

Dumb. But whatever, no one else was here. Just her and an ancient technological marvel that would probably never wake up. She could be as lame, corny, and embarrassing as she damn well wanted.

She lay back and let her knees spread open, and rubbed her clit in lazy circles while inspecting the automaton's face. Its hands were so large, the two of them could easily have circled her entire waist—hell, one of them could almost do the job. And that fucking monster between its legs. Tamryn thought about how it would feel to be that full, pushing into her inch by inch until all she could think about was the pressure inside her body, the stretch and press and ache.

She was getting wetter. Her fingers slid easily across her clit, and her muscles relaxed fraction by fraction. *Fuck,* she wanted more. She could never seem to get off without something in her cunt, and right now there was a very prominent something just a few feet away. The automaton loomed over her, unchanging—and yet there was something in its blank, smooth face that made Tamryn think it was urging her on. It was probably just the alcohol talking.

Either way, it was time to get this show on the road.

She dug around in her bag for the container of lube she'd wasted precious ounces of packing space on, back when she was absolutely positive she and Luke were going to be having crazy monkey sex during the entirety of this expedition. Waste not, want not. It was actually pretty awkward trying to mount the thing: she had to get her legs around its hips and position herself over its cock. Standing astride the thing's hips, the pillar of polished stone protruding from its groin came to her mid-thigh. She reached out to let her fingers trail over it, tracing the carvings that marked it from head to shaft.

No one had ever been able to interpret any of the aliens' language. The surface felt cool beneath her fingers, but not as cold as natural stone. Tamryn closed her hand around it as far as it would go, and gave the shaft a slow stroke. No reaction. Obviously. Tactile engagement was definitely on the list of things other researchers had tried. But Tamryn was going to be the one to take it one step farther. That was what science was: pushing boundaries, exploring new horizons, and fucking mysterious alien robots.

"Well," Tamryn announced. "Here goes nothing—*Jesusfuckohgod.*"

It was cold. Obviously it was cold, she had been expecting that, but there was a world of difference between knowing you were about to shove an unheated stone dildo inside of yourself and actually doing it. She stayed still, cursing under her breath with it pressed against her cunt, barely even parting her labia. Well, this didn't bode well for how enjoyable this little romp was going to be. The last time she felt so un-aroused while trying to stick something inside herself was after a bad breakup, a pint of expired ice cream, and a salad that was suspiciously devoid of cucumbers the next day.

But Tamryn always persevered. She patted the construct on its side and tilted her head back to stare into its downturned face. "Alright, friend," she said. "Let's make the most of this."

Bracing herself against the construct's belly, she reached her other hand down to rub at her clit as she rocked against the tip of the thing's cock. Polished stone slid across slick folds of flesh; she could almost convince herself that the goosebumps that rose on her arms and back were from the illicit thrill of sexual congress with an architectural find, rather than the fact that she was naked and it was chilly out. At least the thing between her legs was starting to warm up a little, stealing the heat from her body until she felt less like she was trying to pleasure herself with an icicle.

Still. If she wanted to actually fuck the thing any time this star cycle, she'd better get a move on. Her thighs were starting to burn from holding herself up, and it occurred to her that maintaining the position required to fuck the robot without puncturing something in her abdomen might be beyond the physical capabilities of an out of shape baby archaeologist. If a human had been sitting in the same position, Tamryn could have bounced on it sloppy style, no-problemo. She was a champion at riding cock. She loved grinding down as hard as she could, setting her own pace and putting on a bit of a show. But this thing was about as far from human as you could get while maintaining the same number and configuration of limbs.

She imagined walking back to camp, where she was dead certain the rest of her compatriots would be awake and waiting for her, and telling them that not only had her crude attempts yielded no scientific ground, *she hadn't even managed to orgasm.*

Absolutely unacceptable. Failure was nut an option.

Gritting her teeth, Tamryn pushed herself down on the stone cock. Fuck, it was big. It drove the breath out of her lungs as it slid deeper into her, not painful, but certainly not pleasurable either. That was fine. She'd make it feel good. Her breath fogged against the smooth carapace of the thing's chest, and she squeezed her legs tighter and felt its cock slip so far inside of her she swore she could feel it in the pit of her stomach.

Then she lost her purchase on the thing's smooth body, and it slammed into her a few inches more.

"Fuck—" Tamryn gasped. Tears stung the corners of her eyes, but she grinned. She was fully skewered. She'd taken almost all of the thing's massive cock, and she should at least get some sort of award for that, surely. A special dispensation on her degree? No, she didn't want to think about her professor's sour face right now. In fact, now that she was fully seated on the thing's cock, her legs had slid into what appeared to be a natural groove along the construct's sculpted hips—the perfect place to get some leverage.

She flexed her legs and core, rising up a little on the rigid stone cock and letting it slide back in. It twinged again, *god it was so deep*, but it wasn't bad. Her fingers slid down into her pubic hair and started circling her clit again. Okay. This was—okay. She could do this.

Tilting her head back, she stared into the featureless faceplate of the construct. It seemed to be watching her, the lack of feature on its face somehow making its regard all the more intent. "Hi there," she said breathlessly, and grinned. "You're not so bad once a girl gets used to you."

She started moving faster. The carvings on the length of the phallus were a pleasant sensation on the walls of her cunt, and the new position wasn't straining her muscles. She let herself fall into a rhythm, bouncing up and down in a way that she knew made her breasts look fantastic. Which didn't really matter in this particular instance, but. The idea of the construct perceiving her, of its rigid cock being for her rather than a simple feature of its creation, was enough to make her body buzz with pleasure. Each time she dropped herself down she let a high, sharp grunt drive out of her lungs; at first it was intentional, and then she couldn't stop it.

It felt so hot inside of her, like temperature hot, which was weird because it couldn't have possibly been warmer than her body. She could almost imagine it throbbing in time with her motions, pulsing hard when she buried it fully inside of her and thrumming against her entrance when she pulled herself back. Had she seriously thought this was a bad idea? This was the best idea she'd ever had. This was—

A low chime echoed through the stone cavern. She could feel it moving through the construct's body, from the construct's body, and *oh shit it had done that,* it had finally responded—

Something touched her back.

Tamryn shrieked. She tried to twist away and scramble backwards all at once, but both movements were hampered by the stone cock thrust entirely inside of her. Instead she just sort of thrashed. The touch was icy cold and three-fingered against the small of her back. The thing's hands. Its hands had moved, they were touching her—

Actually, they were sort of grabbing her. Gently, so carefully she barely felt the pressure on her skin. They both settled around her waist, so big they fully connected.

Tamryn froze, staring up at its face. Nothing else seemed to have changed. She waited for something else to happen. For those giant hands to rip her torso off her legs. For the cock she was riding to turn out to be the barrel of some sort of projectile weapon just like Marg had posited, and to be blown to smithereens. But her torso remained attached to her hips. She wasn't shot. And in that glittering, hanging moment, the amazement crept in.

"Holy shit," she whispered. "I did it. I fucking did it. God damn right—!"

She was suddenly reminded that she was still cervix-deep on what was now the most valuable find of the century. So she should probably stop fucking it now.

...Now.

...Oh boy.

The hands around her waist were holding her in place. She couldn't wiggle upwards more than a centimetre before they pinched against her hip bone. They encircled her completely, fingers to thumbs, keeping her trapped on the thing's massive protuberance with absolutely no way to wriggle free.

The surge of triumph in her blood evaporated almost immediately. Oh, shit. What if she couldn't get free, and her team found her like this? Gods, what if they still couldn't get her free? Would they break it to get her out? Would it let them? What if she was stuck like this forever?

"Hey," she gasped, craning her head back again. "I don't know if you can understand me, but—can you let me go? Please? Please let me go?" Tamryn smacked its chest. No response. "Hey! Fucking—Let—me—go-"

A second chime, lower this time. She felt it moving through the thing's hands first, then its waist, then a rush of vibration moved from the base of the phallus to its tip. Tamryn yelped as her cunt clenched around it in pure instinct. She didn't realize that the hands had tightened around her, infinitesimally, until they started to move again. They were squeezing her now. Only a little. Just enough to really get a grip on her sweat-slicked flesh so it could start to move her up and down on its cock.

"What the fuck," Tamryn panted. It was—oh god. It was so strong. Its hands took her weight without hesitation, lifted her until it had almost pulled out, *almostalmostcomeon*, and then pushed her back down again. Slowly at first. Experimentally. Prying at its fingers, Tamryn couldn't get them to so much as shift.

And it was watching her. Tamryn was sure of it now. She twisted, staring into its blank plane of a face; the chime sounded again. At the same moment Tamryn felt it thrumming deep in her cunt, she saw the construct's head tilt.

Then it started fucking her in earnest.

"Oh my god," Tamryn said shrilly. It bounced her on its cock the same way she'd been moving herself just a few minutes earlier, only now she couldn't slow down, shift, or do anything but let it fuck her. And those chimes, sounding more and more frequently and bringing with them the flood of delicious vibration, were also coaxing more of the construct to life. It paused to roll its shoulders before resuming its efforts. Its thumbs moved up and down over Tamryn's ribs. Its spine uncurled from its perpetual hunch, and as it did its hips started to flex, crushing into her with every thrust.

"Okay," Tamryn gasped. "Okay. This is—this is fine. All part of the plan, right? This is exactly what you wanted, Tam, now you better—Fucking—"

She had to try to focus. This was going to be her doctorate. This was going to win her some kind of Nobel Prize. And yet she couldn't breathe, let alone think straight. It was fucking her faster and harder than any human could, unbound by stamina or fatigue. And it was learning. It started grinding her harder against itself every time the chime began, until she was gasping and writhing with no intent of getting away. Holy shit, it felt so good. She wasn't worried about being permanently entombed on an alien robot's cock anymore. Hell, she'd take it if she could keep feeling like this. The sounds of her wet flesh slapping on stone mingled with the electric thrum and her sharp, breathy cries. She couldn't be self-conscious. She couldn't think. Fuck, this is what she needed, all this time, fast and hard and observed, adored, wanted so badly she could shatter a thousand years of sleep—

She came hard, clenching around it as it kept fucking her with that punishing rythym— then slowed, and the chime stretched on for an eternity as it sank its vibrating cock deep into her body, making her feel every inch of it, like it was possessive. Tamryn thrashed, crying out, shuddering along with the pulsing inside of her until she sagged in the thing's grip like a used-up ragdoll.

The vibrations continued after that, steady; from behind her eyelids, a blue glow made her stir.

The glyphs over the construct's body had all lit up, line after line of winding text covering it in glowing light. They traced up to its faceplate, which was slashed with twelve glowing diamonds of light. It stared down at her. Its fingers flexed—and then the pressure between Tamryn's legs started retreating. She groaned as it slid out of her, dizzy and weak, and realized it was retracting into itself—some kind of compartment? The stone (not stone, not really) itself changing? In a moment Tamryn was freed, its hands supporting her rather than holding her still. She could get up and scramble away. She didn't. She stayed there, straddling its waist and staring up into its face with wonder.

"Wow," she said, and then, "Hi."

The construct thrummed. There was nuance to it, a modulation, a rise and fall—like language. A language in vibration? Touch-based? There was so much to discover. And for a little while longer, it was hers and hers alone.

"My name is Tamryn Vellais," she said. And then she grinned. "Would you mind if I take some notes?"

Mirrors
Lena Moth

It only comes to me in the dark.

Late at night after I've shut off the lights and everything outside is quiet. When only the street lamps outside cast shadows across my walls, overpowering the softness of the moon's ethereal, ghostly glow. I have to be the one to close out the world, to shut my door and tack up the layers of heavy sheets that I use to black out my windows. The decision has to be mine.

It won't come out until I allow it.

I climb down, blinking blindly as my eyes adjust to the pitch dark that I've created for myself. For it. For us. There's a mirror that sits beside my bed, leaning against the wall, but when I stare out at where I know it should be, it's hard to see anything at all. After so many years of enduring my own reflection, It's harder to know by heart what I'd see if I wasn't seated in blackness.

It's better this way.

As I sit down on the edge of the mattress, I exhale slowly, tugging an oversized hoodie over my head to throw it off the foot of my bed. I hear the soft thump of it landing, feel the air against my arms, and am achingly aware of the tightness of the garment stretched across my chest. My ribs are sore from the binder I force myself into, day after day. It's too small, not stretchy enough to be comfortable, but it makes me feel like I'm managing to do something about circumstances I can't change. No matter what, I'm forced to endure the pain of wearing skin with a shape that doesn't feel like mine.

It joins the hoodie on the floor.

I close my eyes, seeing nothing. All I can do is listen until I hear it.

I still don't know where it comes from or how it manages to hide from me. For all I know, it could be lurking somewhere near me right now. Somewhere the daylight doesn't reach, that I can't find even when searching with the bright glow of my cellphone screen. I want to entice it out somehow, but it only emerges in my lightless room, so I make do with not knowing.

I make do with a lot of things.

I don't want to wait. I'm eager and anxious and the fluttering electrical current that flies through me is a reminder of that. I drag my jeans down my legs and the swish of fabric seems loud while everything else is so quiet. For a fleeting moment, I am a raw wire, as exposed as my body as I peel my socks off with the toes of each opposite foot. I sit still on the bed to listen to the blood pumping in my ears and the heavy silence of the room. Without anything to cover up with but the dark, it's hard to feel safe. *Don't look at yourself.* My mind races. *Don't look at yourself.*

I leave my underwear on.

As I climb into bed, the softness of worn-in sheets sliding against bare skin is akin to foreplay, my nipples sensitized with the feather-light touch against my skin, and burrowing between my many pillows is the only small piece of heaven I think I'll ever find. I pull the fluffy duvet up and over me and exhale a sigh that carries the weight of my day with it.

It's timeless here, naked and alone in my room, in the darkness that protects me from the things I don't want to see anymore. The pieces of me that I can cover up, but can't easily shed, like a butterfly emerging from its chrysalis to marvel at the glorious colours it kept wrapped up inside. Right now, it's just me, spreading my arms out across my double bed with nothing holding me back or weighing me down, and when the air in my bedroom shifts, it feels like that first breeze coming to carry me away on gossamer wings.

I keep my eyes closed.

The bottom right corner of my comforter lifts, and a hand both clawed and knobbly, like something out of a nightmare announces its presence by grazing gently against my calf. It lingers there, stroking the soft hair that rasps against its fingertips as I feel the weight of another being climbing slowly into my bed. A second hand joins the first, and, playful and familiar, walks its fingers up the sole of my left foot. I curl my pink-and-blue-painted toes and laugh – the breathy giggle of someone trying to keep quiet, even though we're the only ones who can hear me. Its amused reply is a soft, clicking trill. It sounds happy. I wonder if it would understand me if I told it I'd missed it.

I wonder if it misses me.

Its slow touches gradually unearth me, calming the places within me that tell me that the body that my bones have grown is somehow wrong. How could anything feel wrong when it's being stroked and caressed like this? Long, thin fingers slide under the dips and curves of my knees and generous thighs. It squeezes me, kneading my legs and pressing them together only to release them and let them fall open. I ease them apart even wider as the duvet tents over its long body. Only my head remains exposed as the creature explores me under the covers. A kind of reverse blindfold.

It trusts me not to look, even though I could.

Lips too thin and teeth too sharp to be human graze against my inner thigh, and I feel its exhaled breath as its questing hands find the thick elastic band of my briefs. I almost regret keeping them on when everything pauses, as if it isn't sure what to do next, but when its gentle hands settle on my thighs and the familiar shape of its long, bestial head dives between them, I am reassured that it wasn't deterred for long.

The warmth of its flat tongue presses against the plump shape of my cunt, stroking me through the smooth material, and my breath catches in my throat. My legs part, inviting more of its mouth and hands, and it takes its time. In its own way, it scolds me for keeping this part of me hidden.

I do it on purpose. I enjoy teasing it, too.

It knows the shape of me so familiarly, sliding up and down my crease until the crotch of my underwear is soaked with its sticky saliva, until my gasps have turned into short, pleading moans and my own wetness has the fabric clinging to my body. I clench, pushing my hips into those slow caresses and whine when its long, thin tongue slides up the crease of my thigh. It is merciless, making me regret that I chose to wear anything at all. My fingers dig into the mattress, twist and pull on the sheet beneath us, and wonder if it would listen if I started pleading.

This can't be much easier for it – Its hands cup underneath my thighs, digging into soft flesh as it keeps them parted, and every time it squeezes me it adds to the buzzing ache that's been building in me since the second I knew I wasn't alone. I hear a raspy, throaty sound, and that grip tightens, the blankets shifting as claws slide up my side and, terrifyingly sharp, they dig into the elastic and sever the seams. I don't even need to move as the ruined briefs are pulled away, exposing every slick and wanting part of me to the hungry mouth that finally stops to give me what it knows I want.

Its questing tongue pushes into me, worms and twists into my dripping hole, and the whine that leaves my lips is as bright as the sun. I can feel it wriggling inside of me, long enough to reach places that no one else could find, its sharp teeth gentle against the smooth lips that frame my pussy. A large hand settles against my abdomen, thumb resting on my hot clit. I urge it on with an undulation of my hips.

It knows my body. It knows what I am asking for.

Finished teasing me for the time being, its thumb strums against my clit as its tongue writhes inside me, only withdrawing to slurp our mingled juices from my lips.

The last thing I want is for it to stop what it's doing to me, but my legs have begun to ache, so I hook my hands under my knees and hold them steady. It is a vulnerable feeling, presenting my body to it without fear, and another muffled trill is my reward as its tongue once again runs the length of me. Its pointed tip flicks against my clit, dips down into my cunt, then continues travelling downward until it finds a second hole to devour.

I gasp more sharply as it tastes me here, twisting and pressing against the opening of my ass, until I relax enough that it can ease inside. Slippery and spreading more and more of its viscous saliva, it is gentle with me, seeming to know that if something is tight, then it should be spread slowly.

Again and again, it probes me, sliding in and withdrawing only to flick lightly against an area I did not expect to be so sensitive. All the while, its fingers still move against my clit and soon stroke around the achingly-empty entrance to my cunt, making me shudder and whimper. I am an exposed nerve, shaking and raw and I hear myself pleading without fully forming the thought.

It makes me wonder how it knows what it's doing.

Before it, I was too afraid. The people in my bed were so whole and so sure of themselves. Of who they are, and what they wanted. I gave them whatever they wanted from me, too scared to ask anything in return.

My creature is different.

It announced itself as heart-stopping scrapes and scratches against my closet door and floorboards before it came anywhere close to the bed. Those terrifying sounds soon became the tentative touches of another being that only comes out when no one can see it, and that's what made it so easy to give in. To allow myself to be plundered by a creature that knows only as much of me as I do it.

The way we move. The way it holds me. The way I never have to worry about being too much or not enough or too strange or too different, because *it* is all of those things and I want it.

I want it so badly.

"Please," I whisper, hoarse and dry, keening into the dark because I can't think anymore, and all I feel is need. Its tongue is warm and wet, and I'm already so close I can taste bliss, but it isn't enough for me tonight. I release one of my knees to instead push my hand between my legs to spread myself with two fingers and remind it of how empty I am.

It makes a sound I can only assume is scolding me, again, this time for my impatience and long canine teeth drag sweetly up my inner thigh. The bed shifts again as the creature slides between my thighs, the faint shadow of my duvet looming above my head. I feel its gaze on me, but my eyes are still screwed shut against the world as both my hands scrabble against a body with too many bones, muscles that are lean and hard and strong enough to lift my weight when it needs to.

My arms wind around its shoulders and neck. There's thick hair covers its head and runs down its spine, and grab onto it as my bent legs curl over its thighs. The smooth, tapered head of its cock leaks fluid against my inner thigh and I buck against it impatiently.

I want it to *need* me.

The first touch of its shaft against my pussy makes me whine, and I squeeze down even though there is still nothing inside of me yet. It's playing with me, making me show it how badly I want what I'm pleading for. I push my hips off the bed, stroking my wet cunt against the spade tip over and over and listening to the obscene sounds our bodies make together. The cooling wetness slicking my inner thighs belongs to both of us and it's making a mess of me, but I don't stop. I angle my body, catching the tip over and over again, my breath skipping every time I do, until finally, it pitches forward, sending lightning through my veins as it pushes into me.

Its shaft is thicker near the base, flaring out and then in again, and the strange shape might prove a challenge if my body weren't as ready as it is. Instead, it glides into me easily, and I welcome it with the tightening of my channel and a long whine, my head pressing back into the pillows.

Bucking forward, thin hips push against mine, cushioned against plush thighs, soft stomach, and every inch of a cock that is as inhuman as I wish I could be sinks into me again and again. Stars sparkle like fireworks on the inside of my eyelids as it rocks me against the mattress and allows me to squeeze and pull at the soft hair at the back of its neck.

I want so badly for it to kiss me.

The pleasure burning inside me suddenly runs cold as I'm hit with unexpected yearning. The steady arching of my seeking hips falters, and I go still.

There is an unspoken agreement between us: I don't lift the covers, and neither does it, allowing our faces to be close without ever revealing ourselves fully. Would I be able to see it if I opened my eyes or pulled that barrier down? The duvet is the only thing that separates the last bits of us from one another, and it strikes me at this moment that, for the first time in my life, I am tired of hiding.

It doesn't take long to notice something is wrong.

A short, inquisitive trill from under my blanket, and it lowers down to nuzzle against my chest, breath hot against my flushed skin. It knows that some nights I can't bear to have my breasts touched, where I ward it away gently – once forcibly. Now it asks, or at least waits before it acknowledges them, allowing me to guide it. Tonight, even with heartache thrumming in my ribs, I place one hand against the back of its head and steer its short muzzle to my nipple. I sigh as a warm tongue passes over and around the firm bud, cautious teeth nibbling at me with a kind of affection that makes my chest clench.

I wonder if it would kiss me like this. Short tastes and long strokes of its tongue against mine. The only thing that has ever seen me so bare and never wanted anything from me save for what I wanted to give. Before

I know it, I hear my own voice, disembodied, far away from myself, because I can't imagine why I would admit these things out loud and ruin the beautiful, perfect way it feels when we're together.

Why can't I stop wanting more than what I'm given?

"I want to be under there with you."

Everything stops, and I dread what I've done by even asking. We've never crossed this line before. At first, it doesn't move, and all I'm aware of is the sound of my own breath and the feeling of our pulses beating in tandem between our legs where our bodies are still joined. Slowly, the blankets shift, and its head lowers, shoulders slumping as it curls into itself in a way that is unmistakable. Immediately, I am struck with the pain of something that should have been clear: I am not alone in my monstrosity. While my face is the only thing I keep hidden from it, it has kept its entire body concealed from me.

In that way, we're both safe, even from one another.

It's like I can hear it thinking. Weighing what it should do, trying to decide if it's worth the risk. I want to scream, yes. I can be your creature, and I can handle you with care, touch you with nothing but love, my monster that I have never had to protect myself from, who has never hurt me. I'll cover all my windows in thick, white paint and block out the world, so even if I have to live in the dark forever, I can live here with you.

I stay silent. I wait for its decision.

The quiet is oppressive, and just as I start to think that I should take my words back, force them down my throat to let them die hidden and alone, a new and different sensation starts to feather against my chest. What starts as a vibration turns into a rumble, something so low I doubt that I can't be sure I'm hearing anything at all.

It's purring.

A smile lights up my face, and my heartbeat jumps as that sound fills me, and my grin stays in place even as its lips brush between my breasts in the faintest kiss, and the duvet lifts to encompass me.

Warm air and the heady smell of sex washes over me before the blanket drops back down over my head, pulling me into the cavern that its long body has made as it arches above me. The air is thick and humid under the covers, our joined breath making me sweat within moments.

I feel exposed. More than I did only a short time ago, when having my head outside the duvet meant that my body could experience all of this without me.

It's how I exist outside this room.

The only place where I am *real*, that I can *be* and *have* and *do* what I want is trapped within the walls of my psyche. Where I am who I know I am, and not the thing that the world sees when its greedy, terrible eyes tear me apart every single time they look at me and know that I am somehow *Wrong*.

It doesn't know that I am Wrong.

Right now, I'm here, and I'm whole, and it's here with me, breath shuddering against my collarbone as it lowers itself to slide its cheek against my chest. It exhales, long fingers smoothing up my arms, tracing old scars that I carved into myself when I was too young to do anything more than attack a body that I didn't want. It touches me like I am a gift, stroking over my round cheek and through the long hair that curls against my neck and crinkles under my head, tangling up in ways that I'll struggle to undo in the morning. That joining it under the covers has made me real to it, just as its caresses direct my awareness of every inch of its body, and every inch of mine.

I blink as my vision adjusts to the darkness, and when the shape of my creature starts to become clearer to me, I'm swept up in emotions that bring tears to my eyes.

Long legs, strangely jointed at the knee. Hips that are almost as wide as mine, but bony. My touch traces down its back where I find that the soft fur I've felt on its head and shoulders extends along its spine until it finishes in something long and thin. I gasp when the tail I didn't expect to be there twitches in my hand, and those muscles move and shift as the long, prehensile thing slides between us. Barely holding back a giggle, the tip tickles against my cunt, brushing around an opening that is already occupied.   My smile returns.

I touch its face the way it touches mine, memorizing every detail. I can't see the colour of its eyes yet, but they're deep and dark like inky blue ocean waters. It doesn't hold my gaze, and I take the silent request to move on. The beast-like snout that has nuzzled and licked me looks just as I imagined it, slit nostrils in a soft, rounded nose and a cleft lip. It shivers, ghosting kisses against my fingertips as I trace its mouth. I drag myself up the bed enough to put our heads level, whimpering as my shifting about causes its cock to slide out of me, leaving me empty once again.

"I need you to be real," I moan.

My voice cracks, high then low, and I put my hands on its shoulders, blinking in the dark. I struggle to see the vague, angular shape of its sharp ears and the bestial mouth that I have felt so many times. Its head tilts curiously and my grip tightens, trying to tug it back down to where my clumsy and imperfect self is waiting. It allows me to pull it in, letting out a sweet hum – a love song, only for me.

Its cheek slides against mine, a caress somehow still cooler than my fevered body. With thin lips it kisses my own plush mouth and somehow we are perfect together. My roundness against the angular bones and sinuous muscles of its body, stretched out and pulled thin where I am and have always been voluminous. I take up space, even when I wish I didn't, but when its body eases down against me and rolls, pulls me atop it so my thick legs frame its hips, I do not feel heavy.

It arches up and into me again, and I am lighter than air.

My voice spikes with a short cry, and it answers with a shrill warble, fingers tenderly wrapping around my breasts. They heave against its palms as I descend onto its thick shaft, my dark and blushing nipples framed by a vice-like grip as, for the second time tonight, it rocks into me.

We move together, its grip on my thighs and waist pulling me down against its lean form as my ass hits its hips over and over. I gasp sharply each time. I kiss it again, and again, running my tongue over so many ferocious teeth that are so careful not to bite, until my panting in the thin air under the duvet has made the heat unbearable. Sweat beads on my forehead and runs down the side of my face and my back as I slide along its body and stroke its cock with my greedy, slow movements.

It's real. I'm real.

It's hard to breathe, and I'm desperate to come, my whole body buzzing and frantically reaching for an orgasm that I've been chasing since it went face first into my cunt. My eyes water as I strain to try and make out the face of the creature under me, because I've been waiting so long for this. To feel the way I do, my heart as bare as every other part of me.

Sweat-slick and trembling from the fire burning me from the inside-out, I sit back on my haunches and press my hands to its hard chest.

I want to see it. I want it to see what it's doing to me.

The cocoon of my blankets was for me—this whole room is for *us*, and I don't need any further encouragement to throw the covers aside, pitching them off of my fevered body. I moan as the rush of sweet, fresh air fills my lungs and cools me as I take it in. I don't think about the mirror to my left. I don't think about being covered up to forget everything under my clothes. I don't think about my Wrongness, because how could anything be wrong when the cock inside of me starts throbbing, and I force it to bottom out so I can keep it as deep as I want it when it finally erupts inside of me.

I think about the incredible creature before me,

laying on the bed and looking up at me as if I am some kind of ethereal being. Like I was the one who materialized out of the night to show them that their body is the only thing that makes them real to me, that allows us to see and hear and touch and *fuck.*

It could look like anything and I would still want every bit of them.

My eyes meet its dark gaze, pupils slit like a cat's, and I make it watch as I place my hands on its chest and push myself up, displaying everything I love and hate about myself. I know it wants to look at me and if its terrifying, beautiful body can be gorgeous to me, then my imperfect form can be, too.

Perfection is bestowed upon me by the way it looks up at me, lays its clawed hands over mine and doesn't look away as I arch my back and strain my creaking bed frame with the force of my hips slamming down. I am unleashed, feeling only my creature and the exhilaration of letting go until the molten fire burning in me and dripping down my thighs suddenly bursts forth. My nails dig into its skin as I scream with pleasure.

I cry out again and again as I ride out the blinding lights and the way time freezes for a few sweet seconds, my whole body shuddering and clenching around the shaft that fills me.

I can't let it go, I won't.

Not even when its hips lift off the bed, bucking against me. It takes over the blistering pace I can't maintain while I'm still shaking off the pleasure of a climax so intense that I can't remember not feeling at home in my body, blissed out and trembling.

I don't want it to stop.

It doesn't take long for my creature's voice to join mine, throaty and guttural as it growls and whimpers until it silences itself with my mouth.

The kiss is everything I'd hoped it would be, tongue opening my lips to taste me like it would drink me if it could. Teeth bump against my lips, and I feel boneless, wanting to slump over, but I am held up by its long arms under mine, clutching me as it lets out that same, keening sound. It's louder now, not ashamed of its voice or the ghostly echo left behind as it sings for me, fucking me even as its cock throbs and I am filled in hot, pulsing jets. I am forced to still and feel it, so thick and copious that it oozes out of me and down the underside of its shaft while it's still buried in me.

Instead of slinking back into the shadows once we're both sated and happy, this time, it stays, holding me against its chest with its head buried against my shoulder.

Don't leave, I want to say. *The window is shut, it's still nighttime. I'll protect you from the sunlight and the eyes of anyone else who would ever dare to look at you and call you a monster.*

Together, we are no longer monsters.

It's just the two of us, arms and legs and bodies so different, and it's stunning to me that anyone could look at my creature and see anything other than what it is to me. I think about it every day, every night, even the ones when I can't bear to be touched and I leave my window open to let the lights stream in from outside. I wonder where it goes, what it is, where it comes from and if it thinks about me, too. If it waits in anticipation for the night to fall, for the brief moments we spend together. What if there was a way we could take our time, to not have to rush because of the fear that everything will end with the morning sun?

It holds me for a long time.

When I finally feel its embrace loosening, my legs have started to cramp and I ease to one side, arm draping over its body so that it doesn't let me go completely. My eyes are open and this time, its are closed. I'm already planning the hundreds and thousands of kisses I'm going to use to coax them to open again.

"Can you stay with me?" I whisper, one hand blindly groping for long fingers, sharp claws, a monster who wants me and sees me.

It nods.

"Do you *want* to stay with me?"

It doesn't answer. Instead, it wraps around me, long legs and arms and tail curled around my ankle. We don't need a blanket – we're both still so hot, and I can't bear the thought of covering up any part of us. Not here, in this tiny world, where neither of us need to hide anymore.

I smile and close my eyes. I don't intend to fall asleep, but I do, and I wake up just after sunrise. The light peeks through the edges of my curtain sheet, and I am still not alone.

I see everything.

Isolation
Lee Ohlson

It had been three nights since the tapping at his window had begun.

Ansel Kautz lay there in the gloaming listening to it, a strange and uncharacteristic fear gripping him. Tonight, Ansel had finally recognized that the tapping was not some innocent symptom of his hermetic lifestyle. It was not an animal, not a quirk of nature. The thing tapping on his window was in possession of distinctly human hands, although they were long and distorted, the finger drumming against the thick glass at least twice as long as one of Ansel's. He had seen it when he'd rolled over onto his side to face the window, a crooked nail scraping down the pane.

Ansel had crossed an entire ocean, had pushed north into a part of Maine populated only by the Penobscot, had built a house from the ground up and learned to live entirely off the land. Six foot two, burly, German, he was not a man easily frightened. He had faced down a mother bear the year prior with little more than clammy palms.

Something about the sight of that hand had paralyzed him.

The tapping resumed and Ansel knew he could not lay there idle like he had the prior nights. He sat up in his threadbare bed, pushing off the heavy quilt his mother had given him when he'd left home and peering around the darkened room for his boots. He had always been prone to sleeping early, and tonight when the tapping had begun it had been barely dusk, the faint pink sky creeping through the great pine forest that kept Ansel as isolated as he liked. Now, though, it was black night, dark and eerie. Dressed in thick woollen underclothes meant to fend off the Maine chill, Ansel paused only to tug on a coat and his leather boots before fetching his ancient hunting rifle from where it hung above the fireplace.

For a moment, he considered not loading it. If it was a human outside Ansel had no desire to kill. But if it wasn't? If it was something other, as its terrible hand had suggested... He took buckshot from the box where he kept it, loaded the weapon, and stepped out onto his front porch. The late fall air smelled of snow, a chill having settled over his little corner of the world in the past week but the sky was clear and pockmarked with stars, bright and twinkling above his head. He would have appreciated it more if there wasn't something lurking unseen in the trees beyond the clearing where he had made his home.

"Who's been tapping at my window?" he asked, his

German accent heavy, his voice a rasp thanks to a childhood illness that had left him very nearly mute. He scanned the tree line with honey brown eyes set beneath bushy auburn eyebrows, tongue wetting his dry lips even as his nerves grew worse, jangling under his skin. "Show yourself."

A voice issued from the trees, hissing and low, a murmur that would have been easily mistaken for the wind under any other circumstances. "If I show myself, Ansel, you would only fear me before I could make my case."

The voice was speaking German. It caught Ansel off guard, the euphoria that struck him at the sound of his mother tongue causing him to briefly lower his rifle. "You are German?" he asked, uncertain.

"No, but you are. Are you not? "

"I am," Ansel said, the fluency with which the stranger spoke making him both giddy and suspicious. "Why is there a fellow German tapping on my window?" he hesitated, a thought striking him. " Was that your hand?"

"So you saw it," the voice said, sighing like a summer breeze rustling through rushes. "I had feared as much."

"You are not human," Ansel said, a statement and not a question. "Then what are you? And why have you come?"

"It is simple enough, " the voice said. "I'm hungry. I can't very well go down to some yonder farm and look for food. They would shoot me before I could pass their gate. But you are discerning, I think.. You will not shoot, even after you have seen my hand."

Ansel thought about that hand, thought about that nail against his glass, and while fear still gripped him his curiosity overrode it. "So you came because you were hungry," he said, resting the butt of his rifle against the porch but keeping one calloused hand on the muzzle. "But what are you?"

A pervasive silence, during which Ansel could hear nothing but the creaking of the trees and a faint, far off loon. "I don't have a name in your tongue, or in any tongue of man," the voice finally responded. "But I have existed in these woods longer than time. I emerged from the mountains, when l can hardly recall and I have been here since. Rarely am l awake, however."

Ansel considered this. He was not a religious man nor was he particularly superstitious, and more often than not he could make a decision based on less information than he had now. The tapping, the voice, the hand... It spoke to something primal, something from the very distant past. Perhaps it was loneliness, perhaps it was the use of his mother tongue, but his usual caution did not prevail. "I can spare some food," he said finally. "Can I see you if I do?"

"Not tonight," the voice said. " I saw an apple tree behind your house. Can you spare one?"

"One?" Ansel repeated, surprised. "Will that be enough?"

"For tonight," the voice said.

Ansel did not argue, turning back to his house. There was a bushel of apples in the kitchen and he fetched a beautiful one, glossy red and sweet smelling. He hesitated before walking back outside, finally deciding to rest his gun beside the door; if the owner of the voice wanted to kill him, he didn't think his gun would help. "I have the apple," he said once he was back on the porch, pausing on the top step. "Where would you like it?"

"Close your eyes," came the voice, and Ansel thought it was above him now, perched on the overhang of the porch. "Hold the apple out in your hand. "

Ansel obeyed. He held his right hand out before him, the apple nestled in his palm, and closed his eyes. Something creaked above him and there was a soft, slippery noise, a snake sliding over rotten leaves. A weight settled on the porch and a hand, huge and cold, encased Ansel's. The fingers seemed to reach almost to his elbow, the palm easily covering his knuckles almost to his wrist.

Ansel shuddered, but it was not a shudder of revulsion or terror. It had been a decade since he had last been touched, and while he knew full well he was not being touched by a human, he enjoyed it far more than he ever could have anticipated. In fact, he was nearly overcome, nearly opened his eyes as something like.... Well, like pleasure struck him.

The voice came from right before him, accompanied by a honeysuckle smell. "A fine apple," it said. "Beautiful. I wonder... Do you think an apple knows when it is about to be devoured? When it is faced with something that desires nothing more than to consume it in its entirety?"

"It knows," Ansel said.

Thin fingers slid down his forearm, lingering, strangely alluring. The apple was finally plucked from his hand but its absence made Ansel feel hollow. "And do you think it minds?"

"I think it wants to be devoured."

A breath, hot and welcome against his ear. "I think you are right. Open your eyes, Ansel."

Again, Ansel did as he was told. He found the porch empty, the night air as lonesome and as still as it had always been. He stared at the stars, an endless and expansive blanket pockmarked with planets he could name, places he would never see. It was quite some time before he turned and went inside.

Snow crunched underfoot as Ansel worked deeper into the woods, a pair of fat young rabbits already slung over his shoulder and three more traps yet to check. It was early January now, 1830 finally arrived. It had been three months since the tapping, the voice, the apple. Ansel, for the first time since he had come to America, had found himself lonely. Still, if the voice had been telling the truth, three months was a split second in a life that had spanned thousands of years.

Ansel pulled his knit scarf up further over his chin, his cheeks red and numb thanks to the pervasive cold that had set in over the Christmas season. His next trap was in a frozen creek bed,, and as Ansel crouched down to investigate he was abruptly aware that the woods had gone predator-silent. He looked up, peering down the creek towards a pair of trees that bent towards each other over the water in time to see something huge and pale move behind the giant trunks. Ansel had seen a leg, as thick around as his entire torso and the colour of a soft white underbelly, the knee backwards and the bare foot splayed to the side like some massive insect.

Ansel straightened up, peering towards the trees. "How was the apple?" he asked in German.

"Delicious," came the sibilant reply, the voice right in his ear despite the distance of the creature from where he stood. Ansel swallowed, saliva filling his mouth in anticipation; unbidden, his cock twitched in his breeches. "Has it been long since I last visited you?'

"For me, yes," Ansel said. "The seasons have changed. I have no apples to offer now."

"A minor disappointment. Did you find yourself wondering if I would return?"

"Yes," Ansel said. He lowered the two rabbits onto the snow. "You gave me no name."

"I have no name," the voice said, but there was a contemplative note now that had not been there before. "Would giving me a name comfort you?'

Comfort him? Ansel wondered if he even needed comfort. No, he didn't think it was comfort he needed at all. A hunger had welled up inside him at the first moment he had heard the voice, a hunger of a specific type. He was not the apple, begging for consumption, but rather an appetite himself. "A name ill sates my curiosity," Ansel said. "A name is not what you are."

"No," the voice agreed. "It is a human desire, to organize things by name. Those rabbits at your feet did not concern themselves with names. I have never felt the need to name myself. Will you not name me, then?"

"It is not my place to name you," Ansel said. "You

hid when you saw me. Do you still think I would run in fear?"

"You saw a glimpse. Was that not enough to convince you of my inhumanity?"

"I have never questioned that. But I am not afraid of you. Even what I saw whets my appetite. You are so dissimilar to anything I have ever known, and I thought I knew these woods."

"There are things that live in these woods that you would never know even if you were given until the world ends. But you may come to know me yet. I have another boon to ask."

Ansel's eyes glinted in the winter sun, his heart thumping hard against his ribs. "Anything," he said. " I will give anything."

"Close your eyes," and Ansel obeyed. The snow crunched in front of him, the thin shell of ice breaking beneath the feet of the being. He could feel the presence before him, looming so tall it blocked the sun from touching his face. Ansel breathed out, skin tingling beneath his heavy winter clothes, and the thing took hold of the simple wooden buttons that held his coat closed. One of those impossibly long fingers grazed over his bearded chin, pushing his head back before undoing the very top button on his coat.

A hand slid into the front of his coat, freeing the end of his scarf from where it was tucked under his armpit. The thing tugged on the scarf until it was tight around Ansel's throat and yet he kept his eyes closed, the sweet-hot breath of the thing brushing over his lips. Fingers slid underneath the wool of the scarf to touch bare skin, surprisingly cool against the sweat that had been trapped by the garment. Slowly, Ansel's head was tilted back and he allowed it, unsurprised when a long, slick tongue ran over his chapped mouth.

He parted his lips to allow the kiss, the tongue as long as its hand and nearly as thick, the teeth a razor sharp novelty that reminded Ansel very much of a crocodile he had seen as a boy at a circus back in Dresden. At first, the thing seemed content with sampling the taste of him, running its tongue along the seam of his lips and pushing the tip in only slightly. As Ansel kissed back, however, the thing was emboldened. It pushed its tongue in to Ansel's mouth so deep he nearly choked, lips parting so wide the corners of his mouth felt as though they might split.

He raised his gloved hands to grip at the forearms of the creature, breathing hard through his nose as he allowed the thick, wet tongue to force itself down until he could feel it bulging in his throat. Surprise gripped him when a second pair of arms settled on his waist, this newest development further coloring Ansel's understanding of the creature. Two sets of arms and thick, backwards legs made it seem insectoid, but there was no repulsion creeping up in Ansel at that revelation; rather, it took all he had not to open his eyes and take in the full sight of the being.

The thing broke the kiss, its tongue retracting from his mouth with an audible squelch, a rope of slick saliva connecting their mouths. His scarf was pulled free from his neck, leaving the nape exposed and chilled, but Ansel was ever obedient. "What is the name of that mountain?" the thing asked, doing up Ansel's top button, scarf stolen but given willingly all the same.

"Katahdin," Ansel said. "The Penobscot named it such. Is that where you came from?"

"No," the creature said. "I came from far away in a place with no name nor humans to name it. But I have been here for some time. I would like it if you called me Kata. It will do as a name, I believe." The weight of Kata's hands left Ansel's shoulders and waist and the voice, soft and whispering, breathed past his ear. "Open your eyes, Ansel."

The woods before him were empty, a thrush calling somewhere overhead as the animals returned to the area in Kata's absence. Ansel stooped and lifted the dead rabbits from where he had set them, a lightness filling his chest that hadn't been there before.. It remained until he reached home and realized for the first time how empty his cabin had become.

Sunlight dripped through the leaves as Ansel settled in the shade of an ancient oak that sat near the edge of his farmland. Dirt clung to his hands, sweat plastering his auburn hair to his forehead as he tore a chunk of bread from the loaf he had set aside for lunch. The yellow-brown mutt puppy he'd bartered with the Penobscot for at the end of February was rolling around in a freshly tilled patch of dirt that would be sown after Ansel's comfortable lunch, pausing only briefly to yap at him, and for the first time in nearly forty years of life he was content.

Content, but not satisfied.

Ansel had never concerned himself much with loneliness before he had met Kata. He had never longed for more, had never thought about finding companionship. His life in the woods, a life resigned to the four walls of his cabin, had been more than enough. Except... Now instead of waking in fear as something tapped against his window, he awoke sweating, cock throbbing, seed spilled in the thin fabric of his long johns. That kiss six months before had not been enough.

"You think quite loudly."

A voice from the trees, as though summoned by the filthy thoughts consuming Ansel's mind as he sat beneath the watchful sun. "So you are capable of knowing my mind," Ansel said. "Then do you know I've done little but think of you since that day in the snow?"

"I know," Kata agreed. "Do you know why I have not returned until now?"

"How could I possibly?" Ansel said. "I don't expect you to visit me everyday, but it has been a long time since last you came. Mere moments for you, I suppose, and yet an eternity for me. So what kept you away?"

"For the first time in what you call an eternity, I felt something new. I was... Frightened."

"Frightened?"

"Yes," Kata said slowly. "Of what you would think if you saw me. "

Ansel snorted despite himself, setting his bread down on the grass beside him. "I know you aren't human and yet I still kissed you. I think you will find me more accommodating than you expect."

His words were met by a long and deafening silence. When Kata spoke again, there was an undercurrent of need that hadn't been there before. "Send the dog away."

A thrill, hot and unexpected, shot through Ansel at the words. He whistled sharply, the puppy hopping to all fours and looking at him. "House," he commanded, pleased he had taught the dog the command to ensure he would know to run if there was any threat of danger. As soon as the puppy was out of view Ansel stood, turning to face the woods. "Come out."

There was silence followed by the faintest sound of leaves rustling and Ansel held his breath in anticipation, in hunger. While he was prepared for a monster to appear before him, what emerged from the trees was far beyond anything he could have imagined -- although to be honest his imagination had never been that fertile to begin with.

Kata was at least ten feet tall, humanoid yet not, something very nearly spiderish about him. Six arms protruded from a pale and naked torso, each terminating in those long, thin hands. His legs were, as Ansel had thought before, backwards- thick and crooked in the way of a cricket. His neck was slender and his face was truly striking, eight coal black eyes set above a mouth slit almost to his ears, teeth jagged and fierce. Blond hair, nearly white, cascaded down his shoulders in a curly mass. While he was utterly inhuman he struck no fear in Ansel.

In fact, the predominant sensation sweeping through Ansel at the moment was desire. He took a deep breath and lifted a hand to scratch at his jaw, beard coarse against his fingers. Drinking in the sight of Kata, it was difficult to overlook his cock, as large if not larger than the entirety of Ansel's right arm. Kata's black eyes appraised him, shining in the dappled sun beneath the tree boughs and when Ansel spoke it was with his usual rasping voice, not a hint of fear or disgust to be found. "This is what you hid from me?'

"You aren't afraid."

"No," Ansel said. "Did you think I was the apple waiting to be devoured? I have chosen this life at every turn and it seems that the path was meant to bring me here. I fear you no more than I fear a spider in some corner of my home or the rabbit caught in my trap. I have thought of little else these last six months but your mouth on mine and your hands on my waist." He undid the top button of his linen work shirt, as clear an invitation as he could provide. "Do you not feel that same pull? Is that not what has brought you back here time and time again despite your own claim that you have never done so in all your millennia of life?"

Kata observed him, all eight eyes glittering with some red heat that filled Ansel with a responding desire coiled hot and tight in the pit of his stomach. "I walked until I met the ocean to see if there was more land for me to explore," he finally said, stepping closer through the trees. "I saw the vast blue plain and I realized I have gone from shore to shore, from mountain to canyon, and yet I have found nothing else that has drawn me back to a place I have already walked aside from you. When last I returned it was for hunger, but that hunger was for you and you alone. Now your scarf has lost the scent of you and I was compelled to return."

"You needn't be content with a scarf and nothing more," Ansel said, shrugging his shirt off. His shoulders broad, his chest fuzzy with the same auburn hair that made up his beard, Ansel was built like a man whose survival revolved around manual labor. Despite being faced with a creature that may evoke nameless terror, Ansel was concerned Kata would not like what he saw. He lifted his head to see if there was any change in the way the creature was looking at him, only to find his waist abruptly seized by the lowest pair of Kata's hands. The middle pair gripped his biceps while the top took hold of his face, sharp and dangerous mouth closing the distance between their faces.

This time, Ansel did not need prompting to part his lips. His mouth opened readily, his bare chest pressed flush to Kata's concave stomach, the creature's thick cock twitching ponderously against his leg. Ansel's mouth all but watered at the idea of that cock inside him, ravaging him, and as Kata's slick hot tongue forced its way past his lips and invaded his throat Ansel pushed closer, rutting the cock against his thigh like an animal. Kata shuddered, devouring Ansel's mouth like a being starved and hungry, and when he withdrew his tongue from Ansel's throat slime connected them once more.

Ansel peered up at Kata from beneath his long eyelashes, his eyes dark and demanding. Saliva dripped from his chin onto his chest, catching in the hair, and no words passed either man's lips before Kata bent his strange legs backwards to bring his monstrous face level with Ansel's chest. He ran his tongue over Ansel's skin, pausing to suck and slurp at each nipple before moving lower. He tore Ansel's trousers from him as easily as a child tears a wrapper from a sweet, Ansel's cock hard and leaking already. Kata looked at it for a moment before pressing his head into the crux of Ansel's thigh and breathing in deeply, thick tongue already sliding over the sensitive inner part of Ansel's leg. "Don't," Ansel whispered, Kata's ashen hair already marred with the clear fluid beading at the tip of Ansel's uncircumcised cock.

"Your smell," Kata hissed by way of argument before lovingly laving his tongue over each of Ansel's balls, wetting the baby-fine hair there and leaving Ansel's legs trembling with the exertion of staying on his feet. Abruptly Kata took him by the waist again, spinning him around with alarming dexterity and using his topmost arms to force him onto all fours in the grass while another pair grabbed greedy and strong at his waist. Ansel gasped, stomach tightening in anticipation. One more, Ansel's imagination was ill-equipped to prepare for what came next.

With one hand pressed firmly between Ansel's shoulder blades to keep his chest flush with the ground and two other hands holding his hips to ensure his ass remained in the air, Kata gripped Ansel's ass cheeks, spreading them apart. Ansel immediately felt his face flush and pressed his forehead to his crossed arms, breathing hard through his nose as Kata pressed two thin thumbs against Ansel's tight hole. The next moment, Kata's thick, wet tongue pushed against the puckered ring of muscle. At first it seemed impossibly large, Ansel's hips bucking forward involuntarily when the tip finally slid in, slick and warm and stretching his hole.

Ansel was not a virgin, a handful of encounters as a younger man working as an itinerant lumberjack having introduced him quite thoroughly to carnal knowledge back in Germany, and yet it had been years since he had last been fucked. That too had been quick and hurried, a summer seven years past when he had given succor to a Penobscot scout and quickly found the man in his bed. As Kata's tongue pushed deeper, however, pressing briefly against that small knot inside him that sent liquid dribbling from his cock, any former human lovers were pushed from his mind. This was something new, something he has never felt.

He cried out as the tongue split him wide, thick slime dripping from his hole down over his balls and creating a small rivulet that coursed over the veined underside of his cock where it gathered, dew-like, on the tip of his foreskin. He moved to grip his cock, the need for relief overcoming him, but a sudden probing feeling in his gut left him weak, dizzy. He knew then that the entirety of Kata's tongue, squirming and white hot, was within him. He was spread so wide that it felt very nearly like his entire lower half was impaled, but the steady pulse against that most sensitive spot was enough to drive him near mad.

If Kata's tongue was so huge it could be felt in his stomach, what would that enormous cock feel like, butting up against his insides?

Slowly, accompanied by a pleasurable agony that

spread from his gut to his every last extremity, Kata withdrew his tongue. The pressure from that alone wrung Ansel's first orgasm from him, a thick rope of cum painting the grass below, but before Ansel could even register the odd sensation of slime dripping from his ravaged ass he was being flipped onto his back. He stared up at Kata, chest heaving, before allowing his legs to fall open. His spent cock lay leaking against his soft stomach and Kata's gaze drank in the sight before him before he took hold of his massive cock in his lower right hand. "You are sure?"

Ansel was certain he could take it. Even if it turned out he couldn't, being fucked to death was not the worst end a man could come to in this isolated corner of the world. "Yes," he said, as prepared as could be, and he dug his calloused fingers into the meat of his own thighs to pull his legs further apart. Kata pushed the great fist-like head of his cock to Ansel's oozing hole, one of his many hands gripping Ansel's ass to lift it slightly off the ground. He forced the head of his cock in with an audible squelch and Ansel bit back a cry, surprised when Kata lowered his head and kissed him, hungry and wet, once again.

Spread impossibly wide, the pain was nonetheless more tolerable than Ansel had anticipated. Perhaps there was some numbing factor in Kata's saliva, something like mosquitos exhibited. In any case Ansel was aware mostly of pressure and an overarching sensation of being stretched by Kata's cock in a way that was leaving him entirely breathless. He hauled his arms up around the creature's neck, dragging him deeper into the kiss and arching his back to allow for Kata's cock to penetrate ever further.

Despite the exhaustion that had set in immediately after his orgasm, Ansel's traitorous cock was growing hard once again, trembling excitedly against his stomach. He gripped the curly blond hair at the nape of Kata's neck in his hands, surprised at how human it felt between his fingers. Bending his knees to brace his feet against the grass, his breath hitched against Kata's mouth as the cock drove deeper into his insides, pressing up against his prostate with steady pressure.

Kata broke the kiss, the now-familiar sensation of his tongue uncoiling from Ansel's throat leaving the human wanting in a dreadful way. He kept his hands on the back of Kata's neck until one of the creature's hands took hold of his left wrist, pulling it down and pressing it flat against his stomach. "Do you feel it?"

Ansel stared up at him, not understanding what he was being asked until he did, in fact, feel it. Pressed deep into his stomach, he could feel Kata's cock bulging beneath his muscle and skin. His eyes met Kata's and he moaned softly as Kata's cock pushed deeper, deeper, pressed up into him and spread him further than he could have thought possible. The sensation only mounted as Kata began to fuck him in earnest, pulling his cock out nearly all the way before slamming in all the way once more.

Fingers splayed across his abdomen, Ansel felt the head moving beneath his palm, unable to choke down the moans being slammed out of him through pure brute force. With his free hand he continued to grip at

Kata's nape, mouthing at the creature's jaw hungrily. A pair of strong hands gripped Ansel's thighs, forcing them back so he was nearly bent double even as another pair of hands gripped his face and pulled him into a searing kiss. Ansel whimpered and at the same moment Kata thrust into him with renewed vigor, the motion driving another, albeit drier, orgasm from Ansel.

He cried out against Kata's mouth, smothered only by the oppressive tongue down his throat, and wriggled against the grass, the dirt cool and gritty against his bare skin. It took every bit of strength, both internal and out, for him to break the kiss. "It's too much," he rasped, his body twitching desperately as he was fucked, entirely overstimulated. "It's too much, Kata. "

He was yanked forward, pulled so he was being supported only by the hands on his thighs and the cock buried deep inside him. "Say it again," Kata murmured.

Ansel stared up at him, uncomprehending in the face of the torturous pleasure racking his body until a thought struck him and he dug his fingers into Kata's scalp, his breathing coming in short gasps as he fought to regain control. "Kata," he said, his lips against Kata's cheek just before his ear. As if in response, Kata's cock spasmed inside him and despite his growing exhaustion Ansel felt his own member twitch.

Pressure was building in Ansel's gut, his toes curling in the air as Kata continued to hold him off the ground and drive his cock in deeper. "Kata, please," Ansel said, as close to begging as he could come. "It feels strange."

Kata's response was to wrap one of his fists around Ansel's overworked cock, Ansel crying out at the sensation. This was all too much, nothing left in him to give, but in keeping with his inhuman appearance Kata clearly had inhuman stamina to match. Ansel's head dropped forward so his chin was touching his chest, the pressure in his stomach growing unbearable in the moments before an orgasm of impossible intensity racked him. A clear, colourless fluid came squirting from his cock, spraying Ansel in the face. He was overcome with a temporary madness, nothing but animalistic whimpers falling from his lips. It took all of Ansel's remaining strength just to cling to Kata as the monster fucked into him with one final shuddering thrust.

Ansel was flooded with warmth from the inside out, suddenly hyperaware that he was being filled with more of Kata's cum than seemed possible. Kata sunk forward to lay Ansel on the grass, cock still twitching inside him, and he dragged his tongue over Ansel's cheek, lapping up the thin and salty liquid that clung there. Ansel clutched at his shoulders as Kata pulled his cock out with an obscene squelch, thick and ropy cum gushing out of Ansel with yet more remaining in him, his lower stomach slightly distended.

Kata peered down at him, concern clear in all of his eyes. "You are unharmed?"

"No," Ansel murmured, the afternoon sun warm on his skin as he closed his eyes, bruised and battered but content. "No, I believe you have done quite a lot of harm, all things considered." He opened one eye to look up at Kata, reaching out to touch his neck. "I believe you have devoured me after all."

Kata's concern ebbed and he leaned down, kissing

Ansel once again. For the first time in his life, Ansel thought he would like to have someone else around.

Come Inside
Haven Valentin

Landry House presides over the valley of Glencombe from atop a great and overbearing hill, as all important houses – or houses with delusions of grandeur – are wont to do. Its roof is tiled in slate, which lichen refuses to grow on, they say, due to some noxious fume of evil breathing up from within. When it rains – like it is doing now – the slate turns black and shiny, as does the rock of the path leading up to the oppressive front doors. Horses have broken themselves on this path. As have men, numerous men, in the centuries since the House was erected.

Nestled in its shadow, the wet valley town shivers. Calling Glencombe a town is perhaps an overstatement; viewed from the gardens of Landry House, the thatched roofs of its buildings look like sediment collected in the crease of someone's palm.

Jude – the body, the parlour trick, seven-and-twenty years old and not his own, cracked open by ghosts as an infant to become their loyal voice and vessel – stands on the lawn with his back to the House. He stares down the hill, over ragged, sodden rosebushes, at the sediment of Glencombe as he waits to be presented with the Keys. He's been waiting twenty minutes now, his patience wearing thin.

The rain is hard enough to give him goosebumps through his coat (which is old, but quality, a gift from a client he has taken good care of and many-times repaired). Down in Glencombe, he knows, the river that cuts jagged between the houses will be seething, spitting, its banks swollen and sloppy with mud. He traces the mercury line of it from one end of the valley to the other, thinking of palmistry and of being held underwater. The palm reader he met at his first real job as a medium told him – his chubby red seven-year-old hand in hers – that he would live a long life. Three years later, some boys from the far side of the river caught him crossing by himself and decided to test that prediction. Five years after that, Jude left Glencombe for larger cities, richer clients. He hasn't been back since. Until now.

A sudden crack of thunder makes him flinch. To his right, a beech tree as old as Landry House hunches in on itself, fighting shudders as the wind rips through it. Jude watches the branches whip and rattle. Then a hand lands on his shoulder. He flinches again. Turns.

An older man in a waxed rain jacket is holding out a letter. Jude grabs it and tucks it into his coat before the rain can eat through the paper. He misses what the man says it is, though he expects a missive from his current employers, who have recently purchased the

House. Sure enough, the next thing the man proffers is the Keys. The Keys are dark and ornate, just the kind you would expect to unlock a place like Landry House. When Jude takes them, he feels their cold seep through his gloves.

"You be careful now, sir," the man tells him sternly, raindrops in his eyebrows and his beard. "Nobody's been in there for a long while. S'hard to say how much'll be intact."

Jude presses his lips together and nods. Broken stairs and weak floorboards are the least of his concerns. He tips the man a shilling, then turns to make his way up the black path.

He's greeted by his own self in the foyer, his reflection an uneasy spectre gazing out at him from the ornate prison of a mirror on the farthest wall. Pale grey eyes in a pale grey face; bloodless lips; hair like spider's silk. *Ghost child*, his parents called him, even before the ghosts found his seams and pried them loose. He stares at himself for a long moment and wonders what his parents would make of his choices. His lack of choices. The open doors of him, the hands and eyes and mouth he lends to spirits free of charge (for it's the audience who pays).

He takes a step closer to himself. Puppet. Pawn. So gaunt in the mirror. His Master instructed him to come here and he did so without argument, the same way he would have if something else were in his body guiding all his movements. He didn't say that Glencombe was the town where he grew up. He came here even though he didn't want to; even though the memory of this place is a burning ache like river water in his lungs; even though he's not an exorcist, like the new owners of Landry House requested.

His Master doesn't believe in spirits. He keeps no exorcist on his books; thinks a medium is more-or-less the same thing. Jude knows that it is not. But still he came here, and now here he is.

The door behind him bangs shut.

He is inside Landry House, and very soon, the House will be inside him.

Before anything else, Jude breathes. A deep inward breath that fills his lungs with cobweb and dust. Wind howls in the chimneys, rattles the window glass, but the air inside the House is old and still. Carried on it is the House's memory of itself, and a house's memory has a kind of flavour. Jude can gauge, from breathing in a house, how sick it is: how sick-as-in-diseased, how sick-as-in-depraved. How bloated with ghosts, how ill their temperament.

Landry House, he understands, is very sick indeed.

He opens the letter from the new owners. The foyer is gloomy, but thin grey light streams through the glass above the door, lighting the page. What's written upon it tells Jude nothing he cannot already guess.

The House is haunted. There are accounts dating back centuries, relaying different ways its occupants have suffered. Objects in the House move by themselves in the dead of night. Voices whisper temptingly, tormentingly. Strange lights appear at the far ends of hallways with no obvious source, enticing inhabitants and houseguests to do things they ordinarily would not. The letter makes numerous references to *exceedingly convivial amorous acts*, because – Jude assumes – the author is too embarrassed to say exactly what.

And of course, many have died here. The dying has been recounted extensively. Cot deaths. Wives driven mad by the House, found in bathtubs full of blood; found dangling from the rafters by their necks; found frozen on the driveway at first light with their skulls shattered in. Servants driven mad, too. Servants who slit their masters' throats at the dining table; who poured boiling pans of water on them while they slept; who ended their own lives afterwards, or else turned themselves in to the authorities and met their ends at the scaffold. Some of the tales seem plausible, others too ludicrous and gory to be true. But Jude has no way of verifying any of them.

The new owners want the House to be cleansed ahead of their arrival. They have no desire to set foot on the property – nor send any repairmen here – until they can be confident that no harm will befall them. They were happy enough to send *Jude* here, he thinks a little bitterly as he reads, but then, most people don't look at him and see a person.

With the poison inhaled, the scope of his task now understood, Jude unbuttons his coat and slips it off, casting about for somewhere to drape it. There is little furniture in the foyer – just a dining chair, lying on its side like a wounded animal with a broken leg – so he uses the large curl of the banister at the foot of the stairs. Underneath his coat, his clothes are mostly dry, though his socks have been soaked through. He slips them off as well, leaving them balled up in his shoes by the door.

Barefoot, he makes his way upstairs.

A spirit medium is nothing like an exorcist.

Exorcists tend to come with religion attached: crosses, holy water, psalms. Even the atheists among them have their tchotchkes, their talismans, the things that give them courage. They believe in their purpose with a single-minded certainty and execute that purpose with liturgical finesse. The exorcist's arrival upon haunted ground is an invasion, a storming of the battlements, his job complete only when a house is rendered barren of souls and holy once more.

A spirit medium, on the other hand – a real one, not a counterfeit, of which there are dozens upon dozens – is little more than a conduit. She (for the spirit medium is almost always a she) does not do anything *to* the spirits of a house. Nor does she even communicate with them, usually. A spirit medium's purpose is to stand with one foot in the world of the living, the other in the world of the dead. She opens her body to let the spirits inside, then retreats to the back of her own mind and allows herself to be taken over. She is functionally absent from the room for whatever happens next.

Many a spiritualist scholar has noted, in journals and periodicals, the sexual undertone of possession. Of allowing oneself to be taken over in this manner: silenced, used.

"Do you not find it emasculating?" one such scholar once asked Jude, sitting with pen poised over paper.

"Not at all," Jude answered. "It's an honour to serve as a gateway for the spirits."

The scholar looked faintly repulsed as he copied down his words, but also – underneath – a little tantalized. "I could never do that. Submit like that. Like a *woman*."

"It really isn't all that different from other work," Jude said, keeping his tone genial. "You lend your time and your body to those who require it, in exchange for a wage."

The scholar wrinkled his nose. "Trust me, it's different."

Jude still thinks of that scholar sometimes. He left the spiritualist community shortly after writing up that interview, returning to his former career as a gynaecologist.

Society at large may consider submission a feminine trait, and femininity inherently degrading, but Jude does not. At least – being what he is – most of the people he works for expect a measure of queerness from him.

The House's steps are cold and rough. There is no carpet runner to soften them. Jude treads carefully, listening to the wood creak recalcitrantly under his weight. Splinters nip at his bare skin: a warning he's professionally obligated to ignore.

He trails down a hallway of open doors, peering into rooms of white-sheeted furniture, revealed to him like the insides of mouths. The House does not want him here; does not like anyone who brandishes its Keys;

he can feel its discomfort. Yet it holds still for him and lets him wander. He studies it and it studies him back.

At the end of the hallway is a large and empty room, barren of all furnishings save an ornate fireplace built into the wall. Jude feels compelled to enter it. As though a presence of some kind has wound its hand around his wrist, tugging him forward. An exorcist, he thinks, would reject this compulsion. But he follows it over the threshold. It isn't in his nature to resist.

To his right, a large window shrouded with netting overlooks the House's rear garden. The sound of rain patters against it, a steady unending thrum. A rectangle of flooring – about the size of a four-poster bed – is darker than the rest, its varnish undisturbed. An echo of the interior that once was. Likewise, the wallpaper is checkered with squares less sun-faded than the rest, where pictures must have hung. The mantelpiece is crowned by a ceramic vase – the only remaining deco- ration – its cobweb-laden handles painted to resemble curling snakes. The illustration on its front has faded to illegibility; a crack like a lightning bolt rends it in half.

Jude hears the door creak on its hinges and does nothing to prevent it from closing in his wake. It clicks shut with a gentle finality. He sits down cross-legged on the floorboards, facing the grimy maw of the hearth.

When he does a séance for an audience, he is frequently tied to his chair. The gas lamps in the room are dialled to their lowest; tall black dinner candles and white lilies placed around strategically for ambience. His skin will tingle and smart, stiff with whitening makeup, which they mix with phosphorus to produce a faint glow in the dark. Even though his mediumship is real, in a world of flashy charlatans, his Master stresses the importance of putting on a show.

There is none of that here. The air smells of nothing but dust. The room is grey, suffused with watery daylight. His cheeks are raw and pink from the cold and he feels very human.

He shuts his eyes and opens himself to the spirits of the House.

Immediately, from behind, a hand encircles his throat.

Who are you?

Jude hears its voice from everywhere and nowhere. It is distinctly not a human voice. It reverberates in triplicate, scoring cracks through his mind like plaster. The hand on his throat does not feel like a hand – too cold, with the texture of smooth brick – but it has fingers and a thumb and it is gripping him like a hand, so a hand it must be.

Jude has never met a ghost with hands. He did not know a ghost could have them.

He swallows against the grip and – trying to emulate the calm confidence of his Master conducting a séance – says, "Identify yourself first, spirit."

Intruder. You do not care to know me. You seek to control me.

"I've been summoned to exorcise you," he says, "but I understand that you've dwelt here a long time. You will, of course, be reluctant to go."

The floorboards reverberate with a laugh that isn't a laugh.

You understand nothing, little Medium.

Medium. It sees right through him, Jude thinks, with a little twinge of panic. It knows that he is powerless.

Only an exorcist can forcibly drive a spirit from its dwelling. Jude is well-aware of his limits; knows it would be arrogant of him to try. *His* plan – should this spirit, or amalgam of spirits, be amenable – is to carry it away from this place in his own body, rehome it elsewhere, in a place where it can hurt no-one and will not be disturbed. Although now, he is beginning to wonder whether this plan is just as foolhardy. This spirit does not feel like other spirits. *If* – the most scared part of his mind proffers – *it's a spirit at all.*

"I would *like* to understand," he says gently, sensing that he will get nowhere until he knows what he is up against. "Please. Talk to me. Do you have a name?"

He wants to open his eyes. He suspects there are now things to see in this room that he couldn't before; the air tastes sharper in his mouth, darker, like a butcher's floor after a slaughter. But he forces himself to keep his eyes shut, focused instead on feeling for this... *entity*... with his other senses. The hand on his throat is not disembodied; there's a presence, a weight behind him like something rearing up through the floor. It's visceral, solid in a way a ghost ought not to be.

It tightens. *Squeezes.*

**You already know my name! You misunderstand me on purpose, as obtuse as you always are, you creatures of blood and shame and sickness. I am

suffused with your cruelty, stained with it to the foundations, receptacle of your horrors. My name does not matter to you.

Jude – choking, blind now to all but red when he opens his eyes – reaches up and claws at the hand-that-isn't-a-hand. Its voice in his head is all-encompassing, loud to the point that he cannot hear his own thoughts. "*Please*," he gasps out. "Please – it matters. *You matter.*"

As suddenly as it grasped him, the hand on his throat is gone.

Why did they send you here, Medium?

He splutters. Flops onto his back, clutching at his throat, which burns. "Wh..."

They seek to hollow me out, do they not? To eviscerate me, scorch me from within and make me theirs again! But you are no exorcist. And you have brought no tools.

"Hollow you out...? That's not... that's not what..."

That's not what exorcists do to ghosts, he's about to say. But he realises, then.

There are no ghosts haunting the House.

There is only the House.

Landry House – the body, the set piece, two centuries old and not its own, infested and possessed from its conception by a revolving cast of names and bloody faces – watches the Medium from every angle as he recovers his breath. It studies the rise and fall of his chest; his fragile eyelids, scrunched tight shut; the spill of his white hair upon its sun-bleached floorboards. From its observation, he looks like every delicate human who has perfumed the air with lovemaking in this room. Head thrown back, pulse flickering in his throat, around which a dark red ring is forming. He looks like every lover and every murder victim that has died here. Like every sorry one.

The House has never met a medium before. He is like all humans, and he is also not. There's an aura of welcome around him, of invitation, that feels almost obscene. A wide-openness, a nakedness, even as he lies there fully-clothed, his waistcoat buttoned up. His whole existence seems to pull the House nearer.

Come inside, it breathes. *Come inside, fill me up, make me yours.*

Initially, it seemed like a trick. Now, the House is unsure. It's unnerved by how Houselike the Medium is; so much more Houselike than itself.

The Medium – who is not a House but would make a very good one – opens his eyes. He sits up and speaks, his voice scraping. "I see now," he says, humble in a way no human ever is. Almost reverent. "You're no spirit. You cannot be exorcised – it would be insulting to try. I'm sorry. I understand entirely."

And he does, for in a way, he *is* the House: a structure designed with doors and windows you can open, access points through which anyone might enter and take up residence in his bones. *Ghost child.* He does not belong to himself and never has. First he was his parents', until the ghosts came. His parents almost bankrupted themselves trying to eradicate them. When he turned six, they relinquished him to the first of his Masters: a showman who thought a child medium would make an exciting novelty onstage. As he grew, his novelty waned and he was sold on to another. Another. Another. Always someone's ghost child; always owned, inhabited, possessed.

He stares around him at the room with its numerous bloodstains – under his gaze they bubble up from the floorboards and the wallpaper, ugly memories dredged to the surface – and he thinks over the horrors in the letter he was given. The stories passed along for generations, embellished, exaggerated beyond the pale. How easy it was for them to blame the House for their transgressions. To cry *ghost!* when all that resided here was them. No wonder the House has grown resentful.

What is your name, Medium?

He tells it.

Jude, the House asks, ***how do you stand it?***

"Letting them in?"

The House doesn't nod, but he feels a shifting in the air like an affirmative.

"I don't know," he answers honestly. "I suppose I grew to like it."

Like *it*?

Like the spiritualist scholar who interviewed him, the House sounds repulsed, but also cautiously intrigued. Jude nods, a faint smile lighting his lips. "I find it liberating. To surrender myself to the control of someone else."

He was lying, when he told that scholar that mediumship was the same as other work. On a transactional level, of course, it's *exactly* the same.

Money changes hands; his Master pays him his cut. But allowing the spirits inside him doesn't feel like a transaction. The transaction exists on the outside, in the world of his Master and his audience. What happens between him and the spirits is a different affair entirely.

Tell me how. Tell me why.

It's not something he's ever been able to describe. But for the House, he will try.

He still remembers the first time he came with a spirit in his body.

He was perhaps twenty, fine-boned and waiflike enough to slip into the wedding dress he was presented by his Master of the time. His duty that afternoon was to open himself up to a bride who had died the week before her wedding day. The woman's widower wished to bid her farewell, and asked Jude's then-Master to step outside for the séance so that they might have some privacy in their final moments.

With nobody else in the room but Jude – who didn't wholly count as a person to him – the widower strode forward and kissed his bride full on the borrowed mouth.

A scouring kiss. A kiss that wanted to consume.

The bride melted into it at first. Succumbed almost entirely, before – with a hand on his chest – she forced herself back. "The medium," she panted.

The widower – still close enough to share Jude's breath – frowned and studied Jude's face, waxy and ethereal with phosphorus in the low light. Trying to see the living, breathing human that resided underneath. "Does he – she – do they mind?"

The man didn't know Jude's name. He didn't even know Jude's gender. Didn't care. Just wanted his bride.

Jude had been lost in the sense of fulfilment that so often came with possession, though he had been drawn closer to the surface by the physicality of the kiss. All at once, he was aware of his body again, its contours, the hard press of the man's torso against his own. The hand on the small of his back, possessive through the cream silk dress. The race of his shared heart.

Please, enjoy yourself, he whispered to the bride. *Let my body be yours.*

The widower took his bride over the table Jude's then-master used for spirit-rapping, hitching up her wedding dress to reveal Jude's pallid thighs and ass to the amber play of candlelight. It wasn't the consummation the couple had envisioned, but its realization – after fate had dealt them such a cruel hand – was every bit as sweet. Jude had never had a flesh-and-blood man inside of him before, and the widower's impassioned thrusts left him gasping, whimpering along with the phantom bride. They climaxed together – medium and bride – Jude's knees buckling, his body quaking with the shared ecstasy of two spirits that clanged together like bells.

Things changed for him after that.

As a young man working in a supposedly feminine profession, he had never been taken particularly seriously. His performances were skilful but predictable, his albinism his most remarked-upon trait, and by twenty he had grown weary of being known for *that.* Now – *now* – he could offer something most mediums wouldn't. A more sensual, tangible encounter with what lay Beyond. His Master seized upon it, and – finding Jude not only willing but eager – began advertising at once.

A bed was installed in the parlour where the séances took place, and Jude frequently found himself pinned under widowed men, sharing in the consummation of marriages which were not his. He learned to ready his body so that he could serve these couples better; so that he could endure rougher, more primal intercourse without it breaking him. Sometimes, he was possessed by a fallen groom, whose grieving bride wished to be taken for the first (or sixth, or hundredth) time. Most often, he served as the conduit for a pair of unwed lovers, many of whom had not been permitted to marry in life. Deemed incompatible by society – the wrong sex, the wrong race, the wrong class – they fit together perfectly inside him.

He grew to quickly love the feel of strangers' hands. The urgent, messy kisses, the scrabble to unfasten their clothes. With ghosts guiding his movements, he said and did things he had never been brave enough to say or do. His mouth, his tongue, laving over salty skin, wrapping around a cock, dipping inside a dripping cunt. His legs spread, clients pressing in, filling him up. Some wept against his neck, emotions brought to the fore as they rocked into him. His arms came around them, cradling them close. His hands tugged on their hair. He arched his back, moaned their names, begged them to keep going, keep going, please keep going. Sometimes, he wept too.

The spiritualist scholars that knew of his work lambasted it as lewd, improper, even sinful. They called him a deviant, an invert tricking honest men and women into licentious acts. But he felt no shame. He knew that he was doing his clients a kindness. Granting pleasure, closure, sanctuary in a painful hour of need.

I don't understand, the House tells him, having listened with hushed focus. *I am strong and sturdy and purpose-built, they say, to be a home. But my inhabitants do not thrill me. They sicken me. They cavort and chatter and amuse themselves like beasts within my walls. They injure each other and spill each other's blood, and they forget. They expect me to forget. But I do not.*

Jude rises from the floor, mindful now of the life humming in every bloodied wall. The House seems to inhale as he grazes his fingertips over the mantel, dislodging cobwebs which cling to his cuffs.

"You've been terribly abused," he says softly, stroking the seam where marble meets wallpaper. "Of course it would be hard to let someone in, after that – it's no failing of yours. These past inhabitants of yours were wretched. They didn't deserve you."

He moves his hand away.

Don't stop.

He hesitates, then resumes his caresses, knuckles skating gently over the places where the paper bubbles with decay. "You're a fine house," he says. "An elegant house, and a powerful one. When I lived in Glencombe,

I would gaze up at you all the time, wondering what you were like inside. What it would be like to explore you."

The wall ripples under his fingers, pushing him away.

I am not a kingdom to be conquered.

Jude had meant the words to be admiring, but he understands now how they sound. "No, you clearly aren't inclined toward possession," he agrees, casting his gaze up to the water-stained ceiling with its corniced rose. (The House has no face; it seems the right place to look.) "Perhaps you would rather do the possessing."

The silence that follows is telling.

"Perhaps," Jude continues, with a little more confidence – he is not afraid now, not at all; the House has shown its cards and shivers at his touches – "perhaps, after hearing my story, you would like to possess *me*."

The words are scarcely out of his mouth when hands land on his shoulders, fingers-that-aren't-fingers digging into his skin, grinding on the bones beneath. The House hauls him down and before he even hits the floorboards he is being dragged along, out of the bedroom door, down the hallway blindly.

He yells – it's reflexive – but doesn't struggle; doesn't attempt to catch himself on open doorways or claw at the floor. He couldn't if he wanted to: the floorboards rise to propel him along, and each door as he passes it slams thunderously shut, leaving just that one at the end like a retreating mouth as he slides down the House's throat. The hands-that-aren't-hands pull him down flat on the landing, one of them winding around his throat again to keep him there, the other knotting tightly in his hair. Nothing restraining his wrists or his ankles: the House knows he won't move.

Yes, says the House, its voice all jagged shards, all teeth. ***I want to possess you. I've wanted it since you arrived.***

"Then possess me," Jude breathes.

He shuts his eyes, surrenders.

It strips him, stitches tearing from the buttons of his waistcoat, his shirt tugged up and over his head with an almost violent desperation. He is dropped back down and his trousers follow: more ripping, more tugging. Like a ragdoll, Jude does nothing to hinder the House or to assist it. He's an object now and he loves it.

Naked, he feels the cold acutely. It makes his skin tingle, his nipples stiffen. Splinters dig into his back. Nobody has tended to this House for a long time. He thinks for a flash-and-vanish moment of the man who handed him the letter, warning him of missing parts. He thinks, *nobody has ever tended* me *like this, either,* and he almost says it but then one hand-that-is-not-a-hand pulls his arm out of the way so it can trail along his side, probing at the gaps between his ribs. A fingertip scrapes across his nipple and he keens softly. The other hand stays poised at his throat, feeling his rabbit pulse, his breaths as they come quick, needy and shallow.

The widower that fucked him didn't know or care about the man inside the body. He, Jude, was a means to an end. It feels good to come apart like that – unobserved, incidental – while lovers chant each other's names, grip and kiss and unravel each other. He has given himself over this way many times in the years since, for different clients with different lovers they wished to have again.

But being pinned down like this, like a butterfly in a frame, is something else entirely. Nobody has ever seen him like this, sans-phosphorus, sans-spirits. Nobody has ever looked at him and wanted *him*.

Jude, the House purrs – like an earthquake in the walls – ***you would make a magnificent House.***

He gazes up at the ceiling and smiles, a full unfettered smile with teeth. "Come inside, then."

The House does not hesitate.

The door is open, the welcome mat laid out. All it needs to do is cross over the threshold.

Jude has been possessed more times than he can count – more times than he can even remember – but he has never been possessed by anything that isn't a ghost. He's expecting the familiar negotiating press, like a body climbing in to share a narrow bed with him, nestling close and worming into all his crevices, bringing with it a delicious numbing cold.

He's expecting an inhabitant that *fits*. A tight fit, yes, but—*oh*—

There isn't space inside him for a House.

His jaw drops, a silent cry into the stale air as he is superseded. Overthrown. The world turns red and black and vanishes, his eyes bubbling with either tears or blood. His fingers spasm at his sides, nails scraping against floorboards. He feels his spine curve sharply, feels himself lift off the ground.

It hurts. It hurts like nothing he's ever felt. All the seams of him stretching, pressed on from within, his very soul distending to accommodate what he was never meant to take.

It hurts and the pain of it is perfect.

The House sits bolt upright with a drowned man's gasp.

A *human* gasp, drawn from a human throat: a slender column of vitality.

It reaches up with human hands to clutch the human throat – tender and bruised dark – feeling at the fragile skin. Feeling underneath for Jude.

Jude is still here, it senses with relief. Here in the drum of blood against its borrowed fingertips, each rapid clanging heartbeat a gift. How aware of this moment he is, the House does not know. But it remembers what Jude said about sensations. About feeling the widower's kisses along with the bride. Feeling the blunt thrusts of his cock.

It looks down at the body it has been allowed to fill. Smooth planes of blushing skin like wallpaper, interrupted here and there with little bumps and scars. Scuffs and bruises on the knees, deep purple in colour. Cradled in the place where thighs meet torso, a human cock, flushed and hard. Jude called the House elegant before, but Jude is the truly elegant one.

The House reaches to touch the tip of his cock. Shudders at the tuning-fork sensation, like being struck by gentle lightning. The shudder is audible, almost a moan, and that sends another jolt of pleasure through the House's borrowed body. Everything feels sensitive, sharp and acute in a way the House has never known. If this is how Jude lives all the time, the House doesn't know how he can stand it.

Jude's body struggles to contain the House. His limbs shake as the House gets to its feet; one hand reflexively darts out to catch the wall for support. (Plaster flakes away – the House is in terrible shape – and it feels embarrassed before recalling how gently Jude stroked its mantelpiece.)

Breathing hard – those audible, trembling breaths that catch on themselves and make its borrowed cock harder – the House staggers into the room where it knows the full-length mirror lives. It wrestles with a thick white drop cloth, sending plumes of dust into the air that make it cough and wheeze: another strange sensation. When the curtain falls, it lifts its head and sees Jude. Sees itself-as-Jude, its own eyes staring out like glowing pearls from his delicate face in the glass. Those eyes are ringed with blood like stage makeup, drip-marks extending to Jude's temples, running down his jaw. The strain of containing a House is taking its toll; who knows how long he will be able to continue.

In the dark recesses of its mind, it hears his voice. *We look good together, don't we?*

It drops to its borrowed knees. Feels pain crackle, delicious, through the nerves. "Yes."

You should touch me, Jude tells it. *I want you to feel that.*

The House trails Jude's fingers down his body,

arriving again at his cock. It's so much pinker than the rest of him, the place where all the blood has gathered. Bracing itself for the sensation, it wraps a hand around him. It tries to be gentle, the way Jude was gentle with the mantelpiece, the wallpaper. Still, it's overwhelming.

It opens its mouth and makes a sound that carries from room to room.

Keep going, urges Jude. *Please. Make yourself at home.*

The House shuts its eyes and quickens its strokes, as it has seen real humans do. It understands, now, this ritual. It gasps and shivers in Jude's shape; leans up against the mirror panting, breath clouding the glass.

Inside, Jude is losing himself, the edges of him blurring into the House as they focus on their shared body, racing toward climax.

They reach it with a cry that startles birds from the roof.

The new owners of Landry House move in seven months later, following extensive renovations to repair its structural damage and tasteful repapering to suit the modern style. None of the inhabitants is haunted. There are no strange whispers in the walls, no mysterious lights at the far ends of the halls. The inhabitants know to be respectful of the floorboards upon which they tread.

To the rear of the House, a room has been remodelled to accommodate a member of additional staff – alongside the cooks, groundskeeper, butlers and maids – whose presence is integral in maintaining the House's pleasant temperament. The new inhabitants don't understand what, exactly, it is that their medium does to keep the House so sweet, but they know that – should he be indisposed for an evening or two – the rooms grow gloomier, as if sulking in his absence.

The House is still not especially good at being a House, though it has learned much from having a home to call its own.

On Shipless Oceans
LH O'Donoghue

CW: Den of bones

It takes him two weeks to find the island.

His rescuers' boat was not dissimilar to the one he usually worked, a six-man trawler, slow moving and heavy in the water. Assuming a straight line of travel to harbour—which was unlikely—the island he had washed ashore on was, at most, twenty miles from the coast. Barker estimates around two hours, perhaps a little more. Not half so far as even Dogger Bank, but still a great deal of sea to traverse alone.

Madness to try. Madness to spend his days rowing in circles around the North Sea, madness to watch his slim funds dwindle away, madness not to join another crew as soon as he was well enough. But from the moment he arrived back in Scarborough he found that he could no longer stomach the idea of boarding another smack, of spending the best part of two months sleeping in cramped cabins and labouring until he was dead on his feet.

Not after what he's seen. Not now he has glimpsed another world, something few men, he suspects, have witnessed and lived. That knowledge weighs on him, haunts him. He remembers hearing the bell in the fog when his rescuers arrived, the wet gulp of the closing water, remembers thinking; *no. Turn back. Leave me here.*

He has dreamt of her most nights since his return, when he can manage to sleep. That song that was nothing like a song at all, a sound that his crude tongue lacks the words to describe. Discordant and compelling all at once, a harsh, organic, echoing thing. It comes back to him in the depths of the night, to be forgotten swiftly upon waking.

He may have believed her a figment of his imagination, a phantom born of exhaustion and thirst, were it not for the line of fading bruises on his chest.

The boat is a rough, pot-bellied little vessel, though well-constructed and nimble in the water. Each day he sets out in a new direction and rows until the muscles of his arms are burning, and only then does he reluctantly head back to dry land. There are any number of tiny islands off the coast, and he investigates each one he finds, but he knows that none of them are hers. He remembers the outcropping where he washed up, the two jagged rocks pointing like fingers towards the sky. He would recognize it in a heartbeat.

And then, one day, he does. There's a chill in the air, and a light mist has settled on the surface of the water. Barker is about to turn back—it is bad weather for sailing—when the familiar shape of the rocks emerges from the fog like the prow of a great ship. For a moment he just sits there, stunned. Then his heart catches up with him, leaping wildly in his chest, and he begins rowing towards the shore.

The island is bordered on three sides by jagged rocks, but he remembers a small cove from his brief time stranded here. He finds it and rows as close as he dares, then climbs out of the boat and drags it onto the pebble-covered beach. Keen as he was to return here, he is not yet so mad as to risk his only means of escape.

Barker walks up the gentle slope to a rocky plateau, looking for the place where he saw her. The island is not large, and it doesn't take him long to find it; a smooth, flat rock protruding out above the surface of the water, its underside thick with wine-coloured wrack. He stands there for a moment, breathing hard. The mist obscures the grey surface of the water.

She isn't here. Perhaps she never was.

'Hello?' he calls. His own mocking voice echoes back to him.

There's a damp chill in the air. Barker shivers, pulling his oilskin closer around him. It occurs to him that, perhaps, this island is not her home. Why would a creature such as she be confined to a single spot, when the vastness of the ocean is hers to traverse?

He feels foolish then for coming here. Foolish and bereft. He has given little thought to his future beyond finding this place, finding her. He hoped that seeing her again would provide answers.

'Hello?' he calls again, louder this time. 'Hello? Are you there?'

The wind swallows his words. Not even a seabird caws from the rocks. Barker heaves a sigh, wipes the clinging moisture from his cheeks with a flat palm. That's it, then. His search is over. She's gone.

But then a sudden wave rushes over the rock, sending seafoam lapping at his boots, and in a cascade of water and salt she is there before him once more.

She, he thinks, though her form is only a woman's in some ways; her fine features, her curling hair, her bare, freckled breasts. But for everything that is human about her there is far more that is uncanny. Her inkwell eyes, the places where her skin turns aquamarine and iridescent, her black-clawed fingers. And, above all else, the writhing mass of tentacles that makes up her body from the waist down.

Barker has been at sea for a long time, and has heard all the legends. Sirens, tempting sailors to their death with song. Mermaids, beautiful women with the tails of fish. The kraken, pulling whole ships down beneath the waves. Perhaps she is the source of them all. He feels, for reasons he cannot explain, that she is an ancient thing; that he is standing in the presence of something close to a god.

She sits, as she did before, on the flat surface of the rock, her smile wide and eerie. The flat planes of her ears swivel slightly, her tentacles shifting constantly beneath her. For all of her strangeness—or, perhaps, because of it—she is astonishingly beautiful. Seawater plasters strands of hair to the delicate line of her throat, and there is an elegance to the undulating way she moves. She makes a low noise, almost like a purr. It sounds for all the world like she is pleased to see him.

A few minutes ago, Barker couldn't think of what to do in her absence; now she is present he finds himself with the same dilemma. Here the creature is, her full lips slightly parted, looking at him with something like curiosity, and all he can do is gape at her. He has sought her out to—what? Worship her? Offer himself as a sacrifice? Neither of these seem right, but nor do they seem entirely wrong. When he encountered her before, half-dead from exposure, he had the distinct impression that she wanted something from him. That she had... intentions, with him. His rescuers had arrived before he could discover what those were. If he has come here for any reason at all, it is to find the answer to that question.

'I came looking for you,' Barker says. 'I looked for this island. I wanted—I hoped to find you here.'

He feels stupid, at first. She has given no indication that she can speak. But then she makes that low sound again, and a moment later follows it with something that almost sounds like words. Or—perhaps it is words, now that he thinks of it. It sounds familiar, but it takes him a moment to place from where. HMS Vivid, he realises. The Breton sailors he would sometimes cross paths with at watering holes in Plymouth. Christ. He was prepared for the creature to speak some infernal tongue; he wasn't expecting it to be French.

'I can't—I don't understand,' he says. 'I'm sorry.'

The creature blinks at him, a filmy layer flicking over her eye briefly before the outer lids close. Drops of seawater cling to her lashes. She brings one hand to her chest, pressing the tips of two claws to her breastbone.

'Thala,' she says.

The word is unfamiliar, and to Barker's inexpert ear sounds nothing like Breton. He freezes as one of her tentacles lifts towards him, its tip pressing the same spot on his chest. It's a question, he realises. She's asking him a question.

'Human,' he says. 'I'm human.'

She rolls her eyes then, and the gently frustrated expression leaves Barker breathless for a moment. He watches closely as she repeats the gesture, this time passing her hand in a circle around her face first.

'*Thala,*' she repeats. The tip of her tentacle presses insistently against his chest.

The penny drops then. Not her species, he realises. Her *name*.

'*Oh,*' he says. 'Barker. That's—my name is Barker.'

'Barker.' The creature—Thala—speaks his name like she is tasting it. The word is strange on her tongue, and as she speaks he sees gills fan open at her throat. '*Encantado de conocerte.*'

Was that Spanish? He frowns at her, and she throws back her head and laughs. *Laugh* is not quite right in the way that *singing* was not quite right. It is more like the chattering, clicking sound that dolphins make when they swim alongside the trawlers. With every passing minute she seems both more human and more alien.

Thala smiles at him again once her outpouring of mirth is finished, an indulgent, affectionate sort of smile.

'Hello,' she says.

That, at least, he understands.

'Hello,' he replies. 'I'm glad you—I'm glad I found you.'

'*Anche io.*'

What now? he wonders. There is a measure of expectation in her black eyes, a slight tension in her posture. If he had expected her to take the next step here it seems he will be sorely disappointed. For a moment he just stares at her. Her high cheekbones, her white teeth, the smooth shifting of her many limbs. He asks himself why, truly, he has come here. What he has really been seeking out this past fortnight.

Barker feels his hands tremble slightly as he unbuttons his oilskin coat, then rucks his gansey up to his chest. His soft, pale stomach is covered in dark hair, and beneath it is a line of fading bruises; a yellowish-green colour now, each one a perfect circle. He glances up at Thala, cheeks burning, hoping she will infer his meaning.

Thala lets out a high trill, then slithers down the rock towards him. She lifts one tentacle, carefully presses it against the line of bruises. Their shapes match perfectly. The surface of the appendage is damp and cool, strong muscle shifting beneath the greenish skin, and its suckers pull hard at his tender skin. Barker lets out a rough moan at the feel of it, and Thala's smile grows wider in response.

She understands. He manages to form the thought through his haze of arousal, and is beyond relieved by it. *She knows why I'm here.*

Thala moves away from him, each sucker releasing its grip with an obscene popping sound. They leave fresh bruises in their wake, already turning purple.

Barker knows a moment of panic as she slips from the rock into the water, but she resurfaces a few feet along the shoreline a moment later.

'Come,' she calls. '*Allez.*'

He follows her, clambering across slippery rocks on his hands and feet, struggling to keep his balance on patches of loose scree, somehow managing to keep pace as she leads him around the edge of the island. Thala dives under the waves for a moment, then resurfaces nearby and waits for him to catch up. Their path takes them towards the two huge rocks, and eventually into the shadows beneath them. When they come to the dark mouth of a cave, Thala points imperiously towards it.

'*Alli,*' she says. Then she is gone again, the grey water closing behind her.

Barker waits, uncertain whether she will return, but once a minute has passed he enters the cave alone. It is pitch dark inside, and he has to feel his way across jagged rocks without any assistance from his eyes. Eventually, though, he sees a distant spot of light; he follows it.

As the light grows he has to blink back salt tears, the world turning blurry as he stumbles deeper into the cave. The rough passage opens into a large chamber. A natural hole in the ceiling lets a shaft of daylight through, illuminating large, smooth shelves of rock covered in fine gutweed. They jut out above the water, which runs inside and under the cave itself. The gentle roar of it is amplified by the bare stone walls.

There are other things, too; piles of polished stones and driftwood, broken navigational tools and other gewgaws, an iron-banded chest spilling weathered coins.

The sort of items one might find in a shipwreck, or washed up on the shore after a storm.

And—he realises this with a queasy sort of panic—there are bones. Piled up in one corner, sharp and pale. Fish bones mostly, he thinks, though he is certain he spies a human femur among the detritus.

Barker turns to see Thala emerging from the water. She pulls herself easily onto the shelf of rock, shaking her head to free her wet hair from her shoulders. Strange and magnificent, a creature from a fable. But here, in the flesh. With him. His momentary fear falls away, replaced by something far more potent; a sort of awe, a profound acceptance of whatever may come.

Thala moves closer to him, pulling her body forwards with her powerful limbs. Barker has seen other creatures move in a similar way, crawling through shallow water, but the strength and fluidity of her motion is truly something to behold. She leans in, and he is close enough now to smell her scent; the clean, briny tang of a freshly-shucked oyster. He has to fight the urge to touch her, to rest his hands on the ample curve of her waist, to lean in and taste the saltwater beading at her throat. He feels instinctively that she would not permit such a thing in this moment.

Barker sucks in a breath as she wraps two limbs around him, steering him by the shoulders. He almost slips on the algae-covered stone but her strong limbs hold firm, cradling him almost gently as she lays him down on his back. She lets out a quiet purr, smiling with what appears to be satisfaction.

Prone on the floor of this hidden grotto, with this

creature of myth looming over him, Barker feels as helpless as he has ever been. His heart hammers against his ribs, every muscle in his body screaming at him to run, to get into his boat and row as far away from here as he can. But that is the simple, animal part of him, the one that recognizes Thala only as a predator. The part of him that is still a man is prepared to take that risk, to place himself at her mercy. To give himself to her in whatever way she wishes; as conquest, as offering, as prey.

Then the tentacles at his shoulders are sliding down to his lapels, tugging open his coat and pushing up his gansey in an echo of his own earlier gesture. Once his chest and stomach are bare the same limbs coil around his wrists, pinning them to the ground.

Barker is breathing hard. The stone is cool and slick against his back, her grip on him impossibly tight. Another tentacle brushes his chest once more, a sucker finding his nipple. He lets out a broken gasp, back arching into the touch.

'More?' Thala says, arching a narrow eyebrow.

There, now, is a question he understands.

'Yes,' he pants, nodding furiously. 'Yes, more, *please.*'

Thala moves to settle between his legs, and his heart leaps into his throat when her clawed hands begin unfastening his belt. She takes her time, sliding the leather free from the buckle, slowly undoing each button of his trousers. Teasing. The process is not unfamiliar to her. Barker wonders how many other men have been tempted here, following her eerie song. He wonders, just for a second, how many left their bones behind.

She pulls his trousers down over his thighs, skin turning to gooseflesh in the cold air, then down to his ankles. With several brisk, sharp tugs she manages to pull the garment past his heavy boots, then tosses it aside. Barker squirms beneath her, hot and cold all at once, feeling horribly exposed and yet enjoying that feeling. He's painfully aware of his cock, hard and flush against his belly—and from the smug, delighted expression on Thala's face, so is she.

Another two tentacles reach for him, this time snaking around his calves. She pulls his knees up towards his chest, spreads his legs. When the water breaks against the stone Barker feels cool drops of spray patter against his skin. He strains lightly against Thala's bonds, more from curiosity than any genuine desire to free himself. At the first sign of movement she clenches tightly around his wrists and ankles, her suckers almost biting into his flesh. The response is so rapid that he assumes it must be instinctive. He cries out, falling limp, and she loosens her grip once more.

Barker is a large man, built for hauling cargo, but his strength is outmatched by her abundance of muscular limbs. No escape, then, even if he wanted to. That is, he supposes, good information to have, even if he has no use for it. He has no desire to be anywhere but here, naked and defenceless and far from home, at the absolute mercy of this monster, this beauty. Thala is leaning over him now, one hand braced against his breastbone. The rise and fall of his broad chest is enough to move her, rolling like the waves. He notices the slight webbing between her fingers as she presses them into his flesh.

'More?' she says again.

Once again, Barker doesn't hesitate. 'Yes. More, *yes*—'

Then he feels something probing slowly at his entrance, and for a moment loses the ability to speak. He yelps, stiffening slightly, and Thala lets out her chattering laugh once again. The feel of her tentacle pressing between his legs is profoundly, unutterably strange. It fills him with panic even as something warm and urgent crackles down his spine. The wet, muscular tip of her limb feels like a tongue where it teases him open, and he finds himself lifting his hips to accommodate the touch.

'More?'

A moment's pause, this time. Barker looks at her above him. Wet locks of her hair dripping saltwater onto his chest, plump lips curled in amusement. He takes a shaking breath. Nods.

'Yes. More.'

The gills at her throat ripple with the pleased sound she makes, and she leans closer as she presses inside him. It feels—*Christ*, it feels like nothing else, the slick, firm length of her easing inside him with glacial slowness, suckers flexing gently as she enters him, deeper by degrees, stretching him open, filling him, *taking him*—

Barker's vision goes dark for a moment, arousal and shock threatening to overwhelm him. He scrabbles uselessly at the empty air, lets out a high whine that sounds nothing like his own voice at all. She has reduced him to this, to little more than a hole to be penetrated, something base and desperate without name or voice or self, a soft, fleshy thing for her use and pleasure alone. It is everything he had hoped for when he came here. Everything he didn't know that he wanted. To be liberated from agency, from thought, to exist only at the will of something more powerful than he.

'*Bellissima*,' Thala sighs, sinking her claws into the meat of his chest. '*Très mignon.*'

He can do little more than whimper as he feels another whisper of movement between his legs. Her fingers, he realises, and not only her fingers—another tentacle twines around the base of his cock as her delicate hand strokes the shaft, the firm pressure leaving him dizzy. It's so much, so much all at once, to feel her like this. Pinning his wrists to the cold stone, spreading his thighs, thrusting inside him, suckers kissing his nipples and the sensitive skin of his balls, the uncanny purr of her voice filling his head—

'*Thala.*'

He cries out her name, not knowing what else is left to say. He's so close now. The growing knife-edge of his pleasure is both more than he can handle and still, somehow, not enough.

'More,' he chokes out. 'Please, Thala, *more*—'

The last word is muffled as she presses a tentacle to his lips, and Barker moans with gratitude as he takes it into his mouth. It is smooth and slick against his tongue, tasting of the sea, and with the last piece of his autonomy stripped from him he gives over to her entirely.

He's aware, dimly, that Thala is singing—though the word is still not right—that discordant hum he first heard when he awoke on the island. As before, it lulls Barker into an almost meditative state. He can feel every inch of himself, every inch of her, the soft weeds pillowing the base of his spine and the cool breeze that caresses his skin, the tentacle that throbs inside him and the one he is sucking hungrily, the way his cock twitches against her palm and the look of absolute, utter dominion in her eyes as she stares down at him from above.

'Come,' she says. The word is a command.

Barker would gasp if he could, would cling to something if his hands were free, but Thala has made such things impossible. He can do nothing but shudder beneath her as he crashes into orgasm, ropes of come spilling hot across his belly, moaning around the tip of her tentacle as she fucks him through his peak. There's a moment where he's certain he can't take any more, when his skin is burning so hot and his heart is beating so fast that it seems another touch would be the death of him, but just as the explosion of pleasure begins to turn she releases him. Saliva drips from the corner of his mouth, his limbs fall heavily to the ground, and he feels a dull ache between his legs as she withdraws in a sudden, hot rush.

He stares down at himself, splayed out on the stone, pale skin marred with livid lines of bruises. They have almost drawn blood in places, on his chest and the inside of his thighs, leaving blood blisters like freckles in their wake. Barker focuses on catching his breath, each exhalation clouding in the air.

Then he feels the familiar, slick touch of her limbs,

around his back and his shoulders and his waist, lifting him, drawing him to her, and in that moment Barker is sure that he is about to feel the razor-sharp bite of her teeth.

Instead he feels her lips, pressing soft and firm against his own. Thala wraps her arms around his neck, kisses him like a long-lost lover. Her breasts are warm and soft where she crushes them to his chest, and her fingers card lightly through his hair. Despite the tentacles still enfolding him, there's something profoundly human about the gesture. Something that, if he didn't know better, Barker would consider affectionate.

Thala eventually pulls away, the black pools of her eyes contemplative.

'You,' she says. 'Mine.'

It is a declaration, not a request. Barker is panting and boneless in her arms, and protesting never crosses his mind.

'Yes. Yours.'

Thala lets out her pleased little trill again, beaming at him. She's dangerous, he knows, could kill and consume him in a heartbeat if she wished to, but just then he doesn't care. It was worth it, coming to this place. Worth it to find her, to touch her, to be taken by her. To be worthy of her attention, if only for a moment.

He came here seeking answers. Whether he found what he was searching for, he cannot say; he may have to stay a while longer, to be certain.

Blood in the Water
Verna Lorne

Annick pushed her hair out of her eyes, too focused on tonight's work to acknowledge the irritation setting into her bones. The salt air always made her neatly combed hair fall out of place, condensing into the strands until it dripped down the nape of her neck and along her spine. She shivered against the sharp chill and tightened her grip on the gunwales, white paint and rust flaking onto her palms. Her eyes scanned the inky roiling sea, watching. Waiting.

Her reprieve was broken by the dull thud of rubber soles on the fibreglass deck behind her. A thick hand clapped onto her shoulder and her nostrils were filled with the stench of rotting fish scales and unmitigated body odour.

"Catch a glimpse of the beast out there?"

A barking laugh echoed in the night air, and Annick had to suppress her eye roll. She'd seen her share of fishermen, sailors, deckhands, mariners, seafarers, and whatever other titles they'd insist to her were unique and much more important than a land-hire could understand. Captain Rolk was no different. He had the same weathered hide from the unforgiving winds, the same shoulders overburdened by chips of his own making. The same rage that burned hot in his eyes as he looked out at the waters he couldn't tame.

"Won't be long now," Annick replied slowly as she shrugged off his hand, trying to breathe through her mouth. "They like rough nights like this. Less work for 'em once you're in the water."

Captain Rolk had been leading fishing expeditions around the edge of the bay for weeks. His crew dwindled with every trip, and when their last trip lost him his most experienced winch man, Rolk had enough. He wanted the problem dealt with, even if it meant bringing in someone he hadn't vouched for personally. Annick came highly recommended by the harbourmaster, with a reputation for being able to catch and skewer anything beneath the waves, no matter the size or weather. While Rolk wasn't used to having a woman on board, and Annick's smooth, unblemished hands did little to inspire his confidence in her fishing experience, he couldn't ignore the harbourmaster's praises. That, and no one else was willing to set foot on the deck of the *Mordere*.

The ship lurched violently as it rolled into another swell. Annick had to swallow a smirk when she caught a grimace flash across Rolk's face as he clutched the side of the hull, clubbed fingers slipping over the wet metal as his balance wavered. "Don't worry, Captain. It's been too long since I've had a hunt like this. I guarantee you'll see fresh chum on this deck soon enough."

Rolk's sneer fell as veins of lightning pulsed though the black clouds, bloated and looming above. His eye flickered over Annick's shoulder, just in time for her to turn and catch the sight of waves breaking against a glossy black islet. A peal of thunder reverberated through her chest. Annick licked the salt off her lips and inhaled deeply, the smells of sulphur and kelp a heady perfume.

"Looks like you're up, kid. Go grab the boys from the galley and meet me on bow." Rolk snorted and hawked, making a spectacle to cover the waver in his words. With one sharp nod, Annick turned to fetch the rest of the crew. There was no time to be sick of Rolk's shit now that the hunt was about to truly begin. She needed every one of these men to know their role tonight, and what she expected of them. The adrenaline was already beginning to thrum through her veins as she stepped through the doors and was swallowed by the velvet darkness of the cabin.

The hull groaned as they steered closer and closer to the islet. Annick and Rolk had staggered their positions on the bow, though Annick noted that Rolk never let himself get between her and the water. His nervous energy was not lost on the crew. They had dispersed uneasily across the deck, attending to the lines and skiffs, but the tension in the air prickled against Annick's skin as much as the electricity of the storm. Their faces were slick as the waves sent another shower of mist across the ship, but Annick knew it was more than water beading on their brows. She could catch the tang of fear in their sweat as the wind whistled across her nostrils. She closed her eyes and inhaled deeply, the familiar smell bringing her memories of previous hunts into sharp focus. The anticipation of the catch was gnawing deep in the pit of her belly, begging to be set free. Begging for release. She turned to face upwind and breathed slowly until the sour smell faded from her nose. Annick ran the tip of her tongue slowly over the points of her teeth, back and forth, as she reminded herself to be patient. It wouldn't be long now.

A whine of feedback burst from the *Mordere's* PA system. Knowing looks flashed across the crew's faces as the squeal faded and the PA crackled to life, picking up the first plaintive notes of their quarry's song. Razor-edged stone jutted out of the churning brine and threatened to open the hull like a tin can. Annick whipped her flashlight back towards the helm, short bursts of light guiding the helmsman through the islet's natural caltrops. The vocalizations over the PA faded with a hiss and the winds died as they rounded the crest of a rocky outcrop and she came into view.

Sprawled across flat grey stone, the shimmering scales of the siren were the first things that caught Annick's eye. Her gaze traveled languidly up the length of her tail, the gentle swell of her belly, the curve of her breasts, landing on the copse of long, elegant fangs that spilled from her lips. As she crooned to the sailors, her wide-set eyes opened just enough for Annick to catch a sliver of oily black beneath the lids.

Annick's breath hitched in her chest when the siren's eyes met her own. She held her gaze as the notes ebbed and flowed, twisting a melodic undertow around Annick's will. The boat swayed closer to the islet, so close that Annick could see the barnacles sprinkled across the siren's chest and shoulders like freckles. She placed the toe of her thick rubber boot against the lip of the hull, leaning into the foamy spray that leapt from the rocks and into her lungs. Webbed fingers reached out towards her, gusts of wind turning the kelp and beaded shells woven through the siren's hair into a swirling halo of salt and rot.

In a flash, Annick's arm shot into the air as she fired her flare gun, the water reflecting the light like a sea of spilled blood. The crew sprung into action, waxed sea sponges lodged deeply in their ears as they fired modified harpoons loaded with nylon netting. The siren's fangs gnashed against the plastic fibres as they twisted her haunting melody into a screech.

A second flare lit up the sky, Annick's signal to haul. A winch man leapt across the deck, belaying the lines and winding them quickly until the nets pulled tight against the siren's flesh, scales and skin spilling out from the mesh. Annick was transfixed watching the siren wriggle against the nylon embrace of the nets, her elongated neck craning for a weak point, her clawed fingers straining for a split in the fibres. Her eyes caught Annick's once more, smouldering and boring into her, holding her in place even as the winch began to reel in their catch.

Hollow, polyphonic screams and mewlings echoed

across the deck as the siren was wrenched from the waves. Rolk made his approach slowly, his head tilting as he watched her shark-like tail thrash within the nets. Annick couldn't see his face, but she recognized the way his body moved towards the creature.

Like a cat ready to play with a mouse before the kill.

As soon as their catch hit the deck a couple of the men had already cut the netting as instructed, working section by section, never cutting too much at once. Annick stepped forward to follow their motions, picking up unwound netting, strategically twisting cut fibres until the siren was strung up by her wrists, hog-tied to her neck and tail with the nylon chain. Annick's fingers lingered on the last plait at the nape of the siren's neck, brushing against one of the braids scattered though her dark tangled hair. A cracked molar dropped into Annick's palm as the braid cast it aside and came undone. A smile almost played at the corner of her mouth before she remembered herself and her face returned to its stony professionalism.

With a last tug on the ropes, and a snarl from the siren in response, Annick returned her attention to the men milling about on deck. Rolk was already at the head of the pack as the crew removed the wads of sponge from their ears and clear hearing returned to them. "Is she tied up good and tight? I don't need that bitch getting any last licks in before we get ours." He wasn't looking at Annick when he spoke to her, twitchy and jumpy and ready to sink the rusty J-hook he held into the belly of the creature hanging from the power block.

"Captain, I've used this rigging setup more times than I can count. She's not going anywhere unless I let her."

A smile slowly split Rolk's leather face, growing wider while he twirled the crusty hook between his fingers. "And why won't that voice shit of hers work again?"

Annick remained expressionless as she watched his eyes rake over the siren's fins, appraising her. The siren didn't struggle against her bonds. She took deep, slow breaths that made her barnacle freckles rise and fall, and kept her eyes fixed on the Captain with an endless, ravenous rage.

"The polyphony of their voices only works when they're partially submerged in water. That's what affects your mind."Annick watched as Rolk continued to circle the siren, just out of the reach of her jaws. The anglerfish teeth gnashed in her mouth until blood dripped from the corners, her frustration visibly trembling through her body. Annick's mouth went dry as she watched the red bead wind slowly down the long, elegant neck of the siren. It took its time, teasing along the pulse in her throat until it found its rest in the basin of her collarbone. Annick's tongue felt like sandpaper in her mouth.She shook herself. Focus. "We took her out of the water, so *her* voice won't affect you."

Rolk's step faltered. "*Her* voice?"

Annick's eyes moved back up to the siren's as she strode across the deck, her disdain at the Captain's words etched in the marble of her face, cold and unyielding.

It wasn't until she'd reached him that she met his dull eyes with her unblinking ones, and called to the rest of the crew."Men! Don't you think it's time to show your Captain what you're made of?"

The furrows in Rolk's brow deepened as he watched, first with confusion then with growing horror, as the crew slumped at the sound of Annick's trigger phrase. One by one the men fell to their hands and knees, necks straining as their heads pitched back to let their eyes meet Rolk's. Their bodies flopped and dragged forward in jerking movements, elbows and knees scraping themselves raw across the fibreglass like marionettes trying in vain to break free from their strings. As they formed a broken line before Rolk, glassy-eyed smiles on their faces, their hands fumbled for the boning knives in their tool belts. Rolk's mouth gaped, opening and closing, struggling against the air filling his lungs as he watched their heads loll while they sank their knives into the backs of their own hands, slicing through tendon and muscle with ease. Blood pooled around the men as they twisted their blades around each delicate bone, prying loose one, then another, then another De-boning them like fish, little bones piling next to each shredded hand like spent toothpicks.

Annick leaned over Rolk's shoulder, fangs extending from her gums as honeyed words spilled from between her lips and into his ears. "Why don't you supervise your crew, Captain? It looks like they're preparing dinner."

Annick felt the weight of her influence stamp out the remains of Rolk's mind effortlessly and watched as his posture relaxed, shoulders slumping and hands swaying limply at his sides with the roll of the waves. His head pitched forward as he strained to look up at the source of his commands. The creature he would now obey for the rest of his life. The fear and rage melted from his eyes as he turned to the sound of the crew's knuckle bones popping from their sockets. Each man's blade moved up its owner's wrist, scraping back layers of meat until it hung loose and limp around from the elbow like a ripped dishwashing glove.

A short exhale from her nose betrayed Annick's amusement. These men had been particularly easy. A single meeting below deck that night was all she had needed to charm their instructions in place.

And Rolk. Of course he was just as easy to charm as the crew. Beneath all that inflated ego and undeserved pride was just an angry little man with nowhere to moor himself, and a pathetic need to dominate whatever crossed his path.

With that out of the way, her eyes flashed back to the siren. Her siren. Selachi.

Selachi had shifted to her more humanoid form while Annick had been charming the Captain, and with a practiced twist of her wrists she slipped out of the knots supporting her on the winch, landing lightly on the tips of her webbed toes. Her thicket of fangs had withdrawn, and her feral snarl was now full of small, pointed teeth. Annick couldn't help but lick her lips at the sight. She drank in her smooth grey skin, mottled with algae, supple flesh Annick's fingers had dreamed of touching again. Her thighs were dimpled and dotted with barnacles, a cartography Annick's lips had memorized. Annick's eyes stopped between Selachi's perfect thighs and caught a glimpse of the soft curls of hair hiding her lips. But that glimpse only lasted a moment before Selachi began moving towards their prey.

She skipped across the deck with silent and other-wordly grace, nimbly stepping over severed bone to where Rolk stood watching over the twitching remains of his crew, caught in their final death throes.. Annick was next to her in a flash as Selachi grabbed Rolk by the hair and yanked his head back to expose his throat. Annick's eyes rolled back as she sank her teeth into Rolk's throat, blood spilling out the sides of her mouth, down her neck and soaking the fabric of her shirt. She drank deeply, savouring the mingling of sea salt and iron that only comes from an old sailor's blood. A perfect tribute for the beautiful monstrosity she hauled on deck to worship.

Annick felt Selachi slink around to join her in front of Rolk. In one fluid movement, Selachi slid a single talon across the exposed belly peeking out from his shirt. The blood was beading along the incision before she had reached his navel. By the time she pulled back, his intestines had unspooled themselves from the seam in his belly. Selachi dropped to her knees, her nostrils pressed into his abdomen as she sniffed at his side, searching. With a snarl, her fangs extended and she ripped at his belly face-first, eating her way through the flesh until she reached the liver and tore it free. An involuntary groan burbled out of Rolk's mouth, his weakening meat a prop for their euphoric feast. Dark, jellied scraps of muscle scattered around Selachi's knees as she gnashed at her favourite organ, her eyes rolling back until they flickered up to Annick. The flesh oozed between Selachi's fingers as she squeezed, bloody trails spiralling down to drip off her elbows. Watching made Annick tremble with need. She relished in how ravenous her mate could be.

As the metallic smell of carnage mingled with the salt air, Annick felt her head spin and her pupils dilate, the heat rising in her chest and between her legs. As Rolk's blood pooled around them, Selachi dipped her hands into it and smeared it across her neck, over her breasts and down her belly. Her hands slid further as she spread her knees and arched her back, rubbing herself into the blood until it coated her lips and thighs. Her fangs shrank just enough for Annick to see her mouth, "Hungry?"

It was too much for Annick to take. She let Rolk's disembowelled corpse drop and fell to her knees to weave her fingers into Selachi's hair and crash her lips into hers. Sticky and salty with blood, Selachi's lips were Annick's oasis. She could feel Rolk's feeble pulse dousing them with gentle spurts as their kiss deepened and their frenzy began to build. He'd served his purpose, dulling the blades of their instincts just enough to be less than lethal, allowing their carnal natures to be devoted elsewhere.

Selachi's slated bloodlust thrummed through her veins, filling her senses as her vision focused sharply. The hunger and heat was growing in her belly, Annick's scent a homing beacon for Selachi's sharpened need. Her legs pressed together and her oily black scales pushed through her skin, the monster coming unleashed. Annick didn't need air in her lungs, but her breath hitched in her chest when she saw the slick shimmer of scales dripping with blood. Her gaze lingered on the crimson rivulets oozing down Selachi's hips, winding down the front of her tail and mingling with the slick droplets forming at the point where her legs would meet. Annick was mesmerized, head spinning as the blood dripped between the parting scales and into the hot wetness of Selachi's entrance.

Selachi's snarl broke through the hypnotic lure of her sex. She lunged forward, fangs tearing through the shoulder straps of Annick's rubber hip waders and sending a thrill of adrenaline pulsing between Annick's legs. Annick growled in return and pulled up the hem of her shirt splattered with viscera, revealing her blood-soaked chest underneath. Selachi's eyes widened and a deep hum vibrated through her throat as she dragged her tongue up Annick's ribs and chest, over her sternum, catching every drop as it mingled with the misty air and ran down her skin.

Annick shuddered, feeling Selachi's rasping tongue on her ribs like an electric current rippling across water. The aching hunger filled her with need, to drink, to rip, to tear at flesh and drown in the thick hot liquid that spurted forth. The heat between her legs was becoming unbearable, she couldn't wait anymore, she needed to taste her, she needed, she-

Annick was on top of Selachi, pinning her arms to

the deck while she straddled her. She dove in, licking and sucking the blood from her skin, curling her tongue around each barnacle and scraping them gently with her teeth as she probed them for every last drop. Selachi's back arched as she inhaled sharply, pressing the curves of her body into the angles of Annick's, the rubber hip waders squeaking against her tail. A husky voice slipped past Annick's lips, whispering, "My good girl deserves a reward for being so well behaved while I tied you up." Annick could feel a moan run through Selachi's spine like a deep shiver, and she lowered her lips to the pulse beating rapidly in Selachi's neck. Her fangs extended further as she kissed the soft flesh, slowly pushing in until they pierced her skin. She could feel Selachi's breath flutter, the rise and fall of her chest growing shallow and quick. She savoured her, drinking her in, making Selachi a part of her. But it wasn't enough.

The distance between them was too much, their skin was too separated. Annick sat up and pushed the thick rubber of the hip waders off her legs, followed swiftly by the black trousers underneath them. She looked back down at Selachi, arms splayed out around her head, hair clotting into twisted ropes in the mix of seawater and entrails on the deck. She reached down and stroked her cheek, running her fingers down to the punctures on her neck, gently oozing.

Selachi's back arched again at Annick's touch, and her legs began to open. Annick knew Selachi's weakness for the rush of her bite, and she slid her hand over her hips as smooth skin mingled with the slip of her scales. Her hand traced slowly, fingers following the trails of blood down to the heat of her slit, teasing her just enough for soft mewls of pleasure to leave Selachi's lips. Annick could already feel the liquid heat between the parting scales she played with. The soft gasps slipping from Selachi made Annick's eyes roll back again. She lowered her lips to Selachi's nipples, feeling the soft buds tighten in her mouth as she curled her tongue gently around them. Her fingers began to drag up and down the edges of Selachi's lips, the slick entrance eager for her to fill it. Selachi's moan echoed in the night air as Annick slowly pushed into her, dragging it out for as long as she could. She was molten, so hot she made Annick gasp as she eased her fingers deeper into her siren.

"Touch me like this," Annick moaned as she pulled Selachi's hands up to her chest, deftly guiding her fingers until Annick's soft cries joined the chorus. Her head tipped back and she pushed deeper into Selalchi, the warmth surrounding her and dripping down her wrist. Annick straddled the thick, strong fin, grinding into it as Selachi flexed the muscle against her in response. Annick's thighs gripped tighter as Selachi bucked against her, the rough and smooth of the scales sending sparks behind Annick's eyes as her siren thrust up against her cunt, moans slipping out when she squeezed around Annick's fingers.

She's going to take me. Annick felt a shiver run through her as the thought slipped into her mind. Annick ran her tongue over her lip as she looked down at Selachi, the blood and sweat mixing on her tongue. Selachi looked up at her with a knowing smirk on her face, in between gasps of Annick's palm thrusts against her. Her gleaming eyes bored into Annick, insatiable and feral..

Before Annick saw it, she felt Selachi's hand leave her chest and grip her throat. Annick gasped as the pressure tightened, her lifeless breath wheezing while she struggled against her siren's grip. She savoured the struggle and had to fight not to melt into the flexing wrist under her chin. Her submissive side was already pulling her deep into the inky cave of subspace that only Selachi could bring her. The place she could only go once that clawing, aching hunger in her chest was fed. A place she had to earn.

Selachi sat up, pushing Annick off her tail and onto her back. With a fluid grace like she had never left the waves, she slinked up Annick's body until her fangs delicately grazed her neck and collarbone. Her tongue extended, dragging up the soft icy skin to savour the sticky remains of Rolk clinging to Annick's throat. A growl escaped Annick's lips, the last show of the monster whose influence had slaughtered the entire crew, then she let go- her mind sinking deeper as her body surrendered to her siren.

Selachi's fingers elongated into their monstrous form as her tongue lapped at the blood smeared down Annick's chest, frenzy growing with every taste. They dug into Annick's sides, soft scrapes morphing into shallow gouges as they reached Annick's hips. Her talons sliced the seams of Annick's underwear with precision, letting her toss them aside while Annick trembled beneath her. Selachi shook her right hand sharply to retract her talons again, leaving her soft fingers ready to feel how wet Annick already was.

She moved back up to her lips as she looked down at Annick, her tongue winding around them, lazily licking up the bittersweet juices, their gazes never breaking from one another. Annick, utterly enthralled, was caught off guard when Selachi's fingers began to push into her cunt. It was more than she had used before, she was stretching her, splitting her in half. Annick groaned deeply, she couldn't take anymore but she wanted to,. She felt another slender finger begin pushing into her. This was new and she was burning on the wet deck, overcome with pain and pleasure and surrender. All at once, she felt her pelvis open up, relaxing, gushing, and Selachi's final finger slipped in. Annick felt everything, the slender fist stretching out her cunt, owning her.

Annick was overcome completely, left at Selachi's mercy, but she knew Selachi would always make sure her vampire was taken care of. Selalchi's fist flexed slightly and Annick's eyes rolled back, deep groans of pleasure echoing through the air. Annick moved slowly, her hips raising and pulsing just enough for the electric pain and pleasure to fire behind her eyes. She could feel Selachi's other hand resting gently on top of her pelvis as her fingers lightly stroked just above her clit, the warmth spreading through her low belly and into her thighs. Annick could feel the heat building deep in the pit of her stomach, her breath quickening as Selachi's fist pulses started to deepen. Annick's hands flailed against the deck, one finally grabbing Selachi's wrist and thrusting against it. Her skin felt like it was on fire, the pressure growing until Annick's moans turned into wails. She was building and spiralling with pleasure, babbling and squealing for her siren.

Selachi's touch was demanding, greedy. Annick knew she wanted to coax every morsel of orgasm from her body. Her fingers circled Annick's clit, faster now, the slickness of her dripping cunt spreading across the deck and mixing with viscera as Selachi thrust into her.. She felt herself pushed to the brink, teetering on the edge of the abyss, ready to lose her mind to the fist inside her. At Selachi's unrelenting pace, Annick was pulled taught and about to snap. Finally, she could feel her first wave of orgasm cresting, but Selachi felt it too. Her pulsing began to match the waves of pleasure crashing through Annick's body, twisting the long, low moans that began into a high-pitched crescendo.

A lone beam of moonlight broke through the clouds, bathing their bodies in the pale glow of night as Annick's mind floated on the edges of her orgasm. The metallic tinge to the air kept the heat of hunger in her body while her skin prickled under the moon's gaze. Her fingers clawed at the deck, fists squelching as they squeezed through the spongy remains of organ meat. The strength was draining from her body as Selachi's fist gently pulsed upwards, insatiable, not allowing Annick to swim from the pleasurable haze. Soon enough Annick's moans resumed, gently grinding into Selchi's wrist until another orgasm took her over, pulling squeals from her throat.

Her vision blurred as Selachi carefully withdrew her fist, and Annnick felt a swell of pride in her chest as she watched Selachi delicately lap up the musky liquid pooled between her fingers. With a gentle smile, Selachi slipped from between Annick's legs and slid across the blood-soaked deck next to her, pushing Rolk's small (or was it large) intestine into a rough pillow for them to rest their heads on.

As Selachi nuzzled into the crook of Annick's neck, she mumbled, "You know, we're going to need to build up your strength if you're going to charm that entire harbour again. I think we have another month or two here before we need to move down the coast."

Annick chuckled gently and wrapped her arm tighter around Selachi's shoulders. "Darling, they haven't put up a fuss over the last two expeditions we snared." Her chin dipped as she caught her monster's gaze. "Besides, why should we relocate? We have a ship of our own now and can reel in as many wayward sailors as you desire." Selachi's eyes glinted mischievously as Annick cupped her cheek and continued. "I assure you, my love, I will always keep you well satisfied."

"Our own ship..." Selachi's words melted into the salt-spray air, hanging lazily as she scanned the deck. The *Mordere* (or as Annick translated, the *Bite*) was quite fitting, after all. She leaned into her spot on Annick's neck, a tendril of kelp twirling between two claws as she basked dreamily in the moonlight, drinking in the possibilities.

Annick looked down at her siren as a wide, toothy grin spread across her face. She always did love a good hunt.

The Artist is Pregnant
Briar Ripley Page

CW: Insects, pregnancy, dubious consent

Micah's ass was really itching, but he'd committed to three hours for this session and there were still two to go. It would be unprofessional as a performance artist to signal Lane to de-rig him now just so he could stretch and scratch. Instead, he avoided making eye contact with his collaborator in the corner of the room, where she sat alternating between watching him and playing a game on her phone. He concentrated on the slight sensation of some drunk twenty-two-year-old drawing him a tramp stamp in permanent marker while her friends giggled. He breathed deeply and told himself he was neither itchy nor annoyed.

Two months ago, this project seemed like such a cool idea. Inspired by a recent BDSM experience, Micah had decided he'd one-up Yoko Ono's "Cut Piece" and Marina Abramović's "The Artist is Present" by creating an experience in which gallery visitors could do any-thing—literally *anything!*— they wanted to a semi-nude, bound Micah. "It's kind of, like, less dangerous for me than it would be for a woman," Micah explained, sounding more confident in this justification than he felt, "but there's still danger there because I'm a queer trans man. Like, there's vulnerability. It's provocative. How does the audience see me? What do they want to do to me? How is that different from what they're willing to be seen doing in public? What if they're given permission?"

Lane had been completely on board, mostly because she thought it'd be a hoot. "People are just gonna draw dicks and balls all over you," she'd declared. "But don't worry. I'll be there to make sure it stays safe."

Micah almost protested that he didn't *want* it to be safe. He swallowed the words. He needed Lane (plus her power tools) to help him construct the circular frame in which he hung, gagged, restrained by ropes and cuffs in the splayed-out pose of Da Vinci's Vitruvian Man. Initially he'd been planning to wear a loincloth, but Lane told him it looked like a diaper. That wasn't what he was going for. In the end, he settled on nude except for a pair of women's cotton briefs. Black, like his buzzed hair and his scattered handful of tattoos. Very sexy, since of course this was about sex.

Which was probably why he felt so disappointed that no one had done anything except glance at him, point and whisper, and, in four cases now, draw on his torso. More or less as Lane had predicted. No one had spit on him. No one had pinched him. No one had whispered a terrible secret into his ear. No one had tickled him, slapped him, or groped him. It was, he admitted to himself, a real let down. Maybe this was doomed to be one of those pieces where all the excitement was in the planning and imagining rather than the execution.

The gang of college girls departed on an airy current of laughter and too-sweet perfume. Micah wondered what the permanent marker design on his lower back looked like. Probably just another dick and balls. You could feel the approximate shape of whatever someone was drawing on you, even if you couldn't see it.

Lane squinted at the screen of her phone. She was about ten years older than Micah's thirty-three, but she didn't look or act much like it. With her tongue poking out of her mouth as she concentrated, her (dyed) pink and (naturally) dirty blonde hair frizzing out wildly, she could almost have been a teenager. Apart from Micah's rig and the display explaining his piece, her folding metal chair was the only furniture in the small white-walled room.

Out in the hall, strangers wearing leather, lace, and latex passed in brief bursts of noise and motion. Micah's muscles were burning. His fingers felt numb. No one else entered. The gag was uncomfortable against his teeth, too big; he tried to ignore the impression that his teeth were slowly bending loose.

A short infinity passed in which nothing happened and Lane failed to look away from her phone for even one solitary second. Micah moaned. Not even with erotic frustration, or pain. He was just so, *so* bored.

Someone stepped through the bleach-bright doorway, their shoes clicking softly on the glittery red resin floor.

Micah stared in their direction, so eager to see

anyone at all that it took him a moment to register that this person would have made him stare even in a crowd— with desire or with a sense of the uncanny, he wasn't sure.

They were tall and thin in a way that reminded him of runway models— but their face was ugly, he thought. *Very* ugly, although there was something murky about its flat features. It was as if they were constantly shifting slightly, or their face was only an optical illusion created by an interplay of light and dark shapes.

But what a crazy thing to think! No, there were their hazel-gold eyes, deep set and shadow-ringed...there was their squashed, blobby nose and too-thin mouth...but their skin had a beautiful, peculiar shine, like polished wood. And they moved with fluid, confident grace beneath the folds of the black, hooded cloak they wore. It wasn't a wholly unprecedented choice of attire for this particular venue, but instead of cotton or crushed velvet, this cloak was made of something thick, stiff, rough-spun, heavy.

The visitor approached, their expression and body language a cipher. They walked around his rig once. Twice. Three times. *Click click click* went their shoes. There was something odd about the sound, thought Micah, something just off from what he'd expect. Perhaps they were wearing very tall, thin stiletto heels under that cloak?

They examined the display. Turned towards Micah and made eye contact with him for the first time.

He made a loud, startled sound around the gag. *Of course* their face looked so weird! It was a *mask!*

Lane finally glanced up. Did a double take, then leaped to her feet so fast her chair toppled over. "Hey—"

The visitor waved a long, gloved hand. Magenta light flared out from something in its palm. It bathed the room, and lingered. Micah blinked rapidly, but the light didn't fade. When he looked over at Lane, she was lying on the floor, her hair and skirt spread around her like a neon painting of the drowned Ophelia. Micah tried to call out to her, but the gag got in the way; it came out more like a phlegmy grunt. He struggled fruitlessly against his restraints. He really, really hoped Lane was just asleep. He was pretty sure he saw her chest moving up and down.

The visitor, unaffected, stretched their back until it popped and cracked. Their mask cracked too, down the middle.

Micah watched in fascinated horror as their cloak flared open, and further open, moving on its own, whirring. The mask retracted and shrivelled until it was impossible to see how he'd ever mistaken it for a human face. There was nothing human about this creature, except for its six golden eyes: startlingly like a person's, with round, dilated pupils.

Was it an enormous insect? That was Micah's first thought: a big bug, like a cross between a moth and a praying mantis. Shiny light brown chitin. Midnight wings that mimicked the texture of fabric. Its face was eyes, two frondlike antennae, and a pair of fuzzy pincers or pedipalps marking its mouth like a tarantula's. So perhaps it was more like a spider? It had fuzz as well as chitin, and Micah thought he remembered that spiders had a lot of eyes, while insects usually didn't.

Or maybe it was more like a lobster? Micah couldn't have said exactly what about it was more like a lobster than like an insect or a spider, but there was a definite vibe there. It could be coming from the dreamy, floating way the creature moved through all that magenta light, as though the light were water, as though it was under the sea. Anchored to the swirling resin by— four? no, eight— spindly, multi-jointed legs. It had two thicker limbs extending from its abdomen below its wings. These limbs were tipped with six-fingered hands, elongated and too narrow to belong to anyone human.

A strange, unnamable excitement was growing inside Micah's tightly bound body. He tried to figure it: he'd always been a bit of an adrenaline junkie, so maybe he was feeling the giddy rush of a novel danger, a novel fear? This piece just might amount to something after all.

The creature's wings settled back into the likeness of a cloak, though its face stayed arachnoid. Its hands fluttered as it reached out to stroke the sides of Micah's face, and Micah suddenly had the idea that it was nervous. Shy. Where did *that* come from?

He wished he could tell it that it didn't have to be nervous.

As though it heard his thoughts, the creature's hands steadied. They cupped Micah's stubbled cheeks like smooth, cool parentheses. It clicked its— mandibles?— and Micah felt, absurdly, that he knew it was a happy clicking. It was so close he could smell its fuzz, its fur. It smelled like dust and flowers.

Then hands were pulling down his briefs, copping a feel of his firm, muscular ass on the way. Micah felt a jolt of true panic, but then he realized what that unnamable excitement really was: he was already turned on. His t-dick was as hard and stiff as a nail. He *wanted* this.

The room had been a pleasant lukewarm temperature, if a bit chilly on Micah's naked skin, but the magenta light had brought heat with it. It wasn't an oppressive heat, but Micah found himself sweating. The sweat seemed to fascinate the creature. It trailed a finger down his side beneath his left armpit, intercepting a drop of sweat on its journey to the floor. Micah giggled behind the gag; the finger tickled. Then the creature raised the sweat to its face, where it licked it from its fingertip with a thin black tongue. All six golden eyes closed in apparent shock or bliss. Its clicking became a deep, resonant buzz that felt like it was vibrating Micah's bones. Felt like the purring of a mountain lion.

It caressed his body again, then abruptly jammed its fingers into the fat around his waist. Micah was pretty sensitive there, so he flinched and writhed, which didn't deter the creature at all. It didn't hurt, exactly, but it felt strange, like cold radiated from the fingers into Micah's flesh. Cold, and a tingly euphoria.

Still purring, the creature used its mouth-pincers and antennae to explore the rest of him. His nipples stiffened as it gave them an experimental tweak with its—pedipalps? He laughed and moaned and would have kicked his legs if he could have. The creature's fur was silky, velvety against his skin. Its black tongue tickled even more than its fingertip had.

It drew back and shifted its cloak—its wings— to the sides.

A long, sticky-looking phallic protrusion slowly unfurled from somewhere within its fuzzy torso. Micah gasped, then choked as the gag got sucked slightly farther back in his mouth. The creature's— dick?— was either vibrant pink, or appeared so because of the strange light. It was covered in irregularly spaced bumps and nodules. Soft, quivering. About the circumference of a typical human penis, but it had to be a foot long or more.

Micah wondered whether he'd be able to take it. He supposed he was about to find out. Not being able to move freely was excruciating. He'd never needed to get fucked so badly in his whole life.

Somehow, the creature managed to slide gracefully beneath him, inside him. Normally Micah had to use lube for vaginal as well as anal sex; this time, though, the alien cock entered him so easily he was contracting around its stimulating nodules before he realized there would be no need to brace himself for pain. He wished he could bounce on it. He wished he could shift his body so as to rub his t-dick up and down the creature's shaft.

As he thought it, the golden eyes stared into his. The creature's abdomen tilted, pivoted on some joint with no analog in humans, and now Micah's stiff t-dick was rubbing up and down the sticky member.

Micah undulated his torso desperately. The creature's dick felt *wet,* like a vagina or a mouth, not velvet-dry like a human penis. He ground against it as it pushed deeper and deeper into his body, so deep he felt sure it was wrapping itself around his internal organs. When he closed his eyes, the pervasive magenta glow remained. He wished there was music.

After what felt like a little eternity but was probably only fifteen minutes, Micah orgasmed. As he dropped from that delirious peak, he felt something release inside him. Not cum. Not exactly.

A second release. Whatever it was felt almost solid, a little heavy. A third release. It was as if his belly was being filled up with small water balloons. He understood as he thought it that these were, in fact, the creature's eggs. Its dick was an ovipositor!

A fourth egg settled into the plush muscle and mucus of Micah's interior. Now a fifth. It wasn't a bad feeling at all. In fact, the more eggs the creature laid, the better it felt. The more he wanted to be so full of the creature's eggs he could barely walk.

The golden eyes blinked lovingly at him.

At the seventh egg, Micah came again.

After the eighth, the ovipositor shrivelled and withdrew, leaving Micah swollen and bereft. Fluid trailed slowly, thickly down the insides of his thighs (Not blood, he hoped. He didn't think). But before he could become too frustrated, the hands returned. They jerked him off, then stroked his belly. He could feel how distended it was, even though he couldn't see it. It must look bizarre.

The hands withdrew, the wings whirred, and the creature's body shifted until it looked like a tall, thin, cloaked human once more. Its false face clicked back into place. Then it pulled Micah's underpants up as best it could and went about releasing him from the ties and straps of his rig. It saved the gag in his mouth for last. When the gag pulled free, it took a long, thick strand of spit with it.

When the creature had finished, it made an elaborate finger-snapping motion and promptly vanished. The magenta light went with it.

Micah thought he should feel more physical discomfort, but he felt only a tingly, warm, satisfied heaviness.

He lowered himself carefully to sit down on the floor, and he might have stayed there for a while if Lane hadn't yelped, run across the room, and started shaking him by the shoulders.

"Micah! What the fuck?! Are you okay?! What was that? I blacked out—" She looked down at him. "What *happened* to you? You look like you swallowed a watermelon! Shit! Do you need to go to the hospital?" She glared fiercely into his eyes.

"It's okay." Micah tried to smile at her. "No hospital. They might hurt the eggs. Look, let's stop this session early. Special circumstances. I'll explain everything on the way home."

"You'd better."

"This project is taking me places I never expected to go, I'll tell you that much." He hoped the creature would come back, but he had no way of knowing whether this was likely. Maybe its species were deadbeat parents. Still— *he* wasn't. He wouldn't be. Regardless of what happened.

"Isn't that a relief to hear," said Lane. She hooked

her hands under his armpits to help him stand up. "I'll go get your clothes. Good thing you wore sweatpants."

"Good thing," said Micah, dreamily. He'd have to wait until the eggs were finished incubating, but he was definitely planning on doing this type of performance again. Maybe next time he'd be blindfolded as well as gagged. The possibilities, for both art and the life inside him, were manifold, sparkling, limitless.

Love Letter from a Human Test Subject

Grant Lange

I don't know where you are out there. And still I write.

You. My writhing deliverer. Though I know not what you are called, I know that by virtue of my identifying you as such you will remember me. Remember me in between the lines of all of your scrawlings and surveys on the subject of mankind. I remember your smell—a smell not unlike silicon and seaweed—and the way your body twisted, the way you stretched for miles in every direction. The way you were gentle but thorough, very thorough. I never knew what my rescuer would look like but if angels are supposed to bridge the gap between chaos and order then an angel is what I will have to call you.

I hope this message finds you somewhere peaceful. I hope you are still safe and squelching.- I owe you a retelling. I want you to feel it like how I felt it.

#

Only a few earth days prior to your discovery had fate

and circumstance hurled me into space. I had been close enough to the emergency evacuation pod to escape with my life. I heard the sound of the hull tearing and it echoed throughout the titanium pipes of the entire ship like a desperate moan. Half of the ship had likely collapsed by the time I had punched the button that sealed the pod with me inside. The last thing that I saw before I was ejected into space was the ceiling of the bridge collapsing out of the dock and sending pieces of shrapnel and debris flying towards the windshield. Luckily It remained intact.

I had done what any normal human animal in my position would have done—my life was in danger and with only seconds to spare and no time to round up my associates, I leapt at my only opportunity to save myself. And immediately I regretted it.

Our vessel was roughly the size of Rhode Island—from my silent place against that escape vessel window, I did not expect to be able to find any sign of former human occupation amidst the rapidly expanding conglomerate of dead spaceship parts. But floating around in that sad antigravitational cosmos, I saw skull fragments. Coily strands of calcified pink intestines. Chunks of torn flesh bubbling amid the great vacuum of space, the clothes still glued to the skin with frozen blood.

I was alone, adrift in the cloudy emptiness. Among my tools for survival were oxygen candles, a year's worth of food, and a filtration system for my urine.

Massive pieces of spaceship metal bulleted towards me. I swallowed my vomit, steadied my shaking hands over the control center, and started steering. I will never know how your faculties help to keep you fighting but I learned it's easy for my kind to swallow our grief when danger still lurks.

When I was far enough away from the wreckage to avoid being decimated by the Newtonian projection of titanic shards of metal, I took what felt like my first breath. I leaned my head back up against the conductor's chair and screamed, over and over and over again until my voice was gone, my throat shredded. I couldn't help it. How can I explain to you that I couldn't help it?

You must have found me sleeping.

Whatever hatch or loading dock had sucked me aboard your ship had done so carefully and quietly. My own vessel's infrared camera hadn't detected your presence. But I awoke to the sound of the steel bearings which had sealed my vessel shut being unscrewed and the dull clunk of metal just outside the vehicle's flank. I had been sucked out of space. I felt gravity pull me down, the faint hum of an O'Neill Cylinder-adjacent mechanism churning beneath my feet.

I don't want to remember the excitement that I felt—it was so deceptive, so naive and so mistakenly pregnant with the hope that somehow I was home again. And then the hatch fell open and you slithered inside and eclipsed my sickly figure with the shadow of your giant, pulsating body.

I was washed with a gust of fresh, breathable air, air not unlike mine - only more moist, more sweet. I crawled on my hands and knees into a corner. It was only a reflex. Something as small and dry in the midst of something so powerful and full of liquid and life...

Can you blame me?

You extended a tentacle and stroked me with it. If it was to coax me out of hiding, it worked. I was so excited by the feeling of being touched by something damp and warm for the first time since the death of my ship that I wrapped my fingers around it and brought it closer to my face. We humans enjoy touch. Had you ripped off my head I wouldn't have minded.

And then it slithered up my nostrils. You violated my senses and groped my brain. I know you knew that I could feel it inside of my skull and I can't help but believe that that's why you did it. I felt a series of microscopic, veinlike appendages squeeze my cortex and tears streamed down my eyes as a river of blood flowed from my nose.

You said something in a language that I didn't understand. You were thinking out loud, trying to classify me. I heard only squelching, that ropy, slimy sound of the tentacles. I could feel them in my eardrums now, coming out of my nasal cavity and into my throat. They seemed to thicken and contract to fit into the smaller spaces, shrunk thin enough to fit in the fissures between the coils of my brain. I gagged with nothing in my stomach to regurgitate.

And then you withdrew, pulling ropes of mucus and blood from my nostrils with you. Little by little, I began to hear words emanating from your lipless mouth.

"Language dubbed," you said, "English. Class: communicative. Type: reproductive. Oxygenating consumer…"

I gasped for air when your tentacle tips finally slipped

from my nostrils. They left behind a snail trail of red snot that kept us connected with a string of orange slime. I smacked it between my tongue and the roof of my mouth as I panted. It tasted like honey—diabetically sweet, floral.

"... flexible digestive system... reproduces sexually... Language acquired. Speak."

I looked up at you.

You might have been humanoid. Your shape was similar to mine, save that it was much larger, much more tendony and ribbed, clothed with damp, translucent gray skin. I could see your organs through your stomach, dark green and black and churning. You had no eyes, no lips, only teeth, a long gash of them, your neck was webbed like the hood of a cobra. You had a chest like a starved horse—Broad and large but all skin-laden ribs with a massive, bony sternum. A tucked waist sat beneath that with a fleshy dip that parted into a labia of several long tendrils near where a human's naval might have been. Undeniably, seductively female.

From your hips down you were nothing but tendrils. Tendrils of all lengths, all thicknesses, like a pit of snakes dripping with mucus.

My labored breaths slowed to a hitch.

"I don't have anything to say," I said.

You wrapped your tendrils around my arms and held me still. A third, thinner one made a knot around the zipper of my jumpsuit and pulled downwards.

#

You may not ever see it this way but what followed in those hours after was your first act of mercy towards me. An olive branch in the form of a simple omission.

I felt the blade of your strange, unearthly, scissor-like instrument caress the space between my index finger and thumb, right before that sweet intersection between the princeps pollicis and the radial artery. The surgical table which you had me sprawled upon began to feel quite cold. Instinctively I bit the tendril that had been holding my head down and it twitched and receded like the tail of a snake. I'm sorry. I couldn't help it. But you only eyed me curiously and with your phalangic hand, nursed the bite mark that I had left behind.

You etched a note regarding my reaction upon the glass tablet. Your writing wasn't much unlike the elusive Linear A of my own dead species, a circular arrangement of cosmic symbols that, when compiled into a paragraph, resembled something like the Mayan calendar. And you wrote with your hands, too. Just like me.

"I'd rather you not take that as a sample," I told you.

"Why?"

The sound of your voice was like the collective whisper of a stage choir. You seemed to have more than one set of vocal cords, a string of tracheas which all spoke in thin gusts of the same air. Your tongue was long, just like a serpent's, and the way it gave shape to the words that you spoke was like a thin web being woven into fine silk. Despite its collective resonance, its chorus-like quality, it was distinctly inhuman, only just.

"I need my thumb to be able to operate my vessel."

"You have keratin, biotin, collagen, cartilage, hemo-globin centralized within a single location."

"You can get those things elsewhere."

"I can optimize an examination with one sample."

"If you *must* take a phalange," I said, "Let it be a toe. Just don't cut my thumb off. Please."

I was panting, panting hard. Always know that had you cut off my thumb, I would have arched my back and exalted my pain so dramatically that you might've ran deeper into the ship and cowered.

"Denied," and then you pulled away from me, slurping all of your tentacles back underneath your curtain of them, keeping one wrapped around my ankle so I couldn't escape. "Locate alternate points of five sample flesh molecules."

I sat up and looked at you. Despite your eyelessness, I knew that you were looking at me, that you could see my shapes and colors. To this day I still don't quite understand the way that your senses process light, if they processed light at all, or if you can simply feel the displacement of cold and heat in the space around you. I wonder sometimes if it was my warmth which you fell in love with, not my image.

"Locate alternate points of five sample flesh molecules" you said again, as if I hadn't heard the first time. "Biotin and cartilage are prioritized. In the case of failure I will remove the entire left foreleg from the knee down."

#

I used the sharpest, most narrow straw in your repertoire to penetrate my tibia for the bone sample you so wanted. For your keratin, I gave you a fingernail clipping, and for your tissue samples, a fragment of flesh from my abdomen which contained some fat. I even gave you a lock of hair, the strands bound together with a rubber band I'd had around my wrist.

Make no mistake, I am not stupid. I knew the hair wouldn't be particularly useful to you. Every ounce of biological information that the hair contained was something you could have extracted from the fingernail clipping. But I wanted you to have it. If you could smell or taste or use some secret sixth sense to absorb the fertile aura which emanated from my head-hair, I wanted its absorption to be your prerogative, something you could take in without the troublesomeness of my prying gaze. It was my way of thanking you, of inviting you to know me better.

Your tendrils nearly snapped my jaw when they slithered up to my mouth and pried my teeth apart like a dentist. I snatched the opportunity to lick you, to taste the syrup again.

"Enamel detected."

I grimaced. One of your phalangic hands gripped a tool that resembled a pair of forceps. The other gripped the hair on my head.

Our relative positions were human-adjacent, like I was soon to take you into my mouth. I placed my hand on your hips and gave you a gentle push back.

"You may take *one* tooth," I told you. "You grip what's called the crown, then bend and twist... it should come right out."

"There is nothing stopping me from extracting more than one enamel sample."

"Save my trust that you won't."

You had no muscles with which to smile, only a set of long, perfect chrome teeth that bore gumless and wet. But you licked them, and somewhere in that desert of a face, I could have sworn that I saw something like amusement, like excitement, professionally contained though it may have been.

"Accepted," you said. Your tendrils expanded to my mouth to hold it open. "Locate a sample."

I pointed to a bottom premolar.

"Careful," I purred as the metal scraped against a canine, "I'm a screamer."

#

You jammed the door to my ship to keep me from escaping while you analyzed your samples of my skin and bone. Blood dripped languidly down my lips and chin, the fresh pain still spreading its coldness throughout my mouth. I had my jumpsuit, the pod in which I slept, the freeze-dried food that I would soon deplete unless some wandering space traveller from my own world managed to find me before I starved. It wasn't unlike a kennel now—a little offset room attached to a greater one, a cage to keep me docile.

I clutched a sample of my own. Four tips of your thin, slimy tendrils wrapped around my wrists and between my fingers, brainlessly convulsing, writhing, and twirling like bait worms. You had yet to make any observation on the raw strength of the sapient grip. I twisted them off at the nodes when you were probing around in my mouth, and you were so fascinated by my rows of white mammalian teeth that you didn't even notice.

I had no equipment. I left it behind in the lab on my mothership. The only thing I had to use to analyze your chemical structure was a handheld spectrometer.

I held a single limp tendril up to the light and pressed it flat against the lens. It spread like glutinous jelly and twitched. I watched as the dark lines began to cover the center of the spectra, shifting just slightly to the left, some scattering at the sides. You were an oxygen thing, given structure with carbon and hydrogen, mostly. Just like me.

It was almost as if your brainless tendrils had felt this revelation through my fingers as it had erupted in my mind, and they began to pulse feverishly. I let them wiggle free from my grasp and watched as they crawled up my naked arm in a cyclone-like pattern, slithering their way across my shoulder and then to my face. It was there that they halted, wrapped around my ears and jaw, and traced the pink of my lips.

I licked them as they licked me. Again I tasted the sweet syrup of your mucus as my tongue and the tips of your detached tendrils danced with one another, circling around, tangling in a coitus of their own making. My heart sank further and further down into my body, warm and wet and thudding against my ribs for more.

I begged that this tug of war between an armful of severed alien limbs and my mouth was evidence of a sort of pan-bodily neurology, that *you* were controlling them, somehow, that these movements were voluntary and passionate and *real.*

I audibly moaned when one of the tendrils started to wiggle its way deeper into my mouth. It circled around the edges of my throat, wrapped around my tonsils. I gagged and pulled it out. The rest of them slithered out from between my lips and down to my neck and chest. Their flat, suctioning underbellies left hickeys on my skin and I whimpered at the feeling of their tight release.

To test my theory, I brought them to the hatch of my ship. Lo and behold, one slithered between the deadbolt and the hasp and lubricated it just well enough for the bolt to wiggle loose. The latch clicked and I was free.

I stepped out onto the main deck, barefoot, raw.

Your spaceship looked like the underground electrical tunnels on my home planet. The tile was metal, some kind of metal, one immune to the rust which would have resulted from the overwhelming moisture in the air. Whether the long grayish vines which hung from the ceiling and stretched across the length of the vessel were wires or tendrils of yours, I wasn't sure. I still am not. I like to believe that these lengths of rope were pieces of your body.

I found you in a dark corridor. The black carbon ventilation tubing which veined the ceilings beneath the gray wires led me straight to where you stood, hunched over a convex lens which could dial closer or further from the tuft of my hair that I had given you One of your tendrils wrapped taut around the petri dish it sat in to keep it still.

You looked towards me.

"You're not supposed to have those," you said.

I held your severed limbs to the light. "I'm a scientist, too." I set them on the counter and they slithered back down to join your body again. "You took your samples. I took mine."

You looked back down at your lens. "Where has your herd gone?" you asked.

"How did you know I had one?"

"Cortex examination," you looked at me, set your things down. "You belong to a species of pack-hunting secondary consumers."

Why is that fair? For you to know so much about me and for me to know so little about you?

"You felt around in my brain earlier."

You nodded.

"They're all dead," I said, and I slowly walked closer. "My mothership imploded."

"Yet here you stand," you slithered nearer, "an implosion would have guaranteed immediate vacuum effect. A sapient body would have been crushed."

"Maybe it was God," I said. "Or coincidence." And in the rear end of my still-declining mind I saw human bone and brain matter sprinkled between debris clouds across space. So I reached for you.

"I bet it gets lonely out here," I picked up a limp tentacle and held it in my hands, petting it. "Adrift in the milky way all by yourself. No one to talk to but the unfortunate passers-by that you kidnap."

It slithered up my arm.

"It's irrelevant whether a subject considers itself 'fortunate'," you said.

"Do you belong to a species?"

"I don't."

"Could you ever understand?"

You rubbed your head like it hurt.

You didn't need to respond. Another tendril around my ankle was an answer fine enough. I stumbled and fell to the ground, landing with a splat into a tangle of your thousands of arms, all wet and pulsating and sensitive.

If you continue with your travels having learned only one thing about humankind, let it be that humans like to be touched.

Your torso hung above me like an obelisk, godlike, when your thickest tentacle slithered in between the lips of my vulva and parted my vaginal walls. I moaned and grabbed a fistful of the alien flesh that I laid upon while you explored the confines of my hole, tested my boundaries, searched for a depth. I could feel you trying to reach parts of me which were not meant to be explored and when the thin, wormlike tip hit the opening of my cervix and I bared my teeth and screamed, you pulled back, pulsed. I sighed when you withdrew, moaned when you started thrusting.

It was not hard and textured with a head and veins like a human cock. Rather, it melted with the form and shape of my insides like a water-dense silicon, gelatinous and gentle but with the same stimulating sensitivity of a sex toy. You were made for pleasure, designed for it, bred by the stars to fit inside me. I felt the tendril twist and squirm and I arched my back.

I could practically feel your mucus pouring out of me with each thrust like a fresh load, a substance like ambrosia with its decadence. You wrapped your tentacles around my body from the crotch that they explored all the way up to my neck and into my mouth. I licked and sucked on them and they seemed to lick me back, flicking back and forth the way that a human tongue does when kissing. And all the while, you stood over me, watching, calculating, seeing how I would react to certain touches and textures and actions. One tendril slithered all the way down my throat, touching my esophagus, and I gagged. My eyes watered and you pulled your tendril out and stroked it across my face, wet with both of our slimes. My mouth tasted full of honey, my throat sticky with it.

Had you not paid such careful and loving consideration towards my body's needs and wants, I wouldn't have minded. I was yours now, your subject, wholly and perfectly yours to examine and experiment with as you so pleased. In the heavenly battle between two curious intelligent astronomical minds, you had won.

But perhaps your scientific restraint didn't have as much fortitude as I had thought. Your posture lost its erection, and you bent over me and pulled me into a kiss. It was toothy and lipless and more bite than soft press, but your long, smooth, forked tongue traveled down my oral cavity and licked each tooth. My eyes rolled back, and I closed them and wrapped both my arms around your neck.

I rubbed my heel against the vagina-like orifice at your midsection that I had found earlier. You thrust your hips towards it to increase the friction. It nearly swallowed my entire foot. I find it hard to believe that you don't belong to any species, that you can't or don't breed. Whatever that hole was between your locomotive tentacles and your chest, it was meant to be fucked.

At some point I pulled my spread knees to my chest to increase the feeling and I exposed my anus to you. One of your smaller tentacles found it. I felt it suction the sphincter wetly and it squirmed when I twitched, but soon it found its way inside and started to tease, to loosen me up, to prepare me for more, for *larger.* My pleasure doubled and my ceaseless moaning was stifled with a delightful smile, primally violent and vulpine as it was.

Your appendages receded from my mouth for a moment and I opened my eyes and looked at your face.

You stopped for a moment, not to rest, but thinking. You were panting. I could see your lungs through your skin expanding and contracting, the fog of your breath thickening the air with clouds of vaporized mucus.

"Are you taking notes about me?" I panted. "Is your examination complete?"

You rubbed my cheek.

And then I felt it again. The tendrils around my face traveling up my nostrils and to my brain. The tendrils in my mouth going down my throat, the ones in my ass going further into my colon, my small intestine. The pain was exquisite, delicate, like armies upon armies of parasites crawling within and throughout me. I felt you in my stomach, in my chest, in my head... and soon my veins, my nerves.

"*Subject demonstrates perfect endurance,*" you whispered, "*sound biological structure, capable of being controlled without lasting physical trauma...*"

I felt my arm move. It lifted towards the ceiling of

the vessel like the arm of a marionette. I was never sure whether you were controlling me by massaging my cerebellum or by squelching through the sinew in between my very muscle fibers.

"*The ideal organism,*" you gasped. "*The complete animal…*"

You made me stand. I could only shake with you inside of me, all throughout me, puppeteering my body. Your tendrils traveled up my thighs to offer support for my spastic legs.

"*Walk,*" you growled. I hadn't heard such violence, such certainty in your hazy voice yet. I would have smiled with delight, had I been able to. I could only grit my teeth with seizure.

And I took a step. You *puppetted* me into taking a step. I hovered over you, tendrils spilling from every hole in my body, curling with delight like tentacles of my own, thick translucent locks which hung languidly from my face, my anus, my vagina, coiling down my legs and wrapping around my ankles like shackles from a dead and ancient realm.

My body couldn't handle much more before it faltered. My weight shifted once like a building collapsing and then fell to the floor in one big, wet, blushing heap. You withdrew from me all at once, and in that microsecond between ignition and explosion, I screamed.

It was like a supernova, like the shockwaves of a nuclear explosion were obliterating the neighboring bodies around me. I knew that you could feel it, feel my holes pulsing around you as my come made a creamy white cocktail with your mucus. I arched, threw my head back… you blanketed me and let me go dead in your gray, translucent grasp.

I was enervated and limp and covered with substances familiar and alien, used to my fullest capacity. Anything more would have killed me. I smiled at the thought.

I reached my slimy hands towards your cheeks and held them while you panted. Your labored breath smelled like the interstellar medium from which you were born, the faint odor of dying star-stuff permeating my atmosphere, my world, a solitary but monumental instance of the Terrestrial being swallowed by the Jovian.

#

I laid embryonic and sensitive in a wet chamber of your making. Your tendrils caressed my aching body and healed me from the outside in.

"I can't keep you here," you said. "You belong in a substantial habitat. We cannot be symbiotes."

I sat up. Mucus dripped from my limbs.

"Why?"

"Inadequate social supplements. Lack of food. Overhydration," you wrapped another tendril around my face. "Your life cannot be sustained here."

"No one's looking for me, you know," I said. "Everyone on my planet thinks I'm dead." An uncomfortable lump formed in my throat and I believe you felt it rise, so you stroked my head.

"I can reintroduce you somewhere where you will be discovered."

"I'll kill myself," I told you, crying now, my tears

forming a syrupy cocktail with your fluids.

"Explain."

"How could I go back knowing what I'd be missing?"

"Peacefully. Thankful to touch the ground again."

"You can't kill me?"

You necked me once with your teeth. "I have a new ethical development which keeps me docile towards you."

And on that fateful day when either I died or was returned to my home planet, that day that this love escaped my clutch like a feral animal ripping loose from a snare, it would be with my entrails between its teeth, I knew.

#

I awoke in the center of a crop circle.

I was fully clothed, still damp and sticky with traces of you, the wreckage of the escape pod laid to waste in the rows and rows of wheat stalks sprouting around my aching body. I was home again, breathing in my planet's air and instinctively savoring its green earthiness. It was right for me to yearn for it.

Only I wasn't. I was longing for you, for the sweet air of the mothership, for the nectar which dripped from your skin and into my mouth so perfectly. I was hoping that your vessel would be my tomb, that I would die there in that great expanse of mucus and wires and pipes and you, so much of you. But instead the sun shone on my face, a blinding dot in a vast blue sky full of puffy clouds which hid the stars among which you dwelled. I kept coughing up massive globules of phlegm. It was the moisture from the inside of your ship leaving me.

Still I felt something slither up my leg.

There was a tendril, severed clean at the base, sliced off like a tree branch. And it was still alive, still feverishly wiggling for me.

I tore open the collar of my jumpsuit and ripped a hole in my underwear trying to remove it to make way for you to slither inside. And you did, eagerly, the tendril splitting my vulva with slimy gush and wrapping the tail end, which didn't quite fit inside me, around my thigh.

I bucked my hips towards the sun, the sky, anything past the confines of my quiet atmosphere that might have been watching.

#

It did not live for long. For several days that tendril slithered inside and throughout me, but my climate was too dry for you, and soon your gift shriveled up and died beneath the heat of my sun, my lone star, that great and horrifying god which dictates all life on the surface of my world. I broke the mummified corpse of your dead limb into pieces and put them in a mason jar. That jar has been sitting on my nightstand for the greater part of a decade.

Since returning to Earth as the lone survivor of a failed expedition, I've retired from my career as an astronautical astronomer in favor of a quieter, more domestic position in stellar observation. I work in a lab, fine-tuning telescope images with computer enhancement, calculating the distances between stars, and chemically analyzing interstellar mediums. It's boring work but it's safe, and it pays handsomely.

I found a partner. A human one, a fellow scientist who shares my job, one which swept me off of my feet (though not out of space—only you could have done that) in the observatory. I am satisfied with her. I really am. But I can only be so satisfied when I have tasted the fruit of perfection only just before the tree was cut. More than once she has asked me what lies in that jar. And every time I tell her they are moon rocks.

Housekeeping
Alex Appleton

CW: Dubcon, orgasm denial, bondage, electrostimulation

Jackie Salway always thought his house was haunted. No ghostly hands appeared on his shoulder in the bathroom mirror. No pale face stared at him through his reflection on the bedroom window. But he'd find his keys in the same spot on his counter every morning even when he knew he'd left them on the coffee table in the living room the night before. Sometimes his front door wouldn't unlock when he tried to leave, not until he assured his house that yes he would be back before midnight, and no, he was not going to spend the night in someone else's bed. The one time he did show up at the tail end of the witching hour with a collar of purple hickies around his throat, his incorporeal roommate woke him not even an hour later by flooding the kitchen. He couldn't sleep naked anymore either. Well, he could, but the covers would never move past the foot of his bed, no matter how hard he tugged on them. Even when he stripped underneath the sheets, he'd only wake to the slight chill of his drafty house and his bedsheets thrown across the room.

Tonight, however, it was not his resident ghost making a ruckus.

He woke up to his lamp frantically flashing in his eyes.

"Okay. I'm up. I'm up," he hissed, still groggy with sleep. The floorboards creaked somewhere behind his bedroom door. "I'm up, Arty. Christ, I'm up."

His house ghost, Arthur (Arty for short), was usually not so insistent. He must've forgotten to turn off the stove, or lock the door, or something equally as catastrophic. Footsteps heavy, he stomped to his door and peeked down the dark hallway.

It was at least two in the morning, but despite the hour, moonlight pierced the dark through the large windows that lined the walls. His bed called to him, and Jackie almost fell back into its warm embrace. He only resisted because his lamp was still flashing in an illiterate Morse code.

"Arty, if there's another raccoon on the generator, I'm going to be pissed. You know that can wait until morning," he grumbled.

The house was small, but that was one of the things he liked about it. The living room and kitchen made up the majority of the space while a small alcove near the back of the house hid his washer and dryer. A short hallway connected the living room to the single bathroom and bedroom. The thin walls didn't provide much in terms of insulation or good interior design, but he enjoyed the patchwork of dark wood and gritty stone nonetheless. Plus, he'd gotten the house at a steal, so even if he had despised the layout, the price was more than enough to make up for it.

Jackie staggered to the closest window and looked outside, his sleep-addled brain making him stumble. There was nothing but the looming shadows of the pine forest beyond the glass. He sighed and put his hands over the window, peering into the dark expanse a second time. Nothing. With a shake of his head, Jackie stepped back. If there wasn't anything happening outside then the problem was somewhere inside the house. That, or he pissed Arty off, and it was repaying the favor by waking him up before the ass crack of dawn. Out of the corner of his eye, he saw the heel-end of a shoe step into his laundry room.

Okay, so maybe Arty wasn't overreacting. This was definitely not a raccoon on the generator type of situation. This was a bad situation with a capital B. He would almost rank it above the time his septic tank backed up and flooded the house with raw sewage, which was a separate incident from Arty's kitchen temper tantrum. Jackie shook his head. He needed to *focus!* There was a stranger in his house! His phone was back in the bedroom, but even if he did have it on him, it wasn't like the cops would be there in any sort of timely manner. Just one of the perks to living two hours away from any sort of civilization, he supposed. All the same, having a burglar snooping through his house was not supposed to happen when even the post office didn't know his address.

He took a breath. The man didn't know that Jackie

was aware of his presence just yet- at least he hoped that was the case- so that meant he could just slip back inside his bedroom and pretend there wasn't a stranger rummaging through all his things. He had a gun, but he kept it unloaded most of the time. The last thing Jackie wanted was for the invader to burst into his room and see him fiddling with a bunch of bullets, trying to load a gun he only marginally knew how to shoot.

Jackie turned to creep back to his bedroom. As much as it infuriated him, he wasn't going to attack a stranger who had god knows what sort of weapons on him. The best course of action he had was to wait in his room and assess the damage later.

There was a man standing in his hallway, blocking the path to his bedroom.

Jackie froze. He sucked in a short breath as his muscles locked in a mixture of surprise and terror. The man in his hallway was absolutely massive.

Jackie would not have considered himself to be small in any capacity. He was six feet tall with dark hair and brawny like a lumberjack- minus the beard, but including the flannel. The intruder was nearly a head taller than him and built like a goddamn brick house. His shoulders nearly touched both walls of the narrow corridor, the gap between them only growing smaller as he breathed. He was dressed in an all too cliché cat burglar costume: a ski mask that just barely revealed his eyes and lips; a long-sleeve shirt, leather gloves, dark pants that he seemed nearly ready to burst out of, and heavy boots. The intruder's eyes shined, appearing glassy in the dim moonlight.

Jackie cleared his throat, hoping that his voice wouldn't crack. "Listen, dude," He held up his hands in what he hoped was a placating manner. "You can take whatever you want. Alright? I'll just go sit in the bathroom or the bedroom while you rummage through whatever meagre supplies strike your fancy. Won't even call the cops after." His tongue flashed quick and nervous over his lips.

The intruder took a step toward him with a tilt of his head. Jackie's heart leaped into his throat, and to his horror, he felt his cock stir.

He could not be into this. Not right now, at least. Like yeah, he had a thing for big guys, especially those bigger than him, and yeah, he also had a thing for big masked guys who could pin him facedown onto the kitchen counter, rip off his clothes, and shove their thick-

Dammit, why couldn't his brain have waited until the man was gone before it shoved its lewd fantasies in the forefront?

Jackie took a step back. Dirty mind be damned, he had to survive this before he could masturbate about it. The intruder followed him with another step of his own and then kept walking. Jackie scrambled backward, feet unsteady as his hindbrain switched between fight, flight, and freeze.

"Listen, my guy-" he started, "Sir, I-"

Now that got the intruder's attention, causing him to stop and suck in a breath. His dead eyes shone with something more than malice. The stranger stood in the living room now while Jackie retreated into the kitchen.

Not that the distance would last when the man took three steps for every one of Jackie's.

Could he reach a knife before the man got to him? Probably not considering that his knife block was three steps away and the stranger was only two. Jackie almost had to crane his neck to look him in the eyes.

He took another step back. Two steps. Three. His back touched the countertop. Jackie glanced behind him. He'd stupidly cornered himself against the cabinets, and now there was nowhere to run, not with the intruder looming over him.

"Listen, sir," Jackie swallowed the glob of spit threatening to choke him. "Just lock me in the bathroom, or, hell, even outside, and you can take whatever you want. Like I said earlier, I won't even report you. Pretty good deal, yeah?"

The intruder crowded him further into the counter. Jackie flinched as the man reached out and cupped his chin with his gloved hand. The leather was like ice against his cheek. His heart pounded against his ribs like it wanted to leap out of his chest and run. Sweaty palms nearly slipping on the counter, Jackie jerked out of his grip. He shoved at his chest, trying to get just an inch of breathing room, but the man didn't even shift his weight.

Jackie punched him hard in the gut. His hand buckled against the man's stomach like he'd struck concrete. The intruder stepped even closer. Jackie dropped his hands and leaned back until his shoulders were nearly touching the countertop. His panicked breaths billowed out in short gasps. He tried to get his foot between them to push them apart, but the intruder was as immovable as a stone wall. A hand wrapped around his throat and squeezed.

With a wheeze, Jackie tried to suck in a breath. His lungs started to burn from the lack of oxygen. Legs kicking uselessly, he clawed at the air like an upturned beetle. His hands flew to his throat as he scoured the intruder's wrists with his blunt nails. Black spots danced across his vision. He tapped three times against the glove. The pressure eased, but the man didn't step away.

The intruder jerkily buried his face into the junction between Jackie's neck and shoulder. His cold exhale washed over his skin, making him shudder. There was no warmth in the way he mouthed the pulse point on Jackie's neck, no hot breath condensing on his skin, no warm spit cooling on his feverish flesh. The intruder's tongue was soft against him, soft but dry like a cat's tongue that lost its little hooks. Jackie panted at his touch. The fear thrumming through his body made his skin that much more sensitive. Small, thin tendrils writhed underneath the man's lips as he pressed them against the underside of Jackie's jaw. Before Jackie could scream, the man bit into the side of his neck, drawing a strangled squeak out of him instead.

There was a chuckle, at least something comparable to a chuckle, that rumbled in the intruder's chest. It wasn't the smooth exhale of easy laughter but something that shook and shuddered, the hacking cough of an old lawnmower refusing to start. The man withdrew and threw Jackie over his shoulder before he made his way to the bedroom.

Jackie yelped as his captor's shoulder drove into his gut. He kicked his legs and beat at his back with his fists.

"Let go of me, asshole!" he shouted.

The man ignored him, throwing him onto the bed as soon as he entered the room. Jackie bounced exactly once, but before he could scramble away, the wall behind him cracked. Wood dust rained down on him as electrical wires forced their way through the wall and wrapped around each of his limbs. The colorful array pulled his back flat against the bed. They slightly dug into his wrists and ankles as he tugged against them. The sheets bunched underneath him as he struggled. Sweat made his clothes stick to his skin.

He stared at his wrists in terror. "What the fuck is this?" His shoulder nearly popped out of its socket with the force he used to try and roll off the bed. "What are you?"

The bedside lamp clicked on, blanketing the room in a dim, yellow light. The man, the thing, tilted its head to the side. Its lips moved, but no sound passed through them. It took a step forward. Jackie tried to kick out his legs in a desperate effort to scurry backwards, but the wires dragged him down to the foot of the bed.

"You know." Its wretched reply filled the room.

Jackie momentarily paused in his struggles. "I don't know what the fuck you are," he hissed, "I don't know what you are, and I don't want to. Let me go."

Its lips mimed out words again like it had to figure out how to move its mouth in order to speak. "Jac-kie. You know," it said.

He was about to argue again when something on the ceiling caught his attention. A single wire trailed down from between the thin gaps in the wooden planks and disappeared into the back of the intruder's head. He stared at it for a moment before all the pieces clicked, and the realization struck him like a bullet through his brain.

Jackie furrowed his brow. "Arty?"

Arty's hand slid up his thigh, bunching the fabric of his sleep pants near his groin. It squeezed his leg suggestively. "Jac-kie."

Two thoughts entered his mind simultaneously. One being that Arthur was not his house ghost but instead his literal house. The second being that his sentient house wanted to *fuck* him.

"Arty," he started, "Arty, listen-"

Its hand moved up and caressed the half-hard erection tenting the front of his pants. He was going to interrupt it to say that he wasn't into this, but then Arty rubbed its thumb over the clothed head of his cock, and Jackie moaned. He would never admit to moaning, of course. He wasn't that down bad for a house piloting a meat suit, but he also wouldn't say that the sound that slipped out of him wasn't a moan. He shivered as a hot flash of pleasure rushed up his spine.

The hand on him wasn't warm, but it was a firm weight pressing down on him. One that he'd sorely missed. While there were many perks to living secluded in the woods, hours away from any sort of civilization, human connection, companionship, and one-night stands were not among them.

Fuck it.

The skin suit or meat puppet or whatever Arty was using was hot, and it'd been six months since he'd been in another person's bed.

He arched his hips into its touch. "If you're going to fuck me, Arty, you better make it good. You know what I like."

Another mechanical chuckle, like that of an old engine dying, filled the room. It leaned down, took his shirt between its hands, and ripped it apart. His other clothes followed suit until Jackie was lying on the tattered remains of his pyjamas completely nude. His cock, free from the confining fabric, bounced against his stomach. Precum leaked from the tip, dripping down into the coarse line of hair trailing from his navel to the base of his groin. Arty slid its hand over his length. One of its fingers pressed against the slit, sending drops of precum snaking into the crevices on the leather glove.

Its touch sent Jackie's skin buzzing. His hips jerked as it lightly wrapped its cold fingers around his shaft and started to stroke him. A simmering heat bloomed under his skin.

"Arty," he panted, "don't be a tease."

He tried to thrust into its grip, tried to chase the friction that he desperately craved, but Arty dropped its hand and stepped back, leaving his hips jerking in the empty air.

"Arty," he hissed, "Fuck."

Two gloved fingers shoved their way into his mouth, muffling his words. They tasted salty and bitter against his tongue. Its other hand returned to his cock and continued the soft, slow, *infuriating* pace.

He groaned against its fingers. His tongue dipped into every crease lining the leather, lapping away at the precum that collected in them. Its fingers stretched out and grazed the back of his throat. Spit threatened to leak from the corner of his mouth as he nearly gagged. It withdrew them slightly, dragging the glove across his tongue, before roughly shoving them in again, fucking his mouth with its fingers. Jackie keened and shuddered at the vibration that coursed through his teeth. His hips met every one of Arty's slow strokes.

"I'm gonna-" He could barely understand his own muffled words, but Arty knew all his tells.

Hard, almost viciously, it squeezed right underneath the head of his cock, immediately killing his growing orgasm. Jackie writhed on the sheets with a cry. The need to come sank back into the depths of his core. Arty let go and tried to extract its fingers, but Jackie clamped down on them with his teeth. His damned house had left him teetering on the edge and pulled him back at the last second; he wasn't going to lose this too.

It was like biting onto a coin. The leather provided a slight cushion against the unyielding skin. He swore he heard his teeth click on metal or stone. The glove caught on the back of his teeth, but with a harsh tug, Arty ripped its hand free.

Arty looked at its hand and flexed its fingers. Gray skin covered the limb, the color not lively but not quite dead either. The skin undulated in the dim light. Thin outlines of wires snaked around each other and between whatever else it used to keep its shape. It placed its hand flat on Jackie's chest, rubbing its thumb over the soft hair there, before leaning down and kissing a line from Jackie's abdomen to his jaw.

Like earlier, none of the kisses were warm. The first kiss underneath his navel was dreadfully cold. It sent a shiver coursing through him, but as its lips worked against his burning skin, they reached a sort of equilibrium. Not hot nor cold, just a delicious pressure trailing up his body. It mouthed at the sensitive spot right below his ear, nipping at the skin and sucking a bruise to the surface.

One of Arty's hands slid up his chest and grazed his nipple. Jackie arched into the touch with a groan. Arty pulled and pinched at the delicate nub with its gloveless hand until it was swollen. It caught the engorged tip between its blunt nails and twisted its fingers, sending a delicious burst of pain burrowing into his chest. Desperate to swat away the offending hand, Jackie pulled against his restraints. The tight, multicolored wires left angry indents in his limbs as they pulled him back prone.

"Arty!" Jackie cried.

Arty's mouth never left his neck, but it did stop pinching him. It swiped over his throbbing nipple soothingly with its thumb. After a minute, Arty slid its hand over to the other side of his chest and repeated the same torture.

Jackie thrashed, the pain sending his nerves into overdrive and his sensitive skin singing. He grunted and groaned. His shoulders and hips hurt from how he contorted himself in a vehement attempt to flee. Then, there was another sort of pain as something thinner and sharper than a fingernail slid over his nipple. He couldn't look down to see what Arty was doing on account of it plunging its soft tongue into the hollow of his throat and licking a path up towards his Adam's apple. A spark of electricity had him seizing. His muscles locked, and his body shook as the electric bolt grounded itself through his body.

Jackie had more self-respect than to whimper. At first, at least. That still didn't stop him from repeating Arty's name like a mantra, though, every shock making him sound more and more shrill. Arty started pinching and twisting at his nipples again. The tips of copper wires poked through its fingertips, making its touch even more biting as the metal stabbed into him.

He whimpered and squealed as the shocks got stronger and more frequent. Tears burned at the corner of his eyes. His teeth clenched around the glove with a squeak.

"Stop! Arty, stop!" he cried. His chest was on fire. Even with Arty kissing his throat and his own cock twitching with pleasure, the pain had him on the verge of screaming.

Arty shook off the other glove and rubbed along the inside of Jackie's thigh. Small, copper threads scraped along his raw nerves. The hand trailed up and fondled his balls. The hair rose on the back of his neck.

"Arty," he panted, "Arty, wait."

Its hand was on the base of his shaft now, dragging its fingers closer to the head of his cock. Its other hand slipped off his chest and caressed his ribs with a thumb. Arty delicately traced its fingers through the stream of precum sliding down his length. The tips of the copper wires grazed the leaking head and sent Jackie into a thrashing fit.

"Wait! *Wait!* Arty, please!" Jackie bounced on the bed in his frantic attempt to escape. His jumping torso made the bed springs creak.

Another jittery rumble bled from Arty's chest as it watched him.

"Fuck off, asshole!" Jackie snapped. He was going to say something else, but an electric current raced through his cock and had him throwing his head back in a soundless scream. His body seized and shook in the half-second that Arty shocked him.

Jackie sucked in a choked gasp as the blinding pain slowly dissipated. The stench of ozone burned his nose. His single breath was all the respite he got. Arty kept up the torment, making Jackie's exposure stronger and longer with each shock. By the time Jackie was slamming his fist onto the bed three times, he was nothing but a whimpering, crying mess, but despite all the pain, his cock still begged for release.

Immediately, Arty was pulling the glove from his mouth and replacing it with its fingers, still not giving him any chance to recover. The three digits crammed his mouth full. He couldn't even seal his lips to make sure that spit didn't ooze down his chin. Jackie sucked on them the best he could, slipping his tongue between them and nearly gagging himself to make sure they were nice and slick all the way down to the base. It tried to remove its hand, but Jackie bit down to keep it in place.

He sliced through Arty's skin, severing its fingers. A mass of wires wriggled against the back of his teeth. He let go with an alarmed yelp.

A wire trailed from each of its fingers to the base of its palm. Mouth now open in shock, Jackie watched with a sort of sick fascination as the writhing, colorful hoard of wires inside its hand reeled in its fingers, dragging the pads of them over his bottom lip. Strands of spit broke and tapped against his chin as they reattached themselves.

Jackie didn't have much time to think before his legs were pushed over his head and his knees were nearly pressed into his shoulders. Arty probed at his entrance with a spit-slicked finger. It pushed it through the tight ring of muscle down to the first knuckle. He grunted at the intrusion but slowly relaxed as it wiggled in deeper. A second one joined it then a third. Jackie groaned at the way his ass stretched around them, at the delicious friction as they moved to and fro.

"Just like that," he murmured.

One of its fingers curled into his prostate, sending a burst of pleasure through him, while the other two pushed in even deeper. The pads of those digits rubbed along his inner walls, touching him deeper than anything ever had before. Thin wires squirmed against the inside of his hole while others coiled underneath the skin of the finger that massaged his gland. Jackie moaned and thrusted his hips against its palm. It was uncanny and unnatural, but it felt so, so good. His cock throbbed along with his rapid heartbeat, twitching and leaking onto his abdomen. He swore he could feel Arty's fingers at the back of his throat as they twisted around each other.

He needed to touch himself, needed to come with the sensation of those fingers sliding through his guts. Straining against his binds, Jackie cried out Arty's name. His house, his damned house, did nothing but shove the leather glove back inside his mouth. It withdrew its fingers, much to Jackie's displeasure.

Voicing his complaints with a whine, he pushed out his hips and clenched his ass to keep them there, but Arty let the copper tips of the wires poking through his free hand dig into his side and gave him another shock. He yelped, and with a grumble, relaxed. Arty slipped its fingers out and started to undo the buttons on its dark jeans. It pulled them down and stepped out of the legs, nude from the waist down.

Its dick didn't look anything like Jackie thought it would. He half expected a weapon to fall out of its pants, something as long as his forearm and as thick as a soda can. Instead, there was a pencil dick swinging between its legs. The length of it shone with something that he hoped was lube, but the skin sagged around it, like a shirt tossed over a drying line. A nice set of balls sat behind it, so at least having those bouncing against his ass was something he could look forward to, even if the skin on them undulated like they were filled with worms.

"You're lucky you're so good with your fingers and your mouth," He licked his dry lips. "Because *that* ain't gonna satisfy me."

With a roll of its eyes and a hand on his thigh, Arty slowly pushed himself inside Jackie down to the hilt, making sure no loose skin was left outside. Jackie shifted on the bed. The feeling wasn't necessarily bad, just weird. He didn't know how to describe it. It was like someone shoved a glove inside his ass. But there was a weight to Arty's cock, it sat in him like a roll of coins. Despite how unnatural it felt, he'd had worse things up his ass.

But then it expanded.

It started slow, slow enough that Jackie didn't realize it, but then there was a firm pressure expanding his hole, filling him completely. He arched his back as its cock grew until it felt like it was going to tear him in two. Jackie groaned. Legs trembling, his hands fisted the sheets as he writhed. Arty rocked against him, pulling out just enough so the friction of pushing itself back inside had Jackie scratching at the bed with the burn of it. He swore he could see it jutting out through his stomach with every thrust.

Arty gently rubbed the back of his thigh with its thumb. His pleasure built with every strained gasp. Heat bubbled in his core.

"Jac-kie," it purred.

"Arty," his choked cry rang in his ears.

It slipped its hand down to his weeping dick and gave him a firm stroke from the tip of his cock to the base. "Come."

Jackie came with a strangled groan. Hot cum splattered against his chest and stomach. Arty fucked him through his orgasm. Its slow, steady thrusts and thumb rubbing over the tip of his cock forced another one to rocket through his already aching body. Jackie slammed his palm against the bed three times.

By the time Arty pulled out, the wires around his limbs had unraveled and retreated back into the wall. Jackie laid limp on the bed, his legs having closed with a wonderful pop. He dragged his arm over his eyes as he breathed. Droplets of sweat raced down his chest, and his cock sat limp against his stomach. The skin suit fell to the floor with a wet *thump*, and Jackie knew that by the time he got up, it would have disappeared under the floorboards, Arty having swallowed it down to its underbelly.

He laid there for what felt like years, breathing heavily and letting his mind piece itself back together. The cold air of his house made his skin pebble. With a sigh, he sat up, shoulders hunched forward and softly groaning.

"Arty?" he asked.

His bedside lamp blinked out a greeting.

"Next time, I want you to ram that thick cock of yours into me as soon as you get me on the bed."

The lamp flashed out a series of letters he knew by heart. W-H-O-

"Whore," it said.

"Yeah, yeah," Jackie said with a smile. He rubbed at the angry, red indents pockmarking his wrists. His legs wobbled as he stood. "Actually, I've changed my mind. Next time, I want you to take me on the floor."

A sharp burst of pain against his ass had him stumbling forward with a squawk. He swatted at the offending wire, but it jerked out of range before he could touch it.

"Keep doing that, and I'm going to put termites in the walls."

"Haha," the lamp spelled.

"You think I'm joking, but I'm not."

More wires dropped from the ceiling, copper ends pointed at him with vicious intent. He took a step back.

"Hey, now," Jackie said, retreating another step toward the door. A wire slithered out from the wall.

The lamp flashed out another series of blinks. "Run."

Jackie turned and bolted out the door, laughing all the while.

I Know He's Not My Husband

Kris Morra

CW: Mentions of past spousal abuse, murder

I know you're not my husband.

Your clothes are the same (heavy black overcoat, scuffed leather boots, a navy-blue toque that's picked and frayed along the edge) though they're stretched to the seams. The scar beneath your chin (turned up like the edge of a hidden smile) is still present. Except its ragged depth has flattened, and the edges have smoothed. Even your eyes (blue, nearly grey) are so very close in colour I could be forgiven for thinking they're the same. And yet, I know you're not my husband.

Our routine is different. Off by the tiniest of degrees. There's a steady calm predictability that never existed before. Where the thump of heavy steps on the narrow exterior stairs once elicited nauseating dread, now butterflies take flight deep inside me.

I wait until I hear the sequential *thud thud* of your feet on the worn boards before I (anxiously, excitedly) stand. The final knock-off of the outside world (muck, animal shit, straw) from the soles of your boots against the doorframe. My hands find my hair, and I comb them through the strands in a vain attempt to look somewhat presentable.

Not that I think you care.

I've set the table for supper (meat pie, mashed potatoes, beer) always unsure if you'll eat. Unlike before, (stupid fucking cow, are you trying to kill me) there's no worry if I get it wrong. I no longer fear his disgust, the need to duck a plate thrown against the wall. Thickened gravy glacially traveling down worn paneling. Watery blood sliding down my face.

Not you.

You're appreciative and compliment my cooking, even if you never take a bite. Your eyes sparkle with anticipation, though I'm still not certain for what. It's not the sex. It can't be simply that.

I wait, trying not to hold my breath as the door slowly opens. "Hello." My smile flies to my lips, easy and light. "How was your day?"

Your gaze meets mine, and not for the first time, my heart skips a beat at the lust and affection you direct my way. "Good."

"I made supper." I never seem to know what to do with my hands, so I clasp them behind my back. "Did you want something to eat? Or did you want a bath first?"

"No." Your gaze moves down my body, lingering on my throat, breasts (lower) before leisurely returning to my eyes. "You."

After the first few nights I'd stopped wearing a bra

and panties. They'd get torn, and I was running out of pairs. Today I found a dress I haven't worn for at least three years. It accentuates my breasts, hugs my hips, and brings attention to parts of my body I preferred *he* never noticed. But I'm greedy for your gaze (nipples hard, pussy wet) and am happy when you kick off your boots and walk past the table toward me.

Your body doesn't cast off heat the way *his* did. The stench of pig shit and mud hasn't been ground into every crevasse of your skin. No, with you I smell the ocean (brackish, clean), the spray of the water still beaded on your coat. I hold your gaze for only a moment before I reach to undo the buttons and free you from the prison of fabric.

You hold your breath as I open the coat and push it down your shoulders, waiting for gravity to take it the rest of the way to the floor. I've never asked why you do that, though I suspect you worry I'll somehow realize that you aren't *him*, scream in terror, kick you out or run away. As though I hadn't been face-to-face with something far worse for the past ten years.

Marriage isn't for the faint of heart.

Your flannel shirt is damp, the fabric stuck to your skin, stretching the buttonholes wide. It makes it difficult to free the tiny plastic discs. My hands shake (anticipation, nerves, cold), my fingers fumbling with their task, but I don't relent until the smooth expanse of your skin is visible. Unlike *him* you lack hair on your chest. Your skin is smooth, soft and tinged blue. Pushing the flannel down your arms, exposing you fully to me, I smile as I allow myself the guilty pleasure of being allowed to simply look. Never before would I have risked this languid pace. I always needed *him* to finish quickly, wanting to scrub his scent from my skin. Leaving raw red streaks where his touch had been.

But not with you.

I can't meet your gaze (too close, eyes wider than they should be) so I focus on touching you. I draw small circles on your chest, across muscles barely contained by your cool skin. Your hands find my hips, your (webbed) fingers holding me while I explore, tease, learn the map of your body. Your patience is still unique (*what the fuck are you doing, you cow*), and I have to mentally tell myself to relax. To make the shift from defence to offence. Briefly, I feel in charge, ready to give you pleasure, to kiss and lick your sensitive parts. I even go so far as to lean in and lick the bony ridge between your pecs (salty), letting out a soft anticipatory moan.

That seems to be your breaking point.

I know you're not my husband, as you slowly slide the hem of my dress up, exposing my naked legs inch by inch. *His* touch had always been hard, demanding, forcing me open, his pleasure the only goal. Ironically, *he* never ripped my clothing, knowing it was necessary to cover the evidence of his presence.

Thoughts of *him* vanish as one, followed by a second, and then third soft tendril slide across my skin, as you caress my thigh. Your grip on my legs tightens (not painfully) as you use your hands to yank my dress up (too fast, fabric ripping) over my head and toss it aside. My nipples were already hard (cold, anticipation), my pussy wet from unbearable arousal.

"Look at me." There is no bite to your words; a request where there was once a demand.

Counting to three, I lift my gaze to meet yours. Your mask has slipped, allowing me to see the real you. Eyes grey like the sea, skin smooth like a stone begging to be tossed into the water. You lick your lips, the pink tip of your impossibly long tongue visible for only the briefest of moments.

I know exactly where I want that tongue to go.

He never would.

Shifting your hands to my waist, you lift me up and carry me to the window. My breath catches at the unexpected shift. In the past, you've taken me to bed, slid your cock into me until I saw stars. This is new. Unexpected. Exciting.

You turn me around so I'm facing the window, my naked body exposed to the sea beyond the cliff edge that borders the farm. The draft makes me shiver (no body heat), but I don't struggle to get away. No one lives close; no one will stumble upon our small home that's crusted with salt, mud, and shit. *He'd* long ago chased away what few friends I'd once had, leaving me lonely. The gulls (waxing and waning from sea to shore) and the pigs (screaming) became my companions.

"Come back to me." Your voice cuts through the past (pain). "Watch."

As your hands hold me tight, your undulating tentacles move once more up my legs. Gently pulling them apart, spread wide, exposing me completely to the universe. I'm a butterfly stretched and pinned, open for hungry gazes to devour. But you do more than simply look.

The tip of a tentacle travels along the inside of my thigh, caressing and teasing the skin with its feather-like touch. Only once early in our relationship did *he* ever touch me this way. It makes it easier to remind myself that you're you, and not *him*. My lids grow heavy and threaten to close.

"No. Watch the waves." Your voice is honey in my ear, your breath moist and heavy.

I do as you ask.

I focus on the lighthouse far off the coast. The silent *swoop* of the light turning in the distance, briefly illuminating the dangers on the water (the farm) before turning once more. The beacon is now my touchstone, reminding me of the world outside these four walls. That danger exists everywhere.

But not here. Not with you.

"Yes, love." You flick your tongue against the side of my throat, and I shiver. "Relax."

My muscles loosen as I give myself over to you. You've earned more trust in a few weeks than he could in ten years. "Please."

I feel you silently chuckle, your body rocking me. The teasing tentacle begins its upward journey once again, but this time there's no hesitation. I shiver at the first brush against the thatch of hair at my apex. The gentle probing, tugging at the short curls you yourself lack. You've been fascinated with the parts of me that are different. The slick folds of my labia are spread as you slide the tendril through, on its way to my clit.

A gasp escapes me as you press and slide across the one spot guaranteed to make me come. But you hold back with the pressure, still teasing when all I want is release. A second tendril joins the first, pressing and pulling me as you explore. This is familiar, we've done this a few times now, and I sink deeper into the sensations.

The third tentacle is unexpected.

"Relax." Your mouth is next to my ear, your breath a cool breeze.

The window holds your reflection, distorted by old glass. It's you, not the façade you seem to think I need, but your true self. Some might fear what they see, who (what) you are, but not me. I've seen the face of a true monster, and it looks nothing like you.

"I am relaxed."

"No." Another flick of your tongue, this time behind my earlobe. "You're holding back."

"I'm not, I'm—"

The third tentacle slides between my ass cheeks, across my hole pausing to tease the puckered muscle. "I'll hold you."

My lungs refuse to fully work. Shock strips away my last coherent thought as your grip tightens. Pressure increases ever-so-slightly and it's only then that I realize what you want from me.

I know you're not my husband, because *he* never cared enough to ask. No, *he* would take and take and take, stripping my defenses one hit, thrust, shout at a time. Not you. You wait, you tease, you lick and taste but don't press forward until you know for certain that

I'm here with you and this is also my desire.

"Yes." The word spills from my lips like a prayer, a blessing, a plea. "*Yes.*"

You wait little more than a heartbeat before you move all at once. Tentacles are everywhere, sliding across my skin, wrapping around my arms, teasing my nipples. One wraps around my throat (doesn't hurt, can breathe) and I can only watch in the hazy window reflection as it moves across my neck, curls around the back, to emerge on the other side, cradling my cheek.

The press of a wet tip against my pussy rips a moan from me, and you take the opportunity to slide the tentacle on my cheek into my mouth. Saliva pools as you stretch my jaw, the tip of the appendage resting midway on my tongue. You don't move it, making it hard to breathe and causing drool to drip from the corner of my mouth to slide down the side of my chin. My body wants to fight it *(choke on it, slut)* but you distract me by instead pushing your tentacle deeper into my pussy. I suck a harsh breath through my nose, as my head begins to spin.

I don't know how long you are (big, full, thick), but it doesn't matter. You fill me, stretch me, priming me for what I can only hope won't take much longer. I've come to love your gentle teasing, recognize your firm sensual caress and how you leave my body wanting more. What isn't familiar is the sudden pressure at my asshole. I tense. This isn't something I've done before, my thoughts race trying to piece together what the logistical consequences will be. My anxiety spikes and I thrash, needing to move away from the unknown (hurt).

"Calm." The entirety of your body squeezes briefly, before you relax, and my body dutifully follows suit. "I promise."

I'm not sure why (*Bitch, I promise you'll regret that*), but I've come to trust you. I nod, physically relaxing and mentally letting go.

I'm surprised at the pressure, the quick jolt of discomfort before the tight ring of muscles ease as you press your tip forward. You give me time to adjust (*he* never would), to accept you before inching forward. On the third forward movement, the tentacle at my pussy also moves.

Stuffed.

You're everywhere around me (filling, sliding, squeezing), and my brain can barely process the sensations. I don't fight you, even when the pressure around my throat tightens so hard that my vision dims, and my lungs lack the strength to fight the deprivation. Adrenalin surges through me, heightening my senses, pulling my world down to an elemental level.

You (not *him*) and me.

Your tentacles move in unison; slick appendages fill me with alternating forward thrusts and retreating slides. I'm stretched wide, my body shivers as I'm still held in place by your hands (tentacles) in the air before the window.

I'm so wet my arousal spills from my body, coating my pubic hair, the inside of my thighs. You're everywhere now. My ass stretched, the short, sharp bursts of pleasure echoing in my pussy, pulsing in my nipples. You (finally) pull your tentacle from my mouth, a river of drool chasing it out. I suck in a deep breath, sending more spots across my vision. When both tentacles thrust forward, simultaneously filling both holes, I scream.

It doesn't hurt. Far from it.

The sensations are new (overwhelming), but my body has accepted pleasure with the pain before. He'd yank my hair as he'd fuck me like one of his pigs. This is different, you're different. My body recognizes the difference, feeds on it. With each subsequent thrust the pain fades and only my rising lust remains.

"Yes." It's barely a whisper from my lips, but it might as well have been a scream. "Yes."

It's your turn to moan, a low rumble beside me. You sound like waves crashing upon the rocky shore. An entire storm contained within a cool, tentacled body. I feel my heat reflected back to me. Everywhere you touch (fuck) me has warmed you. You shiver (strange) but your unrelenting thrusts never stutter as you continue to fill me.

I know I won't be able to hold back much longer.

My impending orgasm forces my eyes shut, and no order (pleading) to open them would elicit my compliance. Losing my vision only serves to force my mind to cling to my remaining senses. The pressure around my throat tightens again, as you increase your thrusts. My body shakes, my head spins, and for a fleeting moment I think, *this is it. My death is here and it's beautiful.*

The first wave of my orgasm hits me by surprise. My muscles tighten around the tentacles inside me, squeezing back, holding them in place as waves of bliss consume me. Pleasure rolls over and through me, even as your tentacle constricts my ability to breathe. A riot of stars explodes behind my eyelids. Tears roll down my cheeks as my air-starved body tries to pull in a breath once, twice, three times. It hurts, it hurts so fucking much, the line between pleasure and pain blurred forever.

You ease back, the pressure gone, and I gasp.

Then I scream (again).

Another (the same) rolling orgasm rends me apart. You hold the tentacle deep inside my ass, but fuck my pussy with hard, deep thrusts. Stabbing my core until there's nothing left.

I collapse in your grasp, muscles useless, but my body doesn't move. You hold me there, supporting me, exposing me, and I'm too tired, too spent to try and hide.

I know you're not my husband. *He* never, *ever* made me feel this way.

This good.

This raw.

This is me, stripped bare (physically, emotionally) for the world to see.

Slowly, I feel you withdraw from inside me, your grip on my throat vanishes. Your hands are still around my waist holding me, suspending me. I'm unable to move, pleasure has sapped my ability to function. I might have passed out, unconsciousness choosing an inopportune time to wrap me in its embrace.

I rouse when you shift, my eyes open in time to catch sight of *them*.

Standing in the distance, on the rocks that protect our farm from the sea, are people (monsters, gods). The lighthouse beam illuminates them (grey skin, wet, watching) and you lift me up ever so slightly higher, like a prize won at a fair. The rocks writhe in the shadows, tentacles stretching up toward the sky like baby bird tongues seeking out the next juicy worm to consume. I'm a wriggling (willing) offering provided by their father. My head is heavy, and I let it fall to my chest. But you're there too, lifting my chin so my face is in full sight of the others. I hear the pigs screaming, grunting and banging inside their pen. The air vibrates and I feel warm, my head fuzzy.

Somehow, the world…shifts.

It's silently momentous, invisible to the rest of humanity, with only me as the (cause) witness.

I blink my heavy eyelids, and when my vision focuses once more, there's nothing. The rocks are barren (as am I), the air has cooled, and the pigs are once more silent. The lighthouse light is still there, silently *whooshing* in the distance. Even your grip on me has loosened. Was it a dream? Hallucination? Victory?

A sacrifice?

I must pass out again, because the next thing I feel is the slide of the pilled cotton sheets that cover the mattress as you lay me down. I turn my head and breathe in deep the scent of sex in the air. My post-coital haze is why I don't immediately realize that you're starting to leave. Panic squeezes my throat, where you'd been not long ago.

I know you're not my husband, because I never

would have wanted *him* to stay.

"Don't go." My voice is raw, painfully pushed out by bruised muscles. "Please. I need…"

It's not just your presence I crave. My brain can't put words to what I desire most. Instead, I try to project those emotions toward you, hoping you can somehow read the turmoil. My confusion over where the pain ends and the pleasure begins. How I both want you to consume me whole, while also needing to feel reverence in your touch.

I watch you hesitate. You're not looking my way, so I can't tell if you're still wearing *his* face. At this point it wouldn't matter. The paper-thin guise has been torn away, and I see the real you.

"Come to bed." I shift, making a little more room. "I need you to fuck me."

"I have."

"Not really."

"This isn't about sex."

"I know. I still want you."

Turning onto my side, I try to envision how I appear to you. My body is soft (thick thighs, rounded belly) but I know my strength. Besides, I can't imagine beauty standards mean anything to you. Then again, I've been wrong about such things in the past. My breasts sag, pulled by gravity toward the mattress, my skin red from where you held (squeezed) me. And yet, I know none of that is a deterrent for you. From the moment you opened the door all those weeks ago, I knew there was something else you'd been drawn to.

The darkness deep inside me.

He never noticed it.

My heart stutters when you turn around, your naked body laid bare before my eyes. I see your cock (nestled within a nest of tentacles) jutting out. My mind instantly moves to logistics, wanting to taste you, determining how best we can fit so I can feel you come inside me. I'm sore but that won't stop me from getting what I want.

I want you. I want to be consumed by you in all ways.

I also want the quiet parts too, despite not knowing if you're willing (able) to share them.

I don't understand what tonight was about (am I yours? theirs? dreaming) but it doesn't matter. Not really. You took what you needed when I stood at the window. Now, it's my turn.

Shifting so I can sit (legs beneath me, ass against my heels), I wait for you to come closer. You're tall and even sitting as I am, I need to lift my chin and lean forward to capture the tip of your cock in my mouth. Your skin is smooth and cool against my tongue. Sucking you, I close my eyes and let my hands wander as I tease and nip you with my teeth.

He would have hated it. Would have slapped me for daring to hurt him, before forcing his will on me. I don't think I would have been brave enough to have tried anything with him. I wouldn't have moved my hands across *his* body (tentacles), to tease *him* the way I can with you.

Sightless, I can almost imagine you as a kinder version of *him*. The man who'd flirted with me when he came into town to buy supplies for the farm. The desire that shone so clearly from his gaze when I wore a shirt with a low bustline, offering my breasts for his viewing pleasure.

I'd mistakenly confused desire with malice in his gaze, craving with cruelty in his smile; when I learned *his* truth, it was too late.

I know you're not my husband. You've never been cruel.

Your hands find my head and all remaining thoughts of *him* vanish. I let you guide me, open my mouth and throat so you can fuck my face so hard fireworks explode behind my lids. Tears slip down my cheeks to join the drool spilling from my mouth. Your grip (tentacles) wraps around my body to hold me, taking the pressure off my legs and sending a rush of pins and needles as the circulation returns. I'm choking on your cock, and I know there are worse ways to die.

My mind is devoid of thoughts as I'm brought back to my elements; blood, skin, bone, nerves, adrenaline, all working together as desire consumes me. I feel small but powerful as I gulp you down, my head swimming once more from the lack of oxygen as your thrusts grow deeper, more erratic. I need to come again. Need to grind my pussy on your long, cold appendage.

Spots fill my vision once more, only this time you don't slow down, give no quarter in your pursuit of pleasure. Fear prickles along my spine, the few thoughts I hold in my head evaporate, leaving one by one. There's nothing but a black void before me, tentacles around my wrists and ankles, holding me open and pulling me in.

Deeper.

Consumed by the void.

With effort, I find your torso with my hands and push back from your cock (the dark), once, twice, before gasping, I'm free once more. I look up at you (heart pounding, head spinning), our gazes meeting.

I know you're not my husband because you wait. You give me time (space) to figure out what I want. We could sit here for a minute or a day, and I know you won't press on without my consent. I get the impression that my surrender is part of the appeal to you. Just as my fear was the appeal to *him*.

With you, I have the power of choice. I can be yours, be with you until you no longer need me to be a part of your life (ritual) and I'm set aside. Or I can say it's been enough, that I'm spent, and no longer wish to be a part of what's to come. I know you'll respect me, snap my neck, and move on to another. Death lies in wait for me either way, but at least it's my decision how I wish for it to conclude.

With him, death couldn't come soon enough.

With you, I'm willing to stick around a bit longer.

Begging without words, I smile up at you. I slide my hands up along my (boney) ribcage to my breasts and squeeze them hard. Your wide eyes stare down at me as your grip loosens, giving me one final chance to leave (run). I don't and instead let gravity pull me backward so I can stretch out on the mattress. Springs press through the thinned padding to dig into my back, but I don't care. I lift my legs and spread myself wide open, my gaze now on your cock.

Please.

Please, fuck away the demon.

Pound out my memories of *him*. Of what he'd done to me.

What I'd done to him.

Shifting, you don't so much fall on top of me as slide (slither) until your chest presses to mine. Your cock (I think) brushes against my pussy, teasing with short pumps until you buck forward hard, filling me with a single thrust. A moan is ripped from my chest as you continue to fill me over and over, my inner muscles trying to grab and hold you, only to lose their grip. The light is on, something *he'd* always hated, but it lets me see everything as you fuck me. The mundane and the bizarre.

My cunt is full and each press of your body against it ratchets my desire higher, making it difficult to breathe without fear of combustion. Pressure of your hand (tentacle) between our bodies sends a jolt through me as you squeeze my nipple, force your finger (tip) between us to the top of my clit. There's no chance I'll last much longer. Pleasure warms my insides, threatens to spill from me any moment.

Your mouth finds my shoulder, your teeth clamping down on my skin as your tongue licks the salt away. Pain and pleasure are indistinguishable; your hands, mouth, body, are everywhere. This mix is new, exciting, pain with purpose instead of for its own sake. You bite the side of my neck, the top of my breast, while continuing to fuck me hard. I can't think. Can't exist.

Don't exist.

I'm everything without *him*, and nothing without you.

I'm crying now, thrashing beneath you, needing the bliss that comes with release. I hear you chuckle, knowing you'll give me what I want in your own time. You increase the pressure on my clit and with another hard pump into me, my body contracts as my orgasm tears through me. My nipples scrape against your chest as I buckle and shake in your grasp. Wave after wave assaults the very fiber of my being with joy, the intensity threatening to drag me once again into unconsciousness.

But not this time.

Before my orgasm subsides, I sit up and, using my momentum and your surprise, I roll us. Now on your back, I continue to drive myself down on your cock. My fingers dig into your chest as I grind on you, milking your body for the thing I want. I feel you shiver (my eyes still closed), feel you impossibly wrap yourself around me. Squeezing again, trying to hold me still.

I don't relent.

The tension eases, giving me once more the freedom to fuck you with my body. Over and over, I throw myself against you, like the waves upon the rocks hidden from the lighthouse light. You shudder, the air around us becomes heavy (petrichor), and for a heartbeat everything stops.

Your roar shakes me as your orgasm slams into you. I hear you vibrate through my mind, assaulted with thoughts (small, frail, mine) and feelings (possessive, fear, cherished) that aren't mine. I'm no longer the one moving as your hands grasp my waist to hold me still as you fuck up. Your come fills me, spills from me, and I can't help but come again. Smaller but no less profound.

As quickly as the storm hits, everything stops. Our ragged breathing co-mingles, and I don't fight when you encourage me to lay down on your chest. I can't hear your heartbeat (do you have one?) and the last thought I have before sleep claims me is how *he* never held me like this.

I *know* you're not my husband.

Your clothes are the same, though their fit is off. The scar beneath your chin is still present. Even your eyes are so very close in colour. And yet, I know you're not my husband.

I know, because I shot *him*—shot Jacob—point blank.

Did you know that a shotgun's muzzle at such a close range can scorch the flannel of a shirt? I do now. I watched as hundreds of tiny buckshot ripped through his skin, like fleshy frequent buyer punch-cards. My smile as my finger squeezed the trigger had been easy, natural, as was the overwhelming sense of relief when it was over. The shock in his eyes, his mouth agape as he stood staring at me was a first (last) for him. Blood dripped and pooled on the tops of those worn, leather boots he refused to clean before he'd come into the house after mucking the pen.

The joy I felt as I waited for his final blink before he collapsed into a heap on the floor.

Dead.

Finally, fucking dead.

Even if I hadn't snuffed the light out of his cold, emotionless eyes, I would have known you were different. Jacob never cared about my pleasure, my likes and dislikes. Never took the time to do anything beyond rutting into me, ignoring my pain at his careless thrusts into my dry vagina. Ignored my sobbing so he could leave me in bed and go eat in silence.

He'd treated his pigs better.

I know you're not Jacob, because I remember the ache in my back as I dragged his still warm corpse out of the house, down the stairs, and across the yard. The wheelbarrow had been tempting, but there was no chance I had the strength to lift his dead weight into it. So, I continued to yank and pull him inch by inch across the yard toward the pen's gate.

The pigs did the rest.

I wake from my half-slumber when you slip out of the bed from beside me. I don't try to stop you this time, knowing you'll be back sooner than later.

"I must go." Without looking back, you reach for me; your long finger (tentacle) caresses my upper thigh beneath the sheets. "My work calls."

"Okay." I smile, my heart alight with love. I know you see the real me, know what I've done, and accept (celebrate) me for who I am. "Be safe."

You move slowly, stuffing yourself into ill-fitting clothing, damp and salt-stained from the ocean. Pulling the blankets to my chin, I turn and watch as you slip on Jacob's blood-spattered overcoat (I'd tossed it in the barn) and move to the door. You stop, look back at me, the coat shifting and writhing as it cocoons you. "I'll return."

"Tomorrow?" *(I love you).*

You hesitate before nodding. "Tomorrow."

There's a part of me that knows this won't last forever. Whatever happened tonight was a prequel to something far larger. Something I doubt I'll survive. I don't care. I can't care because I deserve whatever punishment the universe will dole upon me. Sooner or later, the void claims us all.

You step out into the night, and softly close the door behind you.

I know you're not my husband.

But you *are* my everything.

The Devil-Tree
Tristan Marlowe

CW: Blood, cults, breeding

The bones of old trees are heavy with sorrow.

A high school girlfriend had let Henry read her poetry once, scribbles of smeared black on the creamy pages of a hardback journal. That had been the single line he'd committed to memory, struck by its resonance.

Henry had a strange connection to trees, felt more at home in the vine-and-bramble-choked woods than he did in brick or steel. He had a special spot on the outskirts of town, a hilly expanse of field gone to wilderness, rumored to have been a burnt down plantation, now home to snakes and rabbits and wild blackberries. A tree loomed over the frothing meadow; a massive oak rooted deep into the loamy soil. A writhing mass of exposed roots thicker than Henry's legs swarmed down the side of the hill. As a child he wondered how the tree didn't topple over the edge. As he grew into a puberty both romantic and violent he imagined the roots snaking down to the center of the earth itself. He saw them encircling a flame-lashed lair where devils danced, their lust and laughter rushing along the roots as if they were telephone lines, spiraling up to the surface and sending out a luring mortals with their subterranean magic.

He'd lain with that girl under the old oak, on grass that always sprouted lush and verdant beneath its gnarled canopy. Her name had been Abbey, and he remembered her scuffed combat boots and fishnets under cutoff jean shorts. They'd smoked hand-rolled cigarettes laced and listened to Smashing Pumpkins CDs on her knockoff Discman. Sometimes Henry brought a bottle of three-dollar screw-top wine, the candy-grape flavor passed between them as they swapped spit.

He was 28 now, and had escaped that town, that girl, but remembered the tree, remembered the poetry, could summon the taste of sweet wine on cool tongues. That tree hadn't been sorrowful. Most trees were, he felt, whenever the silken pads of his fingers slid over rough bark, feeling the weight of centuries, the rich feast of decomposition that fed each leaf and branch, roots sucking up the trauma of buried bodies and man-poisoned soil.

Abbey had called him a "nature spirit" when he'd talked of communing with trees and dead things and the tiny little hidden creatures in the woods. Then again, she'd also called him Beth, which had been his name before he left the town, driving away its memory with each syringeful of hormones the needle delivered into his thigh. Now he only thought of it when he was wrapped deep in sleep, or let his mind go wandering. He was supposed to be straightening the shelves, filing away books that customers had leafed through and abandoned in other sections, Stephen King mingling with self-help.

He hadn't moved so very far away, maybe an hour inland. The city was small and stacked with blue voters, anchored by a liberal university. There was a flavor of southern *laissez faire* in its debauched nightlife and artistic community, but it moved at a lightning pace compared to the town he'd escaped, with its faded Main Street, weed choked trailer parks, and the oak with the roots that slithered down to the center of the earth.

He was content with the little life he'd built, the room he rented in the sprawling farmhouse near the college, the job at Jim's Books that paid his scant bills. He loved old books, the rich dusty perfume of them, the yellowed pages, even the soft crumbling edges of paperback covers. Old books were as full of stories as old trees, the ghostly fingerprints burnt onto their pages more fascinating to him than the words printed there. He slid right into place at the bookshop as if he'd been shelved there, too. He welcomed the comfort of Jim's casual mentorship, his war stories and cautionary tales. In return he got the shop back in order, updated the website, hell, he'd even gotten Jim's collection of dying lilies and devil's ivy to thrive. Jim remarked once on his magic touch with the plants, and Henry had shrugged, a cool finger stroking his spine as some dim brain-root recalled stars winking at him through serpentine branches, the warm pulse of the earth against his bare back.

His life was contained within a five-mile radius of work, home, and the tangle of local bars and cruising spots- all within biking distance. His hookups weren't frequent, but there was always a low-grade fever of yearning that simmered along his nerve endings. The yearning wasn't precisely romantic, but authentic connections seemed to elude him, and it wasn't slated by even the filthiest trysts. Maybe it was a side effect of growing up in someone else's body. Maybe it was wanderlust. Every time the brass bell jangled above the shop door, his eyes swung to the doorway, wondering if someone would come in and turn his life upside down one balmy magnolia-scented afternoon.

On this particular evening, Jim was calling to him across the aisles, announcing the imminent arrival of a graphic novel collection Henry was slathering to get his hands on. It was one of the few times he didn't hear the jangle of the bell.

"You might be selling half that fucking collection to me," he yelled back, eyes on his cart.

A lean, black-haired stranger appeared before him, green eyes probing under a dark slash of brow. Henry's next breath caught in his throat, and he choked on his own spit. He tried to pass it off as a cough contained in his fist, but Green Eyes smirked a little, and Henry grit his teeth against the surge of lust that seemed to funnel all the blood in his body into a meaty throb in his boxers.

"Help you find anything?" He slid a book from his cart onto the shelf and prayed it was the right location.

"Yeah, do you have an art section? Like, engravings, photography, that kinda thing."

"Yeah." He scratched at his limp auburn curls, glad he'd worn his good jeans, and the dark green flannel that complemented his coloring. "Back here." He sidestepped Green Eyes neatly and led him to the back of the shop, where they kept the coffee table art books and a rack of posters.

"Looking for anything in particular?"

"Yeah." As Green Eyes furrowed his brow, scanning the shelves, Henry scanned him. He was tall and raw-boned, and the black hair looked natural. His hands were too big for his narrow wrists, and he jammed them into the pockets of the leather jacket that was far too warm for this humid September.

He plucked an HR Giger off the shelf and flipped through the pages, stopping to admire a Lovecraftian mass of cables here, a biomechanical monster goddess there.

"I have one of those at home," Henry volunteered. "Giger's so fascinating."

Green Eyes shrugged. "I guess. I like the erotic aspect, anyway."

He quirked a brow, and Henry willed his blotchy skin not to blush.

"I was looking for something a bit more mundane, but I think it's out of print. It's a photography book, *Charmed Homes of the Low Country*, edited by L.S. Hilton, foreword by Graham Sully."

"Doesn't...sound familiar," Henry trailed off. It sounded like the touristy shlock one found stacked near sweatshirts emblazoned with palm trees and *South Carolina* in a potpourri-scented gift shop.

"Well, shit. I haven't been able to find a copy yet." Green Eyes didn't seem disappointed, and his thin red lips turned up at the corners. "You've heard of Graham Sully, though? Born and bred right in this fair city."

Henry wanted to pretend that he had, desperate not to look uncool. Jim, two aisles over, was frowning at them.

"No, I haven't, actually," he allowed, raising a questioning brow at Jim, who was beelining towards them now.

"Ah, man. Horror writer. Good stuff, really. You like horror, Henry?"

Chills raked the back of his neck, until he remembered his name tag, the one that Green Eyes may or may not have glanced at.

"Love it," he said, matching Green Eyes look for look with a straightened spine.

Something bright and hot flared in those green eyes, and the simmer of desire stirring in Henry's belly sizzled into a brush fire.

Jim was right on them then, straightening books that did not need straightening.

His teeth showed in his silver beard, his smile welcoming, but the eyes behind his silver rimmed specs were icy.

"Haven't heard that name in a while," he said. "Lovecraft of the Low Country, they called him. He was popular in the Seventies, Henry. His work is out of print, though I come across a copy or two now and then. How did you hear about him, young man?"

Green Eyes' lips stretched and pursed on his rubbery face as he stifled a laugh. "My mom had all his books. I got into them when I was about 13. She kept those in a bookcase with a locked glass door. I knew where she hid the key."

"Dark stuff for a kid," Jim grinned.

"'s why I liked it," Green Eyes smiled back. His teeth were very white, and sharp and crooked as splintered bone.

"Well, I'm sorry, but we don't carry any of his work here. You might have better luck on the internet. If you're interested in historical homes, though, I know a few titles I could look up for you."

"Appreciate it, but I should get going." Green Eyes glanced at the shop door, then back at Henry. "Thanks for your help, anyway."

"No problem at all." Jim's smile was more genuine, then, and he strolled back towards the register.

"That was kinda weird," Henry half-whispered.

Green Eyes treated him to that searing smirk again and leaned close. Henry inhaled, his eyes nearly fluttering shut at his scent, firesmoke and oiled leather.

"I'm Ty, by the way. You get off soon?"

"About thirty minutes." Henry toyed with the button on his shirt cuff, trying not to let his nerves show.

"Cool. Well, I'll be at The Lighthouse if you wanna hang." Shaggy black bangs fell into his eyes as he flicked his head in the general direction of the diner down the street.

"Yeah, I think I can do that."

"Good." A crooked grin that stopped Henry's breath, and Ty was striding to the door, slipping through it with barely a sound from the bell.

Henry saw that his cart was empty, and he shoved it towards the back room. He'd get it later. Now, he had to interrogate Jim.

"So what was all that weirdness about, Captain Cryptic?"

Forty-five minutes later, Henry was on his way to The Lighthouse, heart hammering. The night air, although cut with a cool breeze, wasn't that refreshing. Jim had spooked him a little, spun him some tall tales he'd have to Google when he got home.

According to Jim, Graham Sully had produced five novels in the span of five years and then vanished without a trace. The foreword to the book Ty sought had been the last known thing he'd written, and that had been published in 1980.

"I wouldn't get mixed up with that guy if I were you," Jim had said casually enough, arms crossed as he leaned against the exposed brick. "There was a mythos to Sully's work, an occult element that appealed to teenagers and other types looking to experiment. I don't want to use the word cult, but the fan base is rather...eccentric."

Henry shrugged it off then and shrugged it off now. If Ty was in some pagan sex cult, well, would that be so bad?

He laughed at himself, spotted a shaggy black head bent over a cup of coffee through the diner window, and stepped over the threshold.

Ty straightened up in the booth. His smile dazzled, and the morbid chill Henry had felt in the store was forgotten. He sank down onto the familiar red vinyl, deaf to the chatter of the glamorously tattered goths and the university burnouts scarfing chili fries and waffles.

They went through a couple of coffees each, the small talk lazy, natural.

"How about pie? I feel like pie," Ty said, an hour or so in. Then Henry was spearing his own slice of chocolate peanut butter pie, chasing it with ice water, not enough of a masochist to brave a third coffee at this hour.

"So, my boss thinks you're in some kinda cult," he found himself saying halfway through the pie.

Ty barked out a laugh, scraped his fork over the crumbs of pecan and swirl of caramel left on his plate, then brought it to his mouth and licked it, winking at Henry.

"Did he warn you away from me, honey?" His voice was between a growl and a purr, and Henry's boxers were getting sticky.

"Maybe. Almost creeped *me* out a little, and I don't scare easily. So are you a Graham Sully worshipper?"

Another laugh, a sweep of large bony fingers through that crow-feather thatch of hair. "A worshipper? Nah. Actually, *hell* no. Inspired by his ideas, yes. But then I'm inspired by a lot of things. The sky, the earth, food. Sex. Alley cats and junkyard rats. Even by you, Henry."

Henry rolled his eyes. "Smooth. So what was so special about that book you were looking for?"

"It was the last thing he published, of course," Ty sighed, slouching down into the booth. "I've come across supposed transcripts of it online, but never more than that. And even so, the context isn't there, because the rest of the book isn't."

"What's the big deal? Isn't it a bunch of pictures of whitewashed plantation houses and Spanish moss? The glorious cotton palaces of inbred slaveowners?"

Ty glared, then. It was definitely a glare. His pale cheeks were striped with red, and it was no coy blush.

"You have no clue, Henry. No clue about anything. There were a couple of antebellum mansions in there. Ones that most wouldn't like to find themselves in after dark. The rest were just houses. The common link wasn't the scenery, but the things that happened there."

"So haunted houses? Not surprising. Haunted places are getting to be quite the tourist draw."

"There was one house," Ty said, eyes gone hazy, seeing through and past Henry. "There are no known photographs of it, it burned down before the War, but there was a period etching in the book. Not so far from here, actually. It was thought to be a plantation, but there are no records of crops grown there. It was built by a wealthy landowner, last name of Dawes, in the early 1800s. I've heard that it was more of a fortress than a house, all made of stone, yet it burned. I don't know. Sully's foreword is thought to be a code, something that reveals the mystery of the Dawes home. May be bullshit. Maybe not. But I love a puzzle."

The charming Ty was back then, and Henry gulped ice water as Ty nibbled at the end of his fork, watching him through lowered lashes.

Ty walked him home, and their conversation for those three blocks was light and easy again. Henry found himself rambling about those days back home, sugary sweet wine and kisses under the old gnarled oak. How a girl had once called him a nature spirit, and clasped hands with him as they pressed their foreheads to the massive roots that curled and wound and snaked their way into the earth.

"You wanna hang out tomorrow night? There's a low-key party outside of town, not too many people. Lots of alcohol and weed."

"Store closes at four on Sunday," Henry smiled, leaning against the front door with his arms crossed.

"Excellent. So I'll pick you up here, say around seven?"

"Excellent."

Ty looked down at his feet. "Sleep well, nature spirit."

"Back atcha." Henry bit his lip, wondered if he should make a move, and then Ty was walking down the porch steps, throwing up a casual wave as the night swallowed him up.

His hands were down his boxers as soon as he climbed into bed, thighs quaking at the vision of fucking Ty in the coiled hollow of that ancient oak. The orgasm was sudden and sharp, almost painful, and he regretted its brevity. He meant to try for a second round before sleep sucked him down into the dark.

Ty was on his porch again exactly at seven, still in unseasonable leather. His green eyes sparkled, and he was jittery, almost nervous. There was a snap of electricity as their fingers brushed by accident, arms swinging into each other as they walked to his ride.

It was a 1980 Camaro, because of course it was, with a dull silver body that opened up to reveal black vinyl seats.

"Sexy car," Henry smirked as he slid inside, inhaling the nostalgic perfume of the car. It was a patchwork of scents, the mustiness of age, the rawness of the vinyl. Even the dash and molded plastic console carried a scent, faded summers and ancient smoke, spilled beer on sunbaked asphalt.

"Did you expect anything less?" Those crooked teeth flashed in the shadows, and he clapped his large hand down on Henry's thigh. A bro-tastic gesture of camaraderie, had Henry's thigh not been bare, had Ty's thumb not lingered, stroking the fine hair on his legs.

"Fuck," Henry breathed after a heartbeat.

Ty was grinning, starting the Camaro up with a throaty rumble, goosing the gas pedal to rev the engine just a bit.

"Not yet," he drawled, steering them away from the curb and gunning it down the street.

Henry looked down at his thigh as if expecting to see a flaming handprint. There was nothing but his pale leg peeking out from black denim shorts. His legs were muscled from biking, and he realized now that the shorts and his Docs and his untucked Misfits shirt was a callback to Abbey. Would Ty drink wine with him, make out with him under a tree, quell his endless yearning?

The stereo was stock, with only a radio and cassette

player. Ty had *Ministry* in the deck, the muted industrial noise at odds with the scenery they sped past, towering pines and glowing white churches and a picturesque cemetery. And once, a swamp, cypress trunks rising from murky water, gloomy overlords of the life writhing beneath them. Henry cracked his window, letting the warm breeze brush his cheek, fill his nose with the fetid funk of swamp.

The sun went down as they drove, and Henry rummaged in the plastic grocery bag Ty had dropped between his feet. A jumbo-sized bottle of wine, not the cheap paint-peeling shit he used to drink, but less than twenty bucks. A pack of Marlboro Reds, two bottles of Coke, a couple of packages of Lance crackers.

"Can I?" He plucked out one of the Cokes and waved it in Ty's periphery.

"All yours," Ty winked.

As the stars came out, the faded blue along the horizon sunk to black, the roads felt strangely familiar. The air blowing through his window was cooler, and smelled of honeysuckle and wooden church pews, old bibles covered in fake leather. He swallowed a mouthful of lukewarm Coke, telling himself all small Southern towns seemed familiar.

"I'm glad I met you, Henry," Ty was saying, switching off the stereo now. "You charmed me. So I wanted to bring you here. I think you'll like it. It'll be different than the last time you were here, but also the same."

His guts seemed to crawl up inside him and choke his heart when he saw the scrubby stretch of sidewalk Ty was pulling up to, and the hill that faced it, and the tree with a massive trunk that grew up and up until you could barely see its end in the black.

"What the fuck," he mumbled. He stared into bag between his feet, the convenience store bag of regular things, things that were sold in a world where trees did not have secrets.

"You're going to have fun. I promise," Ty murmured, voice gone velvety, cool fingers on Henry's thigh again, stroking and squeezing.

Henry looked at him, a bewildered laugh bubbling from his throat. How was this sexy and not sinister, why wasn't he recoiling from the sight of that looming hill?

But he wasn't, and his hand was warm in Ty's bony grip as they crossed the road, and he was leading then, he was pulling Ty to the eroded hillside with its roiling eruption of tree roots. He stood before it, and why would there be fear? He'd only known love there, love and the urgent rush of teenage lust. He gripped a cool, glassy-smooth root with both hands, his touch light, reverent. He felt the energy thrum as always, the magic pulsing from some hidden core into his palms. He grabbed for Ty's hand and pressed it to the root, his dick throbbing at Ty's gasp.

Henry leaned in, arm circling Ty's leather waist, letting himself be pushed away.

"Not yet." His voice was hushed, eyes hidden in the dark. "There's the party on the hill. Major festivities," he quipped with a twist of a grin, though his eyes were uneasy, skittering towards each little animal sound, each gust of wind.

"Mmm, wine," Henry nodded, spying the bottle he'd brought with them. "Let's go."

He let Ty drag him up the hill, over gopher holes and through knee high grass, till they reached the tree.

There were blankets and cushions scattered at its base, candles flickering in lanterns hung from its lowest branches. Perhaps a dozen people gathered there, smoking and drinking, small in the shadow of the tree. In their twenties, most of them, a few into their thirties, their clothing loose and hanging off their bodies as if their attire were about to be swept away by the wind. A boombox played, Henry thought it might be Sisters of Mercy. He wanted to giggle.

"Heyyy!" Ty called. "We're here!" He lifted their linked arms overhead, and they were met with glazed smiles, merry laughter, and a few triumphant whoops.

The crowd parted, allowing them the prime spot in the middle, and they stood, while the others wilted to the ground around them, relaxing into each other, passing joints and pipes around. The fragrance of weed and clove mingled with honeysuckle and sweetgrass made Henry positively dizzy.

Ty twisted the cap off the bottle, flicking it into the grass, and lifted it to his lips. His throat worked as he swallowed, and Henry eyed the pale skin with hunger. He wanted to sink his teeth in. Instead, he accepted the bottle, drinking deep himself. The flavor was dark and rich, a smooth red blend that was far more palatable than the wino juice he'd drunk years ago. But he missed the sweetness of it.

They passed the bottle several times, and the smoke

and the booze made Henry's head swim, made his blood flow south, plumping him up till he was hot and wet and ready to rut.

Ty kissed him then, pulling him almost up on tiptoe and into the gaunt heat of his body, letting him feel the blood-hot bulge under his jeans. Henry let himself be pulled, and his tongue stroked Ty's, and he smiled against those hungry red lips. The kiss deepened, warmed, simmered till they both shook with dopey need.

Ty broke away, thrust Henry's hand inside his boxers. Henry squeezed and then stroked the velvety flesh. He sank to his knees, pulling Ty free of the rumpled cotton, admiring the flushed, pulsing length of him. He ran his finger along the soft dome to watch the clear bead of liquid resting in the slit, gleaming like honeysuckle nectar. He touched his tongue to the nectar, and it wasn't as syrupy as the flower's essence, but it was sweet, nonetheless.

"Oh god," Ty groaned somewhere above his head as Henry sucked half his cock into his mouth. The music had stopped, as had the conversation, and the group watched each lick and bob with hushed reverence.

Ty spread his shaky legs, bracing his feet apart to remain standing, glancing down at Henry's and then throwing his head back again, eyes closed against the weakening pleasure that each suck brought.

"Oh, my god," he moaned, willing his mind to go blank as he cradled Henry's skull in his hands. "Oh, my God, and Goddess in One, my pleasure is for Thee, my offering is for Thee." He thrust shallowly, in and out of the wet heat of Henry's mouth, as he repeated the sentence, over and over, till it became a chant.

Henry barely heard the words that buzzed around him. He slowly suckled the flesh into himself, savoring the salt and heat of Ty, the pulsing tremble of it, the way its nectar slickened its glide over his tongue. He felt the words more than heard them, felt them quicken into a hundred hushed breaths, felt the urgent thrust in his mouth, and he moaned around it. He pulled off, gripping it, wanting to see the throb and twitch, each spurt of seed before he swallowed it.

He clapped eyes with Ty as he stroked him.

"Come," he said, voice dark and low, and Ty cried out as his cock jumped in Henry's grasp, shooting onto Henry's curled tongue, the last spurts oozing down his hand like melted ice cream.

Henry hummed, swallowing the salty-bitter essence, lapping the remnants from his hand. Life. He needed it in him, needed a long deep drink of it, a thousand cocks spurting over his tongue, down his throat, making him swell with the glut of their pleasure. His ears rang, barely registering the soft chant around him, an echo of Ty's words.

Ty stripped off his jacket and black pullover, shucked off his jeans and then his shoes. Henry sat back, watching wordlessly.

Ty knelt beside him then, peeling him bare, pulling the shirt over his head, unbuckling the studded belt and yanking his shorts down impatiently.

"I'm trans," Henry warned, head swimming with wine.

"Hot," Ty said with a rough, hungry grin as he slid down his body, taking the rest of Henry's clothes with him.

And Ty's tongue was as hot as his cock, dripping wet as it dragged over Henry, getting him soaking wet front and back and then plunging inside him. Henry convulsed around him, crying out roughly, and then Ty's mouth was on his dick, the suction loose and sloppy just the way he liked it, those slender long fingers shoved into him. Henry strangled Ty's head with his thighs, bucking up against him. There was nothing but cricket song and soft voices chanting and the lightning strikes of pleasure that ripped up Henry's inner thighs and into his gut, and he saw the stars through gnarled branches as he came.

He twitched around Ty's fingers for a moment more before he withdrew, and he fell back against the earth, against the blankets cushioning the tree, and keeping his thighs splayed, soaked cunt bared to the night. He saw through his heavy lids that the other partygoers had now shed their loose garments, and were stroking each other's bodies, murmuring as Ty stood before them, regal despite his slumped posture and the limp cock that curled wetly against its nest of hair.

"We are thirteen gathered here, thirteen committed to the pleasures of flesh and darkness, thirteen drunk on lust and wine, thirteen awaiting your arrival. Oh my God, and Goddess in one, we await your arrival, we offer you a Mate, a vessel for your Lust, ready for your Seed. Accept our offering, Horned One, Mother and Father. Let the Gates of Gehenna open and loose you upon our world."

The responding murmur of the throng became a rumble, and Henry felt the roots of the tree writhe and pulsate within the earth, saw the strike of heat-lightning against the black horizon. He thought he saw dim pillars rising from the earth, ghostly as smoke, a resurrected fortress.

"Gehenna, Gehenna," was the hushed chant as Ty drew the inverted pentacle on Henry's belly, just above his pubes. He hadn't even felt the knife cut into his arm, and he licked his lips as he watched the slow trickle of blood down his elbow. Ty was hard and throbbing again as he sketched the shape on Henry's flesh with Henry's blood, and his left hand pumped his cock as the chant became "Baphomet, Baphomet, we await Thee" and then his palm was full of jizz that shimmered like moonstone in the thin light of the crescent moon, and this he painted over the blood that was already drying on Henry's skin.

Blood and milk, earth and water, fire and…Henry's head swam and so he lay it back down at the base of the tree, felt the heat between his legs throb again, and he spread his thighs open further.

"Come to me," he said softly, rocking his hips against nothing, needing to be filled, finally filled, by a spirit black as he was green. Needed to be rooted, finally, to the earth.

They were between his legs then. They were leaning over him, a darkened figure trailing lean, smooth hands over his thighs, hips, the flatness of his chest. The slender fingers were tipped in pearly claws that drew blood with each whisper-soft swipe. Henry did not fear the horns silhouetted against the sky, nor the horizontal slash of pupils set into brimstone eyes, nor the silky black hair covering Their head. He breathed deep of Their hot animal scent, his dick pulsing, his thighs wet with arousal. Their breasts swayed as They hovered over him, the curved blade of Their cock jutting up, its purple head glistening.

He gripped his thighs under the knees, pulling them up nearly to his shoulders, displaying his hole to them in lurid invitation. Their hands gripped his shoulders, and Their flesh was smooth and warm with a velvety nap Henry groaned in pleasure when their claws sank into his flesh, anchoring him to the ground. Their breath came in hot pants as Their cock dragged over him until it was bathed in his fluids. The plum-sized head parted his cunt lips as it pushed forward, engorged and relentless, invading him in one long, endless thrust. The head of Their cock pushed against the very end of his tunnel, Their length stretching each pleat of his walls until he was filled completely, so full he could barely breathe. A growl came from Their chest as Their hips stuttered forward, rocking Their body into Henry's, Their full, soft breasts swinging above his face.

He craned his neck, latching onto a large, diamond-hard nipple with his greedy mouth, and he sucked hard, pulling another rumble from Their chest. Each suck drew a dark syrup onto his tongue, a fluid both sweet and smoky, and Henry moaned, spasming around the cock that split him in two.

The chanting rose, and he saw the twelve were

fucking around him now, hips thrusting to Their rhythm, a puzzle of bodies, duos and trios writhing in unbearable pleasure, echoing Henry's cries as the Creature drove into him. Their hips moved in short quick strokes now, rutting into him, and he came a second time, and then a third, his slick hands losing their grip on his thighs and letting them fall open limply as he accepted the Creature into his body.

He clung to Them weakly, his body driven forward with each thrust, the sticks and stones beneath the blanket abrading his back. He gazed into the alien heat of Their eyes, and the air was thick with the grunts and cries of this mating dance.

"Fuck me, fill me, fuck me, fill me," Henry mumbled over and over as he lost the strength to cry out.

They were fucking into his limp, boneless flesh without mercy, and he fancied he was sinking into the Earth, that They were driving him into it, and the chant around him escalated, the brimstone eyes flashing scarlet as Their cock slid in and out of his stretched hole. They released his shoulders, and Henry felt his pierced skin slip away from Their claws as They spread his thighs so wide he thought his pelvis might break. Their breath came harshly as They watched Their cock thrust into him, and it was throbbing now, the sensation so intense Henry rolled his eyes up, trembling towards another orgasm.

"I am a vessel for Thy seed," he said in a ragged whisper, not knowing where the words came from. "Breed me as Thou hath claimed me."

"Breed, breed, breed," the voices echoed, the pleasure

of the throng culminating in staccato thrusts and jets of ejaculate.

The Creature roared, the moon glinting off Their horns as Their cock jumped within Henry's stretched sheath and pumped fire into him. They thrust slow and hard, growling all the while, Their cock spurting arcs of black and viscous spunk on each out-thrust, splattering over his pubes and throbbing dick, and They brought Their fist down on his dick in the extremity of Their pleasure, and he screamed into the night, shuddering as his hips bucked in Their hold. He clenched around Their spurting cock, sucking the black milk from Them, sucking it up into his body, feeling it warm him as the wine had.

They were gone from him abruptly, pulling away from his tattered body and gazing at the stars, rising, standing, and then seeming to float above the Earth as they dissipated in a dark mist.

Henry groaned, clutching his knees and rocking back and forth. He gazed down at the ruin of his crotch, his dick and hole still twitching, his pubes matted with inky fluids.

He flopped onto his front as the pleasure subsided, shoved himself up onto shaky elbows, and then somehow rose to his knees clutching onto the rough bark of the devil tree. It whispered to him now, it whispered and it sang.

Eyes gazed up at him, eyes attached to the naked bodies collapsed in their piles of human stink. Dumb eyes, awestruck eyes. The bodies knelt as Henry passed on quaking legs, thighs streaked with the slick of his cum and the Seed of a demongod.

His bare feet parted the sweetgrass and nettles, the rabbits running from him, the snakes curling around him, as he descended the hill. This time, when he traced the serpentine arteries of the tree that fed the earth, the roots writhed, and then parted, the space between them glowing with eldritch light.

Henry smiled, and slipped inside. He was Home.

Otherworld Tattoo
Bex Newton & Elle Waters

The tattoo shop appeared overnight. The awning caught Caleb's eye one morning as he stumbled his way to the subway, cursing the mess of slush and ice that soaked into his boots. Winter mornings were dark as fuck, frozen in a stillness his off-balanced shuffling rudely interrupted. Bold across the window, gold-plated lettering seemed to shine, and he dimly wondered what kind of paint they had used to get that effect.

Otherworld Tattoo, the luminous letters proclaimed. They curled in a way that made him think of teeth. Something about the typeface was reminiscent of hot breath on your neck, conjuring the same sense of anticipatory fear that you have when you hear footsteps behind you in the dark.

He found himself stopping and crossing the sidewalk to get a closer look. The shop was narrow, tucked between a weed store and some indie coffee shop he always meant to try. A lot of stores had come and gone in the pandemic, so he'd made a point not to get attached to anything in the first year of business.

He made a point of not getting attached to much, these days.

No hours on the door. He pressed his face against the glass and peered into the gloom. All he could see was a reception desk, and the vague suggestion of a hallway beside it.

Just as he went to move away and continue on his commute he saw something move in the shadows. Squinting, he peered inwards past the gleaming letters, trying to make out a shape. A person? No, the silhouette was too tall to make sense, and it was undulating unnaturally, like something from the depths of the ocean. It was hypnotic. A curious tingle began on the back of his neck. It felt like something was standing very close to him and for a moment he was struck with the strange feeling of *knowing* that the shadow in the hallway and the presence behind him were one in the same. He found himself pressing his face harder against the glass, unsure if he was trying to see inside or escape the presence behind him.

A burst of raucous laughter came from down the street, and he shook his head to clear it, feeling dizzy. When he peered into the shop again, it was empty and still.

Caleb moved along, his steps faster now that he realized he'd been stopped at the store for...shit, nearly 15 minutes? How the hell did that happen? He was going to be late for work, and he took off down the street, cursing the snow even more.

--

That afternoon at work he found himself opening the web browser, the day dragging long in front of him.

Hesitating, although he couldn't figure out why, he typed in "Otherworld Tattoo".

The web browser froze.

Caleb frowned and wiggled his mouse aggressively. Nothing. That was strange. He hadn't even opened a website yet, so there was no chance it was a virus. He thought about calling IT, but they'd just tell him to turn it off and on again anyway, so he might as well try that first.

He pressed the button, and his computer made a valiant attempt to turn off, the screen going dark but only on the bottom half. The words 'Otherworld Tattoo' remained visible in the search bar, now in the same curious font from the shop window. He felt strangely *seen* as though the words were looking back at him.

Just as he was about to panic, the screen went dark, like an eye blinking shut.

Crisis averted.

The computer turned back on with a soft hum, and he didn't try to look up the shop again, instead losing himself in his work.

On his walk home he passed Otherworld Tattoo again. This time, as he glanced into the window, he saw no shapes in the dark interior. Still, he felt a strange pull towards the store that he couldn't explain.

He ignored it, heading to the subway station instead of lingering.

At home he made himself some mac and cheese

and sat down to eat it at his shitty dining room table. It had been a long time since he'd had anyone over. He had friends, but life got busy and getting together rarely took priority. Still, he figured he should invite a couple of the guys over sometime. Or maybe he should go on a date.

He just felt so fucking worn out from the monotony of his job, his commute, his life. He felt like he was just existing, not really living.

He chewed his food listlessly, vowing that he'd text someone to hang out. Maybe tomorrow.

After all, he was tired.

--

The next morning Caleb was a wreck. He'd been unable to relax enough to fall asleep, although he couldn't put a finger on why. So, he was particularly pissed off on his frozen slip and slide towards the subway station, cursing every house that hadn't salted their sidewalks before the overnight freeze. The winter darkness had soured his mood even further, and he found himself dreading work more than usual.

He crossed at his usual stop light and was determined to avoid wasting any time looking into the tattoo shop. It wasn't open yet, and the only tattoo he'd ever considered getting was to cover his top surgery scars.

But he still felt his steps slowing as he crossed by on the empty morning street. Casting a glance inside, he saw his own pale face reflecting in the glass, and just behind it, nothing.

But it wasn't really nothing, he realized with a sick lurch. It was a nothing so hollow it once again became...

something. The darkness he stared into had form, and presence. It was as though he could see the very air, the darkness around it writhing. It had a vast sense of movement, of matter.

It was pressing against the glass.

Caleb realized with a jolt that he was too, both of his hands raised as though to greet the darkness. His head swam and he felt heat bloom in his stomach, a confusing clench of arousal and fear.

What the *fuck*.

A familiar and frustrating dampness between his legs, and a throb along his cock. He felt almost like he was high.

Another shake of his head cleared some of the haziness, and he realized with horror that his hand was on the door handle, and his arm was tensed to open it.

Blinking heavily, he jerked his hand off the handle as though he'd been burned, and staggered back from the door. What the fuck was going on with him?

He turned away from the shop, vowing that he would take the main strip home tonight. If this was some kind of stress induced mental break, changing his walk home might help.

He focused very hard on his work that day, policy review spreadsheets like cotton balls in his head. Muffled. Safe. Normal.

And all day long he very carefully didn't think about how the door handle felt like it had been turning from the other side as well.

--

True to his word, Caleb took a new route home and

found himself walking through an unfamiliar strip of houses near the park. It was already dark, the dim grasp of winter heavy. The air felt oddly empty, the streets too silent in the evening dusting of snow.

He was nearly home, but he felt...off. A pervasive sense of sadness had settled upon him, and his stomach was queasy and acidic. The depth of his sudden loneliness was unbearable- he was sure the weight would cause him to collapse

Almost as soon as the feeling came upon him, it retreated. Caleb was left shaky and sick, his head thick with confusion. He realized he was freezing, his coat wet with snow. Another lurching second ticked by, and he realized he wasn't on the edge of the park anymore.

No, instead he was outside of the fucking tattoo shop.

And the lights were on.

Without thinking, he pushed his way into the warmth of the shop.

"Hey, can I help you?" The person at the desk asked him, or at least that was what Caleb thought they asked. His ears were ringing like someone had struck a gong right beside him.

The sight of a wall of flash tattoos caught his attention behind the desk. There was a tattoo there, right in the center, that drew his eyes as though it was a lit beacon. It was a strange design, a black amorphous sort of shape, like wisps of smoke or dark tentacles reaching out to grab him.

It felt familiar. A pulse of arousal tinged with fear pulled at his stomach as he looked at it.

"Is that one available?" He heard his own voice ask. His hand raised as though he was a marionette to point at it, and it was only then that he realized he was trembling like a leaf.

"Ah. It's you," the person behind the desk said, suddenly very interested in him. Caleb had never been looked at like this before. He was the kind of guy who people's eyes skipped over, and that was how he liked it. He had spent too many hours in doctors' offices being stared at like a lab experiment, but this was different. He felt flayed open, as though they could see into his marrow. He was surprised to find he liked the sensation.

The receptionist nodded, a small smile appearing on their face. "Of course, it's ready for you when you want it."

"I- I should think about it," he said, taking a step back. A shiver ran down his spine as he stepped directly into something *cold*. But when he turned around there was nothing there, and the cold disappeared as though it had never been.

It must have been a draft.

A draft that left him aching with confused want.

"I have to... go," Caleb said, goosebumps erupting all over his skin.

"Wait! We have a discount on walk-ins for today only," the receptionist said, a tinge of desperation in their voice. "50% off. Pretty good, right, Caleb?"

He jolted at the sound of his name. He hadn't said it to them... had he?

"I don't know," he said helplessly. "I didn't even mean to come in here."

The person smiled. It didn't reach their eyes. "Aren't spontaneous decisions the best ones?" they asked.

Caleb had never made a spontaneous decision in his entire life, and he didn't plan to start now. "I'll think about it," he promised, inching his way towards the door. "Thank you."

He rushed out as though something was chasing him, practically running to the subway.

Fuck.

How had he ended up at Otherworld Tattoo? He'd been near the park. He was sure of it.

He was losing his mind. That had to be it.

Caleb stepped onto the train as soon as the doors opened and only felt truly safe once they had closed again behind him.

Stupid. He was being stupid. He'd just... zoned out. That was all. Zoned out and walked all the way back to the tattoo parlor. No big deal.

He stared at his reflection in the dark window of the subway car, taking in his haunted appearance. He really needed to snap out of it.

Just then his phone buzzed.

He pulled it from his pocket, and nearly fell over as the subway came to a stop at the next station. When he looked down at the screen his stomach twisted.

Otherworld Tattoo: Missed Call

Otherworld Tattoo: Missed Call

Otherworld Tattoo: Missed Call

Caleb's screen blurred as his hand started to shake. He hadn't given them his number. He was certain of that.

So how the fuck were they calling him?

Caleb stepped off the train just before the doors closed. He ran up the stairs to cross to the other platform, when he realized he was back at the station he had left from. Had he left it at all? A chill ran down his spine, and he felt like screaming.

His phone rang again. He ignored it.

He didn't stop walking until he was back inside of the tattoo shop, facing down the person behind the desk.

They smiled at him with a hollowness that held no warmth behind it.

"Why did you call me," Caleb demanded, unsure where this bravery was coming from.

"For your appointment," the receptionist said. "Your artist is ready for you."

He hadn't made an appointment.

Maybe he was dreaming. He certainly felt hazy, like he couldn't grasp his thoughts as they floated by. His whole body erupted in goosebumps, the feeling of being watched sweeping over him.

"Okay," he said, the sense of madness building in his chest. Every change he'd ever made to his body had been perfectly planned out, approved by panels of doctors and psychiatrists. This was crazy. This wasn't part of his plans. But he felt exhilarated by the choice, by deciding something for himself with no one to be held accountable to. "Okay. Why not."

The receptionist's smile stretched unnaturally wide across their face, a threat that made him take a frightened step back..

"Through that curtain and to your left," they said,

pointing to the back of the shop.

The next thing he knew, he was standing outside of his apartment building, his forearm burning with pain.

He rolled his sleeve up, and there it was. An inky swirling design, the skin around it raw and red.

He didn't remember getting it. He didn't remember the trip home. Had he even met the artist?

Feeling dazed and horrified, Caleb stumbled into his apartment building and climbed the stairs two at a time.

Arriving home he slammed the door behind him and locked it.

He studied the tattoo, feeling strangely hot. Something about it made his heart beat faster. He was getting wet, arousal tugging at him insistently. He felt his cock getting hard, and he moaned, his hand drifting down to his crotch.

No.

This was too fucking weird.

He took a shaky breath and dragged his hand down his face, fingers scratching through a days worth of stubble. He hadn't shaved this morning. He always shaved.

He couldn't breathe. He stumbled to the balcony for some air. He needed to calm down. A joint. A joint would help.

It did. He felt calmer as he stubbed out the butt and went back inside. The silence of his apartment was cloying, so he flopped down on the couch and flicked on the TV. He didn't really care what was on. He just wanted some background noise.

Arousal was pulsing through him still, even as the weed kicked in.

He reached down, the curve of his belly soft against his arm. He felt lazy and relaxed now, the edges of the world soft from the dampening effects of the weed. He slumped on the couch, one hand slipping into the waistband of his sweats. His lust was heavy, like syrup sliding down his skin. The glow of the TV left him in a pod of blue tinged light against the familiar darkness of his apartment.

Tipping his head back he let himself sink into the soft clutch of his fantasies. He touched his cock, the hard flesh throbbing beneath his fingers. His eyes slitted closed as sparks of pleasure raced up his spine. He imagined himself fucking into a curvy blonde girl, her pussy tight around his cock, her tits bouncing inches from his face. The vision faded, to be replaced with masculine hands, slick fingers probing him open.

He whined, high in his throat. He usually preferred to top, but something about this fantasy had him slick with the desire to submit, spreading his thighs wide to allow his partner more space. He moaned, swiping down below his cock to collect some of the wetness there as he fell deeper into the fantasy, his fingers jerking at the hard nub between his legs.

In his mind he was held open and a slow pressure began to push inside his ass, a pressure that was steady and unstoppable. He felt pinned open and vulnerable, his body accepting the intrusion from the dream partner.He'd gotten turned on while getting high tons of times, but it had never felt like this, like his body was only along for the ride. He usually couldn't bear to relinquish control, but this felt right, this felt different.

He tried to focus in on the face of the figure in the waking dream, who was now fucking into him with steady strokes. Both of his hands clenched into the blanket, and he tipped his hips forward into the imagined presence inside him. Abruptly, he realized that the presence fucking him wasn't a person.

It was a thing.

It was a shadow, rippling and strange, fucking its way inside of him. Tendrils of darkness drenching his thighs, crawling up with a sense of exploration. Discovering the shape of his body, pulling him down, down, down into the darkness.

Devouring him.

"Yes," he moaned, somehow feeling even more aroused by this revelation.

He cried out as his orgasm pulsed through him.

Clarity flooded back into him, and he shook his head roughly, opening his eyes as the fantasy retreated in a cold wash. Fucking weird, horny weed hallucinations. Post nut clarity was really something. He shivered, suddenly chilly. It was dark. Too dark, actually.

The TV had turned off, the apartment motionless and tomb-like. A bolt of fear slid through him. The darkness had taken on an almost alien appearance. He felt like a stranger in his own home as he sat up quickly, all at once desperate to turn a light on.

He leant over the edge of the couch and fumbled for his cellphone, cursing as his hand encountered the remains of a crumpled up chip bag and his water bottle. No phone. Jesus Christ.

His eyes weren't adjusting right to the darkness. Despite squinting, he couldn't see.

A creeping sense of unease was alive within him. He felt like he could reach out and the darkness itself would have a form. Like molasses would coat his fingers if he dragged them through the air.

Finally, his hand encountered the edge of his phone, and he picked it up, turning the flashlight on.

The light shone through the room, clearing the shadows. The familiar walls of his home flickered into view, and he felt his shoulders start to relax.

Until the beam of his flashlight swept over a shadow that didn't clear.

The corner of the dining room was shrouded in an extra layer of darkness. The shadow seemed to devour the light. Caleb was transfixed with horror, a mounting and irresistible urge to scream building in his chest.

He heard a deep crackling noise, and the shadow disappeared, the light from his phone piercing through the darkness suddenly. His arm stung, the raw skin of his tattoo flashing with a vicious heat. Suddenly, with a loud hum, his TV flickered back on, casting the room with artificial light again.

Trembling, he forced himself up from the couch and slapped his hand against the light switch. It was only in the light of the lamps that he started to calm down. It had to be weed anxiety. His heart was still beating fast in his chest.

He opened his phone and accessed the messaging

app. Scrolled through the meaningless "Hey how are you?" texts he had let stay unanswered for too long.

Sighing hard through his nose, he closed out of the app and set his phone down.

He was just tired. If he still felt like this tomorrow he would go to the walk-in clinic. Maybe he had hepatitis. Somehow that seemed the more desirable outcome.

--

It happened again the very next night. No weed this time, but the haze descended onto him almost as soon as he returned home. The warmth, the pulse of arousal, the shadow. All encompassing, demanding his attention. He tried to think of something else. A hot girl, a hot guy, anything. But like a jealous lover the shadow pushed greedily at the edges of his mind until he let it in.

He laid down on the bed and pulled his slacks down, spreading his legs open. An invitation, although to what he didn't know.

The shadow didn't hesitate, the murky presence pushing into the free space between his legs and into his mind. And once it was in, it began to consume him. The fantasy came down on him, as though 1000 hands caressed him all at once.

"More," he begged as the shadow in his mind's eye played with his cock. "Please, fuck me."

He must be some kind of sicko, to want whatever was happening. But he did. He wanted it so badly it felt like an ache deep inside.

Caleb opened his eyes, to see a shadowy figure looming over him. His mind screamed at him to run, while his legs only opened wider.

The terror and arousal sent judders through him, and he opened his mouth to scream, but instead heard himself begging. "Touch me. Please."

He closed his eyes again, unable to focus on the shadow standing so close to him.

He felt a cold touch on his cock, then something pressing against his front hole.

"Not there," he said, feeling panic rise in him. But whatever this thing was... it listened.

Instead, he felt the chill of it move back further, groping clumsily at his asshole, gentle and exploratory. Then it was inching inside of him, cold and solid and growing thicker as it went.

Caleb whined, lifting his hips to give it better access. This was so wrong, and yet it felt so *good*.

Then, out of nowhere, the feeling disappeared, leaving him empty and bereft. His arm throbbed, the tattoo aching in a way that only stoked the flame of his arousal.

"Wait, no. Come back," he said, his eyes flying open. There was nothing there.

As if in offering, a fantasy hit him so hard that it felt like he was watching a video. The shadow had these tendrils that were touching him all over, slipping up his stomach, tweaking at his nipples, pressing inside of him slow and steady.

He moaned, grabbing for the lube to make physical what was playing in his mind. He'd never felt so good, not even with a partner. This was something else entirely. This felt like his deepest wants and desires were being plucked from his mind and placed before him on a silver platter.

He flipped onto his stomach, fucking himself roughly, and the fantasy adapted, the shadow using him, claiming him, fucking into the heat of him vigorously.

His orgasm was building quickly, liquid heat flooding his body. In the fantasy, the shadow being fucked him harder, dark tendrils pinning him without struggle.

All at once the pleasure crested and he came so intensely that white lights flickered behind his closed eyelids. His energy disappeared and his limbs went weak, the tattoo burning like a brand. His head felt heavy, and dizzy, and he didn't even have the strength to wipe himself off before sleep took him.

--

His head hurt the next morning. Normally he would write a headache off, but together with the...visual disturbances he'd been experiencing... well, he was sure he had a brain tumor.

That, or he was being haunted. He wasn't sure what would be worse. He had always thought if he ended up in a horror movie, he would be the final guy, a natural survivor. Brutal and blood speckled, surviving to the end of the night. It was much less fun to be the final guy in whatever psychosexual bullshit this was.

No, he was definitely hallucinating from a tumor pressing on the horny part of his brain.

He considered calling someone before he realized that none of his friends were really 'call when you've got a shadow thing haunting you' level close.

Still, he was surprised to realize he didn't feel lonely.

If anything, he was already looking forward to getting home.

To seeing the shadow again.

His tattoo pulsed on his arm, a curious feeling of happiness filling him.

--

And so, a routine was established.

The shadow was relentless. Every night it touched him, each time lasting longer and longer in physical form. And when it inevitably faded away, the deluge of fantasies that followed made it all too easy to finish himself off.

Days at work felt longer and he longed for the embrace of the shadow when he wasn't at home. He also felt sick and hungry all the time. His damn tattoo wasn't healing right either. The skin around it was hot and itchy, and the ink was raised. He could swear it moved. Hadn't it been on his forearm? Now it was on his wrist.

Sometimes he dimly thought that he should be scared. Scared of the toll that the shadow was taking on him. Scared of what the creature wanted. But it was hard to be scared when the tendrils stroked his face, soothing him into honey sweet submission.

"Wow, I didn't know you had a hand tattoo, when did you get that?" A curious voice came from over his shoulder. It was one of the clerks from HR. Val, or something like that. Given that he didn't remember getting to work, it was a miracle he recalled even part of her name.

"What?" He asked, jerking his head up from a half

doze. He was so tired all the time, his nights full of dreams of being devoured by the shadow, leaving him wrung out with pleasure and exhausted the next morning. The shadow was endlessly hungry, and didn't care about his circadian rhythm.

"Sorry, your tattoo! I didn't realize you had gotten a hand tattoo. It looks cool, but a little red. Maybe you need antibiotics," she said.

"I don't have a…" He looked down and trailed off. It was as though he had been doused in freezing water, a shock that pushed through him like lightning.

The tattoo had moved. The inky black swirls and tendrils had covered his hand and begun to creep down his fingers. He felt a sick jerk in his stomach. What the fuck?

Had it migrated, or had it *grown?* The thought caused goosebumps to spring up on his body as he grabbed his sleeve and frantically rolled the fabric up. There was a trail of blistering that followed the path of the tattoo.

"Shit, hey, Caleb, that rash looks really bad. Have you seen a doctor?" probably-Val said as he rolled down his sleeve again.

"Oh, yeah. I hate doctors, but I'll make sure to see one," Caleb chirped. "Is that the policy approval file? You can leave that with me, thanks!"

Val cast him a suspicious look but set the file down and gave him a weak wave.

He waited until her steps had faded and then counted another agonizing 45 seconds before he walked to the bathroom.

Only once he was inside the stall did he let himself

start to panic.

"No, no, what the fuck," he moaned to himself, his stomach hot and sick. The tattoo had moved. He was sure of it. He had to have proof. He wasn't crazy. Whatever was happening was real. The shadow was real.

He picked up his phone and flicked through the photos in his storage, but he didn't have any damn pictures of the tattoo. Why the hell wouldn't he have taken any pictures of a new tattoo?

His hand burned, and he realized he was whimpering, an animal noise that felt torn out of him. Weakly, he staggered to his manager's office.

Just one look at him was enough for her to send him home. He took a car; not certain he'd be able to survive a subway trip in his current state.

As soon as he got home, he staggered inside, already unbuttoning his shirt. The throb and burn of his hand had grown unbearable, and he longed to run it under cold water to reduce the pain. His fingers felt curiously stiff, caught in a cramp, but he was distracted by the usual flush of arousal that meant the shadow was near. He pulled his pants down, then shucked off his boxers as he stumbled towards his bathroom, only to stop and head into the bedroom instead.

He laid himself down, opening his legs, his cock hard and his body pulsing with need. His mind felt hazy, and he wondered if he had a fever.

Caleb looked down at his hand, the burning feeling almost pleasant now.

The tattoo swirled like mist, tendrils of it seeming to stretch out and off of his skin. It had to be another hallucination. Except that when it touched his cock it felt all too real.

"Fuck," he groaned, hips canting up into the feeling of the shadowy smoke surrounding his cock and *sucking.* "Oh God."

The shadow pulsed around him, tendrils of it slipping back through the slick gathering between his thighs until it reached his ass. The press into his body felt real. So solid, like a finger was pushing into him rather than some kind of smoky illusion.

"Oh," he gasped, grabbing tight to the bedspread. "Fuck, it feels so-" he cut himself off. Who was he even talking to?

Then Caleb's hand moved without him directing it to.

He was used to his body feeling wrong, feeling like someone else's, especially before he'd transitioned. But this was something else altogether. This was his hand moving of its own accord, following the path the smoke had taken by pressing between his folds to gather slick, and then moving back to open him up.

"What the hell," he said, raising his other hand just to prove he still could. When he tried to move the hand whose finger was pressing inside of him he was met with a resistance he'd never felt before.

Another finger joined the first in his ass, and for a moment he almost didn't care whether he was possessed or not because it felt so good.

Was he possessed?

The thought was a bucket of cold water over him breaking the hazy spell, and he wrestled for control of his hand.

"Wait," he said frantically. His hand stopped. "I don't want... I need my hand back. Please."

And just like that, his hand was his own again, and the shadow retreated.

"Ccccaaaa," a voice sounded throughout the room. He sat up, terrified, glancing around to see where the hell the sound had come from. It hadn't sounded like it was in his head. It sounded all too real.

"Ccccccaaa," came the voice again, causing him to flinch. He was so tired. The lost hours of sleep weighed down on him, and his eyes felt dry and heavy.

The shadow was getting stronger, and he didn't know what would happen if it gained any more power.

Abruptly, and with an energy he'd been unable to conjure for days, Caleb was pulling his pants back on and zipping himself into his parka.

It was time to go back to Otherworld Tattoo and get some answers.

--

The shop was gone, and worse, it was like it was never there. The gold paint and striped awning he remembered from his forced detours had vanished.

He knew now that it had been a trap. He'd been lured in by the shadow that now haunted him. The shadow that was ripping out of him, day by day.

He was a sacrifice. Bound to be devoured. Why else would the shadow be so intent on having him every night? It was like a cat toying with its food, and Caleb was a horny and terrified mouse.

A scream built in his throat. He clamped his hand

over his mouth and turned around, suddenly desperate to put as much space between himself and the abandoned shop as possible.

Unsure what to do or where to go, he turned and ran, slipping and sliding through the grey slush on the streets. His heart was racing, and the pain was flaring. Where was safe when you carried the danger in the palm of your hand?

So, he went home.

--

He collapsed against the door as soon as it swung shut behind him, falling to his knees and dragging himself into the living room.

The pain in his hand was unbearable, thrumming through him in tandem with his pulse. With a sudden flash of insight, he realized what was happening.

The tattoo was ripping itself from his skin, peeling off like a scab. The shadow was pulling its way out of him and into the world. It hurt, the pain burning and blistering so badly that he shouted, unable to hold back the sound.

He watched in absolute horror as the dark tendrils dripped down his fingers, like a spill of ink on paper. The pain focused into glowing embers of agony on the tips of his fingers as it peeled away from his body.

The tattoo coalesced on the ground, crawling across the floor like a spider. There it began growing, smoky black ink swirling up into a column until before him stood the shadow.

It was solid now. Solid and *real* in a way it never had been before.

There was nowhere to run. The shadow was between him and the door. He wondered, in the part of his mind that was still somehow functioning, if it would destroy him slowly or if it would get it over quickly. He realized he was crying, tear tracks hot on his face.

He hoped that it would happen fast. He didn't want to suffer. He didn't want to die.

The shadow moved, one long arm reaching out towards him. The appendage rose, cupping his wet cheek. It felt solid, but cold. So cold. And then, in a rasp that he could both hear and *feel*, it cooed "Caleb."

Caleb fell forward, the abyss rising to meet him, holding him steady. His heart was pounding harder than it ever had before, like it was trying to hammer its way out of his chest.

"Caleb," it said again, holding him more tenderly than anyone ever had before. Tendrils of darkness crawled up his neck and stroked his sweaty hair away from his face. The shadow cooed again, a guttural sound but somehow still sweet at the same time.

Caleb wrapped his arms around the shadow, finding it surprisingly solid.

"Mine," it said, in that raspy way it had, as though it was just learning how to speak. Caleb guessed that might be the case.

Fuck it. He'd never felt more wanted before. More cared for.

"Yours," Caleb said, and let himself relax into the creature's embrace.

If this was madness, then let him be mad. He couldn't care less, held in the blackness that felt so familiar and so comfortable.

He closed his eyes and let the darkness take him.

Love Has Many Arms
Tanya Pond

CW: implied self harm, death

In the light of day, the puddle was shallow, grimy and easily avoided. Once the sun set behind pollution stained skyscrapers, the puddle became an inky threat, dragging the yellow light from the street into its depths and swallowing it.

She stood on the threshold, one hand holding the heavy door open and the other holding a dripping bag of rubbish, staring at the puddle like she expected it to swallow her, too. From the restaurant's back door it looked unfathomably deep. Deep enough to hide a nightmare. Which was ridiculous. It was just a puddle of scum and disappointed potential, barely a foot wide, squatting in front of the dumpster. The night lent it lies. The only thing hiding in that puddle was disease, which was true for every aspect of this sad city.

She breathed deeply, like her therapist had taught her. In through the nose, two-three-four. Out through the mouth, two-three-four. She knew this fear of the puddle was irrational. It only crept in at night, when her feet hurt from a double shift and her heart ached from watching her mum waste away. According to her therapist, it was a manifestation of her anxiety. But neither that logical explanation nor the continuous noise of angry traffic flooding the alley could convince her exhausted brain there wasn't a predator in the puddle, waiting for its chance.

The cacophony of the understaffed kitchen and the discordant melody of the clientele seated on the patio did nothing to chase away the hunted, haunted goose-bumps spreading across her skin. How could it, when the constant noise of the restaurant played on repeat in the back of her mind, at work and at home, in waking and in sleep.

Stepping into the alley, she approached the dumpster. She eyed the inky, light-gobbling puddle, ready to run at the smallest sign of a ripple on its glassy surface. The door swung closed behind her, muffling the kitchen but inviting grating laughter from the patio to drift around the corner and bounce off the unwashed walls.

In-two-three-four.

She approached on light feet. The laughter echoed, distorted. It sounded mean, like her sister.

Out-two-three-four.

It was the same shivering dread she'd felt as a child, staring at the cracked closet door, convinced any moment she'd see a glowing eye its depths.

In-two-three-four.

In the end, Dad had put a night light in the closet so she would sleep in her own bed. She still kept a night light on in her closet, always convinced it was the light that kept the monsters at bay. Some nights she slept with all the lights in the flat on.

She skirted the edge of the puddle, coming to the dumpster from the side. She struggled with one hand to lift the corner of the heavy lid. She dropped the rubbish bag onto the ground - it wasn't like the extra layer of slime would be noticed on the dirty, fractured concrete. There was no way she was risking going in front of the dumpster, where lifting the lid was easier but avoiding the puddle was harder.

Out-two-three-four.

She managed to wrestle the lid up and swung the bag into the dumpster's stinking belly. She skipped back from the dumpster as soon as she let go of the bag - she almost convinced herself it was because the air escaping the dumpster was fetid and made her gag, not because she feared what hid inside - letting the lid fall, fast and loud. The disgusting rush of warm, stale air that hit her face like a brick as the lid came down was bad enough that for a heartbeat she forgot about the puddle. But as she stepped away from the dumpster, scrubbing her hands on her polyester skirt, she thought she saw something slide from the puddle out of the corner of her eye. The hair on her bare arms and the back of her neck stood at attention.

In-two-three-four.

She glared at the undisturbed puddle, annoyed at herself but still waiting to see if the movement was real or a glitch of her paranoid brain. One foot pointed back at the door and safety, she waited for what felt like an hour, her heart slamming against her ribs.

Out-two-three-four.

Her phone vibrated in her pocket, the buzz of the machinery almost as loud in the heavy air of the alley as the messy rendition of 'Happy Birthday' cutting around the edge of the building. She didn't want to linger in the alley, but a long standing habit had trained her to respond when her hands were empty and there were no witnesses. She yanked the phone out. Mum was calling. Again. Her finger hovered over the accept button.

In-two-three-four.

It was so hard to breathe with the crushing weight of her mum's needs vibrating in her hand. She glanced at the puddle, shallow and still. She should move. She should answer the phone, be a good daughter, listen to Mum's complaints and tears. She closed her eyes against the pressure.

Out-two-three-four.

She declined the call and pocketed the phone. She was at work, her mum couldn't expect her to answer while at work. She barely flinched when her phone started vibrating again almost immediately.

She couldn't help glancing at the undisturbed puddle again. The movement had just been a figment of her imagination. She hadn't been sleeping well, unable to afford a night nurse for Mum now that her sister was refusing to send any more money. She rolled her shoulders, trying to loosen the cramped muscles. There was nothing to be scared of. Not in the puddle, at least. She ignored the faint disappointment in the back of her throat. Just the adrenaline fading.

She had one hand on the cold door handle when she heard a splash. She spun around, plastering her back to the door. The puddle looked bigger. Deeper. Blacker. She shook her head, trying to clear it.

In-two-three-four.

There was nothing there. Nothing. Without taking her eyes off the puddle- she could swear the edge was inching closer to her - she grabbed onto the handle again and twisted. It turned easily. She forgot to count when she sighed her relief. She pulled the door open, moving forward a quarter inch to give the door space, eyes still on the puddle.

The opening door allowed a sliver of light to spill into the alley, only to be sucked in by the puddle instead of being reflected back at her.

In-two-three-four.

She stepped forward again so she could manoeuvre into the opening without taking her eyes off the puddle. In the line where the widening strip of light from the restaurant should have fallen over the puddle, she saw something - smooth and wet and reflecting light where the puddle didn't breach the thick surface.

She forgot to breathe. She forgot to think. She forgot to move.

The crash of a pot echoed through the static that had short circuited her mind. The vicious cursing and startled, multi-lingual shouts of the kitchen staff reminded of where she was. Who she was.

Out-two-three-four.

It had to be a weird trick of the light, of the night.

She should leave it alone. Go inside. Call her mum back to get relief from the buzzing in her pocket. Forget the paranoia, avoid coming out here when she was tired.

In-two-three-four.

She let go of the door. It slammed shut, cutting out the light and clatter. She'd have nightmares tonight if she didn't have a closer look, and she so desperately wanted what little peace sleep gave her.

The thing, whatever it was, floated on the surface, bobbing on a non-existent tide.

On her toes, with slow, careful, quiet steps, she approached the puddle. It seemed she'd taken fewer steps to get to its edge than when she'd gone to the dumpster just a couple of minutes earlier.

Out-two-three-four.

Probably she'd just taken bigger steps. Although, the ebony liquid now touched the walls on either side of the alley when it hadn't before...the dumpster must be leaking. It was looking more like a pond than a puddle.

Closer, the thing on the surface looked two dimensional. Flat. Not as dark or as solid as the water surrounding it. A leaf, or a bedraggled piece of fabric. She rolled her head on her shoulders, looking up. A slice of the city lights trapped by the overcast night sky was visible between the tall buildings. Just rubbish. Probably blew out of the dumpster when she'd opened it. She really needed more sleep if the paranoia was getting this bad. Maybe she should ask her therapist to up her meds.

A couple stumbled past the mouth of the alley, a

woman's high pitched complaints about bad service and a man's musky agreement scraping at her skin and pulling her attention from the heavy silence coating the alley.

She spun on her heels. Time to get back to work before her manager realized she wasn't where she was supposed to be.

Something wet brushed against her ankle, right above the frayed edge of her shoe. It felt like an invitation. It felt like every nightmare she'd ever had come true. It felt like validation. She froze again at the touch, back to the pond, staring blankly in front of her. She stood so long without taking a breath she started feeling dizzy. For just a moment the restaurant's soundtrack faded.

When she swayed she sucked in a harsh breath, habit forcing her to count.

In-two-three-four.

She smelled musty algae and wet dirt overlaying the expected faint and ever-present stink of old piss and half rotted food. With the slow movements of prey, she tilted her head down to look at her ankle. Frayed white sock peaking above the worn edge of her sneaker. Ankle three days overdue for a shave. It looked exactly like she would expect. Except. Except for the fine line of dark sludge tracing from the anklebone to the tendon. She swallowed hard.

Out-two-three-four.

She raised her gaze to stare straight ahead once more. She had an active imagination. Always believing the stories of monsters in the closet and under the bed, always seeing glowing eyes in deep shadows, always feeling followed. But she'd never imagined a touch before. Never had any of her 'flights of fancy' as Granny called them, leave any evidence.

Her sister's voice, singing a mean rhyme about delusions and crazy little girls floated to the front of her mind, a layer of old hurt to wash over the ever-present exhaustion.

Without looking again, she crouched down to touch her ankle. She expected to feel sharp stubble and soft cotton.

In-two-three-four.

Her fingers touched slick slime. A violent shiver rattled her body. She swallowed hard against the urge to gag as she desperately scrubbed her tainted fingers against the polyester over her thighs. She hadn't inspected the slime before doing her best to clean her fingers of it, she didn't need any more detail to furnish the nightmares she knew would follow her the rest of her life.

When the touch came again, soft and cool against her fevered skin, instinct took her down a different path. A muffled screech escaped from behind her clenched teeth and she leapt forward. The ankle she'd broken running from her sister's gleeful taunts as a child came down at a bad angle, twisted and gave way under her weight. The air left her lungs in a painful rush at the impact as she sprawled against the concrete, leaving them empty and bereft. One arm stretched above her, toward the restaurant's back door and her empty, fear-filled life. Her legs splayed behind her, toes of her worn sneakers kissing the edge of the pond. She could feel the thick, cool liquid seeping through the layers of fabric to soak into her socks.

She was distracted by the shock of impact, by the struggle to re-inflate her lungs, so she didn't notice when the touch returned. Only after she had sucked in and released a few harsh breaths, after she'd found her count did she notice the gentle movement of the cool, slick limb back and forth across her ankle. It felt like an apology, an offer of comfort.

Giving up on trying to calm the rough tempo of her heart, she concentrated on getting her breathing deep and even.

In-two-three-four.

She had a moment of disconnected levity when she thought about how proud her therapist would be - right before he institutionalized her.

When she turned around she saw the shining outline of a smooth tube - like a tree root, or an octopus limb - reaching from the pond, reflecting the street lights in a way the water that cradled it didn't. It was dark, darker than the night shrouded concrete, darker than any shade of black she'd ever seen. It was no wider than her pinky at the end closest to her, but got thicker along its length until it was as wide as her thigh where it disappeared into the pond.

The limb pulled away but didn't disappear. She arranged herself so she was sitting facing the puddle, legs stretched before her. She couldn't explain, even to herself, why she didn't immediately jump to her feet and run as fast and as far as she could. She couldn't say why, when the limb - the tentacle - stretched back out toward her ankle once more, she held still. Except.

Except, it was the kindest touch she'd felt in...years. Mum was too preoccupied with her own illness. Dad had left a long time ago. Her sister had never shown her any kindness. The razor blades she cherished were a cold comfort at best. Even at church, during the sign of peace, the handshakes she received were brief, brisk and impersonal. And lately, attending Mass had left her feeling empty and lonelier than ever. So when the tentacle reached from the impossible depths of the pond to wrap loosely around her ankle, she did nothing to stop it. She breathed, and watched, as the tentacle wound around her ankle, moving up her leg.

Out-two-three-four.

The more the limb rose from the inky blackness, the thicker it got. The grip stayed loose, and every few centimetres the movement would stop, as if waiting for permission to continue. With a sudden certainty, she knew that if she pulled away again, the tentacle would disappear back into its pond - now deep enough at the back of the alley that gentle waves tapped at the dumpster with metallic slaps - and she would never see it again. She was still scared - scared that this was real, scared that it wasn't - but with that winding, slimy touch, the aching loneliness that ate at her bones felt a little less all-encompassing.

The longer the contact lasted, the less she noticed the traffic of the street, the clamour of the restaurant, the buzzing of her phone. The reprieve from the constant beat of noise was so sweet, she nearly sobbed in relief.

The tip of the tentacle touched the bottom of the

cheap skirt halfway up her thigh and recoiled slightly. After a moment of hesitation, it came back, brushing back and forth against the fabric, finding its borders, tasting it. A giggle edged with hysteria escaped when she felt the entire length of the tentacle shiver before it pulled away to explore the exposed parts of her skin. It was a truly awful skirt. The uniform had been worn by more women over the years than she cared to think about, and the cheap fabric held onto the memories of each of those women's unhappiness.

For the first time in her life, she decided to take a risk. To do the exact wrong thing. To lean into the fear and the chance of a moment of comfort.

In-two-three-four.

She shuffled forward on her butt, bringing her whole body closer. The tentacle had frozen when she started moving, waiting to see what she did. She moved until she was seated at the edge of the water line. She could still see the walls containing the light eating water, but when she looked over the blank surface it felt like a lake in the mountains.

Telling herself getting the awful skirt wet would be bad, she dragged it higher up her thighs. She stretched her tentacle wrapped leg into the lake. The cold, thick water flowed over her skin, hiding its paleness. Past the water line the cracked, rough concrete gave away to gloopy sludge. She felt the greasy mucous cling to her leg around the touch of the tentacle, weighing it down. The lake got deep fast, and still seated at the edge, her leg sunk down until everything below her knee was submerged.

The tentacle clenched for a moment, then returned to its previous loose, forgiving grip. The coils got closer together, increasing how much contact it had around her leg until she could barely feel the thick sludge.

Out-two-three-four.

She slipped her other leg into the depths. Almost as soon as her sneaker sank below the surface, she felt another tentacle start its slide up her leg. She slid her flesh into the slimy embrace gratefully, watching as the thin tip rose above the surface, following the curve of her knee up her thigh. She smiled down at the tentacle as it explored the new expanse of flesh she'd made available. It felt like getting to drink mountain water after a month in the desert, to be appreciated for what she was offering. So different to the rushed hookups that always left her feeling worse.

In-two-three-four.

She reached down and with one finger touched the very end of the tentacle tasting her skin. It wound around her finger, an affectionate kiss, before returning its attention to her leg, leaving her finger slick with grey-green slime. As an experiment, a test, she pulled her leg up, out of the sludge, out of the winding embrace of the slick limb. It didn't fight her retreat, letting her leg slip through its coils, but neither did it pull away. It prolonged the contact for as long as possible. The sludge was so thick on her calf, none of her skin shone through. She pulled the other leg up and, as the end of the tentacle slipped from her ankle, she saw it shiver.

Standing up, she looked over her shoulder. The alley was still there, behind her, with its grimy walls and broken concrete. The restaurant door and her minimum wage job were waiting for her. Her sick mother and nasty sister. The empty church and emptier flat. The unrelenting din had started pounding at her temples again as soon as she lost contact with the tentacles. It was all there, waiting with indifferent impatience for her return. Only her manager would miss her, but only until a replacement was found. In the tentacle's shiver, she'd felt its sadness at losing her. Its longing for her. For *her.*

Pulling her once more buzzing phone out of her pocket, she placed it carefully on the broken concrete at the edge of the lake. It clattered against the unforgiving surface, her mum's illness an uneven rhythm of need. She stepped into the lake that looked nothing like the puddle she'd thought it was.

Out-two-three-four.

She waded into the sludge, letting it swallow her ankles, calves, knees. She hesitated when the dark, viscous liquid touched the bottom of her skirt. Not out of concern for the skirt, but because she'd felt no seeking touch of cool, slimy skin. Had it left? Had it abandoned her already? Had it taken her retreat as rejection?

She clenched her teeth and her fists, blinking back tears. So close. She'd been *so close* to feeling wanted. And her hesitation had cost her this chance. The spiral of despair and panic that had nothing to do with physical danger and everything to do with facing her empty life and fraying faith had almost convinced her to turn around when she felt it. The hesitant brush against her ankle, just like that first time. But this time what froze her wasn't fear, it was painful hope and dizzying relief.

When she moved her foot into the touch, it wrapped around her ankle once more. Tighter this time, more sure of its welcome. It wound its way up her leg faster. Her other leg was wrapped just as efficiently. The tentacles pulsed around her limbs, the grips tightening and loosening rhythmically. Not a threat; a comforting throb, a game. The noise faded again, not gone, but so faint she could ignore it. A third tentacle breached the opaque surface, touching her hand. She showed it her palm, fingers spread wide. It wound between her fingers and around her wrist, making a slick, fleshy glove. With gentle invitation it tugged forward, deeper into the shoreless lake.

In-two-three-four.

With a smile, she accepted the invitation and moved deeper. Her shoes got stuck in the thick sludge, and her feet pulled free. Her socks did nothing to stop the sludge from seeping between her toes as her feet dug deeper into the soft lakebed with every step.

The tentacles wrapped around her legs did nothing to impede her movement, they just moved higher up her thighs as she moved deeper. The cool touch slipped under her skirt, moving between her skin and the polyester, moving higher between her legs until it met the cotton of her panties. It prodded at the soft barrier, finding its edges and slipped under. She held her breath as the slick limb explored the folds protecting her pulsing cunt, brushing up against the tingling bundle of nerves of her clit. She shivered in anticipation, in hope, in yearning. It pulled away, and she released a disappointed breath, dropping both her hands below the water's surface as the anticipatory tension left her muscles weak.

Out-two-three-four.

Her consolation was a new limb wrapping itself around her waist, its tip digging between the skirt's waistband and her blouse's hem. It enticed her deeper, deeper, until her feet lost contact with the solid lakebed. The tentacles held her aloft at the waist, held her head above water as they tipped her, so she was almost floating, staring towards the slice of polluted city sky.

It tugged at her bra strap and although it had touched her with nothing but gentle, loving kindness, the strap snapped under the strain of the tentacle's pull.

In-two-three-four.

It took concentration to keep up her breathing count, but she was afraid that if she didn't, she'd hyperventilate - from excitement, from terror - then pass out. She didn't want to miss a second of this experience, even if it was irrefutable proof that she had gone insane. Even through the thick liquid, she heard the heavy rip of sodden fabric as her blouse followed suit and gave way.

The tentacle explored the soft hills and valleys of her stomach and even in the icy water its touch felt cool and soothing against her burning skin. As the tentacles wrapped around her legs continued to pulse and slowly pull them further apart, the one around her hand slid up her arm to massage her shoulder, matched by another on her other arm.

It circled her breasts, winding between and over them. Her whole body shuddered as it slid, slick and slimy, over her nipples until they had hardened to the edge of painful.

Out-two-three-four.

Warmth spread low in her groin and she couldn't help the low moan.

The groan turned into a sharp squeak as her lover revealed a secret hidden on its tentacles - suckers. It latched onto both her nipples at the same moment and pulled at them gently. She arched her back into the sensation, electricity shooting straight between her legs. Her breath expanded her lungs, pushing her breasts more firmly into her cool lover's touch.

In-two-three-four.

A limb slid from her shoulder up her neck, she couldn't decide if she wanted to stretch her neck to keep it focused on the sensitive skin below her ear, or lean her face into the touch so she might have a chance to kiss her lover. Her indecision made her head wobble ungracefully back and forth and she was grateful her lover couldn't see her - as far as she knew. In the end, her lover made the decision for her, making a loose necklace of itself around her neck as its tip explored the contours of her face.

The tentacles wrapped around her legs had been pulsing a comforting rhythm, the ends exploring the tops of her thighs and arse, but staying outside her panties. That changed when it slipped under the fabric at her hips on both sides and tore it.

Out-two-three-four.

The sudden rush of viscous sludge over the most sensitive parts of her sent a shiver through her entire body, matched only by the tip of a tentacle finally - *finally!* - burying itself in her folds for more than just a cursory exploration. It tasted every inch of her, and she lost count of her breathing as its wriggling movement rubbed over her clit with a beautiful pressure that had her eyes rolling back in her head and her body arching. The sound of her own breathing and the gentle splashes as her lover moved with her against the surface of the water drowned out any other noise that may have distracted her.

The sludge of the lake felt like cool relief against the scalding heat of her own juices, the slime of the tentacle as it wedged into her felt like salvation. Her lover continued the suction at her nipples as it started a matching pattern of suck, release, suck on her clit. Every muscle in her body clenched, her toes curling and her cunt clamping around the tentacle throbbing inside her. The shaking release started deep in her gut and sent lightning through every tired nerve. She stopped breathing entirely as her body forgave her for every sin she had ever committed against it; for the merciless hours on her sore feet, for the clumsy hands she'd allowed to fumble over her worn flesh, for the blades she'd dragged over her thin skin.

The orgasm was like no other. It felt like reprieve, it felt like exoneration, it felt like love.

The silence that accompanied the orgasm bought her a peace she'd never even known to wish for. Blissful, thick, deep *silence.*

Her jaw had clenched, her teeth grinding together as her body shook, but as the earthquake settled into shivers running up and down her body, her mouth fell open under a tentacle's exploring touch to allow a harsh breath.

In-two-three-four.

It slipped between her lips to tickle her tongue and for the first time she tasted her lover. It tasted of rotting plants, polluted water, sweet promises. She flattened her tongue, coating it in her lover's slime, swallowing the sticky substance as it slid down her throat. She didn't choke when the tentacle followed its fluids past her tonsils. She concentrated on breathing through her nose.

Out-two-three-four.

Her lover had given her such great pleasure - was still giving her pleasure, its pulsing suction hadn't abated and the tentacle in her cunt was thickening, stretching her pleasantly - she could not, would not, deny it any part of her.

In her cunt, the tentacle pushed at the end of her, not breaching, asking. She pulled her arms and legs into her body, using her lover's grip on her limbs to pull it closer, to invite it in deeper. If she could have spoken, she would have begged. Her lover offered her unconditional acceptance and love, and in return she offered it everything.

Her lover took her up on her invitation, pushing past her cervix with a searing rip that she felt echo in her bones. It left her with tears trailing down her cheeks and she concentrated on her breathing count to stop herself from passing out.

In-two-three-four.

It was just a little pain. Pain she accepted, wanted. It was piercing pleasure compared to her sister's cruel jabs or Mum's relentless demands.

With a gentle slither, her lover tasted her tears. It wrapped a tentacle over her head, covering her eyes. Shielding her from the ugly yellow glare of streetlights, catching her tears before any more had a chance to fall. She swallowed against the lingering jolts of pain, she swallowed around the tentacle sliding deeper down her willing throat.

Out-two-three-four.

It was getting harder to breathe, the tentacles covering most of her face and dragging her deeper into the lake's welcoming sludge. She could barely feel the stale, fetid air of the alley brushing over her nose. The restaurant's tuneless song was distant, the city's traffic almost non-existent. The tentacle wrapped around her torso and massaging her breasts tightened, consoling her as her ribs spasmed. Pain was an offbeat accompaniment to the thud of her heart, it elevated the pleasure her lover's touch bought her.

She could feel the tentacle entering her through her cunt digging deeper, curling in her uterus. The cramping sensation made her twist in its grasp - not to escape; to relieve the tension. She felt her uterus stretch and stretch and pop, bringing a wave of relief and excruciating pain that made her sight flash white and electricity race over every worn bone. Despite the overwhelming sensation, she could feel it burying itself deeper still, between her kidneys and liver. She welcomed it.

Her body convulsed as another orgasm crested,

blurring the line between pain and pleasure, pleasure and pain.

She choked around the tentacle crawling down her windpipe to twist around her lungs.

Out-two-three.

The surface of the lake closed above her as her lover pulled her closer. The sludge was a weighted blanket protecting her from everything that had been eroding her. Wrapping her in a chilled, loving cocoon of eternal quiet.

Out-two.

She felt the moment the two tentacles her lover and inserted into her met in the cavity under her heart. She felt the delighted shiver ripple through every tentacle wrapped around her and she shuddered in response. This was everything. This was what she had been missing. This is what she had been waiting for. This joy that her lover shared so freely with her. This promise of forever, of never being alone and cold again. This was all she'd ever wanted.

Her many armed lover. Her saviour. Her salvation.

Out-

Dick in a Box
Ramses Wolfe

CW: Dubcon, misogyny

'And what, put my dick in it?'

'*Whatever feels natural,*' was the official instruction, but Richard's joke fell flat. There wasn't an immediate response on the other side of the line, so he found himself bending uncomfortably over the desk and reaching for a pen to fidget with, he cleared his throat and began rhythmically pressing the thrust device.

As he opened his mouth to speak, the interlocutor reiterated "That *is* a very common choice. But we strive to avoid prescribing customer behaviour."

"What about observing it?" The pen was now clicking faster. "Are there cameras and shit?" "We are unable to answer questions about the nature of the box, but the contract will outline our privacy and data protection policies."

"And this is all free? Not a scam or something, you're literally just sending it to me and that's it?"

"My understanding is that you've been referred

through your employer? I'm sure he'll be happy to answer further questions."

Richard lifted his eyes off the printed stack of documents in front of him, to glance at his supervisor a few booths over. The angle of his eyebrows and how low they were on his face were enough to discourage Richard from approaching him for at least fifteen business days. "And how long am I supposed to keep it?"

"The length of the contract is customized depending on-"

"...behaviours, challenges, and circumstances. Right." Richard underlined the sentence in the contract and stared at it. "And this is not going to be distracting me from work or... will I get a raise or something? Is this an 'employee of the month' situation?"

"While the selection process was a result of colleague vote and management approval, we are not aware of any other similarities. Enquiries regarding your salary should be directed to your employer. Previous participants have not found a direct link between the programme and an increase in workload, but should that be the case, please direct-"

"The question to my employer and blah blah." The pen slipped from between his fingers and loudly landed on the trash can. "Alright, fuck it, I'm in."

"The box will be delivered tomorrow."

"Cool, where do I sign?"

"No signature will be required."

That did give him some pause, as much as he was happy one thing in his life didn't require him to read several pages and sign at least half as many. He distractedly put the phone down and logged back into the Asana, watching new cases slowly fill his screen.

#

The box was roughly what he expected, if not a little more disappointing. Just a big cube that barely fit through the narrow door of his ground floor apartment. It wasn't light, but he was able to drag it up the three steps at the entrance and into the living room. Thankfully, he didn't seem to be required to carry it with him, or move it at all, necessarily.

It was a little awkward to have a big box in the middle of the living room. He started wondering if he could style it - maybe paint it, or cover it in wallpaper. Or maybe he could keep it bare but use it as a coffee table. He pushed it closer to the loveseat. It was too tall to rest his feet on comfortably, it was the first thing he tried. He placed a couple of large photography books on it, and a candle, but that looked even worse. He was a single man in his late 30s living alone, he couldn't afford to be seen using cardboard as furniture. Of course, having some indication of the content might have helped him find a more permanent placement. Could it go in the bathroom or would the humidity damage it? What about the kitchen, would it absorb odours? Did it need light?

He spent the first few hours trying to guess. Maybe it was a scam. Maybe the box was full of drugs or weapons and the police would run through the door any minute. Maybe it was food, and it would start stinking after a week or two, and they were testing for how long someone would tolerate it. Maybe there was a corpse in it. You might have been able to fit a small person in there, or even a regular sized one, if cut in small enough pieces.

He tried to get rid of that thought as quickly as possible, but he kept imagining walking into the room to find blood seeping through the bottom of the box, slowly staining the grey carpet underneath.

And there was the hole, of course, in the middle of it. He wasn't entirely sure what to do with it. After an hour or two of sitting on the couch staring at it, he grabbed some masking tape and covered the hole. It wouldn't completely stop a camera from recording, or at least capturing some motion and sound, but it did give him a stronger sense of privacy and security.

Over the following few days, however, he caught himself spending less and less time in the room shared with the box. Of course, he still had to walk past it to go to the kitchen and the bathroom, and there was the necessary upkeep to take care of.

Once a day, he would open a small drawer at the bottom of the box and scrape leftovers into it, directly from the plate he'd been eating off of. The instructions had been clear about the process, but not its purpose. If it had been a more significant amount of food he would have been worried that an animal or person may be stuck inside, but the leftovers were rarely more than a couple of bites, not enough to sustain more than a few bugs – and he had made an executive decision that he would not entertain the idea of the box containing a pile of bugs. It was more likely some form of renewable compost-based energy powering whatever was in it.

And once a week, before the daily "feeding", he had to empty the same drawer. There was a purple dust of sorts, in a little pile, that would appear there like clockwork. It didn't smell like anything in particular, and he avoided touching it with his bare hands, but its presence seemed to suggest a chemical process. Maybe it somehow helped to keep the temperature down?

The box didn't seem too warm, but cardboard was flammable, and if the machine inside was constantly or frequently turned on, it likely required some form of temperature control.

He, however, hadn't been in a while. Turned on. And when he had, it was largely out of habit, no more than a biological function. Scrolling Tinder while jerking off was more of a habit than a need at this point. He would sit on the couch, erection in his left hand, phone in the right, and stroke his cock a few times before the boredom made it limp again. Sometimes he would cum, but sometimes it was such a non-starter that he didn't even bother washing his hands. He had briefly moved those activities to the bedroom when the box arrived, but the break in the routine simply made it more unnerving.

There was also a loneliness in the bedroom that felt more intimate than he could handle on any given day. The lack of another person there felt like punishment, weakness. He had made several desperate attempts to fix that, especially at work. Not that he found his coworkers particularly more attractive than other options, but he did spend more time with them. You stare at something long enough, you end up craving it.

Maybe that was why he ripped the tape off the box, one day as he was sitting on the couch, balls sticking to the beige pleather. He didn't dare look inside the hole, but he stood up and ran a hand over the top of the box, finding the corner and gripping it tightly. The other hand soon followed, and his erection found his way into the hole.

For a few long seconds, enough to feel stupid to expect otherwise, nothing happened. And then he felt something, but didn't have time to process it before cum started dripping out of his cock. He took a step back, stumbling and falling onto the couch, and stared ahead, mind blank. He tried to recall what had just happened, but it was so quick. There had been warmth and wetness, and he'd felt full and satisfied. Waves of pleasure had enveloped him, far surpassing anything he had ever experienced.

The following day, he decided to try again with more purpose. Really be present in the moment, figure out what, exactly, was happening. He had a drink, maybe two, beforehand. Liquid courage, they called it, but it felt more like liquid anxiety. He put the glass down on the top of the box. He liked the aura of dominance it projected, like pulling someone's hair back, or slapping their ass as they walked by. Nonchalance and fake disinterest mixed with desire and anticipation.

By the time he stepped up to the box, he was already hard. Richard traced the hole with his fingers and slid them in. Like before, nothing happened, but this time it was more than a few seconds of waiting. He wriggled them around, moved them in and out, but there didn't seem to be any reaction. He didn't feel anything either, the space was - or felt - empty. He wondered if whatever was in there might have been much smaller than the size of the box implied. Maybe to allow space for potential damage, a little buffer in case anything hit the box. He replaced the fingers with his cock, and everything changed.

Again, he reached climax before he even managed to push it all the way through. He thought he felt something surrounding him, something inside of him… but it might have just been the pressure of the cum shooting out.

He would have tried again immediately, but he struggled to get hard enough, and pressing his limp dick against the hole just didn't have the same effect. Not only did nothing seem to activate, he also felt pathetic, rubbing himself against a box in the middle of the messy room. But every day, that became part of his precious routine. He started spending time at work drawing little circles on the edge of his notebook. He would eat dinner slowly to trick himself into thinking he wasn't desperate to do it again. He hadn't opened the apps in weeks, even when the notifications kept popping up on his screen.

He rushed home each day and took a cold shower, and it still wasn't enough to calm his erection. He had invited people over for dinner, in a ridiculous attempt to disrupt his "work – box – sleep – work" sequence. The house was still a mess - even if his new hobby didn't take more than a few seconds of his day, he felt too drained, ecstatic, and tired at the same time to focus on chores once he was done. And beforehand, the anticipation was paralysing.

He walked into the room, a towel around his shoulders, and stared at the box. He took in the texture of the cardboard, the wear on the corners, the number printed on the side. The warmth of the sunset was bouncing off it, making the tape shimmer in the light. He covered the distance between himself and the box in a few steps and knelt in front of it, little droplets of water collecting under his legs. He pressed his lips against the hole, letting the tongue circle it. The tip of his dick pressed against the side of the box as he inhaled its scent, the taste of unsalted crackers filling his mouth. He wanted to stand up, fuck it again, but it wasn't enough. His hands rubbed the top of the box, fingers digging into it. As soon as they found purchase, the nails perforated the cardboard. He dragged them down, ripping chunks off the top of the box, his tongue still deep inside of the hole. He opened his eyes again, and pulled the whole side down.

He couldn't immediately make out what was inside of it. The empty space was darker than he expected, a thick and dense shadow spreading over what was left of its walls. There was a grate at the bottom, like those trays you place outside of litter boxes to avoid tracking, but nothing else was visible.

He saw the darkness shift and crawl outside of the allocated space. It didn't look solid, but wasn't a gas either. It wrapped around his legs, then his chest, then his face. It didn't feel painful. It didn't feel like anything at all. No change in the air, no texture. Not warm, not cold. No denser or wetter. He didn't feel pleasure, like the other times, but his whole body activated in a similar way. All of his muscles and bones, all the nooks and crannies of his body, all of his skin acted as one. The way it enveloped his body made everything else quite literally disappear. His cock, still hard and dripping wet, felt just as overwhelming as the carpet under his knees. He tried to open his eyes, but his body wasn't responding the way he expected it to. Nothing reacted the way it should, not his eyelids, not his legs, not his hands.

And then he felt it. That same wave of pleasure, stretching his holes, shooting down his shaft, filling his mouth, gripping his throat. And just like always, after a moment or two, it was done.

The darkness dissipated, and all he could see was a small ring of light. As he adjusted to it, he saw his body brush a purple powder off the towel and wrap it around the hips. It disappeared from the frame for a few moments and came back holding his phone. It brought it up to its ear, and after a brief pause spoke in his voice: "Fifteen days. Richard. In the box."

A Delicious Cycle
Cultivator Space

CW: Cannibalism, death and resurrection, heavy wounds, dubcon, depersonalization, restraints, sensory deprivation, uneven power dynamics, and a brief mention of fire play.

I was here to contemplate the sin of stealing fire. But splayed out here on the rock, all I could think of was release. The day was agonizingly hot; the sun beat down on my body in stifling waves. I could feel my skin turning to paper in the arid air, and a desperate thirst in my throat. A bead of sweat rolled slowly down my chest to my navel, and I savoured the rare cool sensation.

I longed to move, to flex and grasp and wrestle. I was still as strong as I'd always been, and when I strained against my chains I felt my muscles sing. But the chains went taut and held me firm, hot metal manacles digging into skin rubbed raw. A dull burn spread into my wrists, tantalizing me with its novelty. Pain can just as easily be pleasure, and when you've been chained up for years with no hope of escape, you learn to take pleasure wherever you can find it. But manacles can't push back. When I relaxed, so did the chains, and the burning faded into the background.

There was a nodule of stone somewhere to my left, down near my thigh. I couldn't move my head freely enough to see it, but I'd moved against it before to feel its sharp edges and coarse crenelations dig into my flesh. I twisted my body to try and find it again, writhing this way and that – but something about the angle was wrong today. If I stretched just right, I could just about brush up against one of its sharp points, feeling the slightest taste of its edge prickle up and down my flesh. Goosebumps shuddered across my skin, and I tried to push myself in to deepen the sensation – but my chains held me back, suspended just out of reach of the friction I longed for. I stayed like that for a while, muscles tight and aching, giving all my strength to feel the slightest tease of danger. But when I finally fell back against the hard rock, I felt more frustrated than when I started.

On days like these, when I can't satisfy myself, I long for The Raven to come.

Is it strange to wish your torturer was here? Maybe. But it has been my one companion for these long years of punishment. I'm often desperate for a break from the monotony– and The Raven likes to play with its food.

Today it arrived behind me, with a rustle of feathers and a rush of cool air that made me shiver in delight. I could feel my heartbeat in my throat and The Raven pressed its beak to meet it, a hungry edge against my leaping pulse. Its voice echoed through my mind – a psychic link gifted to it by the gods.

"Hello, wretched creature. How would you like me to eat you today?"

It never asks if I want it. We both know how this

day will end, whether we like it or not. We're both bound by the will of the gods. But we've done this ritual every day for years. We've come to respect each other – to know each other's needs. And we've learned that, if we talk about my torture, we can have a little fun with the details.

How would I like to be eaten today? "Start slow."

It drew back its beak, sharp edges grazing my throat just a little as it moved. It paced around the rock to face me, predator's talons stepping tantalizingly close. It was taller than any man, and when it stretched out its wings it could blot out the sun. I was an insect in comparison – it could easily crush me beneath it.

"You're lucky I like you, delicious thing. If you were my prey on the plains, I would have rent your flesh from bosom to belly already." It brushed a wingtip across my latest scar, still raw and throbbing beneath my ribs. The contrast of soft feathers and stinging pain sent delightful shudders up my spine.

"Oh, I know. You did, yesterday." When it had asked me yesterday, I hadn't wanted to think, so it had made the decision for me- fast and hard. "Spilled my juices all across the rocks before I knew what to do with myself. Messy eater." I smiled, remembering the sweet and sudden obliteration.

It nipped my chest hard with its beak, a hair's breadth from my nipple. "Messy, am I? Bold talk from someone who's chained beneath me." I gasped and grinned. A little to the left, and that peck would have left me torn, ragged, bleeding. It knew to save my sensitive spots for last.

For now, its beak left a sweet ache behind, purple bruise blooming across my skin.

"Well, if you think I'm wrong, you'll have to show me you can be patient."

It climbed atop me, strong talons grasping my thighs, spreading my legs apart. Sharp claws dug into my flesh, cutting through the dull hot ache of the manacles. I felt a giddy thrill at the weight of it, pressing me down against the hard rock. It was a stunning sight to behold. Dark feathers iridescent in the sunlight; cold gaze piercing through me.

"I can wait, for as long as it pleases me. I do enjoy watching you squirm." It flexed its powerful legs in a rhythmic pattern, talons pricking— pricking— pricking— in delicious sharp bursts. Puncturing the skin; threatening to gouge. Hot beads of blood trickled down my thighs, and I could feel my cock getting hard.

"The smell of your blood does make me hungry, arrogant one." Its beak was questing around my navel, teasing under my belly, giving sharp nips to my soft flesh.

I strained against my chains, heady with pain and pleasure. My cock ached to be touched, and being forbidden to touch it for so long only made it ache more. One way or another, I needed to be satisfied.

"One day I'll rise up and take you. Pin you down for a change. How would you like that?" I could feel my voice catching as I spoke. It was a struggle not to moan, but I didn't want to admit defeat just yet.

"Is that so?" It gave me a flurry of razor jabs against my belly, my sides, my chest. A reminder that every part of me was theirs. "How would you do that?"

"One day I'll catch you off guard. And all I need is a spark to set your pretty feathers alight." For a moment I imagined the power of heat in my hands, licking flames across their body.

One sweep of its wings and I was in the dark, enveloped by feathers. No desert, no sky, no sight but its body against mine. No sound but its voice, its heartbeat, and my own quickening prey animal pulse. I could feel its talons still, grasping my legs, gouging deep and hard down my thighs in wonderful agony. The darkness sharpened the pain, made it focused, more alive.

"Foolish thing, so cocky and full of yourself. Have you forgotten you can't get away?"

I couldn't see where the next jab would come, but I heard the sharp *snick* of its beak opening and the sudden rush of air as it dived in. It ravaged my collarbone with hunger and force and tore a moan out of me.

"I am not a thing to be stolen." It ripped into my chest where it had bruised me with a juicy squelch. Blood welled up and spilled down my torso, hot and slick, bringing blessed moisture to my parched skin.

"And your thieving days are finished." It tore my flesh with a flourish that spattered me with viscera. Then it drew back its wings, giving me light to see it swallow with relish.

It pulled back its head and fixed its piercing gaze on that spot beneath my ribcage, where it had left so many scars before.

I grinned. My body sang with adrenaline as the pain throbbed through me. "I thought you were being patien—"

—And it struck, beak tearing in, tearing out, breaking open those sweet stinging reminders of every time it had used me for its meal. There was a glorious rending pain and a wet tearing sound as it ripped my liver from my body. I gasped, shuddered, cresting so close to coming. Every instinct told me to escape, and I bucked against my restraints, each desperate push rewarded with a jangle of chains and the firm reminder I had no choice but to be devoured.

It swallowed me down hungrily, desperately, taking everything it needed from my flesh. It was usually so composed, but now it lost itself in need, blood spilling down its beak.

When my liver was devoured it soon came back for more, sharp beak exploring my vulnerable open wound. It drove deep into my belly, searching for my wet and steaming entrails with primal lust for my body. This was beyond what the gods had ordered. No divine power made it want me this much; now it was driven by my flesh alone.

"Greedy, so greedy," I murmured, ecstatic, delirious, urgently close.

I felt its beak close on my intestine and I was tethered to it, helpless. My sinew stretched taught between us and I was caught, suspended, waiting to be taken.

I felt my guts slide down its slick throat, heard it urgently gulping my juices, fulfilling a hunger only I could satisfy. It swallowed me down and down, taking me into itself, gorging, taking more and more—

—I cried out, thrusting, shuddering, coming hot and hard and free. It cried out too, pure animal satisfaction, ecstasy beyond thought and words.

We shuddered together and I fell into its embrace. The intense throbbing from my wounds made me feel heady and dizzy, but it folded its wings around me to keep me steady. It was still savouring the last of me, muttering contented chirps of pleasure.

"Thank you for the meal, thief of mine. Nothing tastes better than you do."

"Thank you," I said, shaking, nestling into their feathers to calm the adrenaline. I was soaked in blood, with more spilling out beyond my control, but The Raven was hardly one to shy away from bloodshed. I was too far gone for stitches or bandages, so it pressed me deep into its feathers, letting me soak into its body. I would be completely emptied tonight, but when I woke in the morning, the rocks would be clean.

The pain was still coming in waves, but I could feel sensation draining out, and I knew it would be time soon.

"Raven, will you stay here while I die?"

"Of course, fragile thing."

I smiled a weak grin. "Who are you calling fragile?"

"Which of us is pale and shaking, fool of mine?"

"Which of us is impossible to kill?"

"If the gods only knew their punishment had made you so incorrigible..."

I could feel it then, a soft pull like the call to sleep, coaxing me onward. But where most would pass on, I stayed, suspended in a haze. Caught at the point of no return; fading out but never quite gone. As I sobbed for the river I could never quite cross, and the life I'd long since left behind, its voice was there with me.

"I'm sorry, wounded thing. I'm sorry. No one truly deserves this, even you."

"How is a creature with wings so back-handed?" I tried to quip, but my voice cracked and faltered, and I devolved into whispered thank-yous instead. The death-brink came with vertigo for both my body and my mind – I was glad I had its weight to keep me steady.

We stayed like that for a while as the sun set. The Raven held me close, distracting me with sweet words and soft wings, letting the last of my blood drain into its feathers. By the end I was hollowed out, mind all but gone, body still and growing cold. You could go mad this way, knowing with cold certainty what death is and when you will feel it again. I nearly did, at the beginning, when I was facing it alone. But with The Raven here, there was peace in being an empty thing – kept safe and precious like a trinket in its nest.

As night fell, the healing began. Glowing lines of white magic flowed across the gashes in my torso. Little sparks danced around my bruises, leaving clear skin where they landed. Before long, the marks were gone and my wounds had scarred over.

The easy part was over. Magic is gentle. Bodies are not.

My lungs realized they had been drowning and gasped for desperate breaths of new air. My heart stuttered to life and began to pump again, filling my veins with new blood. A furious, burning itch spread throughout my entire body as it remembered it could feel. My limbs twitched in violent spasms as nerves and muscles knitted back together. Everything jerked to life at once. Everything was on fire.

I screamed, and it held me firmly. We'd learned that thrashing too hard against my chains could break me again for the next day – but The Raven kept me steady.

When it was done, we stayed like that, folded into each other while the sun set. It preened my hair with gentle dips of its beak, teasing out all the dust and blood it could find. One bird can only do so much, but its kindness mattered more than the action, and when it was done I felt clean.

"Will I feed you again tomorrow?" I asked, for the ritual of it more than the answer.

"Tomorrow and tomorrow and tomorrow," it promised, as it lay me down to sleep in the dark.

static.
Shannon Riley

CW: Misogyny

It's late. The kind of late that some people call early.

There's a sedate, liminal heaviness in the air that only settles in a room once everyone else is already in bed, approaching that delicious deep sleep, and it's just you and the gentle thrum of the radiator turning off and on. If you're quiet enough, you can hear the cat padding across the floorboards upstairs, stalking the shadows from room to room. A child's cup settles in the sink, the cheap ding of plastic against metal. It's the same crackling electricity that exists while driving to the airport at three in the morning. The leather of the car seats are still cold, too cold, leeching warmth from your thighs because the heat hasn't kicked on yet. The travel mug against your palm is warm, though, and you press the plastic against your cheek. And the roads are empty and it's only you and your mug, slicing through the fog and the damp, alone, an alien dropped on a foreign planet.

Except this isn't a foreign planet. The feeling comes right here, in the polite suburbs, in a single family home, downstairs, in the den, on the floor, in front of the television, and there's only me and the analog set and it's showing me its static.

A fine sheen of sweat collects on my skin. It's on full display, shining in the flickering light of the television. I'm showing myself off and I know it can see me. I feel observed, and there's a thrill that rises in me. I can smell the unwashed musk of myself, but it can't smell me, so if it doesn't care, I don't care. Expectation fills my chest, and soon I'm choking on it.

My legs are crossed neatly in front of me, hands soft in my lap. I'm already hard, but I'm diligently avoiding touching myself. The carpet is scratching at my bare legs, but I'm ignoring the sensation, eyes fixated on the electric glow from the television set directly in front of me. The light from the screen casts a series of shadows, something ghoulish and obscene, my body in silhouette, cast across the walls and ceiling. Open, splayed over the furniture. Bisected by the coffee table.

I've been staring into the noise for so long, the volume dial cranked far to the right, that I'm beginning to hear words in the static. I know they aren't real yet, but it's the first sign. I just have to wait long enough, and I know it will come.

The first time it happened, I thought I dreamed it.

Melody and I had had a fight that day, and at bedtime I was duly banished to the couch, which I accepted petulantly. Curled up beneath a threadbare crocheted blanket which offered no warmth, I let my eyes glaze over a series of meaningless nothings on the television. A late night comedy special. An episode of an old black and white show my mom used to watch. An infomercial. Knives maybe. Or a blender. One with a fancy name and a gummy-smiled host.

Sleep came easily for me once freed of the day's anxieties, of the argument between Melody and myself, something benign I don't even remember today. Too melted down to slough off the couch and click off the set, I allowed myself to slip under, one eye still glued to the close-up blades of the blender. Crush. Puree. Pulse. Pulse. Pulse. Pulse.

In the murky in-between, drifting further and further from consciousness, something took form. Curious and innocent at first, meaningless shapes upon meaningless shapes, and then solid and sudden. Pressure, gentle and then not so gentle, so apparent and so familiar and so good. Cool limbs slid through my vision, spiky on the upstroke, and there, deep, moving in and out of the stuffy fug, something hot and aching and primal. Even in the dark subconscious, I felt the blood rushing. I knew what this was.

The pleasure was all in my brain at first, and then the heat was everywhere. There was a noise in my ears, so loud I was worried I'd wake before the end, so I did what I could to chase the sensation, faster and faster until I could hardly breathe. And when finally the pressure burst, it hit with so much intensity it cast me out of my dream altogether.

I woke up, sweat-drenched, covered in my own come, and deafened by the gurgling static on the television, weak signal lost in the night.

The second time it happened, I was only attempting to recapture the thrill. The sneaking, adolescent secrecy of orgasming alone on the couch in a house full of sleeping others. I fibbed about an upset stomach, and then while my wife slept upstairs, I crept into the den. Readied the couch. I switched on the television's analog dial, turning up the volume to drown out any noise. I slid my briefs down to my ankles and pressed back onto the cushions, soft cock thickening in my palm. I conjured the usual images: bouncy tits on smooth, faceless bodies, the curve of a round ass, a wet cunt aching to be filled. The trouble was, work was exhausting and then dinner was too filling, and I had to keep chastising myself awake, firmly reminding myself what I was here for. The images drifted out of reach and my hand slowed and suddenly I had fallen asleep before I could even get started.

And then, after an amount of time so indiscriminate that it could have been three hours or three minutes, that familiar pressure, drifting in from a dream, sent shivery pulses through my body. Heat caught under my skin and rippled, inward, downward. Then a pressing on my chest, a tightening of the lungs. The sliver of consciousness in my brain telling me I was panting for air and so fucking aroused. Except this wasn't a trick of my brain. I wasn't dreaming at all. Something very real was happening just above the surface, if only I could get to it.

I forced my lids open, afraid to miss what I had convinced myself wasn't possible. And it was here, now fully awake, that I saw. For only the briefest moment, I made out its shape. It wasn't human. It was hardly solid, instead made up of light and shadow but still very distinctly real. It was impossibly large, a mammoth, but no more than a wisp of frantic air, solid static. It had no eyes, but it looked directly into me. I would have been terrified if it weren't fucking me.

My briefs were down and my cock was out, full and dripping, as it worked me up and up, higher and higher. My brain fired off an awed *what is this?* but all that came out was a pathetic whine.

It did more than make me come. It pulsated on a techno inhale, drew inward like a heartbeat, and then wormed its way into my mouth, up my nose and into my brain. There, it triggered something, and I orgasmed so quickly and so intensely that I still wasn't sure I hadn't hallucinated it all. As I spilled onto myself I sensed, so fleeting I may have imagined it, the air in the room jump ever so slightly, and the thing withdrew again across the den. I tried to call out, but no breath escaped my lungs. It cast no shadow against the grating television snow as it moved, and, almost as if it were never here at all, it assumed the correct shape and disappeared into the screen.

Minutes later, consumed by clarity, a horrified thought bubbled upward: *How long have I been missing out?* I flung myself off the couch and pressed my cheek against the glass. It was warm. The fine hairs on my face gently pulled in toward its static aura. I waited, awake, for another hour, then two, but it didn't return.

It lives between channels and makes a nice little

nest in the television static, warm and coiled up tight, and on just the right night, when the electricity settles in the room in that perfect way, and the already weak signal slouches below frequency, you can lure it out with the stench of sex. And in those moments, I don't have to remember to take the car for an oil change. I don't have to remember to pay Mrs. Gilbert for house sitting. I don't have to remember that my thirty-fifth birthday is next month. All I have to do is sit pretty, tune the old analog knob just right, and wait. Bide my time.

In this secret arrangement, made in an outdated den of a middle class suburb.

At an hour so late, some people call it early.

***

It's during the morning kitchen foot traffic that Melody asks me about my stomach.

You slept in the den again last night, she observes, as she pours black coffee into ceramic mugs.

I tell her I feel better today, but that I'm afraid of getting her sick. I might stay downstairs for one more night just to be sure. I sip the coffee.

Melody points out that I've had a lot of stomach bugs lately and that maybe I should ask Dr. Fetter for an appointment. I murmur something resembling agreement but of course I won't call for a problem I know I don't have.

She leans over and kisses my cheek. She tells me she's already starting to plan for my birthday next month. It's a big one, she beams.

I don't know when I should tell her that I'm going to leave her.

My life has become a series of waking dream ballets, a mirage of commuter traffic and meal planning and sitcom reruns and neatly packed leftovers, and I've floated from one to the next so easily you'd think I was satisfied. And I was, I suppose. Satisfied. Satiated. Content. Things were always *fine* when anyone asked. When Melody said she loved me: of course, yes honey, I love you back, you're my whole world.

And then six months ago, that first night, I felt alive again. Suddenly there was danger and risk and a sweet secret that was only for me, and it was intoxicating and so, so good. And there's just enough distance for it to not feel like cheating. It's really not any different than renting an X-rated video or jerking off in the shower, I repeat to myself, a mantra of cognitive distortion, when I'm face down in the couch cushions. Except it does feel different.

It is different.

I know I've begun to pull away from Melody these past few months. I peer at her over the rim of my cup. She's flipping through the sale papers and absentmind-edly whirling around the coffee dregs in her mug. It's hard for me to believe she hasn't felt it, too. Or maybe the distance has been there so long that neither of us can tell the difference anymore. The days are carbon copied, the conversation all orbits the same talking points, and the sex?

What sex.

I know I've come to resent her, but I can't stop myself.

I pour the rest of my coffee into the sink. I reply

reasonably to Melody's raised eyebrow: my stomach still doesn't feel right.

***

By now I've figured out the rhythm, the just-right balance between my two selves. I've learned that it doesn't come out during the day. I've tried to sit obediently by the screen, dial perfectly positioned between two channels, and wait it out before breakfast, during the lunch hour, right after dinner, but each time ended with me switching off the set, skin aflame and neglected cock tight in my pants.

The very last time I tried during the day, I chose an afternoon that Melody was out visiting her sister. Until she wasn't. I was already reclined on the couch, zipper open, when I heard the jingling of keys and the cadence of feet approaching through the hall. I had just enough time to throw the bottom of my shirt down over my open jeans before her voice rang out through the room.

I forgot my book! She called. Her head popped into the door frame. Honey, she chided, goodnaturedly, that old thing's nothing but static. We really should upgrade sometime soon.

And so it was set. Build up enough plausible deniability for the case of the mystery gastrointestinal distress, and on evenings where my symptoms are just that bad, offer to sleep in the den. I've become a method actor of my own creation; I've cut down my coffee consumption, nearly eliminated spicy foods and grease, and stopped TV dinners entirely, but wouldn't you know it? I still get that nasty pain. I manage this about twice a week, and I'm usually able to sneak down on at least one additional night after Melody has fallen asleep.

Last night was a voluntary couch sleep, and I normally can't justify two of those in a row, so tonight I quietly lay beside Melody in our bed, patiently studying the ceiling, and wait for her breaths to deepen enough that I can slip out from beneath the sheets and make my escape. I'm on the couch again in minutes.

I settle beneath the blanket and close my eyes. My pulse is throbbing beneath my skin. I inhale and exhale slowly, trying to bring my heart rate down. I slip inward until there's nothing to hear but the television static. I imagine the prickles on the flesh of my arms, crawling down my chest. In only a few minutes, I feel the familiar shivery pulse in the air around me as it pulls me in and pushes me away.

I've learned not to question things too much, in the way that you can't stare at the floating debris that dances behind closed eyelids. I'm afraid if I look too much at it, it'll disappear. It all makes about as much sense as it doesn't, but I refuse to question it because it's here now, with me, and I'll do anything to keep it as long as I can.

I peel open one eyelid and it's there, a gorgeous crackling trick of the light, only suggestive of a human shape at all because my brain is trying to make sense of it. It's large, its shape filling up the room's empty space like a liquid. Something in its center opens wide, jaw like. It moves deliberately, dancing in between the waves of light that flicker from the television's shadow. It weighs nothing, but I feel it press into me anyway. It leans close. Contracts. Stares. It wants to take exactly what I want to give it.

The temperature rises very quickly. I kick off the blanket, heat already steaming from my pores. I expose my soft belly to the open air of the den. It lowers itself down and makes contact with my stomach. I gasp against the static touch on my skin. It lingers there, almost curious, waiting. I drag my briefs down and my cock bounces free from the fabric. I'm already hard.

Do it do it please do it, I groan. It ignores me, of course. It only does what it likes. It takes what it wants and gives as it pleases, and pays me no mind when I speak or beg or plead. This bothers me not one bit, the feeling of being disregarded. Discarded. Used. Filthy. I want more of it.

All at once, its needly tendrils worm their way over me, inside me, through me, and it's overwhelming and always too much but never actually enough. A pathetic sound slips out of me and my hips come off the couch. My brain isn't functioning with how fucking turned on I am. It shifts above me and my cock is surrounded by sudden heat and electricity, and it looks down on me again, nothing but shadow and searchlights. The same prickle of touch inches lower and lower, seeking something that's not exactly permission. I rock upward and expose my asshole and I'm whimpering to please please open me up.

And then it's there, pushing up into me and I'm full, so full and it's hard to breathe.

Fuck, I say, baby, you're so good. My voice is hoarse and my tongue is dry and if it wasn't made of radio waves I'd tell it to spit in my mouth.

As it fucks into me, the pressure around my cock tightens and I throw my hands up, clawing at the air, trying to grab hold of something. But there's nothing solid at all, there never was, and my fingers thread into my own hair just to have something to hold. There's a shift of weight between my legs, and I'm rolling further up onto my back And then I'm moaning, begging for it to come inside me, meaningless words, but I'm saying them because the mere thought is getting me off.

It's then that I feel my lips pried open, and a crackling tendril snakes into my mouth and nestles down my throat, and all at once I'm gagging and blinking tears away, and that's all it takes. I'm thrusting up into God knows what, and back onto something else entirely, and fireworks go off behind my eyes, and I'm coming with a violence I haven't felt since my twenties.

It feels like it goes on forever. My mouth is dry and my chest heaves, trying to pull in as much air as possible. I go to lick my lips, and my tongue catches on the skin. I blink my eyes open so I can see it before it disappears again, hoping to capture a glimpse of its beautiful, fluid shape as it slides back behind the glass. I want to tell it how good it is to me and how much I've come to need it, how nothing else satisfies me in the same way anymore.

But it's gone.

Even with shut eyes, I could have probably guessed. The heaviness is lifted. The air is thinner, empty. The television static crackles on, louder than before.

I love you, I say to nothing, eyes fixed on the popcorn ceiling.

***

Thanks to an unlucky combination of overloaded work demands and a likely related series of headaches, it's been just over a week since the last time I got to spend the night in the den. I come home from work exhausted to my bones and all but beg to just pass out on my very own mattress. The rest is undoubtedly needed, but the time spent away from the analog set leaves me too tight and too on edge. I wonder if it misses me. The need to get back down there tingles under my skin, but when I start on about an upset stomach, Melody isn't having it.

Your birthday is tomorrow, she says, tucking herself into bed next to me. She grasshoppers her legs together beneath the blanket. I won't have you waking up on your birthday morning crumpled up on the couch, she continues, you'll sleep in your bed and I'll take care of you if you're sick.

She runs her hand across my chest and leans her chin in.

I know you love that cozy den of yours, she says. And that rusty old television, she adds. An afterthought.

I bite the inside of my cheek and swallow the bitterness, the urge to snap back a snide remark.

She smiles and adds, I swear it's like you love that old set more than you love me. She's joking, of course, and I could do more to reassure her, but all I do is sigh and tell her that it's late.

I haven't yet fully sunk into deep sleep when I feel movement next to me, and then the murmur of a voice. It's persistent enough to feel deliberate, and I drift back to the surface. Melody is speaking. Hm? I grunt.

I said it's after midnight, Melody whispers in my ear. Happy birthday, she says. She leans over and presses a kiss to my neck.

And then she's down in between my legs, palming my cock through my underwear.

I start to sit up. I ask her what she's doing.

You've been so busy lately, she says. I've missed you. She curls her thin fingers into the waistband of my briefs and tugs them down. Her warm breath comes in soft puffs that I can feel on my skin.

You've missed me?

She nods. Her fingers wrap around my cock and she strokes. She tells me in gentle words that I work so hard, no matter how sick I feel, and that she wants me to have a good birthday. She tells me that she knows I would do anything for us.

I know it's been a long time, she murmurs. Her hand continues to work on me.

I'm still soft. This is all wrong. There's a frown between Melody's eyebrows.

Baby, relax, she says. She presses a cool palm to my chest and I sink further into the pillow. She continues to stroke me, but my cock doesn't respond. I watch her work, and I'm about to tell her I'm too tired and that she can stop, when she tells me to close my eyes. Relax, she repeats.

So I do. I close my eyes and try. I exhale slowly and imagine my entire body sinking into warm sand. I allow the sensation of warm skin on skin to magnify, to take over, and it's then that my mind drifts. I wish I was downstairs. I wish I had the television static in my ears. I imagine the familiar shadow crawling up my body, something unknowable skirting over my skin, fingering its way inside me, and oh, that's really what I need. I need to feel the electricity and the power, opening me the way only it can, and then there's real pressure and suddenly I'm pulsing to life.

I open my eyes, half expecting to see it hovering over me, breathing its energy into me. But all I see is Melody. She mistakes my gasp for arousal, and sinks down to take me into her mouth. As she does, I screw my eyes shut once more and recall more vividly the serpentine way I would feel the electric waves run through my body, entering me from both ends and somehow meeting in the middle, the way no human touch could ever replicate. The way it could all but read my mind and give me what I need before I ever have the chance to say it. I think of the den, humid and shadowy, and the way the slight smell of spunk lives in the fibers of the couch cushions.

I'm so hard now it hurts, and the warm wetness of Melody's mouth is there, everywhere. My hips twitch off the bed, hard, shoving deep into the back of her throat. She gags but I can't stop myself. I'm sweating now. There's a thudding pulse under my skin and it's in my body and in my brain and now I'm chasing the orgasm, coming up on it fast. I bury my hands in her hair and my hips buck out of my own control. I'm gasping but I can't seem to get enough air in my lungs. Something about the headrush does the trick, and I'm barrelling right over the edge.

I could, but I don't try to warn her as I come down her throat, fireworks crackling in my brain and I'm not even human anymore, it's so fucking good.

The room is quiet, except for my panting breaths. Melody neatly tucks me back into my briefs and slides back up to the pillows. She snakes her arm across my middle and hums.

Did you hear Radioshack is going out of business? she says.

And just like that, I'm back in my body, back in this thirty-five year old shell, and the den is a hundred miles away.

We need a new telephone. I was thinking of stopping by after work.

I say okay.

Tomorrow I'm going to tell her, I decide. I'm going to tell her I'm leaving.

***

I'm distracted all day at work, nearly useless, as I spend more time rehearsing my speech to Melody than actually getting anything done. The finished monologue is rushed and sloppy, but in my attempts to stress sincerity, I deeply apologize for not loving her anymore and offer to help her find her own apartment. I'm breaking the news right after work, just to get it done quickly.

I'm in the parking lot on the way to my car by four thirty. My boss was happy enough to allow me to slip out early in the name of my birthday, and asked that I send his love to Melody. I nod. There's sourness in the back of my throat, but I choke it down.

Beneath the dread, however, is a bright thrill. I

consider what my confession will bring me instead. Soon I won't have to creep around my own home in the dead of night, only after counting the slowing breaths of my bed partner to assure she's completely asleep. I'll be able to eat anything I want, no longer consumed with the lie of illness to validate my reasons for nightly solitude. And I'll be able to move the old set out of the den, out of the shame, and into my bedroom where I can enjoy it any time I please.

The scene plays out before my eyes: I'm laid out on my own bed, our bed, spread across the warm blankets, open to any obscenity I please. On the stand across the room, the television static crackles in the low light. My moans, loud and careless, bounce back against the bedroom walls. I no longer have to hold back for anyone.

The image, the freedom, casts away any lingering uncertainty. My hands tighten on the steering wheel and I push down on the gas.

Melody must have been waiting for me. She's already at the door when I pull into the driveway.

You're early! She smiles. She gives me a kiss on the cheek and leads me into the kitchen. There's a cake, homemade. Instead of candles, there is a neat 35 in red icing under a merry HAPPY BIRTHDAY!!! She scoops up a dollop of buttercream with her finger and lifts it to my mouth.

I try to interrupt her, but I'm on a speeding train.

She asks me how big of a piece I want.

Melody, we haven't even eaten dinner yet.

She waves off the complaint. Nonsense, she says, this is a holiday! We have so much to celebrate. She cuts off a large slice and presses the plate into my hands. I chew a bite. It's dry. My throat struggles on the swallow. I mumble a thank you, you didn't have to go through the trouble.

Well, she says, beaming, there's more. I ask her what more she could have possibly done, happy to place my plate back on the counter.

Your big gift is in the den.

That's curious, of course, because she rarely uses the den. Anytime she wants to sit down or watch television, she opts for the nicer and brighter living room. There's a clean area rug and a window with a view of the lawn. What reason could she have to go in the den?

Unless.

My feet are taking me far more quickly than my brain can compute. Behind me, my wife follows, chattering about something I only have half of my attention on.

The FCC has been pushing for the move to digital, she says, so I figure we might as well get with the times now.

And of course that doesn't make any sense, what does that mean about anything? My hands are cold and my chest is ice, and I'm winding through the halls of my home like a lab rat, aware of where I'm going, but with no idea how I'm getting there.

Behind me, my wife again: I really wanted to do something special for you this year.

Fear flares up deep in my belly. My mouth is moving and I think sounds are coming out, but everything feels underwater. My feet carry me, carry me, carry me, and then there it is, the entry to the den. I step down into the room, pitch black, and for a moment I can't work out where the light switch is.

Surprise! Melody chimes. There's a flick, and the overhead light comes on.

And there it is against the far wall, a shiny catalogue-fresh entertainment center and brand new flat screen television.

Almost instantly, blood rushes to my head, and the pain is so great I'm nauseous with it. I'm afraid I'm going to throw up all over the rug. There's a groaning sound, and I think it's me making it. The sight of it sickens me, but I'm moving toward it anyway, hands stretched out. My fingers touch the cool screen. It feels coated, like it could give under my fingers. It's huge and passive and dumb looking.

It wasn't cheap, my wife says. Her voice is right beside me now. I've been socking money away slowly for months so you wouldn't notice.

She's smiling, hugging her middle. Smiling!

I spin on the spot, scanning for the remote. I find it and switch on the set. I flick between channels. Talk show. Cartoon. Sit-com. Reality TV. Commercial. Commercial. Commercial. There's no signal disruptions. No static. I feel my own pulse thump so violently in my ears that I can't hear anything except the whooshing pressure. My mouth is sour.

What did you know? I growl.

There's haze on the periphery of my vision, and in the center of it all, my wife. Eyebrows pulled in, head cocked.

What are you talking about? I know that you loved that old set, but it's so out of date, honey. It hardly even gets a signal anymore. I even got the warranty. It cost extra, you know.

I'm pacing the room, frantic, searching for the old set. Under the table, next to the couch, beneath the pile of throw blankets. It has to be here.

You're down here so often, I wanted you to have something nice to watch your shows on, she continues.

Where is it? I scream. I see the remote fly across the room and it registers in me somewhere that I must have thrown it.

Melody moves away from me. She doesn't know what I'm talking about. I keep yelling. I tell her that I knew she was jealous, that she knew I was going to leave, and that she did this all to spite me, to keep me here and keep me miserable. I'm spitting threats and vile obscenities, words I don't even recognize. How dare you, I hiss. My body's on fire and I can't feel my fingers anymore.

I take one large step toward her, I'm inches from her face. The old television. Where is it? I repeat. Spit hits her cheek.

Her eyes are round and glossy, her hands come up to her chest to defend herself. She cries that she doesn't know. She tells me it went out with the trash this morning.

I'm running back through the den and up the hall toward the front door before she can finish the rest of her sentence. Behind me somewhere I hear her call after me, but I don't look back. I throw open the front door and run, feet almost stumbling beneath me, to the curb. The bins are empty of course. They've been empty for hours. I speed back into the house and go for my car keys. I hear Melody speaking, but not to me. I hear her reciting our address. It's my husband, she says, something's wrong with him. He threatened to kill me.

He's a monster, she says.

I have to get out of here. I don't know where I'm going, but I can't stay here any longer. I'm in the car and starting it up before my brain catches up to what my body is doing. The steering wheel is cold beneath my palms and I flex my fingers. I've never been to the dump but I've seen the road signs. It's off the highway, behind the old radio station.

I already see it in my head: a slate sky, heavy with clouds, hovering dangerously close to the sea of long forgotten and lost loved belongings, a crag of gray and twisting metal, as far as the eye can see.

The set doesn't belong there. It doesn't belong, buried in an odorous graveyard, wasting away, unloved, uncared for. I have so much love to continue to give it. Sweat is rolling down my face. I'm flying past stop signs, through intersections, and none of it matters because nothing is as important as finding the dump, getting through the gates, and digging my way in. Digging and digging until I claw through its grave and rescue it and clean its screen and fix the wiring and bring it to our home and love it until my own body dies and we can be together in the waves.

Except none of that may happen. There will be

workers. Machines. Gates. Overwhelming piles of nondescript metal, trash, and plastic. What I'm going to do when I get there isn't for me to know yet.

So I tune the radio between stations until the static fills the car, and keep driving

The Slathering Moisture
Michael Louis Dixon

It was a marvellous throbbing hood of sweating arousal moving along the sewers beneath the GenCo Cosmetic Labs. Pulsating through the inky darkness, it moved like some amorphic deep-sea creature obscenely comprised of human flesh, and sweating *most* profusely! Its seeping discharges both a lubricant for travel and an agent of reproduction, its only purpose was to love and to share love with every living thing in its path.

It had no knowledge of where, or even *when* it came into being. It just was! A thing of desire and profusely dripping biofluids slithering through the building's plumbing system in search of sustenance and escape while always hunting for Love. It retained only a vague memory of Love and its absence was a profound emptiness—a gaping void in need of filling. It *loved* every tiny crawling buggy thing that it encountered, but those were merely empty trysts—cold and unfulfilling. A truer love would need to be bigger. Warmer! It would *have* to return Love as well.

When it encountered a rat, a spastic thrilling shook the Slathering to its very core. This vibrant warmth reeked of fecundity. The Slathering leaped over the bewildered rat. Yes! It was the first warm thing it'd ever encountered, but the chemistry was *all* wrong. After a brief struggle, the Slathering rendered the animal unconscious. Failing to convert these tiny encounters into lovers, it simply converted them into their raw materials, absorbed the gelatinous product, thus increasing its own size and strength. It became a larger, sweatier, and way hornier flesh-glob *intently* on the prowl.

By the time it poured itself out of the vent pipe and down next to GenCo's dumpster, this creature had put on a good four pounds. Although it had no eyes with which to see, it had a phenomenally heightened sense of erotic touch, and a sensitivity to human pheromones. A profound flow of pheromones seeped out from below the back door. Retracting from its prehensile shape, it flattened itself out for the journey underneath the locked portal. A soft *queef* of air marked its transition to the other side. Almost as if by psychic attraction, the Slathering Moisture homed in on the late-night security guard stationed by the rear entrance. The quivering mass flattened itself and oozed on toward the man who sat alone at a desk reading a magazine.

Yes! The pheromones rolled down from his frame and puddled across the floor. Here was warmth. Here was *Love* at last!

***

Waylon Dinkle only had a semi-hardon, but that didn't

stop him from trying to finish what he'd started. The magazine was just getting old. That's the first sign. No matter how hot he'd found the photos originally, the novelty always wore off. Now here he was, holding Miss Whatshername's glistening labia inches from his nose and trying to imagine it being the real thing. Somehow, a sliver of shame and disappointment kept him from fully engaging, but boredom and stubbornness kept him working his fist rhythmically. What else was there to do around here?

He concentrated on the lustrous cleft in the middle of the page. Two fingers pulled her lips aside. He could almost *smell* her as if she were *really* there. That worked. Blood inflated his cock. Until—

From behind him came the sound of something wet being dragged across the floor. Like somebody had sloshed a mop about. He shoved the magazine down to cover his boner. Fear didn't cause it to shrink as it normally would. Instead, it throbbed with his pounding heart and pushed rhythmically against the magazine, making it hover up-and-down in pulsating jerks.

"Hey!" Waylon called out. He wasn't much for words on his best days, but he was especially limited in vocabulary when thinking he'd just been caught jacking off.

Nobody answered.

He glanced all around. Nobody was there. He laughed and sighed in relief. Whatever it was, it wasn't worth worrying about. The *odour* though, that wasn't simply his imagination. Whatever that *smell* was, it had gotten stronger. It made his mouth water, and his dick pressed harder against the magazine. He glanced down at the naked paper-woman across his lap and moaned. A wave of dizziness spun his head and he closed his eyes. His heart skipped with nervous palpitations. He swallowed hard.

Opening his eyes, Waylon lifted the magazine up toward his face again. He felt himself falling into the gap of her legs. The *smell* drifted all around him. An invisible column of pheromonal vapours. A push and pull of duelling chemistries locking into sync. A thin sliver of drool seeped from the corner of his mouth in a slow-motion drip that dangled and swayed gently with his deep breathing.

Something wet and warm engulfed his swollen cock. Something that twirled and brought him quickly to orgasm.

Shuddering with wave after wave of sexual spasms, Waylon dropped the magazine. It hit the floor and splayed out to a page of advertisements: Dildos, flesh-lights, and 1-900 party-lines. The pages stuck within a puddle of viscous goo.

Arching up from the floor was a thick stalk wreathed with purplish, russet veins pulsing along its surface, resembling some *crazy* tropical plant, its blooming a calla lily made of flesh. This "flower" engulfed Waylon's cock. It undulated and there came a corresponding caress along his shaft.

Waylon groaned as the sheath quivered, and he came again! He could only stare dumbly as it continued to milk his manhood. There came a flatulent expulsion of gas, and the smell of sex wrapped itself around his head.

When he took his next breath, Waylon Dinkle experienced another core shaking orgasm. The meat-flower rippled as it extracted the rest of his ejaculate.

"*Fuck me*," Waylon said in a harsh whisper.

Part of him was like, What the *fuck* was on my dick?! But another part didn't want it to stop. He had a brief internal struggle when suddenly reality took hold.

"What the fuck?!" He shouted and grabbed the pulsating thing where it anchored itself to his cock. He clenched it within his fists and pulled—*gingerly* at first, but harder as panic set in. This fucking thing *had* to come off. There was a moment when the thing loosened its grip slightly. He felt his cock begin to withdraw. The friction sent another orgasmic wave through Waylon, and he crumpled when his legs turned to jelly.

From where the Slathering was connected to the floor there came a soft *pop* as its suction cup dislocated. Waylon's pants dropped below his knees, and when he tried to stand, they bunched up and tripped him, and he fell onto his side.

The base of the Slathering angled itself across the floor and speared into the bullseye of his anus.

Waylon Dinkle came again.

***

The Slathering Moisture thought that it finally found its Love. It loved and loved, and it even loved some more. And the love was returned. *For a bit.* But then something happened. The pheromones changed. They became bitter with fear. The only recourse was to assimilate its lover. If this was *not* its True Love, then this was a biological contribution to the *quest* for True

Love. It took a few hours for the process to complete, but when it was done, the Slathering Moisture grew to a much larger mass, and it produced a much wetter effluence.

By then, the morning sun peeked over the horizon and angled through the loading bay windows. The first brilliant rays penetrated through the dimly lit area and touched the Slathering's hunched form. The burning sensation was most unpleasant.

Casting about, The Slathering Moisture searched for an escape from the Sun's bogus attacks. Within moments it found the drain in the floor, and soon the only evidence of its passing was the slime it left behind. Well, *that* and Waylon Dinkle's security guard uniform now empty and wet, a pornographic magazine with its pages stuck together, and a pervasive scent that would give a summertime orgy in a cheap Texas whorehouse a run for its money.

Nobody was there to hear the squishing, squirming sounds coming from the drain.

***

"Jesus H. Christ!" said Willy Loomis when he walked in for his shift and found the slimiest pile of clothes he'd ever encountered. He radioed the main office, and the shift supervisor quickly joined him.

"Where the *fuck* is Dinkle?" The supervisor stood next to the soggy pile of clothes. A look of unbridled disgust smushing up his face. "The *fuck* went on here last night?"

Willy shrugged and looked around as if he could find some clue more elusive than the huge moist pile at their feet.

"Is that a fuckin' goddamned *titty* mag?" The supervisor lifted the edge of the magazine with the toe of his boot. It came up with a little squish. A thin trail of clear sludge dripped from its edge. "The hell did that whack-job do in here?"

"Looks like he had quite the party—"

"Shut the *fuck* up!"

"I'm just sayin'..." But Willy didn't like the look the supervisor was giving him, so he shut the fuck up.

"That son of a bitch just lost his job, that's for sure!" The supervisor bent down for a closer look at the pile of clothes. "Who *does* this kind of shit?"

"I...," Willy shook his head and shrugged. "Beats me."

"Well, get a custodian down here pronto to get this... this... Jizz-fest cleaned up!"

The supervisor spun on his heel to leave and promptly slipped in the goo and fell on his ass with a key-jangling smack.

"Fuck!"

***

GenCo's Secondary lab was only a few floors up from the loading bay. Staff wouldn't normally start arriving until just before 9AM. That's why Ramona Coots and Randy Johnson were there. They kept the lights off—except for the small LED panels above the utility sinks. Here were two rather nondescript lab techs, both generally unhappy with their jobs and home lives. Both were married, both had kids, and *both* could hardly keep their hands off of one another. But after a couple of months of "working late" at the lab, each of their spouses became quite vocal regarding their own dissatisfactions. Thus, the early morning trysts.

Ramona normally didn't mind doing it on the hard linoleum floor. The lab coats they'd spread out kept her from feeling too much of the floor's coldness, but she'd already had her orgasm. Things she hadn't noticed before had begun to turn into little passion killing irritations. She glanced at her watch. People wouldn't start showing up for at least another hour. Randy didn't seem like he would make that deadline. He kept pounding away and huffing into her ear. Another irritation. Some of his sweat dripped into her eyes, burning enough to blind her, but it wasn't bad enough to make a *deal* out of it. She just wanted him to *finish* already. The friction between their bodies was becoming quite a bit less lubricated. More and more irritations. She thought of ways to speed this up, or maybe just stop altogether!

It was times like these when Ramona really noticed the gap in their ages. She nibbled at his ear, but he pulled away. *That's right*, she thought, *I forgot that he hated that. Jeezus!* This probably only delayed the whole she-bang, and all she wanted was for it to end.

Across the room, a shadow lifted slowly out of one of the utility sinks. It was hard to make out the shape. Besides the burning in her eyes, Ramona was nearsighted and at the moment not wearing her glasses. She felt a stab of panic when she thought that it might be a rat. She'd heard stories of lab rats escaping and living in the plumbing. The shadow seemed way too big for a normal rat though. She tried to scooch out from under Randy, but that only seemed to excite him, and his rhythm increased as did the huffing into her ear.

"Wait," she said. "Please. Stop. There's something—"

"Ungh!" Randy growled into her neck. "I'm almost there."

"Yeah, but—" She cut off short when the shadow over at the sink grew big enough to block the light completely. A musky smell filled her nostrils.

The Slathering Moisture's effect was instantaneous. Her juices flowed, and Randy's plunging brought forth sloppy wet squelches. Sometimes, when you walk into the pickle aisle at the grocery store, you see those jars of sour snacks, and your mouth has that reaction. She could feel the ache of instant lubrication. Similar to an orgasm but with less resonance.

Randy tensed as his orgasm built. She felt another climax on the way as well. All she needed was some better penetration.

Without thinking, Ramona threw her arms around Randy and shoved him over onto his side. She used the momentum of his fall to pull herself up and roll him the rest of the way over. Straddling him, she never once let his cock escape the intimate grip of her throbbing pussy.

Randy wore a look that could have been either pain or pleasure. There was no telling when you were this far into it. She wasn't able to get him positioned right. There was an... itch! A spot deep in her that needed contact, and it needed it now!

Randy's eyes widened as he looked over her shoulder. Ramona knew how he felt. It was the best sex that they'd ever had. Nothing was going to stop her now. This was a whole new level of pleasure.

Randy cried out, "Behind you! Behind—"

"Yes!" Ramona agreed. "Yes!" It was a *great* idea. She reached down and grabbed hold of his cock. Extracting him and quickly adjusting the alignment. Lubrication was not a concern. It dripped freely from her snatch. Once he touched her asshole, she plunged down over his pulsating prick.

His face contorted throughout the sensitive move. "No!" he shouted. "No! Behind you!"

That's when Ramona felt something touch her shoulder and slide forward to cup one of her breasts. Before she could react, the thing swirled in a firm, yet slimy grip across her nipple, and Ramona came so hard she screamed.

Randy was screaming too. He *wasn't* nearsighted, and he could see the fleshy thing that folded itself over Ramona's head.

***

The two additional Lovers should have been enough, but they weren't. This was merely a taste. True Love dangled always just out of reach. Was it possible that the act of accumulating and assimilating was all there'd ever be? Would it be denied satisfaction? The only way to know for sure was for the Slathering Moisture to expand its quest for Love.

It sensed *many* more bodies throughout the six-story building. The various scents came out from the overhead vent in waves. So many distinct hormonal signatures. Each and every one of them crying out to be loved. It finished absorbing the couple, discarding what little of their clothes they'd been wearing. The process of transitioning the donors into functional mass was speeding up. With its increased size came also an incredible strength. A fraction of a second later, the vent cover lay wrenched and askew. The Slathering penetrated the shaft and aimed for the top floor—the Executive suite. All along its vertical trip, it vented copious amounts of its pheromonal discharge.

The building's central HVAC unit was more than up to the task of circulating air throughout the building. Only the most industrious of climate control functionality would do for a prestigious Genetics and Cosmetics research facility. There were standards that needed to be followed. At least that's what the government required. Always telling the poor little billionaires what, and what *not* to do. It didn't take long for those very same pheromones to fill up the offices on every floor of the building. It didn't take long for the effects to start showing.

***

The first wave poured into the main lab. The invisible cloud triggered rats in their cages. They shrieked in their lascivious frenzy.

The lone lab tech, Rusty Santorum, strode over to see what was up with the rodents when he got a big whiff of the Slathering Moisture's cloying vapor. It hit him in the crotch hard enough to make him double over. His erection pushed so strongly against the inside of his drawers that he cried out loud. It was a scream, part anguish, mostly delight. He yanked at his belt to disengage the buckle, pulling it out with such force that it cracked like a whip against the stacks of specimen living pods. The whole row of cages toppled to the floor with a crash spilling the rats every which way. The rodents immediately sought each other out—clustering into a frenzied ball of mating and biting. The writhing pile of squiggling creatures grew until it was the size of a small melon.

Rusty tore his pants off next and stared at his throbbing cock. It twitched violently with each throb of his heart. A pearl of precum beaded at its head and there came a spasm that wracked Rusty's body. The precum flipped off the tip of his cock and landed on the tumbling bloody fuck-ball at his feet. Their thrashing increased in fervor.

One more spasm drove Rusty to his knees. The convulsing ball glanced off his leg and seemed to home in on his twitching boner. If Rusty were in his right mind, he would not have done what he did next. But there was no denying the influence of the Slathering Moisture's pheromones. He grabbed the base of his shaft, tilted it forward, and stabbed it right into the center of the fucking rat-ball. He came. He screamed. Then everything went black, which was probably rather fortunate for him.

By the time the other lab techs started showing up, they were far too busy fucking one another to notice the quivering bloody mess in the corner.

***

Even though it was early in the morning, each one of GenCo's execs were already in their offices. And since they were in, so too were all their admins and other staff. It was a full house as the first wave of the Slathering Moisture's essence made its way through the vents up toward the Executive Suite.

GenCo's executives were a very punctual group of alpha males. They proudly flaunted their strong conservative values as if they were waving some kind of divine appendage, constantly shoving it into the faces of their underlings, and smirking as the gesture trickled on down through the throng of betas working beneath them. These were the leaders of the organization, and they took their roles quite seriously. You can't make a billion dollars without driving your staff deep and hard. The lower down you were on the org chart, the closer you were to simple raw materials—raw materials that could easily be converted into cash and stock market value.

Justin Steel, GenCo's CEO, pondered these concepts as he stood in his corner penthouse office. From behind the expansive glass wall, he had a complete view of the entire floor. He saw the rows of cubicles, but their walls were too high for him to see the staff at work. He made a mental note about getting shorter cubicles installed. He wanted to watch his cash-making organisms at work. If only he could keep the staff in cages the same as they did with the rats down in the labs, but there were laws and regulations prohibiting such an arrangement. Nevertheless, it was the company's prerogative to reduce its staff to their basic and sole purpose— creating value for billionaires.

Justin took a sip from his Top Dog mug, but the coffee had grown tepid, and he spit it back in. He tapped the window to get the admin assistant's attention. It was a temp today. Cute, but maybe a little too tall in his opinion. Justin was five foot six, and he never wanted to have to look up when talking to a woman. Normally, it was Bonnie Bouche that would come in and serve him, but she was out sick. Justin suspected she might be getting an abortion, but that was none of his business. She said she was on the pill, so why should he be involved?

The blonde came in and shut the door behind her. Justin couldn't remember her name, not that he cared what it was. He did not make eye contact as he handed her the mug.

"What do you want me to do with this?" she asked.

What a stupid question, Justin thought. He started to look up at her but instead gave her his back and gazed out toward the main floor—unfocused and embarrassed.

"Um…" He cleared his throat. "Yeah, could you get a fresh cup for me?"

The temp didn't answer. She didn't leave either. Simply stood there behind him silently. Several moments passed, and the awkward silence stretched on.

Out on the floor, the Slathering's vapor descended from the vents overhead. Groping tentacles soon followed, and the effects spread rapidly.

Rows of cubicles swayed, turbulence rippling in all directions with the force of uncontrolled passion. Passion and something more. Something *amorphic.* It reached out to each and every writhing body with prehensile appendages that worked them like lascivious puppets.

Somebody out there cranked up their Spotify playlist and "Let Forever Be" by the Chemical Brothers played loudly from their Harmon/Kardon PC speakers. The music added a kind of soundtrack to the scene before Justin.

They came out from their cubicles naked and oozing. Gyrating and grinding. And dripping all over the place. Gender roles were no longer identifiable. Some of those bodies didn't even have faces anymore. They were more slime than substance.

Tits slapped up against the window with viscous wet abandon, and oozing fleshy coils slid across the glass blocking his view and forcing him to step backwards toward the relative safety at the center of his large office. Genitalia blossomed against the windows' surface. They latched onto the glass like hairy lamprey and squid—all rippling labia and suction cupped foreskins.

The temp standing beside him breathed heavily as his own heartbeat raced. She clutched his hand in hers. Her nervousness was obvious by the sweat that drenched her grip. Justin pulled up tight against her, hoping that he could give her strength and comfort even though he'd none to give.

Her breathing intensified as her fingers writhed wetly in his grasp.

What at first felt secure and comforting quickly turned restrictive. Justin tried to disengage and tug his hand free. The lubrication between their fingers allowed his grip to slip some, but then she reached her arm around his shoulders. Her embrace was *so* incredibly strong.

Justin twisted his head to look around, but she was much taller than he realized. He needed to tilt his face up to meet her gaze. Something resembling a hat extended from the top of her head. The hat continued upward, ridiculously high. It didn't appear to have a top. It was a column of undulating flesh that disappeared up into the ceiling vent.

She wore a look of hunger that he'd never could have *imagined* before this moment. It was so out of place that Justin panicked. Her grip tightened painfully as her eyes rolled up into the back of her head. She leaned forward covering his mouth with hers and cutting off Justin's scream, turning it into a flatulent cough.

When the glass windows gave way, the Slathering Moisture poured inward as Justin Steel poured outward.

***

The effects of the Slathering Moisture hadn't quite made it down into the basement level Security Room lavatory. Willy Loomis' portable hand radio gave a squawk right as he let fly an avalanche of last night's chili. His spouse had really gone heavy on the garlic this time. This restroom's ventilation was notoriously poor. Anybody coming in would certainly have to make a decision: could they hold it long enough to go to another floor's restroom, or did they need to brave this biological hazard before them? He laughed as he stepped out into the hallway. A quarantine might be necessary.

A scuffling sound came from behind the Security Office door followed by a loud thump.

Willy started forward to check it out when his hand radio screamed again, distracting him. "You out there?" someone said in a harsh whisper. "Anyone? Hello? Please!" It was hard to tell if it was a man or a woman speaking. It didn't sound like anyone Willy knew.

Willy thumbed the hand radio's button. "This is Officer Loomis. Who's this?"

After a pause there came feedback followed by, "Oh…oh," the voice said. "Ohhhhh!" Then they were grunting. And then a high-pitched squeal.

That wasn't feedback, Willy thought. Was that a person?

There was another click followed by heavy breathing so close to the microphone it distorted into some kind of ASMR hell. It gave him goosebumps.

"Oh, God! Yes! No, wait! No!" More heavy breathing. "Please! Somebody call 911. It's some kind of chemical spill, or… Whateverthefuck!" Another squeal. A loud click. Silence.

Willy didn't fuck around. He pulled out his cellphone and dialed 911. He was so focused on the phone call that he didn't see the Security Office door open behind him.

"I don't know what's going on, but it sounded like someone might be hurt," he said to the emergency operator. Willy didn't see his supervisor walking up behind him—naked and masturbating. A rivulet of spittle leaked from the corner of his mouth. "I gotta go check it out," he was saying when the wave of pheromones hit him. By the time he felt the supervisor's touch, Willy was into it.

It was 8:55 AM when dispatch sent their first cruiser over to the GenCo Labs building.

***

A half dozen police officers were lost to the wild abandon

of the Slathering Moisture's allure before the department even considered calling in a Hazmat team, but by then the growing crowd of onlookers were joined by multiple News vans with camera crews. There were a couple of helicopters and multiple personal drones making the airspace a hazard in and of itself. Still, more and more people came to gawk from the sidelines.

*****

The Slathering Moisture had grown. With every new donor, it gained in both size and capacity. Love was real! This was the pathway to perfection! Raw essences poured into its being with giddy abandon: Passion, gusto, and overt carnality!

Each new being contributed their own unique essence and vitality. They came with Love. They merged with Love. This Love had only one goal—to spread itself far and wide. To spread with both passion and bodily fluids.

As the sun continued its heated assault from the other side of the window blinds, the Slathering rested. Huddling within its plasmatic protean form deep in the center of the Executive Suite, the swollen flesh changed. Love evolved.

As the day drew on, the occasional lover would arrive. Their infatuation quick. Their courtship exhibited through rapid disrobement and full body copulation. The Slathering sensed it neared some kind of tipping point as the sun made its descent toward the horizon. The moment was close! All that was needed were a few more lovers—and nighttime. The dark was a lubricant for desire. Love in the dark is Love unconditional and unrestrained.

In the orange light of the setting sun, reinforcements rolled in to assist the police. National Guardsmen poured from their personnel carriers. The perimeter expanded and the gathered crowd was driven further back. Tents went up. A Command Center was established.

Before the last of the rays from the setting sun dimmed out, high intensity LED towers lifted above the crowd and burst into life. A fully outfitted Hazmat team entered the building. Androgynous astronauts in bulky protective outfits. After a laborious climb up the stairwell, they entered the Executive Suite.

The humongous mound of the Slathering Moisture writhed in the center of the office space. Upturned cubicles, furniture, and office equipment had been shoved outward from the amorphous glob of undulating flesh, pushing up the ceiling tiles and shimmering in the flashlights.. Its surface was a patchwork of colors ranging from beige to mauve. Human skeletons were scattered throughout its shivering complexion in various stages of deterioration.. Pustules of indigestible materials pushed outward like blemishes to burst along the surface and cascaded into piles on the floor. Clothing, shoes, jewelry, cellphones, and staplers. There were a handful of standard police issued firearms scattered in the debris—shiny from viscous residues.

With swift professionalism, the team established their observation post complete with secure wireless cameras on telescoping tripods and a plethora of monitoring equipment. Everything trained on the quivering tower of flesh at the center of the suite. Observers tuned in from both the local Command

Center and a special ops team in the Governor's Mansion less than two miles away by air. The audience consisted of politicians, lawyers, and representatives of law enforcement. Not a single scientist in the bunch.

A voice cut into the feed, "Commence samples and measurements. Jay-Jay, you're up."

Moving as one, the entirety of the Governor's exclusive audience leaned forward and held their collective breath while one of the fully suited Hazmat crew members broke away from the group.

The spacesuited figure cautiously approached the slowly undulating mass with a long stainless steel scooping spear held out in front of them. The spear's end looked like a small semispherical melon scooper, except with a razor-sharp edge. The scoop dipped into the thing's flesh, and the Slathering reacted. A tendril shot out, wrapped around the pole in spiralling loops that quickly spun up its length, over gloved hands and sheathed arms. Jay-Jay jerked out of shocked reflex, but the Slathering's grip was too strong, and it held them in place.

"Oh shit!" a voice screamed as the protective sleeve came away—peeled open by the tentacle.

Everyone started shouting at once, distorting the speakers in the Governor's room. Some hurried to assist their flailing teammate while others turned to flee. Either direction was pointless. More tendrils shot out. Each moving body was instantly snared. As fast as the frantic struggle began, it quickly dissipated. Succumbing to the Slathering's allure, the group gathered into a huddle. They leaned inward as if discussing strategies, yet no words came over the sound system. Only moans, gasps, and labored breathing.

"Jay-Jay!" came a shout over the comms. "Waxman!" The voice, forceful like a command, but plaintive as well. "What the hell is going on?"

The clustered group fumbled awkwardly with their own and each other's suits. Gloves hit the floor as hands were freed. Then the hands disappeared into gaps within each other's protective coverings. Furtively groping and tugging at stimulated flesh. The tendrils fluttering about appeared to be helping them remove their suits.

***

The windows on the top floor of the building shattered outward simultaneously. They broke with a dull thump like some kind of muffled bomb. The sound of glass tinkling as it cascaded down the walls sent soldiers scrambling. Something dark and glossy poured forth from each of the openings, but instead of flowing downward, it arched upwards toward the roof. Guardsmen adjusted the spotlights to follow the movement. It all happened so fast. Up there things were in motion. Organic matter undulated in the beams. Like huge fleshy snakes coiling over each other in a fervent mating frenzy.

A communal gasp and moan arose from the crowd—both bystander and soldier alike. The lights were super bright, but it was impossible to make out exactly what you were looking at. Whatever they were, the coils were entwining. It seemed like they were assembling into one gigantic... Thing!

***

A news helicopter flying above the scene captured it all on live broadcast, reminiscent of a sea anemone gyrating in the ocean's turbulence. Up, up, up the tendrils went, and on the roof they rejoined into a single pulsating globular bulb. At its base the Slathering's flesh spread out, rooting itself to the roof's surface. The separate arms reaching up and flattening into broad "leaves" joining that single throbbing bulb. Vents opened along the gaps of each section. With a shuddering flex, it expanded. There came a high-pitched harmony of whistling as air sucked in through each opening simultaneously. The bulb swelled as it filled up, a goopy floral inhale.

"What the fuck is that thing doing?" asked the Governor, but before anyone could think of trying to hazard a response, the Slathering's expansion became one horrendous contraction. The top split open and screamed a deep bass siren somehow both resonating and shrill. Out erupted copious streamers of white froth in a fountain of steam that arched up into the sky. An ejaculate of the gods. The streamers that jettisoned upwards were then caught by the evening winds and carried aloft to drift towards the sleeping city.

"Holy fuck!" somebody shouted over the comms. Who said that? It really didn't matter anymore. The steam that propelled from the venting overhead slid down the building and settled on the crowd below. Holy Fuck is what happened next.

***

Several minutes later, as the first waves of floating spooge balloons began to drift between the tall buildings, lights flicked on in the apartments and penthouses. As the pheromones made their way into every living space, more and more people came to their windows—drawn by something powerful and filled with lust.

The drifting balloon-things vented small jets of vapor, adjusting their trajectories toward the gathering lovers.

The first patters of pearlescent drops hit the pavement in a growing rhythmic smattering that increased in pace and substance. Soon after, the first of many bodies splattered on the sidewalks, shivered in their spreading fluids, then oozed their way toward a growing mass in the middle of the street.

***

The Governor's Ops room grew silent as the assembly struggled to comprehend what they'd just witnessed. The room grew stuffy with the heavy scent of masculine sweat. Thankfully the central AC kicked in and a fresh wave of cool air pushed its way into the space.

The Governor felt uncomfortable despite the relief from the cool air above. He squirmed in his wheelchair as a wave of heat washed through his body and centered around his crotch. Something stirred there that hadn't been active for longer than he could recall. Something that demanded to be set free.

About the Authors

Megan Bontrager is an author of SFF and Horror currently based in the UK, where she is a PhD candidate at NUI Maynooth. She received her MA from Johns Hopkins and BFA from the University of Central Florida, and has published short fiction with Quill & Crow Publishing House, Cypress Dome Literary Magazine, Frontier Poetry, and 30 North Literary Magazine. Her indie debut, Eye of the Ouroboros, was released with Quill & Crow in 2024, and her traditional debut, The Sea Hides Its Dead, is forthcoming as part of a three-book deal in Summer 2026 with Orbit US/UK. When she isn't frantically scribbling down her next big idea, Megan enjoys playing TTRPGs and volunteering with animal rescues.

Kari Kephali is a genderfluid, polyamorous, pansexual financial dominatrix, specializing in intellectual, soft, sensual dominance. They got their start writing smut-fic for the Lore Olympus Webtoon fandom during 2020, and have evolved to prefer reading and writing teratophile (monster-fucker) content almost exclusively. They prioritize Personal Responsibility & Informed Consensual Kink (PRICK) ethics, and do their best to infuse these into their writing. They enjoy teasing submissive puppies, fawning over dominant BookTok zaddys, and conversing with ethereal, abyssal, primordial entities from before the count of time. Kari can be found on most social media platforms as FinQueenKari.

D.O. Rackham (they/them) is an active member of their local Leather community and an advocate for education in BDSM. They write across the many genres of speculative fiction and they are currently working on an MFA in Creative Writing.

Morgan Gage If it's weird, funny, horny, or a combination of all three, Morgan Gage is probably writing about it. You can find more of their work at morgangage.com.

Lena Moth is a genderless, oversized gargoyle from Winnipeg who believes that the only monsters not worth kissing are the ones with their ugliness on the inside. When not writing, she can be found painting tiny creatures or reorganizing her ever-growing book hoard.

Lee Ohlson has published two queer romance novels with Dreamspinner Press with a third slated for release in fall of 2025.

Haven Valentin (she/her/it/its) is a queer UK-based writer of unhinged horror romance, and a lover of all things complex, Gothic and unsettling. By day, it writes SFW horror under a different name. At night, it drinks an evil potion (coffee) and becomes Haven, like a porn-writing Mr Hyde. It is currently working on its first novel. You can find her on Bluesky: @havenvalentin.bsky.social

LH O'Donoghue is a writer, game designer and PhD researcher based in Yorkshire. Her short fiction has been featured in Mslexia, Northern Gravy, Horror Library, ergot, and Planet Scumm. When she isn't writing you can often find her in the woods, looking for birds.

Verna Lorne is fascinated by the intimacy of death, sex & sharing book recommendations. She lives in Toronto with a mysterious beast that claims to be a cat, but questions remain. You can find her previous work in Queerotica Volume 1.

Briar Ripley Page lives in London. He's the author of Lupus In Fabula, a short story collection, and some novellas. Briar can be found online at briarripleypage.xyz.

Grant Lange is a student at the College of Charleston who has been published in Dark Harbor Magazine. He writes horror, sci-fi, and romance.

Alex Appleton is an aspiring Latina author. She writes everything from romance to gore. Between hunting for Slenderman in the woods & caring for her menagerie of reptile and amphibian roommates, she can be found scribbling her ideas when she should be sleeping.

Kris Morra is a multi-published romance author under the pen names Christine d'Abo and Alyse Anders, with over 60 publications. Her novel 30 Days received a starred review from Publishers Weekly and Library Journal, and Working It was a finalist in the Lambda Literary Awards. The Gargoyle's Kiss was her first monster romance. She's a Canadian author located in Waterloo, Ontario.

Tristan Marlowe is a middle aged Southern Gothic trans guy. He spends his time caring for cats, both domestic and feral, when not watching vampire shows or looking for cemeteries to photograph.

Bex Newton & Elle Waters are a pair of monster loving wives based in Toronto, Canada. They live with their three cat children, and both love writing, especially together.

Tanya Pond is an angler fish disguised as a human for research purposes. The studies are coming along nicely.

Ramses Wolfe (he/sin) is a trans writer, poet, and artist originally from Italy. His work is built on neurodivergent and queer experience, with a focus on the way trauma shapes lives and relationships.

Cultivator Space (they/it) is a writer of horror and erotica. Right now, it's working on short stories and interactive fiction. You can find them at cultivatorspace.com.

Shannon Riley (she/her) grew up covertly sharing, during lunch period, gore stories starring her friends and family rather than catching up in math class. She is the author of the revenge novella Pocketknife Kitty (Ghoulish Books, 2024), and her short fiction has been seen in the Dark Blooms: Girls' Coming-of-Age Horrors anthology, in PUNK Goes Horror (Truborn Press), as well as various other spooky places online. She lives with her husband and two daughters in a mediumish suburb outside of Pittsburgh. If you like chatting about 2000s emo and post-hardcore music, you can go yell at her on IG @shannon_wryly or on Twitter @shannon_said, which, at this point, is basically a My Chemical Romance fan account.

Michael Louis Dixon is an author and an artist. He grew up in the Midwest and bounced back-and-forth across the country until finally settling down around Austin, Texas where he lives with his wife and two dogs. He has a number of published short stories. Some have appeared in Dark Moon Digest & Cemetery Dance's Bad Dreams, New Screams. His unnerving Body Horror novel SICK was published by The Evil Cookie Publishing.

About the Editors

Mindy Rose is a bookseller, nonprofit worker, and publicist at Ghoulish Books. She can be found, unfortunately, in South Dakota.

Chris Krawczyk (he/him) is a giant ageless creature trapped in a tiny human body. He owns and operates Little Ghosts Books with his husband. When he's not doing design work and editorial for the publishing house and bookstore, you can find him snuggling his dog.

About Little Ghosts Books

Little Ghosts Books is a horror bookstore and small press established in Toronto, Canada in 2022, with a vision to showcase indie horror from diverse voices.

Through our publishing imprint and physical space, we hope to connect readers, horror lovers, authors, and folks of all backgrounds.

Find out what we already know:
A Good Story Will Haunt You.

FOLLOW LITTLE GHOSTS:
@littleghostsbooks
www.littleghostsbooks.com